As the shimmering summer sun sets, a dark moon is rising...

Summer Nights with a VAMPIRE

Maggie Shayne
Maureen Child
Alexis Morgan
Linda Thomas-Sundstrom
Meagan Hatfield

Mills & Boon, an imprint of Harlequin (UK) Limited,
Eton House, 18-24 Paradise Road, Richmond, Surrey TW9 1SR

SUMMER NIGHTS WITH A VAMPIRE

ISBN: 978 0 263 89776 0

024-0612

Printed and bound by
CPI Group (UK) Ltd, Croydon, CR0 4YY

CONTENTS

Vampires in Paradise

Maggie Shayne

Chapter 1

"I'm sorry, Anna, but there is no cure."

Anna Seville sat in a chair facing her doctor and friend, Mary St. Augustine, and waited for the punch line. But there wasn't one. Mary was known for her stoic disposition. In fact, since high school, Anna had never seen Mary cry. But her eyes were welling with tears now, and that only added credence to the impossible pronouncement. But all Anna's brain kept repeating was that *this just couldn't be right.*

"There's a mistake somewhere, Mary, there has to be. I'm not…I can't be…dying." Saying the word, though it had emerged only as a whisper, seemed to make it more real. Dying. Ending. Leaving. Her life was *over.*

Suddenly Anna felt cold, and her focus seemed to turn inward, searching for logic or reason somewhere. Anywhere. But Mary's words had just taken it all away.

So she sought for rational reasons why it couldn't possibly be true. "I haven't even been all that sick. Just…you know, tired. Worn out. Lethargic."

"I know. That's one of the main symptoms of this condition."

"But I don't have a *condition.* I've been fine my whole life, and now you're telling I was born with some sort of flaw that—"

"If you'd come to me sooner, I'd have told you sooner. But you've spent your whole adult life dodging health care at every possible opportunity."

"Yeah, and look what happens the first time I give in to the nagging and come in for a checkup. A death sentence."

Mary lowered her head. "Maybe on some level you knew."

Anna sighed. "My mom did, I think. Probably why she was always running me to doctors and being so overprotective when I was a kid. God, why didn't she tell me?"

"I imagine she intended to, when she thought you were old enough. It's not as if she planned to have a heart attack at thirty-nine."

And now it didn't look as if her eldest daughter would outlive her by much, Anna thought sadly.

"What is it, Mary? What's killing me?" she asked, ready, she thought, to hear the truth.

Mary shook her head. "You were born with a rare blood antigen known as Belladonna. It was never detected until now because you've never been a donor or needed a transfusion, or had any major surgeries."

"And if I had been?" Anna asked, instantly ready to blame herself for not being generous and donating blood like any decent citizen would do. She'd always meant to, she'd just been so busy with other things. Her job and all her causes, and her sister's, Lauren's, kids—until they'd turned on her, anyway.

After their mother had died unexpectedly, Anna had become Lauren's caretaker. Her enabler, actually. Lauren had drifted into addiction—prescription drugs, mostly, at the beginning, but that soon degenerated into anything she could get her hands on. She'd had two babies in a row, Nate and Cindi, with no father in sight for either of them. And hell, someone had to make sure the kids had a roof over their heads.

Anna realized that Mary had been talking and she'd been oblivious. She fixed her eyes on her friend and said, "Sorry, I drifted. Would you start over?"

Mary nodded. "The Belladonna antigen is rare. Few people have it. Those who do tend to bleed very easily. Almost like a hemophiliac would. Your mother probably knew this, and that's why she was so worried about every little cut and scrape you got as a kid."

"Makes sense. Okay, what else? Has anyone ever… beaten this?"

Mary shook her head. "Everyone with this condition experiences the same symptoms you've been describing. Onset occurs in the mid-thirties, on average."

She was speaking in sound bites, Anna realized. Uttering a fact or two, then pausing to be sure Anna had heard and understood before moving on. She was watching Anna's face now, waiting for a signal.

"Okay. So far I'm just like everyone else who has this… condition. So what happens next?" She blinked, then focused on Mary's eyes. "Tell me the truth. How bad will it be?"

"It's a very easy, gentle process, Anna. And that's the truth. There's no pain. You'll just keep feeling weaker, more lethargic. You'll begin sleeping more and more. Patients often find that daylight becomes harsh and unbearable, so they tend to become a bit nocturnal toward the end. Eventually you'll just fall asleep and won't wake up again."

Anna nodded slowly.

"Anna, it's usually less than a year from the onset of symptoms to the end. And you've been feeling them for… what? A couple of months now?"

She thought back. "It's hard to say. It was so subtle at first, you know? I just thought I needed iron or more vitamins or something. It's been three months since they got to the point where I was worried." She thinned her lips. "But I knew you'd ask, so I got out my journal. And the first time I made a note about feeling as if I were tiring more easily than I should was six months before that."

Mary's eyes widened just a little. "And yet you didn't come in sooner?"

"I kept hoping it would pass on its own." Anna held Mary's eyes. "And you said it wouldn't have made any difference."

"It wouldn't. Just would have given you more time to—"

"Time. God, time." Suddenly she was eager to get out of the chair, get busy, get moving. If she only had three months to live… "I've got so much to get done! I'll have to put my house on the market, make arrangements for the money to go to Nate and Cindi—and the car, what am I going to do about the car?" She was moving around Mary's office as she spoke, looking for her jacket, that was on a coatrack near the door. Long and deep green, a trench-style coat for the spring rains. "I don't even have a will. I'll need to write one immediately. Where did I put my purse? Oh, God, work. What about work? I have to help them find a replacement for me. And there's that big fundraiser we're doing for the SPCA! It's six months away, and I might not even be here to—"

"Anna."

The firm, clipped nature of Mary's tone reached her. She stopped talking, stopped moving, right there in front of the desk.

"Please sit down. Just for five more minutes. Just sit down and listen, okay?"

Frowning, Anna sat, noticing that her purse was on the floor beside her chair. How had she not seen it right there?

Mary got up and came around her desk. She pulled a vacant chair around to face Anna, then sat down, leaning forward, her arms resting on her legs. "I'm talking to you as your friend now, not as your doctor, okay?"

Anna nodded.

"This is your life we're talking about. Three months, give or take—they're all you've got left. Do you understand that?"

"Of course I do. You just told me."

"And your response was to list all the stuff you have to do for other people. Your sister turned on you when her kids were finally on their own, and you told her you wouldn't keep helping her pay her bills unless she gave up her drug habit. Hell, the kids turned on you, too, after you practically raised them and put them through college, when you refused to bail their mother out of jail last year. They haven't spoken to you since, have they?" Anna lowered her eyes, shook her head. It was true. Nate and Cindi had vowed never to speak to her again for letting their mother rot in a cell. She'd been out in a month and using again, anyway.

"You have time now," Mary went on. "And fairly decent health for a while yet, too. I'm telling you to stop thinking about everyone else and figure out what *you* want to do. What do you want to experience that you never have? How do you want to spend the last days of your life? Figure that out, Anna, and once you do, say 'to hell with everyone else.' And just go do it. They'll all figure things out when it's over."

Anna sat there, blinking. "But if I don't…take care of things, then who will?"

Mary shrugged. "Go on a dream vacation. Write a will while you're there. Pick someone you trust to name as your executor. Mail it to them, and they'll see to it that everything gets handled. They'll sell your house and give the money to whoever you name. They'll see to everything you want just the way you want it. You don't need to do it now. I can't bear to see you wasting what's left of your life taking care of everyone but yourself."

Anna lowered her head, blinking slowly. "But…that's what I've always done."

"I know it is, hon. I know. And you've earned your place in heaven—as well as the right to be just a little bit selfish now that you know your time is limited."

Anna released a pent-up breath. "I'm not sure I even know how. I don't even know what to do."

"Think on it. Don't think about death or dying, or your sister or her kids. Think about what you would do if you could do anything you wanted. Anything at all. What would it be? What would you see, where would you go, what would you wear?"

Anna nodded, her gaze again turning inward as Mary's words stirred visions and dreams she'd left along the roadsides of her life. Her short, empty life. Dreams of sailing. Of the ocean. Of tropical islands. And of a dark-eyed man who loved her with the kind of passion she'd read about in romance novels all her life. The one she'd longed for, dreamed about, fantasized, and sensed was out there… somewhere. She'd always thought he would be waiting when she got around to searching for him.

But she'd never gotten around to it, had she?

"Will you do that for me, Anna?" Mary was asking.

Anna nodded. "I…I will." She nodded harder as she got

up from her chair. "Yes. Thank you, Mary. I'm going to think about this. About what you've said. About what…I… want."

Mary stood, looking at her. "Promise?"

"I promise."

Mary wrapped her in a delicate hug, and Anna knew her friend was crying, felt it in the way her body trembled ever so slightly from trying to hold it inside. "I love you, you know," Mary said, her voice deeper than before. "I love you."

"I love you, too," Anna told her. Then she broke the embrace. "I'll let you know what…what I decide."

"Thank you. I'd love that, but don't feel obligated. From this moment on, Anna, your life is about you. About you doing what *you* feel like doing. Period. Okay?"

"Okay." She stood, too, facing her friend, blinking through tears that matched the ones dampening Mary's lashes. "Thank you," she said softly.

Mary nodded and kissed her cheek.

Turning toward the office door, Anna drew a deep breath and then went through it, not looking back. She didn't slow or think or pause until she was sitting behind the wheel of her car, and about to turn the key.

But she couldn't. She looked around her at all the people passing by, and she wondered how they could all seem so…ordinary. How were they just going about their everyday lives as if the entire world hadn't just turned upside down?

She laid her head on the steering wheel and cried.

Chapter 2

Diego leaped easily from the gleaming hardwood deck of the *Santa Maria XIII* onto the pier without need of a gangplank. He didn't own a dock of his own on the mainland because it was fairly important he not show up at the same coastal port town too often. This one was in the mishmash of peninsulas and islands along the blurred edges of North and South Carolina, where it was often tough to tell which state one was technically inhabiting. He'd used it before. The closest town was Kendall, but this long public access pier was beyond the town limits, in the middle of nowhere, with nothing much to mark it besides one of the most beautiful lighthouses he'd seen. Tall, black and white, simple, but elegant and solid. It seemed as permanent as the rocky peninsula on which it stood. And far more elegant than the man-made walking path, pretty park benches and manicured flower gardens that surrounded it.

He'd tied his sailboat securely and knew she would still be there on his return. It wasn't often he ventured onto the mainland. He viewed doing so as a necessary evil, a task he performed as seldom as he possibly could—about every three months or so. And even then, only by dead of night, when he was far less likely to encounter humankind. He preferred the smell of the sea to that of their sweat and their sex and their fear of all things unknown. He preferred the innocent perfection of nature to the mistrust and cynicism of man. Part of nature...once, yes, man had been that. But he'd veered so far from natural that he no longer qualified. He was all but a machine at this point. He'd lost his connection to his mother.

They would call *him* unnatural, he supposed, but in his own mind, Diego was the most natural creature he could imagine. Not that being a vampire made him naturally good. Some of his kind were as bad as the humans were. Some were worse. Far, far worse.

He walked in silence along the pier, hating that the energy of peace, of blessed harmony, was slowly being overcome by the raucous and unnatural thoughts and emotions of the world of man. He'd tried his best to prepare for the mental onslaught, but, as usual, he'd failed.

He felt anger and rage. Couples arguing, men fighting, parents shouting at their children. He felt the despondence of the homeless and the cravings of the addicts. He felt the fear of the innocent, not yet cruel enough to hold their own among the melee. He smelled the chemicals and exhaust in the air, and he wished for nothing more than to complete his task as quickly as possible and return to his haven, where none of that existed.

And then he felt *her.*

He'd reached the landward end of the pier and stepped from it onto the little path that meandered past the lighthouse. She wasn't far from him—a few dozen meters at most—and her emotions were overwhelming her. They were mixed, but the most prominent among them was sadness. And in spite of himself, he tuned in to her above all the other noise in his mind. He focused on her and listened in, and he heard the thoughts racing around in her head.

My life is ending before it's even begun...

How can it be true? How can it be true? How can it be true?

What will happen? Is there a heaven? Do I deserve to go there?

Should I do it? Can I possibly be that selfish, even now?

What about Lauren? What about Nate and Cindi?

The kids are going to have to learn to fend for themselves, anyway. It's not as if Lauren's capable of taking care of them.

They're adults. They'll manage. God knows I did.

I deserve some happiness.

I don't have much time left.

I could just go. Just buy the boat and go...

God, it would be so beautiful. So peaceful. So restful.

How can I be so selfish?

He frowned, pulling away from her jumbled emotions

and telling himself it was none of his business, anyway. Turning, he started to walk in the other direction, toward the town and the victim he would take tonight. A criminal or an abuser or a thug. No one worthy of using up this beautiful planet's precious resources. Like lancing a boil, removing one of those. He was performing a service. And he only allowed himself the pleasure a few times a year, when he came in for supplies. The rest of the time, those supplies were his sustenance. Stolen from one of the various blood banks, clinics and hospitals that were his usual sources.

He was running low on supplies out on the island. It was time to restock. And while dealing with humans and their world full of misery was something he dreaded, he had to admit that he looked forward to the taking of a live victim on these quarterly excursions. There was nothing quite like the rush of warm, living blood—not to mention the power of it.

Dying. Dying. How can I possibly be dying?

Her thoughts stopped him again, and he turned once more, gazing along the shore, spotting her. She was on the same path as he was, on one of the benches, but farther out on the long finger of the earthen pier, near the tall lighthouse at its tip. The sentinel stood impassive, as always, its black barber-pole stripe flawlessly twining upward, to the sunlike yellow glow at the top. He loved lighthouses. Perhaps because they were as close as he would get to ever seeing actual sunlight again, aside from that reflected in the mirror of the moon.

She was sitting on a stone bench, the lighthouse at her back, her gaze on the sea. He sniffed the air and caught the scent of her tears, of her skin. The soap and cologne she used, the shampoo.

He should stop right there. He should not notice anything more about her. Because what he had already noticed was tugging at him. She was dangerous.

Like Cassandra had been. Cassandra, who'd come to him at the end of her mortal life, knowing exactly what she intended. Making him fall so deeply in love with her that he would have done anything for her. Anything.

And then destroying him once she got what she wanted. When all the while, all she'd had to do was ask.

No, he wanted no part of any beautiful woman in misery. But then, just then, he caught the scent of something else about this weeping woman.

Her blood.

And it was unlike the blood of most mortals. It held the antigen that made her…a relative of his, to put it most simply. She possessed the rare Belladonna antigen. Just like Cassandra had.

Hell, she was one of the Chosen. That made her doubly dangerous to him.

Mortals with the antigen were the only ones who could ever become what he was. Vampires sensed these special humans and were compelled, often to their own detriment, to protect and watch over them. For a vampire to harm one of the Chosen was, it was said, impossible.

He'd only encountered one other. The woman who'd

brought him to his knees with a heartache so crippling, he'd vowed there would never be another. And that alone made him want to leave this one to her suffering. She likely deserved it, anyway.

Again he tried to walk away, knowing now, at least, why her emotions outshouted all the other mental energies wafting on the airwaves this night.

And again his steps halted and he turned in her direction. Compelled, like a feline by the scent of catmint. Every instinct in his body was telling him to help her, to ease her pain, to go to her—while every thought in his brain told him the opposite.

He could not resist going to her. He couldn't.

Sighing, vowing that he would only speak to her briefly, be of help if he could, and that then he would leave and never so much as *think* of her again, he followed the twisting path to the bench where she sat, still weeping.

He stood over her, looking down at her. She lifted her head, sensing him there, but didn't even gasp in surprise. Her eyes narrowed. But she said nothing.

She was beautiful. Utterly beautiful. Auburn curls, wild and thick, falling over her shoulders, and huge blue eyes that seemed to reflect the soul of the sea itself. Her skin was pale already, and she had a sprinkling of freckles across the bridge of her nose, spilling just slightly onto her cheeks.

And in spite of himself, he felt her pain so sharply and so keenly it nearly brought tears to his own eyes.

"There cannot be anything so dire as to make a woman as beautiful as you are weep this bitterly."

She blinked. "I've just been told I'm dying."

"We're born dying, lady. But in truth, there's no such thing as death. We're eternal beings, whether we choose to stay or move on."

Her brows bent toward each other. "I wasn't given a choice."

"You will be. When the time comes, you will be."

Her frown deepened. "How can you know that?"

He shrugged, not telling her that despite his vow only moments ago, he would probably be the one to give her that choice. Not yet, not now. It was too soon. He could feel the life force in her and sensed there was time yet for her. But when the time of her death came, he would return and offer her the choice, or some other vampire would find her and do it. For she gave every sign of being worthy.

Though he'd thought that about Cassandra, too. Blinded by his own treacherous heart.

Not so this time. Not yet. Not if he didn't let himself be.

He would return, yes, when her time was near, and he would ask her if she wanted to live on as one of the Undead. He would offer her that option. He decided it on the spot, which was very unlike him.

She rose from the bench, her eyes staring into his as she blinked her tears away. "What should I do?"

He held her gaze, peering deeply into her eyes, slipping his will inside her mind, and finding it a beautiful place to dwell. Damn, he liked this woman. In her unguarded mind, he poked through all the litter. Obligation. Guilt. Other people's needs. More guilt. He pushed all that aside and whispered, "Let go, Anna. Let go and show me your truest heart."

As he whispered the words, he willed her to comply. He saw her eyes widen when he spoke her name, and then he felt her surrender. Her own will melted under the force of his mind. He saw her standing at the helm of a wooden sailboat. He saw her with the wind in her hair and the sea waves beneath her vessel, riding them like a triumphant Valkyrie.

"You want to sail," he said softly. "You long to be one with the sea and with the creatures who live there, and with the sky and the wind." It stunned him how much her idea of perfection matched his own. "You need to sell the house and use the money to buy the boat of your dreams."

"I do?"

"It's what you truly want." And with those words, he withdrew his will from her mind, leaving open the trail he'd blazed for her, through all the baggage and useless guilt.

"But what about my sister? What about her kids?"

He blinked at her. "Why do you cling to the need to be needed?"

"Is that what I'm doing?"

He shrugged.

Lifting a trembling hand, she touched his face, then drew her fingertips away. "You're not real, are you?"

You were put upon this planet to make the most of your life, Anna. To do so, then, cannot be deemed selfish, can it? His mind spoke directly to hers.

She was looking up at him as if he had spoken aloud, but knowing he hadn't. Her hair danced on the sea wind, almost as if reaching toward him. Her skin was pale, paler, even, than his own. And her eyes…as blue as the sea. Her beauty was beyond anything he'd ever seen.

Don't go there, he told himself. Tell her something to help her, and then go about your business and forget you ever saw her. Do it.

But as she stared at him, a smile toyed with the corners of her full, ripe lips. "I've dreamed of you, I think."

"And when was that?" he asked softly.

"All my life." Her hands rose, one touching the nape of his neck, fingers lingering there, and he felt every point of contact to the core of his being. "That you would come to me now, of all times…"

"I'm just a stranger, passing by and offering unasked-for advice."

"But you knew my name. And my deepest desires."

He should have been alarmed at having revealed so much, but he couldn't seem to drum up a hint of common sense. She was listening to him, and it was helping her. And more. He felt he was touching this woman's soul, and it was affecting him as much as it was her. Why was that? How could it be?

He whispered again to her mind, eager now to help her and then be on his way, because the feelings swirling inside him were beyond anything he understood, and he needed to be alone to figure it all out.

No loving creator would give a woman desires and then forbid her from fulfilling them. It is not selfish to wish to live your life to its fullest, no matter how long or how short it might be. To do so is sacred. It's your calling. It's why you are here. The sin would be to do anything less. I promise you that.

"Are you an angel?"

He smiled at her question. *Follow your heart,* he told her. *It is the guidance you've been given all your life. It shows your true north. It leads you true—always.*

It was a philosophy he believed in. Admittedly, doing so had earned him the worst hurt of his existence, but it had also led him to paradise. The life he led now was blissful, if lonely. And he wouldn't have found it without the heartbreak that came before.

He felt her mind gently sliding into agreement, felt peace settling over her like a soft, warm blanket. Like the velvet night itself. He felt her nodding, and even sensed relief floating into her soul.

He had helped her. And now, he told himself, it was time to walk away.

He started to go, but she caught his shoulders in her small, gentle hands, somehow compelling him to look down into her eyes one more time. And then she rose on tiptoe, her lips moving close to his.

So close he felt her breath.

He whispered, "What are you doing, Anna?"

"What my heart tells me, like you said," she whispered back. And then she kissed him.

The power of it was beyond imagining. He was as engulfed in the kiss—in the woman—as a lifeboat would be by a hurricane. He felt her heart, soft, and loving and pure. He smelled her scents, and heard her heartbeat inside his own chest. He tasted her kiss, and it was beyond anything he'd ever dreamed off. He wrapped his arms around her and held her to him, and they kissed and kissed and kissed.

And then, finally, he gave heed to the sense of self-preservation he'd built upon a foundation of pain and betrayal. He'd thought Cassandra's heart was pure, too. And he'd been wrong.

Sleep, he commanded. *Sleep, and remember me as but a pleasant dream. Sleep, Anna. And when you wake, follow your heart's desire, no matter what. I'll find you again before you die. And you will be offered a choice. I promise you that. But for now, sleep. Sleep, Anna. Sleep.*

Anna slept. He held her against him as her legs went weak, and he scooped her up into his arms and then sped through the night, carrying her at speeds far too fast for mortal eyes to observe him. He probed her mind to find where she lived, and he took her there. An attractive, one-story house with flower boxes in the windows. Yellow. It would sell easily.

He unlocked the doors with the power of his mind and laid her gently on her bed, and then he turned and forced himself to go away. It was, for some reason, far more difficult than it should have been.

An hour later he sank his teeth into the throat of a drunken pedophile in a stinking alley outside the bar the man had been visiting.

But as the rush of the blood hit him, carrying with it the pleasant burn of rum, his mind went back to the woman he'd kissed beneath the lighthouse. He saw her eyes, her face, her hair. He heard her voice, rough with tears. He tasted her mouth, felt her hands on him. He closed his eyes and for just a moment gave in to the fantasy that it was her blood he was drinking now. Her blood, rushing into his throat, warming his flesh, sizzling in his soul, filling him with power, with strength, with vigor and, God help him, with desire—for her.

A surge of ecstasy rose in him even as he released his victim. The man's body fell to the alley floor, and Diego tipped his head back and, in spite of himself, released a growling roar to the night. In that moment, pure primal power and unleashed lust washed through him, and he had no control.

As he brought his head level again, he heard voices, human ones.

"What the hell? Was that a freaking lion?"

"I never heard anything like that in my—"

"A bear? *Here?*"

"C'mon."

Crouching low, Diego pushed off with his powerful legs and shot upward, rocketlike, landing easily on the roof above even as the curious mortals arrived at the mouth of the alley and saw the dead man lying there.

He didn't stick around to see what happened next.

Chapter 3

Two months later...

Anna stood in what felt like the vastness of eternity. There was no clear boundary between the sea around her and the night sky above. The only visible difference was that the sky was dotted with glittering stars and the water was too choppy to reflect them back. On calm seas, she'd experienced nights when she honestly couldn't tell where the mirror of the sea ended and the sky began. Breathtaking. And peaceful.

She no longer feared dying. She imagined that the night sky above was a black canvas, and that behind it there was a light—that beautiful heavenly light talked about by near-death survivors. She imagined the stars as tears in the fabric, giving her tiny glimpses of that warm, loving glow. One more month, give or take, if Mary's predictions were true. And then she would be able to find out for herself.

Below, and all around, her there was water. Blue-black, with whitecaps appearing and vanishing again as if at random. But there was an order to it, she thought. One she couldn't see but felt on some level. There was order to everything. It all happened for a reason.

Beneath her feet, her boat, the *Spanish Angel,* rocked and bobbed at the whim of those waves. She'd furled her sails, dropped anchor for the night. There was a vague and brief rocky shoreline in sight, but only barely, off the starboard side. It was small enough that she suspected it was an island, but she had no desire to visit it. People, tourists, were not what she had come out here to experience.

She stood on the port side, near the bow, staring out at the endless expanse of sea and sky, and letting her focus go soft until the two blended into one. One living, breathing, heaving, moving entity. The great Whole. And she was a part of it. Alive or dead, a part of it she would remain.

Anna was at peace now. That night on the pier, in the hulking shadow of the lighthouse, she'd met an angel. Her own guardian angel, she thought. And the fact that he had the face of her dream lover, who'd hovered just beyond the edge of her dreams since she'd been a teenager, made him even more real.

Yes, she had probably imagined him. Maybe. Her subconscious had conjured just the image she had needed. He had broken through her grief and her worry and her pain, and given her permission to be selfish. To be happy, even, during the waning months of her life.

He'd seemed so real. She'd even given him a name, in her imagination. Diego. It had come to her during that imaginary kiss. She knew his voice, his touch, his kiss. God, his kiss. And that sense of him looking so deeply inside her that he knew her deepest thoughts, fears, longings.

She'd spent a great many hours pondering her angel while she'd been living blissfully at sea. There had been something otherworldly about him, and a faint trace of an accent—Spanish, in his case—the way there always seemed to be when people claimed to be channeling the words of a spirit guide. Or of an angel. He'd had that accent in her dreams, too, she recalled.

Hazy, those dreams. Vague. No real story to them, just images of him, of his eyes blazing into hers, his hand reaching out to touch her cheek. And a feeling of absolute love welling up inside her heart.

She'd thought, in her youth, that those had been glimpses of her soul mate. Her future partner, husband, lover. But now she knew better. She'd been glimpsing her own personal guardian angel. He had come to her that night and told her what she needed to hear. And when she passed from this life into the next, he would be there, waiting. She was actually looking forward to seeing him again.

She'd sold her home and her possessions, and she'd closed out all her bank accounts and cashed in her retirement. She'd quit her job. And then she had bought one thing for herself. Something she had always wanted.

She'd given part of the remaining money to her sister's kids, and she'd invited them to lunch at a fast-food joint where she used to take them when they were little, so she could deliver the money personally and have a chance to say goodbye. She told them that she was leaving the country and didn't know when she would return. They'd accused her of abandonment until they'd seen the numbers on the cashier's checks she handed them. Then their whining had gone silent and the questions had begun.

But by then she'd already been on her way out the door.

The rest of the money had gone for supplies, that she stowed on the gift she had bought for herself. This sailboat. She'd named her boat the *Spanish Angel,* after the otherworldly being who'd come to her on that night when all had seemed lost.

And now she was doing what she had always dreamed of doing. She was sailing down the East Coast, embracing the ocean she had loved since birth. She was riding the waves, and soaking up the sun, and relishing the wind. She was communing with dolphins, and whales, and sharks, and seals, with seagulls and osprey and birds and fish she had yet to identify. She was meditating, and pondering the meaning of life and the universe and spirituality. She was living. For the first time in her life, now that she was dying, she was truly *living.*

She'd saved enough money to keep herself in food and fresh water and other essentials for the three months

Mary told her she might have left, with a little extra left over in case she lived longer. Honestly, though, she didn't think that was going to happen. She was sleeping more and more. And soon, she thought, it might not be safe to remain at sea, with no one at the helm in case she never woke up.

Then again, what did she have to lose, really?

As she stood there with the wind in her hair, she smiled and felt content right to her soul. She was happy, she realized. She didn't have a worry in the world. She had no bills to pay, no jobs to rush to, no phones to answer, no computer to crash, no email to answer, no people depending on her and expecting things of her. All she had to do was sail, and live, and breathe. Eat and sleep. Read and sing. Pray and meditate. Ride the waves, and dream of crossing to the other side, into her guardian angel's open arms. She wondered if it was sinful to feel the way she felt for him. Because her love for him, while pure and powerful, didn't feel at all platonic. But she supposed if there was anything wrong with that, he wouldn't have kissed her the way he had.

If she died tonight, she thought, she would die happy. And she would be even happier when she emerged on the other side. She could feel the antigen tugging her to sleep yet again. She'd managed to stay awake for six straight hours today. That was pretty good, for her.

She went below, to the little cabin, and fell asleep in a state of bliss.

She'd been sleeping pretty hard, as she tended to do

these days, when she realized the wind was howling and water was rolling over her face. It was too dark to see, and she was completely disoriented; nothing in the room was where it belonged, and she couldn't tell which way was up or which was down. And yet, she felt no panic. The water was warm. And if she drowned, so be it. Suddenly there was a crash, and her beautiful boat seemed to explode in a thousand directions, flying away from her like the expanding universe itself and leaving her in the open water, which was roiling, throwing her up and sucking her back down again. Lightning flashed over and over, and she gasped for air, blinking through saltwater to see brief strobing images. Jutting rocks. Broken boards. Foaming froth. Pouring rain. Heaving waters.

The instinctive urge to survive overwhelmed her even as her practical mind told her to just relax into the embrace of the sea. She was dying, anyway. What did it matter? But at that moment, in that instant, all she wanted was to keep her head above water, to keep sucking air into her lungs, and to struggle ever nearer to the rocks that had demolished her boat.

In desperation, she cried out, spewing water with her words. "Help me! Help me, someone!"

Diego was safely inside his cottage, the window shades up and shutters thrown wide, so that he could watch the rain, enjoy the electric light show that nature was putting on tonight. He loved storms. The pure, raw power of them. Right now, the wind was blowing the palms so that their fronds were nearly upright, and the vibration of the airwaves whisking around their variegated trunks made a hum that was not unlike the primal tone of a didgeridoo. The wind, that hum, the thunder, the crashing waves—together they created a symphony, and he listened in pure raw pleasure.

And then, a heartbeat later, his entire body quivered in awareness. Danger. Fear. Panic. What the hell was—

Help me! Help me, someone!

He felt the summons more than heard it, but then realized he'd heard it, as well, just barely. Not only that, but he knew its source, knew it immediately, as her energy rushed into his awareness, filling him. The woman he'd seen two months before, near the lighthouse, the one who'd been weeping. The woman he'd kissed.

One of the Chosen, and one with whom he'd felt an instant and powerful bond.

That made her very dangerous to him.

And yet, he was unable to deny the gut-level drive to help her. He had no choice. Nor would he have done otherwise even if he could have. He pulled on a slicker, a black one, caped. He pulled a cap down over his ears. It would only be soaked through in a few minutes, but he wore it, anyway, then dashed out of his haven and into the heart of the storm.

He could move faster than any living thing. Fast enough so that he would not be detectable to human eyes, nor, he suspected, to most of the wildlife here—though he wasn't entirely sure about that. Still, he pushed himself to preternatural speeds through the storm, until he stood on the windward shore, and there he paused, listening—not just with his ears but with all his senses—and staring intently out at the violent sea.

"Where are you?" he asked aloud, but he sent the words out to her, too, using the power of his mind, knowing that might be the only way she, a mere mortal, would be able to hear him.

Rocks. Water. Can't...see....

He felt a wave smash into her face, felt it as if it were happening to him. It silenced her mind and pushed her downward, and he felt her consciousness fading.

No time for the boat. He shed the slicker and hat, and ran into the water, sensing her near the treacherous rocks that rose from the sea a few hundred yards from shore. He dove, arrowing through the waves toward her. Angling deeper, to escape the surface effect of the storm—which would have slowed him, though only slightly—he sped onward, his senses attuned to the essence of her. Flawlessly they guided him, and in only seconds he was wrapping his arms around her body and shooting upward.

They broke the surface, and he held her so her back was against his chest, one hand pulling her forehead back and up. "Breathe!" he commanded, with his mind and will as well as his voice.

She gulped in air and gasped, gurgled and choked. Water spewed from her lips.

"Again," he told her. "Breathe."

And again she inhaled. Her eyes were closed tight, her

body still. No fight left in her. He turned them toward shore, struggling now. He couldn't just speed through the waves without forcing more water into her lungs. And it was difficult to make headway while keeping her head from submerging once more.

Lifting his own head, he called out, no longer speaking like a man. His voice was a high-pitched chitter instead. And within moments a dorsal fin appeared, pale amid the black water.

"Thank you, my friend," Diego said softly, gripping the slick fin with one hand, holding on to his charge with the other. The dolphin swam rapidly toward shore, chirping happily, the ever-cheerful demeanor unaffected by the storm.

Diego couldn't say the same for his own—although his darkening mood wasn't due to the storm itself, but to what it had carried to his beach. His haven.

A woman. One of the Chosen. And not just any one, but *this one.* This woman he'd met during what he'd taken as a chance encounter two months ago. He'd gone into seclusion forty-five years ago because of a woman just like her. He'd taken refuge far from the reach of human or vampire. And yet, she had come.

Hell, was history doomed to repeat itself—even here?

"Far enough, Layla," he said, releasing the dolphin and giving the animal a pat on the side even as it turned and swam away. His feet sank into the sandy sea-bottom, and he shifted the woman around to face him, carrying her as he strode up out of the waves, onto the beach and then along the winding and well-worn path through the forest to his cottage. His sanctuary. A place where only one other being had ever set foot, at least within his five-century-plus lifespan.

Allowing someone else to visit the island had proven disastrous. He had sworn that no one ever would breech his sanctuary again. And yet, here she was. And there was not one thing he could do about it.

Chapter 4

Anna struggled to open her eyes, but they seemed to resist her efforts. It was no surprise. She had a lot more trouble waking up, and a lot more trouble *staying* awake, lately. She seemed to be becoming almost nocturnal. The sun's energy was just too much for her slowly weakening body, she supposed. Hadn't Mary told her that would happen? The essence of nighttime was so much softer, easier to take. Even on the boat, she'd…

The boat…

Her sailboat!

Her eyes flew open wide, and she sucked in a breath so sharply that it hurt her chest. Her arms flew out, hitting something that clattered to the floor, and she pushed herself upward all at once. And then, slowly, her wide-open eyes showed her that she was not in the ocean, fighting to keep her head above water, being battered by the waves and the storm. No. She was warm, and she was dry. The surface beneath her was soft, and the room around her, one of utter beauty and…peace.

Odd, that she would think that, but that was what it felt like to her. Peace.

The walls were red-brown wood, full of swirls and knots. There was a small cobblestone fireplace on one of them, with a rounded opening, and a glass screen in front. There were flames dancing and heat flowing. Huge windows lined the room, but they were all closed off now, by dark shutters from the outside. There were a few pieces of furniture, all apparently made of raw wood-slabs and coated in thick gleaming layers of shellac. Someone had attached legs to them to create tables, backs to create chairs, added cushions to some for relaxation. The one she rested on was a sort of fainting couch, she thought. She was lying on a brown plush pad, and matching pillows were tucked between her body and the wooden back, which was, she thought as she tugged one of the pillows aside, gorgeous. Hand carved to resemble the graceful body and long swooping neck of a swan.

Sitting up slowly, she looked down to see that her hands were clutching a cream-colored blanket made of the same sort of fabric one would use to make a baby's first teddy bear. So soft. And then she noticed the shirt she wore—it wasn't her own. It was a man's tank-style undershirt. White, ribbed. Her arms were bare. She lifted the blanket and saw she had on a pair of men's boxer shorts.

She tried to remember how she'd come to be here, who

had rescued her from the storm-tossed sea that had devoured her beautiful sailboat. Her *Spanish Angel?* But for the life of her, she couldn't recall anything more than waking in the water, struggling to keep her head above the surface, choking on the brine, and finally losing her battle. Peace had surrounded her as she had gone sinking down. And peace was what she had awakened to just now.

Was this heaven? Did they dress you in men's underclothes in heaven? Did they heat heaven with a crackling wood-fire?

Maybe. If heaven was, as she had come to suspect through all her hours of pondering and meditation, what one expected it to be, then maybe this was her heaven. A private, cozy cottage, where she was warm and safe and dry. She'd always wanted a cabin of wood, with a cobblestone fireplace. If this were *really* heaven, her cottage would be situated on a beach.

Beside her luxurious bed were a pitcher of water and a wooden bowl filled with tropical fruit. There were figs and nectarines and berries. She didn't particularly like figs. Would there be figs if this were heaven?

She stared at the bowl and imagined a juicy steak appearing there. Just to test it out. But nothing happened. Where *was* she?

As her senses expanded, seeking more information, she heard no sounds of traffic outside, no horns or motors or sirens. She didn't even hear an occasional passing car.

She eased the blanket off and sat up straighter, then swung her legs around and lowered her bare feet to the floor. She started to stand, but a wave of dizziness put her right back down. Her head swam, and her body began to complain at her for daring to move at all. Pain pulsed, soft, then more loudly, from her back, from her legs, from her shoulders and one hip. The dizziness became an insistent throb, and she lowered her head into her hands, closing her eyes and moaning softly.

Not heaven, she thought. *Not even close. I'm definitely still in my body.*

"You shouldn't be trying to get up yet."

It was a voice. A familiar voice. Deep and resonant and male, with the accent she'd heard so many nights in her sleep. Her angel?

His hands closed on her shoulders, and he spoke again with concern. "Are you all right?"

She lifted her head slowly, expecting…she didn't know what. A radiant being in white robes with a halo floating above his head?

It wasn't quite that. But he *was* radiant. And so blessedly, blissfully familiar. His skin was light, for a man who was clearly of Latin descent. Oh, the usual coppery tones were there, but it was almost as if it were backlit somehow. And his beloved eyes… Deep brown eyes like chocolate left too long in the summer sun, and lashes so thick she was almost jealous. Her own only looked that way with the help of mascara and eyeliner. He came by them naturally, just like the heavy brows and the full lips.

"It's you," she whispered, and she almost choked on the

tears that welled up in her throat. "I really am dead, then. Why does it still hurt?"

His eyes seemed to well up, or maybe she was just thinking that because her own were wet. "No, pretty one. You are not dead."

Was his voice as beautiful as it seemed? Or was she experiencing some sort of ecstatic state induced by nearly drowning? "If I'm not dead, then…how can you be here with me?" she asked softly.

He frowned, then lifted a hand to indicate the room around them. "This is my home. Where else would I be?"

"Then…you're not an angel?"

His smile was quick, but restrained, too. A flash of perfect white teeth only partly revealed. "No, *pequita,* I am no angel."

"But I know you. I do. I know you. We've met before. At the lighthouse, before I…" Her head ached harder, and she frowned, pressing her hand to her forehead.

"You've been through a terrible trauma. Your mind is playing tricks on you, no doubt."

"No, I *do* know you. I've dreamed of you. All my life, really. When you came to me that night—"

"Your mind is playing tricks on you."

"No. You knew my name that night. You called me Anna. And I know yours. It's Diego."

That seemed to bring him up short. He went still, and his gaze darted away from hers, turning inward, but only very briefly. "I've been speaking to you while you slept,

Anna. I've told you my name several times. But this is the first time I've heard yours."

"Why are you lying to me?" she asked softly.

He met her eyes again, holding her gaze steadily as if to show her how sincere he was being. How truthful. "You've been through a terrible ordeal. That's just confusing you now. And it doesn't matter, anyway, does it? The past rarely does, you know. You are here with me now, safe and sound, and I can get you back to your people just as quickly as you wish. So there's not a thing in the world for you to worry about."

She nodded very gently, even while thinking that she had no "people" to go back to, and now no boat and no money.

"You should lie back down. Your poor body is bruised and battered from end to end. You need rest, so you can heal."

She thought so, too, but didn't obey. Not yet. "How badly am I hurt?"

"Nothing is broken, *pequita,* and I don't detect any internal injuries. I think it would be harder on you to make the journey to the mainland in your current state than it would be to just remain for a few days and let your body heal."

"The mainland?" She frowned and lifted her head again. "Where are we?"

"We're on my island. I call her Serenity, because that is what she has given me."

"Your island?"

"Yes."

"And...you live here with...?"

"With the animals. With the birds. With the ocean waves and the palms and the coconuts. And...with peace."

"There's no one else?"

"No. No one else." He shrugged. "Until now. But I promise you, you are safe with me. I will not harm you. And I'll take you back as soon as—"

"Can I see it? I need to see it—please."

"The island?"

"Yes. Please, Diego, I need to see it."

He hesitated, staring at her as if trying to see more than what she was saying, and she experienced the oddest sensation, as if he were probing her very soul. And then he seemed to make a decision. He bent closer, sliding his arms underneath her body and lifting her up.

"Wait! You don't have to carry me."

"You're in no condition to walk on your own. And it's not the first time, after all." She barely had time to glimpse the other rooms in his home as he swept through them toward a large wooden door that seemed to be made from one single board and was completely covered with the images of animals and symbols, like she would have expected to see on some Native totem pole.

He nodded at the handle, which was a wrought-iron ring. "If you would," he said.

She grasped it and pulled. And the door swung open, revealing...paradise. Stone paths wound in a dozen directions amid exotic flowering plants, the likes of which she had never seen. Orchids, maybe. Birds-of-paradise, perhaps. And others, huge blossoms and tall grasses, all emitting the most beautiful fragrances she'd ever smelled. There was a fire circle in the center of it all, made of stacked rocks, with a bare, sandy patch of ground surrounding it and a chair entirely carved from a tree trunk close beside. Beyond the flowers and paths and fire circle, palm trees stood tall and graceful, along with other trees she couldn't have named. And beyond those she saw a very large roof. "What's that?"

"My workshop. I'm building a new sailboat."

A tiny animal—like a miniature deer—grazed nearby. Its head came up, soft eyes meeting hers, nostrils flaring slightly. But it didn't run away. It looked at the man who held her, and he looked back. Anna watched his face, more caught up in his expression than the odd little animal. He looked at it the way an adoring father looks at his child. He loved it. He smiled at it, and she looked back at the tiny deer as it returned to grazing. Something moved in her peripheral vision, and she glimpsed a peacock strutting along one of the winding paths that led into the forest, its long tail dragging behind.

She looked and looked and looked. And the more she looked, the more beauty she saw unfolding beneath the nighttime sky, that was clear and glittering with stars. And then, slowly, she swung her wide eyes to his again and asked, "Are you *sure* this isn't heaven?"

Chapter 5

Diego was both pleased and troubled by her reaction to the haven he'd created. Pleased, because it gave him pride to share what he had chosen to surround himself with. The natural beauty. The place he'd worked on until it became his idea of paradise. And yes, heaven, because he would never see the real thing, being an immortal. Or if he did, he wasn't sure he would be allowed in. Weren't vampires damned?

The only thing his paradise lacked was the presence of other people. But he'd chosen to make it that way. And he'd protected his solitude with every power at his disposal.

But he was worried by her reaction, too, because she seemed to love Serenity Island just a little bit too much. He didn't want her here any longer than she had to be. And that was a difficult thought to maintain while holding her cradled in his arms, her body resting against him, her arms linked around his neck.

She twisted to look over his shoulder, back at the house, a two-story structure of logs and cobblestones. “It’s like something out of a fairy tale,” she said. “Did you build it?”

He nodded, realized her striking sea-blue gaze was no longer focused on him and spoke. “Yes. Over the course of…several years.”

“But how?” she asked, her wide eyes meeting his once more. “There were lights inside…I saw—”

“I use the sun and the wind.” He pointed with his chin, since his arms were busy holding her. Her eyes followed his gaze to the windmill standing on the highest hill on the island, visible like a sentinel in the distance. He’d had to anchor it in place the night of the storm, but he’d since set it free again. Then he showed her the solar panels lined up on the roof of his home. There were more at the workshop. “Batteries store the excess. I’m never short of power here.”

She drew her eyes from the roof to gaze into his once more. “The world could learn a lot from a man like you.”

“I want no part of the world,” he whispered.

She swallowed, silent for a moment, searching, and he felt almost as if she were probing his mind the way he had probed hers. But she wasn’t capable of such a trick, was she? She was no vampire. And yet he felt himself erecting a mental barrier to his mind, the way he would do were some strange vampire trying to read thoughts he wanted to keep to himself.

"Where did you get the lumber?" she asked at length. "The stone?"

"From the mainland," he explained. "A little at a time. All *Maria* could carry in a single trip, and then back for more when I ran out."

"Maria?" she asked, tilting her head to one side.

The wind lifted her hair and made it dance. He nearly lost himself in watching it.

"My sailboat. The *Santa Maria XIII.*"

She frowned very slightly. "That name inspires about a half dozen questions."

He looked away. "It's just a name."

"Somehow I doubt that." She waited, but when he didn't elaborate, she went on. "And you live here all alone?"

"It's the way I prefer it." Had he sounded a little defensive just then? He wondered.

"I've been doing something very similar myself. Bought a sailboat and set out, all alone. There's something about being one-on-one with the sea and the sky that just—"

"Nourishes the soul," he said softly.

"Yes. And clears the mind. It feels…holy. Like a sacred pilgrimage, somehow. Is that how it is for you, too?"

"I…love this island. And I love the natural beings that inhabit it. Every plant and animal and bird. I'm not quite as fond of people."

She nodded as if she understood that sentiment, but she didn't elaborate. After a few moments she said, "The sky is so clear now. It's hard to believe it was so violent only hours ago."

He carried her to the log chair and lowered her into it, since holding her was so very disturbing. He'd fed, and fed well, hoping to alleviate the natural cravings that he knew would arise in him with her close by. Oh, he couldn't harm her. But drinking from her didn't have to harm her. Quite the opposite, in fact. And warm, living blood was so much more enticing than the cold, bagged liquid that usually lined the refrigerator in his tiny kitchen. He'd created it in case of interlopers, to make it look as if an ordinary mortal lived there. No food in the cupboards, but there were dishes.

Since her arrival, he'd moved all the bagged blood to the cooler in the workshop, so she wouldn't stumble upon it by accident. He didn't need her knowing what he was—not yet. He wasn't ready. And she still had time.

Even as he lowered her into the chair, he sensed the warm, living blood pulsing just beneath her delicate skin. Enticing him. He couldn't remember the last time he'd—

Yes, he could. And it was far better if he didn't.

"It's been almost twenty-four hours, actually, since your ship was dashed against the barrier rocks offshore," he told her.

She shot him a quick look, her brows arching. "I slept the entire day?"

He nodded. "Don't sound so appalled. I did, as well."

"Well, no wonder, after the night you must have had." He lowered his eyes. "And I'm not appalled that I did. I do most of the time. More and more, in fact. But I want to know more, Diego. How did it happen?" she asked. "How did you know I was in trouble?"

He pursed his lips and averted his eyes, knowing that the truth would sound unbelievable. She would either guess that he wasn't quite human or presume he was lying to make himself sound like a superman. And he didn't like either option. So he chose a third. He lied.

"I was out for a late-night stroll and found you lying on my beach, in the surf."

"Must have been a shock to you."

He shrugged.

"So you picked me up and carried me back to your… your home."

"What else could I do? Certainly not leave you there to die."

"And you undressed me," she whispered, her voice going deeper, softer.

"It had to be done. Your clothes were soaked." He paced away a few steps, then added, "But they're clean and dry now."

"I owe you more than I can ever hope to repay," she said softly. "And I'm sorry to have interfered with your solitude."

"It's not as if you had a choice in the matter."

"Still…I'll try not to bother you overly much." She shrugged. "In fact, you'll probably rarely see me. I've become almost entirely nocturnal. There's something about the sun that makes me sleepy. The night, though…

that brings me alive. At least as much as anything can, these days."

He frowned at her, even while wondering if that was a side effect of having the Belladonna antigen. He didn't remember it bothering him when he'd been human, but then again, he'd been young when he'd been given the Dark Gift. Twenty-five. She had to be in her mid-thirties, at least. Perhaps even a bit older. Few of the Chosen lived to see forty. They either became what he was—a vampire—or they quietly died. Mostly the latter, since few ever knew the truth about what the antigen in their blood meant, much less knew a vampire they could ask to transform them.

He realized how little he knew about her and what she was experiencing. He wanted to know more, but not now. She looked tired. Weak.

"You're pale," he said. "We should get you back inside."

"But it's so beautiful out here. Can't we stay a little longer?"

He tilted his head to one side in thought, then nodded his consent and moved to the fireplace. He'd built it by digging a bowl out of the sandy soil, then lining it with stones so tightly interlocked that it was as if they'd been laid with cement. The surface surrounding it was lined with angle-cut stones in an ever-widening circle. He'd cleared the area around that, as well, so that no spark would ever land and set fire to his haven. Usually he used a domed screen to cover it, for even greater protection.

As a vampire, he had more than one reason to fear open

flames. And yet there was something so primal and so pleasing about them that he couldn't resist. His kind had a love-hate relationship and an abiding fascination with fire. Maybe that came from never being able to see the sun.

As always, the kindling stood nearby, and he bent to work, building a small campfire for her. As he worked, she spoke.

"You don't have to stay out here just because I am. If you want to go to bed, I mean…"

"I tend to be a bit nocturnal myself," he told her.

"Really?" She frowned, and he knew she found that odd and wanted to ask why, wanted to dig a little. But she restrained herself with a sigh and moved on to a new subject. "Can you see the ocean from here? I haven't caught a glimpse of it yet."

"From the second story you can. But there's only my bedroom up there. And the bathroom, of course." With a luxurious tub and shower he adored, and a toilet that had been installed just in case his hideaway was ever discovered. It was a cover. But it was a working toilet. It hadn't been used since the last time a mortal had set foot on this island. Cassandra. But he wasn't going to think about her.

"What made you build so far from the shore?" she was asking.

"Shelter from the storms. Privacy from any passing ships that might grow curious. But it's only a short walk along that path to the beach. And you can hear the ocean from here. Listen."

She did. He watched her close her eyes to listen, saw

the way her senses sharpened, and knew the moment she heard the waves whispering over the beach by the way her entire being practically sighed in contentment. Yes, this place had that same effect on him.

And then her eyes opened again. "I know the full name of your sailboat, but not yours," she said. "Who is the man who saved my life?"

He rose from where he'd been hunkered by the fire, put a palm flat against his waist and bowed slightly toward her. "Diego del Torres," he said.

Smiling, she said, "I'm Anna Seville."

But he already knew that. He'd known it from the night he'd met her, two months ago. It was a name that had been whispering through his mind ever since. "I'm very glad you didn't die, Anna Seville."

Her eyes lowered quickly, as if to hide some rush of emotion, and he heard her mind's knee-jerk response. *I'm dying soon, anyway. I thought I was ready, but now that I've met you, seen this place... I'm not sure of anything anymore.*

But aloud she only said, "I'm glad, too. Otherwise, I wouldn't have had the chance to see this beautiful place, and to meet you. Thank you for saving my life, Diego."

"You are more than welcome." He stared into her eyes—and into her mind—for a long moment, then finally decided to say what needed to be said. "And that is true, Anna, despite what I'm going to say next. And I hope you won't take offense."

"You saved my life. I think you've earned the right to say whatever you feel you have to."

He nodded. "You cannot stay here."

She frowned, all the pleasure vanishing from her face.

"A day or two more, yes, naturally, while you recover from your injuries, but once you're well enough to travel, I will have to take you back to the mainland."

Her eyes shifted away from his, and she blinked rapidly. "I understand. This is your haven. Mine was broken to bits by the storm. That doesn't give me the right to horn in on yours."

He nodded slowly. "I'm glad you understand." He wanted to say more, but there was a feeling creeping over him, one he knew all too well. "It's nearly sunrise."

She seemed to shake off the discomfort—hurt, perhaps—his words had inspired in her and looked at him again. "I want to watch it come up over the ocean. Can we?"

"Sadly, no. I have…I have a severe sensitivity to sunlight, Anna. That's the condition that has forced me to become…nocturnal, as you put it earlier. And I need to retire soon."

She blinked, opened her mouth, then closed it again. "I suppose you've heard all the vampire jokes you care to by now."

He felt his eyes widen a little but schooled his expression at once. "More than I care to, in fact."

"Don't let me keep you, then," she said softly.

He nodded. "I don't think you're in any condition to

walk to the beach to watch that sunrise. Not today, at least. Perhaps tomorrow morning?"

She nodded. "You're probably right. If I find myself too weak to walk back, I most likely won't be able to rouse you. If you sleep soundly, that is." She tilted her head. "Do you? Sleep soundly, I mean?"

"Like the dead." He said it with a straight face, saw her expressionless reaction last for an expanded moment, and then she smiled.

"I get it. Vampire joke."

He returned the smile with a wink. "Make yourself comfortable here, Anna. Whilc you were asleep, I stocked the house with fruit and spring water. There are fresh fish in the kitchen if you need more sustenance than that. I caught them for you earlier. Enjoy the day. I'll see you this evening."

She frowned at him, but nodded. "All right. Good night, then." She rolled her eyes. "Good day, I mean. I guess."

"Just say 'good rest.'"

"Okay, that, then."

"Do you want me to help you back inside before I go?"

She seemed to think about it, this involved thrusting her lower lip out just a little, a habit he was already finding he enjoyed. "No," she said at length. "I'll stay outside a bit longer. I think I can manage to limp back into the house when I'm ready."

"Be careful. Take your time."

"I will."

He nodded, sensing that she would not listen to him,

anyway, and walked away, wondering if his secrets were safe. He'd taken every precaution he could think of to ensure they would be.

He'd done much the same when Cassandra had shown up here, only to learn later that her innocence had been an act, and that she had known what he was from the very start and set out on a mission to seduce him, to use him, to get what she wanted from him and then walk away forever.

And that was precisely what she had done.

It was not going to happen to him again. Not ever.

Not even with Anna Seville.

Chapter 6

Anna wasn't afraid of him. That might seem very odd to anyone else, she supposed. Maybe it ought to seem odd to her. Or foolish, even. Here she was, alone, on an apparently deserted tropical island, with the strangest man she had ever met. What did he mean, he'd stocked the house with fruit and water and fresh fish *for her?* What did *he* eat?

He might be strange, but he was also beautiful. She had rarely chosen that word to describe a man, but she could think of no more suitable one. The liquid brown of his eyes and those impossibly thick lashes. The slenderness of his face and the angular jawline. Skin so smooth it seemed unreal.

All alone, yes, but perhaps not lonely. A genius, of sorts. He must be, to have built what he had here. The fairy-tale house, the natural sources of power, the entire layout, that was so very Zen-like with its beautiful landscaping. He'd created a paradise for himself. And no one else.

He was a solitary, ingenious artist who lived his life by night. And whose voice and face were familiar to her. Even his name, Diego, was exactly what she had known it would be. In fact, the only thing about him that seemed strange to her was that he was human and not the guardian angel she'd been expecting.

Maybe she really *was* dead. Maybe this was heaven.

She looked down at her legs, stretched out in front of her as she relaxed in the low tree-trunk chair, that was surprisingly comfortable. The firelight gave her a better look at herself than she'd had before, and what she saw made her suck in a sharp breath that caused a stabbing pain in her sore chest.

Her legs were mottled in vivid bruises that spanned the color spectrum from brilliant fuchsia to deep gray. They looked like contour maps of mountain ranges. There were scrapes, too, but mostly deep bruises. No wonder it hurt to walk. Lifting the waistband of the boxer shorts, she saw that the bruising included her hips and, as she twisted in her seat, her buttocks, as well. She looked as if she'd been beaten with a club.

She held out her arms and saw that they, too, were badly bruised, then shuddered at the thought of what her face must look like. She needed to go find a mirror. He'd said there was a bathroom upstairs, hadn't he?

She would definitely pay it a visit before too much

longer. But first, she was dying to get a look around the island, and his warnings about her being too weak to walk to the beach had fallen on deaf ears. She'd been alone at sea for eight weeks now. She thought she could handle a walk, even with bruises for company.

So she set out, and it did hurt. Every step brought pain, and she supposed that was all the proof she needed that she wasn't dead and this wasn't the afterlife. Yet it did not erase from her mind the knowledge that there was something otherworldly going on here. Something about him, or this island.

Or both.

It really did hurt to walk. Maybe he'd been right, she thought, once she'd traipsed a few dozen yards into the palms. She did seem to be limping a bit more with every step. Still, she pressed on, walking very slowly along a well-worn footpath that twisted and writhed through the forest. And even as she traversed the trail, night began to give birth to the day. The sky paled slightly, and in the space of a heartbeat the hush around her was filled with bird calls as the forest came to raucous life.

She smiled at their songs, their cries, their screeches, and wished she could identify them by their voices. Maybe if she were here long enough she could make a study of them.

But, of course, she wouldn't be here long at all. Diego had made that much perfectly clear, hadn't he?

Such a beautiful place to live, she thought. And then

another thought followed on its heels. Such a beautiful place to die.

She knew she should have felt at peace with that thought. Just as she had come to a peaceful acceptance of her own demise while she'd been at sea. Gradually she'd understood that this was just part of the journey. She'd accepted her own end, had started looking forward to seeing what was on the other side.

Of course, that had been when she'd still thought he would be waiting for her there. Her Spanish angel, Diego.

Now she no longer felt peaceful about it at all. In fact, thinking about her life ending filled her with an uncomfortable sense of foreboding. Of unease. Of near panic. What the hell had happened to her serenity?

She emerged from the tree line onto an expanse of white sand that sloped ever so gently to the sea. Waves rolled in, broke and thinned until they were little more than froth on the sand, and then the sea sucked them back again. Over and over. A hypnotic, healing energy wafted over her, as if generated by the movements of those waves.

Live in the moment, she reminded herself. Make the very most of every single moment. Just like you've been doing for the past two months. Just be in the moment, and don't think too much about the future.

Yes. That felt marginally better.

She sank down onto the sand, drawing her knees to her chest and gazing outward toward the horizon. And she saw the blazing hint of fire that touched the sky at the very end of the sea—for just an instant, until it became a glowing curve. Then the edge of the giant dinner-plate sun, rising as if from the depths of the ocean itself.

It was beautiful here, she thought, smiling. She really didn't think she was going to want to leave.

Diego had slept with his bedroom door locked, something he hadn't felt the need to do since he'd hosted the only other houseguest ever to visit Serenity Island. He didn't need another woman poking around, uncovering his secrets. Perhaps exposing them this time, and his haven with them. There was too much at stake. And he knew, from cruel experience, that once she had what she wanted her apparent enchantment with his home and his island—not to mention with him—would evaporate. Because it wasn't real. He gathered up fresh clothing and took it with him into the bathroom, where he indulged in his nightly ritual of a piping hot shower. It felt delicious against his supersensitive skin. Vampires felt *everything* more powerfully than humans did. Pleasure. Pain, too.

If anything, he thought as he stood beneath the steaming spray, Anna was even more beautiful than Cassandra had been. Her essence, her aura, was like a soft golden glow. The impression she gave was of a pure spirit, good to her core. But tender, too. Vulnerable. Easily frightened. Of course, that could just be what she wanted him to believe. She might be very good at disguising her true motives. Blocking her thoughts. It wasn't impossible. Some mortals could do it. Cassandra could.

Maybe Anna was…

She wasn't in the house.

He realized it as he basked in the shower's pulsing flow. There was no sense of his wounded houseguest whatsoever.

He cranked off the shower knobs, stopping the flow of the solar-heated water, and stood there dripping, cocking his head to one side, feeling for her. Then he frowned. Her essence was there, but distant. Near the beach, he thought.

Stepping out of the shower stall, he toweled off, dressed in khaki trousers and a short-sleeved yellow shirt, then headed down the stairs and outside. His hair was still wet, and he was barefoot. But then, he was nearly always barefoot. He walked, gathering his hair in a band behind his head. The shirt still hung unbuttoned, but it was a warm night, and he loved the air on his skin. Often he didn't wear any clothes at all. Why bother? He was entirely alone here, aside from the animals he so loved.

As he emerged onto the beach, he saw her curled on one side, sleeping in the sand. Close beside her Charlie, a familiar iguana, stood in the stand, poised and motionlessly staring at her face. As if waiting for her to wake up.

Certain she'd been there for a while, Diego knelt beside her, and put a hand on her shoulder. "Anna. Wake up, now."

She smiled in her sleep, twisting a little, rubbing her cheek over her shoulder. "Hmm?"

"Wake up now," he repeated, trying not to notice how irresistibly attracted he was to her in this state. Or any state, he corrected. "Come on."

Her beautiful eyes opened, like jewels shining on him with a power that surprised him. And then, as she noticed the animal so near her face, her smile become full blown. "Well, hello there, little guy." She met the reptile's steady gaze, and her own was nonthreatening. Almost beaming with love. Lifting a hand, she tentatively stroked one crooked finger over Charlie's neck.

The iguana leaned into her touch the way an affectionate cat might do. So much for loyalty, Diego thought.

"I think he likes you," he said, and then he sighed. "Anna, meet Charlie. He's an Acklins iguana, and he's quite upset that he's not looking his best right now. Those browns and greens, though quite lovely, brighten up to oranges and yellows during the hottest parts of the day, or so I've read."

The lizard gave a slow, contented blink, then turning, skittered away into the undergrowth, his very gait a comedy of its own.

Anna laughed. "Do you name all the animals who live here?"

"Only the ones I get to know well," he said.

She was still smiling. It was hard to believe she might be up to no good, conniving or plotting to use him. Hard to believe there was anything other than sweetness in her, when she smiled at him like that.

"I can't believe I fell asleep." She pushed her hands through her auburn curls, that were more beautiful tousled than neat, he thought.

"How long have you been out here?"

She blinked, her gaze sliding from his to the sea, the horizon, the night sky. "All day," she said, sounding only slightly surprised. "I watched the sunrise."

"You're lucky you didn't burn to a crisp," he told her. Then he tipped his head up, noticing the thick fronds of the palm above her. "This tree must like you as much as Charlie did. She protected you."

"She?" Her eyes followed his, and she examined the graceful tree, the way its trunk bent over and its fronds draped low, giving her shade for almost the entire day. "It does look rather feminine at that."

"You must be starving."

"I am." She extended a hand. "Help me up?"

Diego clasped her hand and pulled her onto her feet with him; then, turning, he began walking her back along the footpath toward the house. "Aside from hunger, how do you feel?"

She shot him a quick look. "I'm very sore. Way more than I realized. I hurt all over." She slowed her pace, added a pronounced limp. "I thought I was strong enough to walk down to the beach and back, but…you were right. I think my body took a far worse beating out there on the rocks than I knew."

He sensed that she was being less than perfectly honest and delved into her mind, just a little. He felt her pain, the stiffness, the aches. They were bad, yes. But she was pouring it on a bit more than she would normally do, and he heard, clearly, her rationale. *Don't act like you're doing too well, dummy, or he'll be hauling you back to the main-*

land before the night is out. Besides, you're not doing all that well.

Just as he'd suspected. She was playing it up so she could stay here longer. And that certainly lent credence to his suspicion that she had come out here knowing already what he was and what he could do for her. She had come out here to trick him into sharing the Dark Gift with her.

When all she had to do was ask.

Or maybe…maybe he was wrong. Hell, how could he know for sure?

"Did you enjoy the sunrise, at least?" he asked, to keep her talking. Because the more he conversed with her, the more of herself she revealed. Soon he would see all her secrets.

She stopped walking to beam up at him. "It was most beautiful one I've ever seen, Diego." She met his eyes as she said it, then looked beyond him, shaking her head. "This entire place—it's like your own personal Eden."

"That's exactly how I think of it."

She smiled. "I'm very grateful to you for putting up with my presence for a little while. It's awfully generous of you to share this special place with a stranger. Although…" She stopped there, gnawing her lower lip in a way that made him want to taste it.

"Although?" he prompted.

Tipping her head up, she stared into his eyes. "You don't feel like a stranger to me at all."

Like a magnet, she pulled him nearer. Not physically, but with those eyes. They tugged, and he felt his head begin to lower, his eyelids begin to fall. But he caught himself, blinking free of the spell she'd cast and straightening up again.

She lowered her head quickly, almost as if embarrassed. "I don't suppose that makes any sense to you, does it?"

"It doesn't matter if it makes sense to me. And it's not as if this is the first time you've mentioned it. It's your feeling, and you have a right to it." He set off toward the house again, step by step, though she seemed to want to take it very slowly.

"It's just that…well, it goes back to the worst day of my life, or what I thought at the time was the worst. About two months ago." She looked over at him as they walked.

He wasn't touching her anymore, but it was all he could do not to. He wanted to slide an arm around her waist, to hold her against him. He wanted to help her, because he could feel the discomfort that walking brought, but also the pleasure she was taking in the stroll.

Touching her right then, he decided, would be a mistake. He met her eyes briefly, to let her know he was listening, even though he thought he knew what she was about to say.

"Actually, it goes back a lot further than that. I'd been seeing a face, hearing a voice, in my dreams since I was a teenager. I thought I was seeing my soul mate then. But later I decided he was someone else entirely."

"He?"

"You."

He lifted his brows, studying her.

"But back to that night, two months ago. I'd been feeling…tired. Lethargic. Sleeping more and more, and sometimes during the day, too." She smiled. "Like you."

He smiled back but didn't interrupt.

"It seemed to keep getting worse, so I finally saw a doctor. And she told me…" She paused, as if needing to gather her strength to go on. "She told me I was dying."

Then she looked at him again as if to gauge his reaction. But it didn't seem appropriate to feign shock or surprise. "I'm sorry, Anna. That must have been extremely difficult for you to hear."

"It was. I was…I was devastated, really. But then…then I wasn't."

He lifted his brows.

"I just had to process it all. My life was ending. And I think what I really regretted was that I'd never lived. I'd spent my life taking care of others—people who never even seemed all that appreciative of it. Mary—my doctor—she tried to tell me that, but I didn't really get it, you know? Not down deep. Not until I wandered down to the harbor, where all the sailboats come in. I've always loved the sea, always wanted to buy a sailboat and just head out into the ocean alone. No worries. No cares."

"And what's kept you from doing that up to now?" he asked, honestly curious.

She shrugged. "My sister. Well, her kids, really. She's an addict."

"Heroin?"

"Prescriptions. Anything she can get her hands on,

really. Vicodin, Percocet, Ativan, Oxy." She shrugged. "I gave up trying to help her long ago. She has to want to help herself, and she just doesn't. But she has two kids, and they needed me. So I was there for them. I mean, they lived with her, but I was the one making sure there was always food in the house, keeping the power from being shut off and the heat on. I was the one who bought all their school clothes, and went to all the open houses and parent-teacher conferences and holiday concerts. I was the one who kept Child Protective Services from declaring her unfit and taking them away from her for good."

He nodded, and he knew she was underselling all she had done, minimizing it.

"The kids grew up and headed off to college. Now they both have jobs, they're living on their own—not high on the hog or anything. But they support themselves, and over time they'll do even better. So I stopped paying my sister's bills." She looked at him, as if waiting for his verdict on that. But he said nothing, and so she went on. "See, when I paid them before, it was for the kids' sake, but now it would just make me an enabler. She's not going to take care of herself unless she's forced to. It's the best thing I can do for her."

"You don't have to defend your actions to me, Anna. Not only am I not your judge, I agree with your decision completely. I doubt I'd have done as much as you have, in your position."

She thinned her lips. "I love my sister."

"That I *will* judge. You *don't* love your sister. You love who she could be, maybe who she once was and who she could become again. But you don't love who she is now. A negligent mother, an addict without the backbone to get herself clean. Who could love that? What is there to love in that?"

She lowered her head. He thought her eyes were growing moist. "When I refused to keep helping her, the kids disowned me. They won't even speak to me anymore."

"And how long did all of this happen before you were handed your…prognosis?" He'd been about to say "death sentence," then decided it was too harsh.

"A few months."

He nodded slowly.

"So, anyway, that's where I was in my life that night, as I sat on the pier by the lighthouse, staring out at the ocean and crying and wishing someone would step in and tell me what to do. And that's when I…had this…encounter."

He lifted his brows but didn't meet her eyes. "Encounter?"

"Vision, maybe? Maybe it all happened inside my head. But it was very clear, very vivid. Like it was real. I met… this man. The same man I'd been dreaming about all my life. He came to me, and he held me, and he told me it would be a sin not to live what was left of my life to the fullest, doing what I had always wanted to do most. He said that was our whole reason for being here in the first place."

"Sounds like a very wise man."

"It was you, Diego," she said softly. She stopped walking, staring up at him. Forcing him to meet her steady, probing gaze. "I swear, it was you. How is that possible?"

He had to hold her eyes, but it was very difficult for him to lie to her when she was looking at him so intently. In fact, he didn't think he could. But for the life of him, he couldn't sense deception in her just now. He didn't think she knew what he was, not in that moment.

"Is it possible," he asked, "that you were feeling so low that the man you believe you met that night seemed to…to save you? And that since I also saved you, though in a different way, your subconscious mind has created a connection that wasn't there before?"

She blinked, and a tiny crease appeared right above the bridge of her nose. He had to restrain himself from bending to kiss it away. "I…hadn't thought of it that way."

"It's just a notion," he said. Then he paused, as a tawny-colored bat flew from a nearby palm, swooping and diving right over her head. She caught her breath, ducking at first, from sheer instinct, but then straightening and watching with awe.

"I've never seen a bat that color before."

"That's Buffy."

She grinned so wide he almost laughed. "After the vampire slayer?" she asked.

He was stunned by those words and stared at her, his eyes no doubt wide with horror. "Vampire…*slayer?*"

"The television show. It was…well, obviously you've never seen it."

He sighed, relief flooding him. "No. No television reception out here. Nor would I want there to be."

She nodded. "So then why name the bat 'Buffy'?"

"It's her name. She's a buffy flower bat. They supposedly only live in the Bahamas, but she's living proof otherwise."

She smiled, then lifted her eyes and her hand, wiggling her fingers. "Hey, Buffy." She kept watching the bat's antics. "She looks so carefree. Not a worry in the world."

"What is there to worry about, after all?" he asked.

She tilted her head sideways, looking at him curiously. "Dying?"

"Humans are born dying," he told her. "It's as natural as the sun setting at night. Part of the cycle. It's all fine. Everything's fine." He watched her taking that in, and then, when she seemed to have absorbed it, he went on. "What did you do, after that night when the…the vision told you it was all right to live as you wanted to?"

She met his eyes. "I did what I wanted to." And then she smiled. "I put my house on the market, quit my job, wrote my will, planned my funeral—all the next day. And then I started looking for a sailboat. And you know, it was as if the day I learned I was dying, I finally started living."

"And you've been at sea ever since?" he asked.

"Until that storm, yes. I was hoping my boat would outlive me, but, um, it didn't work out that way. And now I'm not sure what I'm going to do. When I leave here, I mean."

He nodded, saying nothing. The conversation had taken a turn for the awkward.

"Because I have no home to return to, no job, no money, and only another month or so before I'm due to… you know…check out. If it all goes down the way Mary said it would."

"It *is* a dilemma," he agreed, and then he nodded. "Here we are. Why don't you cook some of that fish while I take care of a few chores around the island, hmm?"

She frowned at him, but nodded. "Chores?"

"I'd like to spend some time working on my new sailboat. In the workshop."

She smiled. "I'd love to see it sometime." Then she frowned. "But I'm so tired just from the walk back from the beach, I don't think—"

"There will be another time. You'll love this boat, being a sailor yourself. She's all wood, twice as big as the *Santa Maria XIII*."

She smiled, visualizing. "How close are you to being ready for her maiden voyage?"

He shrugged. "A few more weeks. No longer." He smiled at her eager excitement over his project, a work of the heart, truly. And he found himself eagerly anticipating taking her out to his workshop, showing her the boat, watching her reactions. Damn, she was getting to him. Far too deeply.

She was staring back at him, deep into his eyes, and looking as if she wanted to do more…as if she wanted to embrace him. But she held herself off and said, "Go ahead, then. I'll make enough fish for both of us, if you want."

"No need. I've…already eaten." He hadn't, and that was part of the problem, wasn't it? He was hearing the gentle call of her, the thrumming rush of blood flowing through her veins just beneath her supple, warm, salty skin, and it was doing things to his mind. Making him want to blurt that she should just stay here, with him, for the time she had left. Making him want to take her in his arms, to taste her skin, just a little. Maybe take a sip, one tiny droplet, to sate himself.

Right. And then the next thing he knew, he would begin to care for her. To believe that she cared for him, too. And then he would tell her that she didn't have to die. That she could live by night, endless night, as he did. He would tell her what he was, and offer to share the Dark Gift with her.

And she would pretend shock and surprise, and then calm, beautiful acceptance, and she would accept the Gift. He would drink from her, drain her to the very edge of oblivion, and then he would feed her from his own veins. And she would awaken a newborn vampire, a fledgling with wonder in her eyes.

And then she would leave him, laughing at his naive belief that there would be some fairy-tale ending, some happily ever after, for the two of them. She would leave him, laughing at his innocence, his trust. She would leave him, alone, in the paradise he had wanted to share.

He saw it all playing out in his mind, the memory stabbing into his heart like a red-hot blade. Cassandra laughing at how easily he had fallen for her. Laughing as she told him she had what she had come for and would be leaving now. Calling him a sap—and worse.

No, he would not fall so easily again. Not again.

Chapter 7

He left her at the door, and as Anna watched him go, she felt a sense of clarity. That was, she supposed, the positive side of facing one's imminent demise. Clarity. It suddenly became very, *very* easy to see what was important and what was not. It became easy to know what you wanted and almost impossibly irrational to do anything other than go after it.

And right then she knew what she wanted with that clearness of mind that only a condemned woman could have. She wanted to stay here, on this island, with this man, for whatever time she had left. Because no matter what he said or what tale he told, she knew she had met him that night near the lighthouse. And she knew he was the one she was meant to be with. She didn't know how it could be true. She didn't know what he was, exactly, only that he wasn't quite…normal. Wasn't quite…earthly. Or maybe…mortal.

And it was as that notion hit her that her gaze seemed drawn, almost of its own volition, to the corner of the cabin, way down low where the foundation met the earth. The solid square stones were fitted together perfectly, partially hidden by tall, graceful grasses and ornamental reeds. Still, she saw something in the stone and moved closer, frowning.

October, 1965.

How could that be? He'd said he'd built this place with his own hands. But he couldn't possibly have been here for more than forty-five years. He didn't look a day over thirty.

What the hell…?

She backed away, into the house, with a certain knowing settling into her. He wasn't mortal. But she wasn't dead. He wasn't an angel. He slept by day. He didn't seem to eat food.

Okay, just take a breath, she told herself. Just take a step back here and think on this. Could he be…something else? Something besides human?

That's ridiculous, Anna. It's just...

What if he was? What if he had the power to make her…that way, too? They could stay together then. She could be with him.

It hit her then, that rather than fear or disbelief her mind had jumped right to what had been her goal all along. Finding a way to stay with him. So staying with him was clearly what she wanted, what her heart desired. And she'd learned—from the man himself, in fact—that doing what her heart desired was the only way she wanted to live ever again. Dying or not.

The means to achieve that goal were just as clear: she had to make him *want* her to stay.

What if she was wrong, and he was just an ordinary man? What if the rest was all in her mind? Would it be fair to him to try to make him care for her when she was more than likely going to be dead in a few weeks?

But life was too short to always do what was best for others. He'd told her that. Or she thought he had. So she would spend her remaining time doing what was best for herself.

Besides, she'd told him her condition. He knew she was dying. He wouldn't be entering into anything unaware. She had to make inroads with the man. Somehow.

But he was so different from any man she'd ever known, she wasn't exactly sure how. So she watched him vanish around a bend in the trail, taking a fork they hadn't taken before, and then she went inside the house and explored it thoroughly. There really wasn't all that much to see. Very little food in the kitchen. Almost none. And while there were dishes in the cupboards, most of them wore a thin film of dust, as did the range. The fridge was the only appliance that appeared to be used regularly. Though it, too, was all but bare. Fresh fish, cleaned and ready to cook, lay in a glass dish with a tight-fitting plastic cover. But though the fridge looked well used, there was nothing else inside besides a pitcher of what looked like iced tea.

And the rest of the kitchen looked positively bereft.

How very odd.

There was no dining room, just a big archway that led back to the living room where she'd first awakened. Logs were stacked neatly beside the fireplace, and the room looked far more lived-in than the kitchen. A blanket lay over the back of a chair as if left there by someone who'd been enjoying its warmth. Books on wildlife and local vegetation lay here and there, one open, facedown, as if to hold its place.

Her eyes turned, drawn to the stairway, cleverly made of halved logs. She was pulled toward it, even though she sensed that she was dancing along the borderline of his tolerance. Even in her own mind, snooping was out of line. The bit she'd done so far seemed within an acceptable range, but as she walked up the stairs, she felt worse and worse.

She stood outside his bedroom door, her hand hovering near the antique brass doorknob that had the face of a bear engraved on it. But something stopped her. Something just wouldn't let her invade his privacy by sneaking into his bedroom. His sanctuary. It wouldn't be right.

Sighing, acknowledging inwardly her own disappointment in her willingness to pry, wondering what discoveries she might have made had she pressed on, she backed off and went instead to the very large bathroom that was the only other room on the second floor.

And she was glad she had.

The tub was a giant round Jacuzzi. Beside it, a shower stall twice as large as any she'd ever seen stood invitingly. She opened the etched glass door and saw that it was equipped with six showerheads at varying angles and heights. Wow.

The soaps and shampoos were mostly male-oriented, woodsy scents, or spicy ones. And her clothes, her own comfy pajamas, that she'd been wearing when the storm had tossed her little boat onto the rocks, were lying across a counter. They smelled of mild soap and fresh, ocean air. He'd washed them and hung them out to air-dry, she suspected.

All right, enough with the snooping. It was time to do some basking. Life was short, and there wasn't nearly enough basking being done by most of those living it. She ran the tub full of steaming hot water, which took far less time than she had expected. While it filled, she found several brand-new, still-wrapped toothbrushes in the nearby medicine cabinet and helped herself to one of them.

In short order she was soaking her bruised, battered limbs in the bubbling bath, head leaned back, eyes closed. She was exhausted from her little walk from the beach and her minuscule spying expedition. She'd really discovered very little, except that the man didn't seem to eat.

She was still very curious about him. But she would just keep her eyes and ears open. She would ask him the things she wanted to know. She would look around some more when she had the chance, she told herself. Maybe even try to position herself close enough to the bedroom to get a glimpse inside when he opened the door.

Or maybe get herself invited in there in…some other way.

That idea appealed more than it ought to. Well, of

course it did. She'd been dreaming of this man her entire life. Whether he believed it or not, she had. He was meant for her. Even if it was destined to last only a very little while.

She felt tears spring into her eyes at the notion of dying, of leaving him behind, and they were still burning there as she fell asleep.

She was in the house, though he would be damned if he could tell where. Her scent, however, that essence of Anna, was *everywhere.*

His houseguest had been snooping. The realization made his heart trip over itself, even though he had taken precautions. What if she had found something?

If she had, he asked himself, what was she going to do about it? Besides, hadn't he already suspected that she knew full well what he was? That she was only pretending not to know? Playing him, the way Cassandra had?

His inner voice silenced that train of thought before he could ponder it through to the end. What she might do about it was hardly the point. His secrets were just that: *his,* meaning not hers to go digging around in. And *secrets,* meaning they were not for public knowledge. She had no right.

She wasn't in the living room, but her energy was. It was everywhere, on every shelf, in every corner. Not unpleasant, never that. Her essence was like a soft perfume, but more than a scent. It was her aura. Fragile, but fiery, like the tiny, spitting flame of a stubborn candle in a gentle rain.

And yes, he liked that about her.

But this was…too much. She'd touched his books, running her fingers over the spines as she'd skimmed the titles. She'd walked around the entire room, pausing near every shelf and painting, every stand and bauble, every heavily curtained and darkly shaded window. What had she made of those? he wondered. Heavy drapes of forest green, hanging over matching colored window shades, with shutters on the outside as an additional barrier against the sun. What had she thought about his need to completely shut out the daylight, assuming she didn't already know?

Her essence led him into the kitchen, where she had opened every cabinet and the refrigerator, too. Had she noticed the lack of food? Had she gone looking for what *really* kept him fed? He'd removed his bags of cold, clean human blood from the fridge only a few hours after he'd brought her here. He'd waited long enough to put warm, dry clothes on her, to cover her in blankets and build a fire nearby, to make sure she was going to live, then removed his stores of blood to the cooler out in the workshop.

Not finding Anna in the kitchen, he surged up the stairs, pausing where she had at his bedroom door. He felt the energy of her hand hovering near the doorknob and lowered his head in disappointment, before he realized that her essence ended there. She hadn't turned the knob or opened the door. The sense of her went no farther. She had not intruded into his bedroom. And not because he'd taken the precaution of locking her out. No. She hadn't even *tried* the door.

He felt a smile tug at the corners of his lips, felt the tension slowly ease from his body. His feelings of violation and resentment evaporated, and curiosity replaced them. What had stopped her?

And then a sneaking suspicion arose that caused the smile to falter. Had she simply run out of time? Had she heard him coming and had to scamper away, giving up on her day of prying into his shadows?

He lifted his head, turning and sensing her nearby, in the large bathroom that took up the other half of the second story. The door was ajar, far enough for him to see a naked, water-beaded knee in the tub. It wasn't moving. He stepped a little closer and saw more of her revealed. Her thigh vanished into the water, the sight of it blocked further by the tub itself. Her arm dangled over one side, long and slender and surprisingly toned for one so thin. But she'd been alone at sea for over a month, hadn't she? That would firm a person up, even a sick one.

And she *was* sick. He'd seen it before, the ravages of the antigen going to work on a mortal. Not in himself. He'd been turned before it got that bad, but he'd seen it in Cassandra. It was what had made him want to save her.

He banished that memory from his mind and moved a little closer, pushing the door wider now, but not quite going inside.

Anna was leaning back, her head tipped to rest against

the edge of the tub. Her eyes were closed, mouth slightly open, hair bundled on top of her head, with curls cascading around her like a waterfall. As he stared, she inhaled and snorted a little.

His smile returned. No artifice there. She wasn't faking. She was truly asleep, and judging by the stillness of the water, the Jacuzzi jets, that ran for fifteen minutes before shutting themselves off and requiring you to hit the start button again, had long since gone silent. She'd been there awhile.

And that told him all he needed to know. She hadn't gone into his room because she had chosen not to. As curious as she must be, she'd chosen to respect his privacy.

For the first time, he considered that maybe she was genuine. Not a liar, like Cassandra. Not a user. Not a cold, calculating thief out to steal eternal life under false pretenses.

Maybe she was for real. As sweet and wonderful as she seemed.

And if he took one more step closer, he thought, he might see a whole lot more to like about the woman. But since she'd respected his privacy, though she obviously hadn't wanted to, he figured he ought respect hers in turn.

He backed out of the bathroom without so much as peeking at her body. Besides, he'd already seen it when he'd stripped off her sopping-wet clothes and dressed her in his own. And it wasn't a sight he was likely to forget. Not only because he hadn't glimpsed a naked woman in years, but because she was a beautiful specimen. A tempting one.

But he wasn't going to let his mind go in that direction.

He pulled the door closed, then knocked sharply, twice, to wake her. "Anna?" he called. "Are you in there?"

"Wha—oh!" There was a sloshing of water. "Yes, give me a minute."

"Of course."

More sloshing. Then the distinct sound of gurgling as the water started to drain. Moments later she was opening the door, holding one large plush towel around her torso, with another draped over her shoulders. Her hair was still up, wet tendrils dangling around her neck, and her face was sleepy. Leaning on the doorjamb, she smiled up at him. "I fell asleep in your tub. I'm sorry."

"It's perfectly all right. You're here to rest and to heal. Nothing to apologize for."

She nodded, but her eyes shot lower. "Not much healing that can be done, though. At least, not for what's really wrong."

"The weakness…it's getting worse?" he asked.

"I'm so sleepy all the time. I want to be exploring and playing and relishing what's left of my life, and particularly my time here on this beautiful island with you. But instead I'm falling asleep in the bathtub."

"There's a lot to be relished about a hot bath in an oversized Jacuzzi." He tipped his head slightly. "At least, as far as I recall from the last time I did so myself. You enjoyed it, yes?"

Her smile returned, as he had intended it to do. "Yes."

"Then no time was wasted. And there's still enough night left to enjoy. And since you so enjoyed the sunrise this morning…" He paused there, frowning at her. "You did, didn't you?"

"Not all of it." She lowered her head so that her curls fell damply across her cheek, then peered up at him from behind them with a sheepish grin. "I fell asleep *then,* too."

"Well, then, this will please you doubly. How about watching the moonrise instead?"

She frowned. "But it must be nearly…"

"Midnight," he filled in. "But it's a half-moon. They rise at midnight, set at midday, more or less. Very predictable, the moon."

"Yes, I love that about Her."

He lifted his eyebrows at her personification of the luminary, but other than that, let the comment go. "How quickly can you get dressed?"

"Five minutes."

"That fast?"

"What's to take time with?" she said, lifting the towel from her shoulders and using it to rub her hair. "It's warm outside, so there's not a lot to put on. Not to mention I've barely got any clothes to choose from, so making a selection won't take long."

"Well, we can remedy that. I noticed a few colorful items washing up on the shore, near where the boat's docked. Probably your clothes. Go on, get ready. I'll be waiting downstairs."

He turned to go, leaving her to it. And he wondered why he'd proposed what could be construed, he supposed, as a romantic evening together. Why would he put himself through that, take that risk, just because she had stopped herself from invading his privacy? Was it really all that impressive that she had managed not to do something that almost anyone would see as rude and unacceptable?

Given his experience with women in the past? Yes. It *was* that impressive.

Chapter 8

"Here we are." He nodded toward a tipped-over log that lay on the beach, just where the palm trees met the sand.

They were in a different spot from where she'd fallen asleep earlier. They'd circled the shoreline a little bit farther and come to a cozy cove where he'd built his own private dock.

"You can sit right there," he told her. "I've found that the log makes a comfortable backrest."

But she didn't sit. She was too busy staring at the small sailboat tied to the pier he'd built in a tiny inlet where the water was shallow and mostly still. It was a small sailboat with a large motor attached, though its sails were tightly furled at the moment. The name *Santa Maria XIII* was painted in a beautiful, old-world-style script across the stern. She wondered about that *XIII,* even as she experienced a pang of longing for her own lost vessel. The feeling faded, though, as she noticed colorful items littering the shoreline. Frowning, she pointed. "Are those…?"

He smiled. "Your clothes and belongings have been washing up all evening. I spotted them earlier but wanted to check on you before coming down to gather them up."

"You spotted them…all the way from the house?"

"The workshop."

"That's a long way to see—especially in the dark. You must have very good eyesight." Suddenly her theory was seeming less and less ridiculous. Could he really be…? She couldn't even think the word.

"Excellent, in fact—particularly my night vision," he said.

She tried to hide her look of…well, shock, she supposed. Her crazy supposition was seeming more and more possible. To avoid his probing eyes, she started forward toward the debris on the shoreline, but he held up a hand. "I'll get them. You should rest."

"I'm fine at the moment, Diego. But thank you." She walked with him, and as the frothy surf washed over their bare feet she bent and began gathering up items she'd thought were long gone. A bikini top, no bottom in sight. A pair of denim shorts. A couple of tank tops and a T-shirt. She picked them up one by one, wringing them out as best she could and then draping them over one arm. She located one tennis shoe. A lot of good that was going to do her, she thought, when she failed to find its mate.

"It's better than nothing, though," he said, speaking

as if in response to her thoughts. That was, of course, impossible.

Or was it?

When they'd picked up everything, she found herself closer to the little dock, and she studied his boat for a moment. "It's small," she said. "But nice."

"Wait until you see the new one," he said proudly.

"Don't tell me. The *Santa Maria...XIV?*"

He smiled, but didn't confirm it.

"Have there really been thirteen other boats, Diego, or does the number mean something else?"

"I…are you sure you have all your clothes?"

"Just how long have you been here, Diego?"

He averted his eyes. "A long time."

"And you only go to the mainland…what did you tell me? Once a month?"

"Once a season, if I can manage it. But if supplies get low, I sometimes have no choice."

"I see. And when was the last time you went? For supplies, I mean."

"Just this past April. I was—" He stopped there, then began again. "Or it might have been March. I don't really keep track."

But she knew it had been April. April 10. The day she'd received her death sentence and gone to the shore to process the news. The day she'd met her guardian angel. And he'd been there, too. She knew it now for sure. She'd known it as soon as he'd said April, and he'd seen her know it, and then quickly tried to cover—to change his answer. But it was too late, and he knew it.

"It was you I met, you I kissed that night, wasn't it, Diego?"

He met her eyes again, held them. "Don't be ridiculous. How could it have been?"

She shrugged. "I guess you must be…some kind of… supernatural being. You spoke to me mentally. You knew my name. You heard me crying out for help on the night of the storm. Didn't you?"

He lowered his head, saying nothing.

"How would it hurt you to tell me the truth, Diego? I'm dying, remember?"

He heaved a great sigh, then turned to focus on his small sailboat. "So what do you think of her?" he asked, changing the subject.

"I think she shouldn't be in the water. You don't leave her there all the time, do you?"

"Of course not. Only when a trip is imminent." He looked at her. "I put her in earlier tonight."

She blinked, afraid to ask why, but he answered, anyway.

"You'll be well enough to leave soon."

Was it too soon for her to ask him to let her stay? No. No, it was the right time, but she hadn't worked up enough courage to do it yet. Gnawing her lower lip and trying to compose a rational argument in her mind, she began walking through the warm sand, back toward the log where he'd suggested they sit. "I have a confession to make," she said softly, hoping to work her way up to what she really wanted to talk about.

"And what's that?"

She reached the log, curled her toes in the sand, then turned and sat down, getting comfortable and eyeing the horizon for the promised moonrise. Nothing in sight just yet, though. "I'm afraid I was a little nosy today. I kind of…looked around the house a little."

He nodded. "I know. You didn't go into my bedroom, however."

She felt her eyes widen. "How did you know?"

He shrugged. "Why didn't you go into my bedroom, Anna?"

She blinked, still blown away that he had known. "It would have been out of line," she said softly. "An invasion of your privacy. I just… It was outside my comfort zone, I guess."

"But looking around the rest of the place wasn't?"

"No." She lowered her eyes. "Maybe a little bit."

"So why did you?"

"I was curious. About you."

"I see. And did your explorations sate that curiosity?"

"No, not at all. If anything, they only sharpened it. The cornerstone of the cottage says 1965. How can that be, if you built it yourself?" She tipped her head to one side, waiting, expecting him to at least try to formulate an answer that made sense. But that wasn't what he did at all.

"I'm a very private man, Anna. That's probably obvious to you."

She blinked. "Well, yes. I mean, you live all alone on a deserted island. Can't get much more private than that. But…why? What made you want to live this way?"

He looked away. "I can't help but wonder what part of the word *private* you don't understand?"

"You're being mean now."

He looked back at her. "Sorry."

"It was a woman, wasn't it?"

He rolled his eyes and walked closer, but passed her to bend down near the log. He pulled out a bottle of wine and two glasses, then filled one to the brim and handed it to her.

"Nice," she said. "Aren't you having any?"

"Of course," he said. And then he filled his own glass, sank into the sand beside her, leaned back against the log and pointed. "Look, here it comes."

She fell silent, though her questions were still screaming in her mind. She shut her lips tightly, determined to enjoy this night to the fullest. Relaxing there, she sipped the wine, which was delicious, and leaned back and watched the moon climb into the sky, lopsided and a bit less than half-formed, rising slowly above the water and sending a long beam outward, like a glowing arrow pointing straight from the moon to this very stretch of beach. Pointing right at her. At them.

"That's amazing. So beautiful," she said.

"I agree."

His words were soft and his eyes, she found when she looked his way, were on her. Not the moon.

"Diego," she whispered. "I won't be here very long."

"I know."

"And I won't snoop anymore."

"That's good to hear."

"But I want..." She got lost in his eyes. There was a passion in them that was beyond anything she'd seen before. A desire she'd never seen focused on her. "I want you," she whispered, even though it wasn't what she had intended to say at all.

"That would be a mistake," he told her.

She smiled broadly. "How could it be? I've got nothing to lose, Diego. I'm dying. And my guardian angel told me to do exactly what I wanted to do with the time I had left. And what I want to do right now is kiss you. And so I'm going to."

She leaned up, and he didn't pull away. Her lips moved close to his, then, boldly, pressed against them. He remained motionless as she slid her hands over his shoulders and around to the back of his neck, then threaded her fingers into his hair and held him to her so she could press harder, kiss deeper.

She felt him shudder, and then he gave in. He wound his arms around her waist and bent over her, pushing her back into the sand so that his body was angled over hers, and then he kissed her. He kissed her like she'd never been kissed before, and every single part of her came alive.

"Diego," she whispered. "Diego."

She arched upward against him, felt the hardness of his arousal pressing into her thigh. And then, to her stunned amazement, he rolled away, sitting up, blinking in the night as if his entire being were shattered.

"Diego?" she asked.

He said nothing. She sat up, as well, sliding a hand over his shoulders from behind.

"Please, talk to me."

"There's nothing to talk about. I can't do this with you, Anna. I know where it's going to end, and I don't want to go there again."

She closed her eyes. "I want to stay here, Diego. I want to stay here, on the island with you, for whatever time I have left in this life. It can't be more than a month—six weeks at the outside."

"No." It sounded as if he had to force the word through a space too tight for it.

"But…but I'm dying. I don't have anything to go back to. I'll stay out of your way, I'll do whatever you need me to do, but please, don't make me go back."

He rose to his feet, so that her hands fell from his broad shoulders. She stayed where she was. "You need to leave. And you're obviously strong enough to do so. We'll set sail tomorrow night at sundown."

"Diego, please!"

"Don't beg, Anna. It's beneath you."

"I don't have a damn thing to lose."

"There's always your pride."

"You're a hard, cold man, aren't you?"

He shrugged. "I'm going to my workshop for a few hours. I don't want to be bothered."

"Fine. You go to your damn workshop, you selfish bastard."

He walked away, seemingly unperturbed by her parting shot. Anna sank to her knees in the sand and wept bitterly. And she wasn't even sure why.

Chapter 9

She sat there in the sand, staring out at the half-moon and drinking the bottle of wine he'd left behind. When she was all cried out, she sat in silence for a while, trying to analyze just what was behind her roiling feelings. They were confused and tumultuous, far from the peaceful, blissful state she'd found while alone at sea.

That state, she decided, had been one of calm acceptance. She knew she was dying. She had made a choice to spend her time on the sea, and she had been enjoying every moment of it.

That was no longer the case, and she struggled to figure out why. Why, for example, wasn't her dying request to Diego something entirely different? Why wasn't she begging him to loan her his sailboat so that she could continue on the path she had chosen, to die at sea, maybe sail close to this island again when she sensed the time was near and just anchor offshore, so he could come get his boat when it was over?

That request would have made more sense to her. To him, too, probably. But she had no desire to borrow his boat or head back out to sea. Her only wish was to stay here on this tiny chunk of paradise. And not alone, either. She wanted to stay here with *him.* There was something so…so compelling about him. Something that felt…intimately connected to her. She wanted to touch him, to be close to him all the time, and she barely knew the man. And yet it felt as if she knew him. It felt as if she'd known him all her life.

And loved him even longer.

She was no longer so much at peace with dying. Rather than that calm, blissful state of acceptance she'd felt before, there was now a sense of time running out. A sense of urgency to use what time was left to get closer to him, to this place.

She closed her eyes, lowered her head and sighed. Maybe it was just the approach of her own end making her feel such a wild array of nonsensical emotions. Maybe everyone got all tied up in knots when they knew they were short on time. Of course they did. Why wouldn't they?

Okay, so she needed to get a handle on this. Probably apologize to him, and maybe try to explain what had led to her outburst. And then she would get back to the task at hand, convincing him to let her stay. Because no matter what he said, she had no intention of leaving. He would have to carry her bodily off this island if he wanted to get rid of her. Whether to tell him that, too, was still up in the air in her mind.

She opened her eyes, feeling better, empowered, calm, resolved, and found herself focusing on a stain in the white sand.

A red stain. Like blood.

It was right beside the spot where Diego had been sitting, on the side of him that had been farthest from her. She frowned, bending closer, wondering if he'd been injured and unaware of it, or—

And then she saw the wineglass, sitting empty on the log, and knew it wasn't blood. That stain was wine. She bent closer, sniffed. Yes, it was wine. He'd poured himself a glass, but as her mind replayed the events of the past hour, she realized she had never actually seen him take a single sip of it.

And in her mind she heard the actor Bela Lugosi in the role that had made him famous, saying, in his thick Romanian accent, "I never drink…wine."

"Oh, come on, Anna," she said aloud. "Just cut it out, already." And yet her eyes were glued to that stain in the sand.

She shifted her gaze to look out at the moonlight beaming down on the water, as perfectly beautiful as if it were the backdrop on a movie set. And her mind kept on taunting her. *He's nocturnal. He said so himself. And you've certainly never seen him in the daylight.*

"He hasn't seen *me* in the daylight, either," she argued.

No food in the house. And not just curtains on the windows, but heavy drapes, and window shades, and shutters to boot.

"Just because he doesn't like the sun, doesn't mean…"

You've got to get a look inside that bedroom.

But then her thoughts ground to a sudden halt, as she heard him cry out in what sounded like pain. She was on her feet, turning toward the path back and even starting forward, before she realized she hadn't heard the shout with her ears.

She'd heard it with her mind.

And she felt it still, that sense of him, hurting and in distress, ringing in her head, a feeling, not a sound. She was compelled to go to him. She dropped her wineglass beside the empty bottle in the sand and ran.

He'd been careless. Angry, frustrated, stupid and careless. Because he wanted so very badly to believe her when she told him she wanted to stay on this island…to stay with him. But he'd been told the same thing before. By a woman in the very same circumstances.

He'd taken his angst out on his work, and now the circular saw lay on the floor, its teeth clinging to bits of his flesh, and his forearm was gushing blood at a pace that would kill him in very short order.

"Oh, my God! Diego!"

And then she was there on the floor beside him, and acting without any kind of hesitation or panic or delay. She looked around, assessed the situation and sprang into action, grabbing a box cutter from his workbench and quickly slicing the power cord off the saw. Kneeling beside him, she wrapped the cord around his arm, above the gash, then knotted it once, tightly. Getting up again, she grabbed a big screwdriver and laid the blade atop the cord, then knotted the cord again over the blade to create an instant tourniquet. She twisted the screwdriver, tightening the cord around his arm, and he couldn't help but cry out in pain.

She shot him a look—and he saw tears welling in her eyes. One spilled over and rolled slowly down her cheek. "Don't die," she said.

He couldn't look away. "I…tend to bleed like…like a hemophiliac," he explained. "It's not going to clot."

"I'm the same way," she told him, wonder at that in her eyes, and then she pushed her questions aside. "I can stitch it up."

He shook his head. "The pain—I have a very low threshold for pain."

"Then what? We can't just leave the tourniquet on indefinitely. You'll lose your arm."

"What time is it?"

"What earthly difference does *that* make?"

"Please…"

She shrugged. "About three-thirty, but I'm only guessing."

"Two hours, then."

"Until what?"

"Sunrise," he told her.

She looked at him sharply, holding his head in her lap now. "And what happens at sunrise, Diego?"

He averted his eyes, but he'd heard the knowing in her voice. She'd either known what he was all along or she was beginning to figure it out. "If you can help me back to the house, get me to my room, I'll be fine."

"Before sunrise, right? I have to get you to your bed before sunrise? And then you'll be fine?"

"Yes."

She tipped her head to one side, staring at him, and he saw her deciding not to press him for the truth. Not now, at least, when he was in imminent danger from a cut that shouldn't have been all that serious. And *certainly* shouldn't have bled as much as it had. He saw her looking at the amount of blood on the floor around him, and he read her thoughts almost without trying.

"You're going to have to tell me sometime," she said softly. "But at least now you won't be in any condition to make me leave tomorrow night." She pulled his uninjured arm around her shoulders and got to her feet, helping him to rise with her.

His knees nearly buckled beneath him, and she got a better grip around his waist and said, "Diego, this is worse than it ought to be. It's not that bad a cut."

"It's the blood loss. And the pain. If I make it till morning, I'll be all right."

"Right. If you make it till morning." He looked bad. He looked worse than bad, he looked near death, she thought.

They walked—stumbled, really—together to the house,

and she got him inside. Somehow they managed to get up the stairs, and at his bedroom door he paused, leaning on the wall as if it was all he could do to remain standing.

"Key…in my pocket."

Nodding, she thrust a hand into the pocket of his khaki trousers and felt around, finding the key and pulling it out, and quickly unlocking the bedroom door. Then she helped him inside, into utter blackness.

"I was dying to get a look in here," she told him. "But not like this." Her attempt at levity fell flat, though. They shuffled forward through inky darkness, and then he fell onto a bed that she hadn't even seen. She leaned over him, feeling around to get her bearings. She got him straightened out as best she could. Then, holding her hands in front of her, she made her way back to the open door, guided by the light that came from beyond it, and found, as she had expected, a light switch just inside the doorway. She flipped it on and turned for her first glimpse of his bedroom.

And then she blinked, because it was just an ordinary bedroom, with one notable exception. "There are no windows," she said softly. She looked at him, lying there on the bed. "Why are there no windows, Diego?"

He didn't answer. He was lying still, and his skin was startlingly pale. She hurried to the bed, climbed onto it beside him, kneeling there, her hands on his shoulders. "Diego? Diego, just tell me what to do—please."

He opened his eyes to mere slits. "I…need…"

"What? Tell me what you need and I'll get it for you. Just tell me. Diego? Diego, what is it?"

He stared at her, trying hard to keep his eyes focused, she thought, but she could see the pupils dilating and contracting over and over.

"I'm dying," he said.

"No! No, Diego, you are *not.* Tell me what to do. *Tell me.*"

He tipped his head back as his eyes widened in a burst of pain and his mouth opened wide, and she saw his incisors. She jumped from the bed, moving backward away from it, but only three steps. And then she stopped herself, swallowed hard, stood still, staring at him. "My God, it's true. I've been thinking it all night, but I just didn't think it was possible. You're...you're..."

"A vampire," he whispered. "But you already knew, didn't you? Isn't that why you came?"

She frowned. "You're talking crazy now. It's the blood loss, I guess." She swallowed and moved close to him again. "You saved my life, Diego," she whispered. "And I know you're the one who spoke to me that night so long ago. It seems like forever. But I know it was you. You're the reason I took what time I had left to do what I wanted. You're the reason I'm even here." Lifting her chin, she nodded once, firmly, unsure whether he was even hearing her. And it didn't matter. She was talking mostly to herself, anyway.

She moved to the bed, put one knee up on the mattress, then the other, and leaned close to him. "I'm dying, anyway. I have nothing to lose. Take what you need, Diego. Take it from me."

He opened his eyes and met hers again, and his were glowing now, glowing from somewhere within, glowing and sort of…feral. It was frightening, and yet she couldn't look away. Lifting her hand, she reached behind her head to pull her hair around to one side. She slid her other hand beneath his head to lift it gently from the pillows as she bent even closer. His cool lips brushed against the warm skin of her neck. Taking a breath, then another, she closed her eyes, bracing herself. His mouth parted, and his hands slid upward to gently cup the back of her head. Then his grip turned fierce, and he bit down with a growl that reverberated right to her soul.

Chapter 10

He was lost. Lost in a red haze of ecstasy, of healing, of hunger and of desire. Lost until the luscious elixir that rejuvenated his life force and alleviated his pain finally got around to clearing his head. Only slightly, though. Yes, feeding kept him alive and eased the pain that was dulling his mind. But it replaced that fog with the bloodlust, which was nearly as mindless.

With the force of sheer will, he withdrew his razor-sharp incisors from her butter-soft skin and lifted his head.

She stared at him, her eyelids heavy with the opiate effect of the vampire's kiss and the heavy weight of passion that went hand in hand. In his kind, feeding and sex were urges that were intertwined, and sating one fed the need to sate the other. In the victims, it was very similar. Sharing blood was an act as intimate as—no, more intimate than—intercourse. It was powerful.

As he stared into her beautiful eyes, he wanted her.

And then, drunk with the act he had just committed, she whispered, "Please?"

He blinked against his own aching need, shook his head, pushed her from him. "No."

But she gripped the hem of her blouse and tugged it over her head. Her breasts bounced as the fabric released them, round and full and soft. "I need you," she told him.

And then she leaned over him again, her lips meeting his, opening, suckling his lips and teasing with her tongue. "I've *always* needed you…"

He didn't have a choice. He wasn't made of stone. He was a creature of passions, for God's sake. Blood and sex and life were all blended together in him, and there was just no way to avoid this. He'd never wanted, never *needed,* like this before. Never.

Not even with Cassandra.

He wrapped his arms around Anna and returned her kiss, and it felt as if the fires of hell itself rose up and wrapped around them.

And then it felt like heaven instead.

Her mind vanished, and all that remained was her body, her senses. And pleasure, mind-blowing pleasure that left her quivering and weak. But gradually, very, very gradually, she came back to herself and realized that she was lying naked in his arms, and that she'd just had hours of passionate sex with a man who'd been near death.

No, not a man.

A vampire.

Her mind didn't want to wrap itself around that, but there was no other way to explain what… She raised her hand and pressed it against the skin of her neck. Yes, there were wounds there. Puncture wounds, two of them, tiny, swollen and tender.

He'd admitted the truth. And if that hadn't been enough, he'd bitten her neck.

He'd drunk of her blood.

He was a vampire.

Blinking and waiting for that truth to sink in, to make sense, she decided at length that it never would. She didn't feel afraid of him. She didn't feel any need to run away. In fact, she felt…she felt better than she had before. He'd shown her his true self. He'd let her into his lonely world.

For whatever time she had, she would embrace this new reality. What difference did it make, when she would be dead herself in a few weeks' time?

She sat up a little, propped her tired head on her hand and smiled down at him. He didn't smile back. He lay very still. *Very* still.

"Diego?"

She touched him. "Diego, are you all right?" And then, when he still didn't respond, she shook his shoulder. "Diego, wake up!"

But there was no response.

God, she'd killed him! She'd become so lost in passion that they must have knocked the tourniquet loose and—

Even as she thought it, she turned to inspect his arm.

The tourniquet was still in place, but the wound…the wound was…it was vanishing.

She blinked her eyes, rubbed them, then leaned closer, staring at something that couldn't possibly be real. The cut in his arm was mending itself, the skin pressing together in a kiss and sealing itself. In minutes there was only a faint red line remaining, and even that faded before her eyes, growing paler by degrees.

Carefully, her heart in her throat, she loosened the tourniquet and then stared hard at the arm. There was no more bleeding. How could there be, when there was no cut?

If I make it till morning, I'll be all right.

She guessed it must be morning, then. And by day, it seemed, his wounds healed. But even stranger was that fact that he certainly didn't seem alive right now. He seemed like a corpse. Except, not stiff. And not cold, either. In fact, he felt warmer than he had since she'd been here.

Slowly, she slid out of the bed and stood staring down at him. Should she check for a heartbeat? Did vampires even have one? How could she tell if he were alive or dead? Or undead? How could she know?

Blinking, she backed away. All right, she would just have to wait for nightfall, then, wouldn't she? That would tell the tale. She would wait for nightfall. And he would wake. Or not.

And if he didn't, then she supposed…she would have to bury him.

Tears welled in her eyes and spilled over, and she

rushed back to the bed, flung herself onto it and wrapped her arms around him. "Don't be dead, Diego! Please don't be dead! I don't care what you are. You gave me my life. You *did.* You convinced me to *live,* for the first time, for the only time, with the tiny bit of time I have left. And I am so grateful to you for that. You really are my guardian angel, even if some people would call you a demon. And I don't want to lose you now. Not now. So please, don't be dead, Diego. Please?"

She wept harder than she had ever wept before, even that day in Mary's office. And eventually she fell asleep there, her head on his chest, her arms linked around his shoulders, sobs racking her body every few minutes even then. She slept hard for what amounted to most of the day.

By the time she roused, it was well after 7:00 p.m. Being summer, sundown wouldn't come for a couple more hours yet. And he was still unresponsive, but since it wasn't yet dark, there was still hope. In fact, with his arm showing no sign it had ever been injured at all, she had more hope than before.

She was refreshed and feeling absurdly good. He would wake up. He had to.

She couldn't seem to stop smiling. And her attitude was so positive that she couldn't *wait* for Diego to wake so she could share another perfect, blissful night with him. In the meantime she decided to kill time as best she could. She started with a glorious hot shower, lavishing herself with the best-smelling soaps in his overstocked bathroom.

She got creative then, bundling her hair up on top of her head but leaving it loose enough that curling tendrils spilled around her like a crown of spiral silk. She made a sarong from a nearly sheer silk throw, in a French vanilla cream color that she thought was the height of romance. She searched the house for candles, lined his bedroom with them, and set a lighter nearby. And then, with around half an hour to go, she realized she was half-starved, so she filled her belly with fruits from the island, downed a glass of icy cold water, brushed her teeth and returned to the bedroom.

She lit all the candles, and then she tried to strike an alluring pose near one of them as she waited for him to rouse.

Minutes ticked by. And then more minutes. She began to fear he might really be dead, after all.

But finally his nose twitched. And then it wrinkled.

Suddenly he sat up fast, eyes flying wide, and shouted, "Fire!"

"No!" She hurried to the bed and put her hands on his shoulders. "No, Diego, it's just candles. There's no fire."

He scanned the room, wild-eyed, and bounded from the bed without even looking at her, then stood there staring at the tiny flames that surrounded him. And then, finally, his gaze found hers and a little of the wildness faded.

She smiled, relieved. "Thank God," she said, sliding from the bed. "I wasn't sure if you were going to wake up or not. I mean, when you sleep, it's as though—but then the cut, it healed, and so… Oh, I'm just so glad you're alive, Diego. So glad." She moved closer to him as she spoke, and by the end she was sliding her hands up over his shoulders and resting her head on his chest.

He put his hands on her shoulders, as well, but didn't wrap his arms around her as she had expected him to do. He seemed tentative. Probably just hadn't caught up with himself yet. When you slept that deeply, you must wake up a little disoriented, right? He needed to process everything, to remember the night before, to—

"I need you to put the candles out, Anna. I'd do it myself, but I could easily go up in flames without a snuffer, so..."

"Go up in flames?" She lifted her head, because he didn't *sound* confused or disoriented.

"After last night, I suppose there's no longer any question in your mind about what I am."

She smiled shyly, lowering her eyes even as she lifted her palm to press it to the marks on her neck. But then she frowned. "They're gone," she whispered, her eyes flying to his.

"They heal at the first touch of sunlight."

"Oh. Just like your injuries do."

"Mine heal during the day sleep. The touch of sunlight would be a whole different problem for me."

"I see. And fire?"

"My kind are highly flammable. I only keep a supply of candles on hand in case my power sources fail and light is needed."

"I didn't know," she said. "I'm sorry...about the candles." She quickly went around the room, blowing them out one by one until they stood in total darkness, the scent of smoldering wicks and hot wax too much to bear.

He opened the bedroom door. "Have you eaten?" he asked.

"Yes, I…I'm fine. Full. Thank you."

"Good. The journey will only take about four hours. Giving me ample time to get back before sunrise, but only if we leave within the next—"

"Journey?"

He stopped at the foot of the stairs, turning to look up at her. "Back to the mainland. Did you forget I was taking you back tonight?"

She blinked rapidly, her heart taking the blow that felt like a blade straight through it. Her throat constricted, and though she opened her mouth to reply, she couldn't force out a sound.

"Why don't you…" His eyes moved down her make-shift outfit, that had felt like a seductress's peignoir before and now felt like a silk throw. "Change," he finished.

"I…I thought…after last night…what we shared…"

"It was the bloodlust, Anna." He looked away when he said it, unable to hold her eyes, she thought, probably because he knew he was being a coldhearted bastard. "When a vampire feeds from a living being, sexual desire is…one of the side effects. It's nearly irresistible."

She blinked, her eyes burning with tears. "That's all it was? It would have happened…with anyone?" she asked.

"No, not with anyone. But with any beautiful woman, probably, yes, it would have happened."

"Then it meant nothing," she said softly.

"It didn't mean what you want it to mean. Can we leave it at that?"

She was silent for a moment, but inside, way down deep where he couldn't see—or could he? She was burning with anger, humiliation and rage.

"I gave you my blood," she said softly. "And I gave you my body. And you won't even give me a few weeks on your precious island before I die?"

He lowered his head. "I will visit you again before you die," he told her. "And I'll repay your favor at that time. But until then, it's best you go."

Blinking rapidly, she lowered her head. "All right, then."

Suddenly it felt as if someone were poking around inside her brain. Her head snapped up, and she found his eyes on her, the intensity in them telling her that he was doing *something*. Trying to read her thoughts? So she filled her mind with the image of walking along the beach, saying goodbye to the island.

"If you don't mind," she said softly, "I'd like a few minutes alone. I'm going down to the beach. I'll gather up any more of my things that might have washed up today."

He seemed to relax a little, and he nodded. "That's a good idea. I need to pack a few things for the trip, anyway. I'll meet you at the boat in…half an hour?"

She nodded and headed back up the stairs to his bedroom, where she pulled her clothes on as fast as she could, then grabbed the lighter from the nightstand and tucked it into her pocket.

She was staying on this island. She was staying for the rest of her life. As near as she could figure, that might be another four to six weeks. So she was staying. Whether her guardian vampire liked it or not.

Chapter 11

It was killing him to treat her as coldly as he was. He didn't want to. He wanted to scoop her right up off her feet and carry her back to bed. He wanted to ravish her over and over. He wanted to drink from her again. He wanted to feed her, too. Feed her from his own veins. Share the Gift with her.

But what he wanted had nothing to do with anything. Self-preservation came first. It was what had brought him to this island in the first place. The need to stay solitary. The need to be completely self-contained and not dependent upon anything temporal. And everything was temporal, when you came down to it. Everything. Humans, totally mortal. Lived, died, gone. Houses, homes, rotted with time. Cars fell apart. Money. Jobs. Hobbies. Friends. Relationships, even with other immortals. Nothing lasted.

Nothing but him.

He was meant to be alone. He'd lost sight of that for a time with Cassandra. But he'd learned from that experience, from the pain of it. And he'd brought himself around to being at peace with solitude again. Until Anna had shown up here and brought all those old longings back to screaming life.

If she stayed any longer, he was going to fall in love with her. He was going to let himself believe she really was everything she seemed. Already he felt himself sliding down that slippery path. How many times, just in the past hour, had he caught himself believing in her?

Why was it so hard to let her—make her—go?

She was one of the Chosen. All right. He got that. That meant that there was an automatic bond between them. He couldn't hurt her, not even if he wanted to. And he was compelled to help, to protect, to watch over her. He got that, too. Those things were the case with any member of her caste.

But this…this feeling of her being…being a part of him, of his life, of his soul, a part that had been missing all this time—it made no sense. It was far beyond what he'd come to understand were the limits of the blood link between his kind and hers.

The sharing of blood increased the power of the bond. He knew that, too. But he'd had little choice about drinking from her. He would have died otherwise. But that had only made things worse. Made her feel even more a part of him. A necessity to him.

Probably he was suffering some ordinary reaction

brought on by spending years with almost zero contact with other living beings. Probably it was natural to imagine some supernatural bond with the first female to come stumbling into his life in nearly half a century.

But it wasn't good for him to feel this way. He wasn't going to humor this thing, or even tolerate it. She had to go before he fell any harder for her.

As he thought that, he realized he was actually afraid of her. Afraid of the heartbreak she could cause, of his own vulnerability, of the pain he'd suffered the last time. He, Diego del Torres, who'd sailed aboard the *original Santa Maria,* an immortal, a vampire, was afraid of a small mortal female who'd lived only a few decades.

And no, he told himself, he wasn't going to just let her die. He was going to monitor her condition. He would know how she was doing. This link between them was that powerful—even more so now that he'd tasted her blood. When she got near the end, he would go to her. He would tell her there was an option, let her make the choice.

But he wasn't going to put his heart on the line for her. Or for anyone.

They say no man is an island. But they're wrong—this man is.

He returned to his task of packing a bag for the trip to the mainland. A change of clothes, first-aid kit, toothbrush. He needed a pint of frozen blood, and he'd moved his supply to the cooler in the workshop, to keep her from finding it. Not that it mattered now. As soon as he returned and she was gone, he would move his stores back where they belonged.

When she was gone.

The notion made his heart contract into a hard, painful knot in his chest. Already, he thought, she was causing him pain. If he needed any more proof that he was doing the right thing in sending her away, that was it. Things would only get worse if he let her stay.

I'm going to miss her.

Yes, but only at first. He would get over it, and soon he would be comfortable again. Happy again.

Happy? Again? When have I ever been truly happy?

"Silence," he said to the voice that seemed to be coming more from his heart than his head. He slung his bag over his shoulder and headed for the front door, intent on reaching the workshop and the blood stored there. But as soon as he opened the door he smelled and tasted the acrid burn of smoke on the air, felt the blast of her anger. If he hadn't been so self-absorbed, he would have sensed both far sooner.

He dropped his satchel and ran full speed to the cove, following that sense of her all the way there, stopping when he caught sight of her. She was standing in the shallows, her back to him, watching the *Santa Maria XIII* go up in flames. The fire licked at the night sky with a hunger that rivaled any he'd ever felt.

He stopped in his tracks, too stunned to move, anger surging in him that rivaled hers. "Anna!" he shouted. "What the hell have you done?"

She didn't turn, just stood where she was, feet in the surf, watching the fire leap and dance. The heat of it seared his face, and dangerous sparks rained down around him. "Fire is so beautiful, isn't it?" she at last said softly.

"Why did you do this?" Her refusal to answer his questions made him even angrier, so he strode up behind her, gripped her shoulder and spun her around to face him. "*Why,* Anna?"

"You didn't leave me any choice, Diego."

There were tears streaming down both her cheeks. And his heart seemed to crack a bit, the inside softening, as if the heart of the fire were actually penetrating it. But it wasn't the fire prying its way into his heart, and he knew it.

"The choice was to go," he said. "This is *my* island, Anna. It's my life you're intruding on. You have no right." His hands on her shoulders were tight, might even have seemed menacing, had his tone not had the distinct ring of a condemned man pleading for mercy, he thought. He didn't *sound* menacing. Nor did he feel that way.

"What are you going to do, Diego? You going to hurt me? Or drain me dry and finish this once and for all?"

He bared his teeth in a flash of temper, wishing he could oblige her, but knowing better. He gave her a slight shove as he let go, then paced in a circle, furious.

"It's not in you to hurt me, Diego. We both know that. There's something…something between us."

"I drank from you. That gives you the sense that we

have a bond, but it's just an illusion," he argued. "It's chemistry. Nothing more."

"I saved your life last night. And I gave you something more precious to me than that blood you so desperately needed."

"I didn't ask for that."

"You didn't turn it down, either. And whether you admit it or not, you felt something, Diego. More than chemistry, more than physical lust and release, more than any kind of blood bond. You felt something. I know you did. I was there. Why are you trying so hard to deny it?"

"Because it's not what I want."

She clenched her jaw, and her eyes flashed with impatience, with temper, and with what he thought was the first hint of certainty. She thought he was weakening.

And God help him, he was.

"I want to spend the last weeks of my life here, in this place. This is where I want to die."

"And what about what *I* want?" he demanded, already knowing she had defeated him. Because what could he possibly do now? His only means of transportation was gone. Destroyed, by her hand.

She shrugged. "You're immortal, right?" Turning, she stared at the boat again. "You've got plenty of time to have what you want."

"This is unforgivable," he said. "It's unfathomable that you would go to such lengths to get your way."

"Refusing to let me stay is what's unforgivable, Diego. Especially after…" She stopped there, then waved a hand at the burning sailboat. "This…this is barely even bad. It wasn't that great a boat. You've got a gorgeous one taking shape in your workshop, so it's not as if I'm marooning you out here. You said it would be finished in a few more weeks. By then I'll be dead. And you'll be rid of me." She turned to look him in the eyes. "Until then, you're just going to have to tolerate my presence."

She was hurting. He could feel it in her, practically screaming way down inside. It wasn't anger, as he'd initially thought. It was pain. That flaming boat in front of him right now was no more than the visual evidence of her pain, scorching its way into the sky.

He lowered his head, wondering if he were the cause of all that pain. "Why are you hurting so much?"

"Why? Because I'm dying, you idiot. I'm *dying.* I thought I'd made peace with that, but that was when I thought I had this wonderful, beautiful, wise and ageless guardian angel waiting for me on the other side. But then I come here, and I find—" She bit her lip. "Never mind. Just go finish your stupid boat. And if you finish it before I breathe my last, I'll go. All right?"

He nodded slowly, but he was trying to read more into her words, trying to see the feeling behind them. There was something trying to make its way from the sublevels of his mind, some knowing that he hadn't let himself hear or see before. He felt it. It was knocking on his awareness. "I'll…go work on it now," was all he could think of to say.

"Yeah, you do that. Try not to cut off your arm this

time." And with that she stomped away from him, heading along the shoreline, her pace rapid, her posture angry.

His fists clenched and unclenched at his sides as he watched her go; he felt utterly helpless in his anger and confusion. He turned to stare at the fire, and then tipped his head back and released an anguished shout at the heavens. Why had the gods seen fit to disrupt his peaceful, perfect, solitary existence with *her?*

She walked along the beach, gathering up more of her possessions as she did. A hairbrush, twined full of seaweed. A useless wiry tangle of algae and headphones that had gone with her MP3 player. A book.

She bent and picked it up. Soggy pages, but intact, waterproof ink still legible. It was her journal, the one she'd been keeping since the day she'd found out her diagnosis, the day she'd set sail. She felt compelled to keep it, so she carried it back to the house with her and patted it dry with a thick towel. Then she lit the oven, setting it on the lowest temperature, and set the journal inside, open facedown.

Every five minutes or so she turned the pages, and the process seemed to be working. In between, she handwashed all the clothing she'd scavenged from the beach, then hung each item outside, making use of every tree branch and bush she could find.

As she worked, the birds of the night sang to her, and she paused to just close her eyes and listen to them. Their voices, their songs, seemed full of hope, and the ocean sound beyond them, that gentle whisper of waves washing over sand, an almost inaudible message. They were speaking to her. She was sure of it. Saying her name. Telling her it was all going to be okay. And the stars, glittering above, spelled out the same message in some kind sparkly code. *It's all fine. Everything's okay. Just relax and be easy about all of this. It's fine.*

She stood there listening, trying to hear with her heart the words being spoken to her by nature. And yet her heart ached. She closed her eyes and let the night wind caress her face, but her cheeks burned from the rivers of tears flowing over them. "How can it be okay when I've found the man of my dreams, only to make him hate me? How can it be okay when I've landed in a paradise that can never be mine? How can everything ever be okay when I've found my heart's desire just in time to die and leave it all behind?"

Suddenly her body felt very light. As if she were no longer even inside it. That empty body fell to the sand like a suit without a wearer, and this time it was different from the tiredness she'd felt before, the weakness, the need to sleep. This felt like being taken to a whole new level.

This was, she thought, the end.

Weakly, she lifted her hand and started to drag her forefinger through the warm sand.

Chapter 12

He spent a couple of hours working on what was now his only means of transportation, all the while working through things in his mind. He was trying to make sense of everything bit by bit, and he was still certain she was in the wrong. She was forcing him to do what he didn't want to do, and she'd had no right. It was his life, his island, his boat.

But she seemed to feel she had every right, just because she only had a few weeks left to live. The thing was, that wasn't true. She could live forever if she wanted to. She just didn't know that. Because he hadn't told her.

Why not? he wondered.

He knew the answer. He feared her reaction would be the same as Cassandra's had been. She would accept his offer, declaring her utter delight that they could stay together, after all. And then he would transform her. And then she would leave him.

But, finally, the distant knowledge that had been waiting patiently beyond the doorway of his subconscious managed to slip inside.

Why would that bother you? You've been trying to get her to leave, after all. Why not change her and let her go?

"Because I don't want to be used again, taken advantage of again, lied to again."

Or is it because you don't want to be proven right about her? That you want to believe in her?

He shook his head. "No. No, it's not that at all. I want her out of here before I can fall in love with her, then have my heart broken again. That's all."

But don't you see, Diego? It's already too late for that.

He blinked in stunned surprise at the revelation he'd been denying, closing his eyes to, refusing to see. He already loved her.

He already loved her.

So if she left, either by her own volition or by his order, he was doomed to suffer that heartache again, anyway. There was no way around it.

He had been dreading rejection by yet another beautiful woman to whom he'd offered all he had to offer. He'd been living his entire life in an elaborate design to prevent that very thing from ever happening.

And yet Anna had found him. She'd found his haven, despite all his precautions. And she'd found a way into his heart, despite all his fortifications. Maybe there was something here that deserved a deeper look. Maybe she'd been nothing more than honest with him the entire time.

What about that?

He pondered and nodded, understanding her anger a bit more. From her point of view, he could see how unreasonable he must seem to deny her dying wish. It was only a few weeks, from her perspective. It must seem very selfish to her for him to say no, and so adamantly, too. Especially after last night.

Yes, that must really have added fuel to her fire, he thought, seeing again his burning boat in his mind's eye. No wonder she'd done what she had. She must feel just as rejected as…as he'd been fearing he would feel if he gave her the Gift, and his heart along with it, and she walked away.

Exactly like that, he realized. She'd given him her blood. Her body. Her heart, perhaps. She'd saved his life. And he'd thrown her precious gift back in her face, rejected her. He'd done to her, he realized in dawning horror, exactly what Cassandra had done to him.

The revelation made him stop sanding and rise to his feet. Damn, that was it. He needed to apologize. Maybe even offer an explanation, if she were still willing to listen. And he needed to tell her the truth about her nature, her condition, what it all meant.

He tuned in to her, though he'd been tuning her out for the past two hours. Her essence was very weak, he realized with a frisson of fear. Almost as if she were unconscious or…

Alarm rippled up his spine, and he headed out of the shop and back toward the house, only to find her lying on the ground a few feet away from the tree where she'd apparently been hanging her clothes to dry.

"Anna!" He knelt beside her, shook her a little, but there was no response. His stomach convulsed as he bent closer to listen to her breath. He was relieved to realize she *was* still breathing, but only once every few seconds. And her heartbeat was weak and erratic.

She was dying. God, no.

He scooped her up into his arms and straightened, then paused as he noticed the words she'd written in the sand after she'd fallen.

I've loved you all my life. And I'm sorry.

It felt as if something inside Diego broke open then, like a dam giving way to the floodwaters it had been holding back. His emotions rolled over him like a tidal wave, and tears blurred his vision. He carried her into the house, laid her on the sofa and then, reluctantly, left her there to check on the strange smell coming from the kitchen.

There was a book in the oven, baking slowly on the center rack. He grabbed a potholder and rescued it, dropping it face-up on the counter. The pages where it had been lying open felt slightly crisp, but for the most part, he thought the book unharmed. Warped by having been soaked in seawater and then oven-dried, but aside from that, it was in surprisingly good shape.

He leaned over it, peering at the handwriting on the pages, knowing it was Anna's. It held her essence. Her energy. Her personality was reflected in the shape of the letters just as it was in the shape of her face.

Later, he told himself. He would look at it later. Right now he had to see about the woman herself. He shut off the oven, then poured a glass of cold water from the pitcher in the fridge. He dampened a clean towel with more of the icy water, then hurried back into the living room, where she lay—so helpless, so fragile—on the sofa.

Leaning closer, he laid the folded dish towel on her forehead, cooling her face, then moved it to cool her neck. As he worked, he spoke to her with his mind, willing her to have the strength to wake, just one last time, before sinking into the sleep from which there was no awakening. Not to this life, at least.

Hear my voice and hold fast to it, Anna. Hear my voice and abide by my will. Gather every bit of strength in you and open your eyes. Talk to me, Anna, just one more time. I command it. Open your eyes. One last time, Anna.

Eventually she stirred, moving her head a little, moaning softly.

"There, that's it. Come on, wake up."

She blinked her eyes open, then stared up at him sleepily. "What happened?"

"You're weaker than either of us realized, Anna."

She nodded slowly, spotting the water and starting to sit up, reaching for it.

"Let me," he said, and he got the glass for her, holding it to her lips and supporting her head.

She drank deeply, then leaned back again and said, "I'm not going to last much longer, am I?"

He thinned his lips, saying nothing.

"I'm dying. You don't have to put up with me for a few weeks, after all. Maybe not even for the rest of tonight."

"Stop it. Stop saying that."

She blinked at his sudden outburst. "Why? It's true. I'm at the end. I can feel it. And then you can toss my body on a pyre and burn me to ash, or haul me out to sea and dump me over the side to feed the fish and be rid of me at last. It's not as if I'll have anything to say in the matter."

"You have everything to say in the matter."

"Do I?"

He nodded. "More than you know. Including…" He bit his lower lip. "Including whether or not to die at all."

His words had clearly reached her. She blinked, hope appearing in her eyes for the first time. "What do you mean, not to die at all?"

He licked his lips, rising from his spot beside the sofa to pace away from her. "I wasn't going to tell you this until… well, until closer to your time. But it seems your time is nearer than we thought."

"How were you planning to tell me anything closer to my time if you sent me away?"

He turned to look back at her. She was watching him, her big blue eyes wider than before, more alert, as if the hope he'd just given her had provided a rush of new strength, as well. "I would have found you. And I would have known when your time was close. I would have felt it, just as I'm feeling it right now."

She blinked rapidly, averting her face and trying to prevent the tears that she could not hope to hide from him. "I'm feeling that, too."

"You know what I am, Anna. You've seen—"

"Yes. You're a vampire." Her eyelids seemed to grow heavy again. They fell slowly closed.

He hurried closer, shook her gently. "Stay with me, Anna. This is important." When she forced her eyes open again, he hurried on. "I'm a vampire, yes. But do you know what that means?"

She shrugged. "You have to drink blood to survive." She was whispering now, leaving long spaces between her words, as if just speaking left her out of breath. "You can't go out in the daylight. And you're…immortal."

"For the most part. We can die. There are ways. We can bleed out. We can go up in a blaze quite easily, either due to the sun or accidental exposure to an open flame. We feel everything intensely. Our senses just grow sharper the longer we live, so that they become extremely acute, from the moment we are changed over, increasing exponentially with each passing year. That means we feel pain more acutely, too. It can debilitate or even kill us. But pleasure…pleasure is…amazing."

She nodded weakly, eyes dropping closed, opening once again. "Why…are you telling me…all this?"

"As a human being, Anna, I had the Belladonna antigen. Just as you do."

Her brows knitted tight as her head tipped sideways. "The same thing that's killing me?"

"Yes. Every vampire had it. It's rare. But it means more than just that you bleed easily and die young. It also means that you can become…what I am. A vampire."

He watched her face, wondering if he would see relief and surprise, or the smug look of triumph he'd chosen to ignore in Cassandra, all those years ago.

But she showed neither of those things. She was still waiting to hear more, as if that was not the revelation that mattered to her. Not at all.

"And then what?" she asked softly.

His brows rose. He was puzzled by both the question and her lack of reaction. "And then you'd be strong, immediately strong, vital, alive. You'd be able to hear every birdsong for a hundred miles, if you wanted. Identify every living thing by its scent from miles away. You could read minds, communicate mentally. You'd run faster than a gazelle, jump higher than anything alive. But you'd never see another sunrise. Never age another day. Never eat another morsel of food, or drink wine or water or anything else. These are heavy prices to pay, Anna."

"I don't imagine I'd be eating or drinking much if I were dead, either," she said very softly. "And all the rest sounds very appealing, Diego, but that's not what I was asking you."

He frowned at her. "Then…what?"

She frowned, staring at him as if she could see inside his mind the way he saw inside hers. "There was another woman, just like me, here with you once, wasn't there? This same situation? I can see it. Who was she?"

"There's no time, Anna," he began.

She swallowed hard. "Then talk fast."

Sighing, he nodded. "Her name was Cassandra. She had the antigen, the syndrome was killing her. She found me here somehow. I think she may have followed me from one of my trips to the mainland. She pretended not to know what I was, what her options were."

"Did you fall in love with her?" Anna asked softly.

"Yes. And she pretended to love me, too, but only until I transformed her. It was all she'd wanted all along, you see. But if she'd simply asked…"

Anna lifted a hand to his cheek and turned him to face her. "You've been shutting me out. Keeping me at arm's length. All because of her. A woman who used you and then threw you away without even knowing what a treasure she had found in you. But I'm not her, Diego. I know how special you are. Somehow, I've always known."

He lifted his brows, hope springing to life in his heart. "I didn't want to let you get close. I was afraid you would hurt me in the end."

"I won't."

That was all she said. Those two little words. And just like that, what remained of the granite wall he'd erected around his heart shattered into a million glittering bits. He believed her. He actually believed her.

"I don't want to die, Diego," she told him. "I want to live. I never did before, but now…now that I've seen how good life can truly be—now that I've finally figured out how to live—I want to live. But only if I can live here—with you. I think this place…this is paradise. It's all I've ever wanted. *You're* all I've ever wanted, Diego."

He blinked away hot moisture from his eyes and realized it was tears. He hadn't shed tears since Cassandra. This time he shed them in sheer joy.

"I want to share eternity with you, Diego," she told him. "Tell me that's okay with you."

"It's more than okay. I…I love you, Anna. I realized it out in the workshop. I realized I was trying to prevent something that I had no choice about. It was already too late. I love you."

Her smile was wide, and so bright it was contagious. "I love you, too."

"Then…then you're ready?"

"I've been ready for this my entire life," she whispered.

Diego bent closer, pressing his lips to her mouth, kissing her deeply, passionately, and then slowly, he traced a hungry path around her jaw, down over her neck, to her jugular.

She pressed her palms to the back of his head, and closed her eyes as his teeth broke the skin. *"Now,"* she whispered, "I'm in heaven."

* * * * *

Immortal

Maureen Child

Chapter 1

"Ye doona hae to go wi' me if ye doona want, though ye hae nowhere else to go nae?"

"Huh?" Two weeks in Edinburgh and Emma Madison still wasn't used to the heavy Scottish accent. Though, in her defense, Cute Blond Guy had a much heavier Scots burr than anyone else she'd encountered since arriving for her summer course at Edinburgh University.

He'd wandered into her study cubicle a half hour before, and since then, they'd been flirting. At least, Emma was pretty sure they were flirting. With that heavy accent, it was sort of hard to tell. But he said his name was Derek, and he was *tall.* Since Emma stood five foot eight, she appreciated a man she had to look up at.

Truth was, though, even if he'd been five foot three, she'd have been grateful for the company. For two hours she'd been sitting in a cramped, generic, study room in the university library all alone, wishing she'd gone to the pub with her dorm mate. But no, she'd done the "right" thing. She'd wanted to somehow prove that her parents were wrong and that spending all this money on a six-week summer session wasn't a waste.

And what did she have to show for being so virtuous? A headache, a growling stomach demanding dinner and a weird sense of…unease. She didn't even want to admit that last bit to herself, but the strange sensation of being watched was hard to ignore.

Just one more reason why she was glad Derek had come to sit with her. Being alone in a practically deserted university library was clearly making her jumpy. No one was watching her. Heck, except for Derek and her, she was pretty sure no one else was there at all. So why, she wondered, couldn't she shake the feeling of impending… something?

She was probably just tired. That and the fact that the library was too empty. Too quiet. Too…well, creepy.

The building was new and well lit, but beyond the windows, the night was thick and black and almost seemed to be crouched at the glass, waiting for a chance to sneak in and—

"Will ye?"

She frowned, tried to figure out what he'd been saying before and took a shot. "Will I go with you to the pub?"

"Aye, isna tha what I've been sayin'?"

Well, yay her. She'd guessed right. And a trip to a neighborhood pub sounded much better than wading through more nineteenth-century literature at the moment. Naturally, though, her American-honed cautionary instincts kicked in.

Going somewhere with someone she'd never met? Not a good idea. But on the other hand, she'd come to Edinburgh to meet new people, see new things, shake up her life. No point in not seizing the moment when handed the opportunity, right? She was smiling to herself when she happened to glance at Derek and thought she saw… *something*…shift in his eyes. They went from grass green to gray to black and back again to green in the thump of a heartbeat.

Her stomach rolled, but this time fear was in charge, not hunger. She hadn't really seen that, had she? A trick of the light, maybe, she thought as she noted the slight hum of the fluorescent lights overhead. Emma watched him, and the longer she studied him, the less cute Derek became. His smile was fading, his eyes were narrowing and she had the distinct impression he was losing patience with her.

"You'll nae go wi' me, will ye?"

"If that means no way, yeah, that's right," she said, though she wasn't entirely sure why she was suddenly less intrigued by him. There was just something *off.* Something she couldn't put her finger on. Something that warned her to stay exactly where she was.

"Aye, then," he said, his accent sliding into something less comically overdone. "We'll do this here."

"Do what?" Did she really want to know? She slid her

chair back, wanting a little more distance between them. Derek had changed so quickly, going from flirtatious to vaguely menacing in a split second. Emma wasn't sure what to do next.

Was there anyone besides the two of them in this library? Would anyone hear her if she screamed?

Screamed?

Where had that thought come from? Was her mind already sifting through information about Derek and finding things she hadn't really wanted to notice? Was she sensing trouble on a subconscious level?

Oh, she hoped not.

"Look, Derek," she said, standing and gathering up her books and papers, "this has been fun, but I really have to go."

"Not yet." He stood and Emma swallowed hard. Was he going to try to keep her there? Was he some kind of crazed rapist? On drugs or something? That would explain the weird thing with his eyes, but the thought went nowhere in calming Emma down.

"My friends are waiting for me," she said, forcing a smile that felt brittle. That was a big lie. She only knew two people in Edinburgh and they were both at a pub, convinced that Emma would be studying all night.

"They've a long wait, then." His smile faded a bit then as he cocked his head, as if straining to hear sound in the quiet.

She listened, too, hoping to hear a whole *crowd* of

people approaching the study cubicle. All Emma heard was the hard thump of her own heartbeat.

The steel and glass and chrome library looked innocuous enough—hardly the old-world castlelike building she'd expected to find—but when it was empty, as it was now, it felt sort of…haunted. Of course, Emma had always had a low creep threshold, which was why she never watched horror movies. At sixteen, she'd seen a late-night TV showing of *Friday the 13th,* and hadn't slept for a month.

But that hadn't been real. This was. And she was wasting time. If Derek was hearing someone she wasn't, she'd do well to bring whoever it was closer.

"Hey!" Emma shouted. "In here!"

"Shut yer mouth, woman." Derek's green eyes flashed black, then shifted again until they seemed to roil with flames.

Emma moved back fast, stumbling in her hurry to get away from him, but Derek moved even faster. His feet made no sound, though. It was as if he wasn't really there. And that thought was enough to deepen the chill crawling along Emma's spine.

Then the cold came, settling over the room like an early frost. Her breath puffed in front of her face and ice cracked and covered the study table like a glistening tablecloth. Derek stood in front of her, his lips peeled back from his teeth in a parody of a smile, and the temperature in the room plummeted even further.

Fear spiked inside Emma, slicing at her insides, making

her breath hitch and her pulse race. Her mouth was dry, her throat was tight. There was nowhere to run. The cubicle was small, enclosed, with one way out, and Derek was blocking that path.

To escape, she'd have to go through him, and for the first time in her life, Emma was grateful that she wasn't exactly a delicate flower of a girl. She was an athlete and not exactly anorexic. In fact, her best friend had once said that Emma had enough boobs to build two healthy women.

Right now, though, she'd trade the boobs for a baseball bat. Or an Uzi.

She swallowed her fear and the wild racings of her mind. Why was it so cold? What was happening? Who was he? He couldn't simply be some run-of-the-mill lunatic. There was more going on here, much more, but she had no idea what it was. Or how to combat it or even if she'd live through the next ten seconds.

So the only choice she had was to play dumb. The innocent. To try to ease Derek back into the mildly flirtatious mood he'd been in only moments ago.

"Look," she said, shivering as the temperature continued to drop and her mind screamed silently. "You seem like a nice guy and everything..." Soothe the crazy person, she told herself. Keep your voice even, soft. Don't be threatening, and for heaven's sake don't ask him why his eyes change colors or how he's making the room so damn cold your hands are turning blue. And most importantly, if he rushes you, remember that you played soccer for five years and you've got a hell of a kick.

Good to know that one corner of her mind was still working even while another corner was curled up in a ball keening.

"You're a Campbell, are you not?"

"Huh?" Okay, she hadn't been expecting *that.* What did her mother's maiden name have to do with anything and how had this guy known about it, anyway?

She backed up again, keeping one trembling, nearly frostbitten hand stretched out behind her, hoping to not trip and fall like a dumb heroine in a horror movie.

"You are." Derek sidled closer again, still moving without sound, and now Emma realized he'd done that from the beginning. She hadn't heard him enter her study cubicle. It was more like she'd looked up and there he was. Why hadn't she noticed that before?

Why was she only now seeing that nothing about him was normal? He smiled as if he could guess what she was thinking and now his eyes were black again. Black and empty. "You're a Campbell. I can smell it on you. Your blood sings to me."

Her *blood?* Not only crazy, but a wannabe vampire? Oh, crap. Emma was in deep trouble.

"Give me what I need."

"Therapy?"

Then he was on her. So fast she hadn't even seen him move. So fast she hadn't had a chance to kick him or even to draw in an icy breath to scream. In a blur of soundless speed, he closed the distance between them and grabbed her so hard she dropped her books, and the papers tucked inside swirled in the cold air like overblown snowflakes.

"Step away from the woman, demon."

A deep voice, dark and rich and full of threat, rolled out around them like a clap of thunder. Emma didn't feel the reprieve that voice should have provided, though, because Derek's hands on her arms tightened, his fingernails digging through her long-sleeved yellow T-shirt to slice into her skin. She felt blood trickling down her arms, glanced down to see it seeping through her shirt. She felt sick to her stomach.

"Guardian," Derek whispered, his once-pronounced accent now completely gone, and his voice a raw scrape on the air. "Move and she dies."

"Don't move!" Emma shouted, looking past Derek to the man standing in the open doorway. The instant she saw *him,* she knew instinctively that nothing would ever be the same again.

At least six foot five, *he* had shoulder-length black hair and pale blue eyes. His jaw was square and his nose looked as if it had been broken and reset a few times. His shoulders seemed as broad as a football field and the long, black leather coat he wore over black jeans and a white shirt was just the camouflage he needed to hide the sword he carried.

The sword?

Oh, God. What was going on?

And in that one horrible moment, she realized that she'd

spent a lot of time lately wishing for some excitement in her life. This reminded her of her mother's all-time favorite saying.

Be careful what you wish for.

"You don't belong here," the sword-wielding giant announced, his deep voice nearly rattling the windowpanes.

"Excuse me?" Emma said, outraged despite the fact that Derek's fingers dug even harder into her upper arms.

"I wasn't talking to you," the huge man in the doorway said, those pale blue eyes fixing on the guy with a death grip on Emma.

"Oh. Okay." Well, good, she thought, one half of her mind still worried about that sword, while the other half was happy to have him on her side. Then she turned her face to her captor. "Look, just let me go and we all walk away."

"No, we don't." The man in the doorway looked more formidable than ever as those icy eyes of his fixed on his prey.

"Not helping," Emma told him, struggling wildly to pull free of Derek's grip.

"I'll not let her go," the blond said, and instead of releasing her, he wrapped one arm around her throat and pulled her back tight against him. "She's mine now."

"Yours?" Emma dragged her short, neat nails across Derek's skin, but he acted as though he didn't feel it. She had to escape. Had to get out. How had a study night at the library turned into a scene from one of those movies she hated? How had she, Emma Madison, landed in the middle of some weird hostage situation?

Chapter 2

"You can't win this and you know it, demon." Bain Sinclair stared at the demon he'd tracked through most of Edinburgh and couldn't help the mild sense of disappointment he felt. This miserable creature would prove no test of his strength. Would offer no real battle. Were there no strong demons left to fight in this infernal city? Was this the best demon the worlds had to show him?

Still, as an immortal Guardian, it was Sinclair's duty to capture the damned demon and send it back through a portal to the hell dimension it had escaped. As there were thousands of different demons, so, too, were there many different dimensions. All of them crowding up against this world, all of them housing demons hoping to claim the earth and subjugate humanity.

The Guardians were all that stood between the demon worlds and this one. Sinclair, like his fellow Guardians, had taken an oath centuries ago to protect the human world from those that would destroy it. Even if it were only this puny demon with delusions of grandeur.

"I'll kill her."

Sinclair scowled at the creature who held the woman so tightly. He didn't dare take his eyes off his prey long enough to inspect the hostage. Even small, inferior demons could prove challenging at times, and he'd no wish to see the human woman harmed.

"Get him off of me!" The woman's voice was loud and demanding.

Then Sinclair did spare her a quick look and felt a hard jolt to his system. She was tall, with eyes as green as the highland hills and short, red hair with curls that looked as soft as eiderdown. Her mouth was full and lush, her chin stubborn and her body the stuff dreams were made of. Her curves were as lush as her mouth and desire pulsed inside him with a heat he'd never known before.

Who was she? Who was this woman who inflamed both him *and* a demon? A question that must be answered. But first… Lifting the sword he'd carried for nearly a thousand years, Sinclair moved within a foot of his prey in the blink of an eye.

"I swear I'll kill her," the creature spat at him, his eyes wheeling as he desperately searched for an escape that wouldn't be found.

Pale blue eyes locked on the demon, his features schooled into a calm mask of determination, Sinclair shook his head. "You won't, you wee weasel of a demon. You need her. As you've said yourself."

"There are other Campbells," the demon said slyly.

"Campbell?" Sinclair stopped short, glared first at the demon, then at the woman and then back again. "She's a Campbell?"

Before anything more was said, the woman clearly became tired of waiting to be released. Lifting her foot, she dug the heel of her boot into the top of the demon's foot. The creature let loose a shout of pain, released her and she instantly dropped to the floor. Scrabbling backward on her butt, she moved as quickly as she could, while keeping an eye on the men closing in on each other.

Sinclair took advantage of her courage. Moving quickly, he tossed the tip of his sword high and allowed the Guardian netting, a fine mesh of magically warded silver he'd attached to the blade, to drape across the demon, who was trying to run. Instantly, the creature was trapped, and the more it struggled, the tighter it was held. Only when he was sure his prey was incapacitated, did Sinclair allow himself to turn and face the woman.

"Who are you?" he demanded. "And why are you with a demon?"

"I'm not *with* him—" She broke off and sent a look at the creature trapped within the netting, rolling about on the floor and cursing in an unintelligible language. "A *demon?*"

"Aye."

"You'll pay, Guardian," Derek suddenly screamed in unaccented English.

"Aye," Sinclair muttered, "so your kind always say." Then he focused on the woman, now gathering up her things from the floor and pushing herself to her feet. "Tell me, then. Who are you and why did the demon want you?"

"My name's Emma Madison and who are you?"

"Bain Sinclair. Guardian to this post and the one who's asking the questions, lass."

"I'm not a lass," she argued. "And what's a guardian and you know what? Never mind. I don't want to know what's going on here, who you are, who he is, how you threw that net or any other damn thing. I just want out of here."

She backed away and Sinclair's eyes narrowed on her. She wouldn't be leaving until he knew what was happening. The fact that she was a Campbell didn't set well with him, since Sinclair had died during a skirmish with the treacherous clan centuries ago. But he was willing to overlook that for now, especially since she had a spine. Unless he discovered that, true to her bloodline, this lass was somehow conspiring with the demon world to unleash hell on Earth.

"I'm just going to leave now and you two can—" Her voice faded away as her gaze locked with his, and Sinclair felt her fear spike even as he watched it register on her features.

Guardians were telepaths, able to read the minds of those they wished. Normally, Sinclair turned that power down, not wanting to be assailed by the thoughts of others. But in this instance, he needed to know what the woman knew. Needed to have more information. And in a rush, her wildly disorganized thoughts streamed into Sinclair's mind.

You're both crazy, her mind screamed. *I don't know what you want. Or what he wanted, but right now, all I want is to get back to my dorm room, close the door and barricade it. Maybe this is a dream,* she thought frantically, helplessly, *maybe I'll wake up in my room and realize I'm just jet-lagged or hungover or something and none of this is real and—*

"'Tis real," Sinclair said brusquely, interrupting the wild flow of her thoughts.

"What?" She blinked up at him. "How did you know—What *are* you?"

"Time enough for that discussion later, Emma Madison," he said, turning his gaze back to the trapped demon. "First I must return this one to his hell."

"Hell? Oh, God…"

Sinclair bent down, lifted the demon as if he weighed nothing at all, then slung him, still netted, over his shoulder. "Come. We'll talk, you and I. I've need of answers and you're the one who has them, I'm thinking."

"Hold it," she said, shaking her head, shifting her gaze between him and Derek. "I'm not going anywhere with you."

"Aye. You are. Either walking or across my shoulder. Your choice."

"I'll scream."

Sinclair waved one hand through the air, effectively sealing the three of them in a bubble of privacy. Wrapped in this field of energy, Guardians could move unseen through crowds of humans. And trapped as she was now, with him, the woman could scream her blasted head off and none would be aware of her.

"Go ahead, then," he said, already walking, expecting her to follow, for where else would she go now that he'd trapped her as neatly as he had the demon. "But once you've seen it'll do no good, I'd take it as a kindness if you'd shut the bleeding hell up."

Insulted, enraged and just plain terrified, Emma was dragged in his wake as if tied to him by an invisible tether. She had to run to keep up with his long-legged stride and she noticed as they moved through the library that the building was indeed deserted. Long hallways lit by the flickering overhead lights seemed to stretch on forever. Empty rooms stood sentinel as she passed and Emma's heartbeat quickened. If Sinclair hadn't come to her rescue, God knew what Derek might have done to her.

And he'd been right. Screaming wouldn't do her a bit of good. There was no one to hear her.

The big man stopped suddenly and she collided with his back. It was like walking into a brick wall. He didn't budge. Didn't rock unsteadily on his feet. He was a mountain. The proverbial hard place. And now she was trapped between him and a...demon?

Her gaze fixed on Derek, she stepped back and slammed into an invisible wall behind her, then shot another look at Bain Sinclair. Was he safety or a new threat?

The man Derek had called guardian turned his pale, icy blue eyes on her. Slowly, he raked his gaze up and down her body until she felt as though her skin was on fire. Tiny electrical jolts shot through her system under his steady regard. She took another breath, fought down that sizzle of whatever it was and focused on the most important point at the moment.

She was alone with not one but *two* crazies.

Instantly, Emma pictured the headlines on her hometown newspaper in California: "College Student Killed by Sword-wielding Psycho in Scotland."

Not what she'd been hoping for when she signed up for this summer course. But then she'd never expected to run into a man like this one, either. Who would?

"A new portal's been opened here," Sinclair said, lifting his sword high.

"I don't see anything," Emma muttered, not sure if she should tell the truth or placate the crazy man.

"You will." Then Sinclair began speaking, his deep rumble of a voice rolling out around her like black velvet. Words in a language that sounded as old as time and just as mysterious filled the air and Emma held her breath, half-afraid to face what might happen next.

Then she saw it. A wash of pale yellow light that streamed into the room as it brightened, elongated, becoming what looked like a window into another world.

As Sinclair's voice rolled on, images formed and faded within that window. Colors, shapes, creatures, flickered on and off like a slide show of kaleidoscopic breadth. So many things, too many. And none of it made sense.

"Hold!" Sinclair's shout brought the flickering images to a standstill.

Emma looked into the window of light and saw beyond to a landscape that was so foreign she could hardly take it in. Black trees, twisted into shapes both horrifying and intriguing. Skeletal creatures slipping in and out of the shadows. Twin bloodred suns shining from a black sky, and a hot wind, heavy with the scent of spices, raced through the opening into Emma's world.

"What is that?" She shook her head, looked at Sinclair as he swung Derek down off his back and quickly freed him from the netting.

"There are many hells," Sinclair muttered, keeping a tight grip on the back of Derek's neck. "And even more demons. This one belongs in that hell," he said, jerking his head at the weirdly pulsing window of light.

Derek stared at her, licked his lips with a tongue that was as red as the weird suns staining that foreign sky and then he whispered, "He can't save you from me, you know. I've got the flavor of you now." He lifted his fingers, still damp with her blood, tasted them and sighed. "I'll find you. When he's nowhere near. I'll find you."

"Leave off, demon, and go back to your hell," Sinclair ordered, and gave Derek a shove that sent him tumbling through the window of light and fire.

When he was gone, the portal snapped shut and disappeared as if it had never been. All that remained was the faint scent of spice and the huge man at Emma's side.

"Oh, my God." Her brain was spinning. This was like being drunk without the good time. Nothing of what she'd experienced could possibly be real. So the only explanation was she'd had a stroke or something. Maybe she was even now lying in a dream-filled coma in an Edinburgh hospital. Heck, maybe she was still at home, dreaming about going to Scotland. And if that were true, she wouldn't be anywhere near the country she'd dreamed of visiting all her life.

But beneath her, the floor felt cold and hard and the sultry scent of spices still hung in the air. So no, she wasn't dreaming. This was all real. Impossibly, incredibly, *real.* "What is happening to me?"

"A long story, lass. One better told in safer places." The giant of a man held out one hand to her and Emma wanted to take it. She just wasn't sure she'd be able to stand even with his help.

She needn't have worried.

"I might've known it would be a Campbell to bring me more grief." He shook his head, his long black hair settling behind his back as he grabbed hold of her, pulled her to her feet and, in one easy movement, tossed her across his shoulder—exactly as he had with the demon only a few moments ago. Emma pushed herself up against his back, but she'd no hope of freeing herself, anyway. He was even stronger than he looked.

Locking one arm across her knees, Sinclair muttered something about damned women and blasted Campbells as he stalked from the library and into the cold, clear night.

Chapter 3

Emma's kidnapper/hero lived in luxury.

His palatial estate took up half a city block not far from Princes Street, and outside the floor-to-ceiling windows, the lights of Edinburgh twinkled like fallen stars. Inside the house, she stood in a book-filled study, with a fire blazing in a man-size hearth. Leather chairs dotted the floor as if silently inviting guests to get comfortable.

She was so far from comfy, Emma thought she might never relax again.

Her gaze slid to the man standing with his back to the fire. His coat and sword were gone and still he was formidable. Broad chest, muscular legs and thickly muscled arms—the man was a walking weapon. She should be terrified of him—and yet, there was something inside her that…yearned. That ached for him. Wanted to crawl inside his embrace and stay there. Ridiculous, she told herself.

She was clearly having some sort of delayed reaction to what had happened to her.

"Think, Emma. What would a Cirico demon want with a Campbell?"

"I don't know," she said for at least the fifth time since he'd brought her here to this…palace. For the past hour, he'd questioned her, made her repeat her conversation with Derek and in general hadn't given her a moment's peace. "Until an hour ago, I didn't even know there *were* demons."

"Yet he found you. Marked you." Bain nodded at her neatly bandaged arms.

For a second or two, she remembered him carefully rolling her long-sleeved shirt up and tenderly bandaging the slices Derek's fingernails had made on her skin. In those moments, Sinclair had seemed gentle. But it hadn't lasted long.

"What does that mean exactly?" she asked. "He 'marked me.'"

"He's tasted your blood—"

"Don't remind me—"

"When he escapes again—"

"When?"

Bain nodded. "The blasted demons never stay gone for long. And once he's out, he will find you."

"Oh, God." Her knees folded and she sat down right where she was, landing on an ornate rug that was more beautiful than padded. "What can I do?"

"You will stay here. With me."

A decree, she thought, said with the same tone of authority that an ancient lord of the manor would have used to an annoying peasant. She wanted to be insulted, but, really, she was grateful. And what did that say? She didn't know this guy from a hole in the wall. For all she knew, he could be just as crazy as that…*demon.* But no. Her mind argued with her even as she considered it. He wasn't crazy. He was the hero in this picture. He'd saved her from whatever Derek had had planned. And he'd brought her here and bandaged her—she remembered the soft touch of his hands on her skin and recalled, very clearly, the buzz of sensation just being near him had caused.

So yes, she was grateful to him and intrigued by him and, God knows, she didn't want to think about facing Derek alone—still, she couldn't just stay here with Bain Sinclair indefinitely.

"For how long?" she asked.

Those wide shoulders moved in a lazy shrug as if her question were of no consequence. "For however long it takes."

She shook her head, despite the tremors racking her body. "I can't do that. I have classes. Obligations."

"You will stay."

Emma lifted her chin and narrowed her eyes. She never had been one to follow orders easily. Even when it was the logical, rational thing to do. "You can't make me."

Bain smiled at her as he walked stealthily across the room. "I can and I will. Where would you go for help if not to me? The police? They'd think you crazy. Lock you away and then the demon would have you."

"Damn it." He was right. But that wasn't her only option. She could catch a plane and—

"Would you think to run to your home in America? Would you lead the demon to your family?"

She glared at him. "How are you doing that? Reading my mind?"

"For you, Emma Campbell," he said, not bothering to answer the question, "there is no one but me."

"Madison," she corrected absently, hating to admit that he was right. She couldn't very well take a plane to California, leading Derek right to her family's door. "My name is Madison. My mother was a Campbell before she married."

He sneered and in that movement she saw him as he should have been. Standing on a Highland mountain, hair blowing in a cold wind, bare, muscular legs braced wide apart, a kilt flapping at his knees and his plaid tossed over one shoulder. The image in her mind was so real, so detailed, it was more like a memory than imagination.

Oh, Emma had read plenty of books with Highland heroes, and Bain Sinclair was the personification of every one of them. Arrogant. Proud. Determined. Funny that she'd never before realized how annoying those traits would be in real life.

"The Campbells have been known for treachery since time began," he said, sneer still in place. "Diluting that blood through marriage does not change it. I knew many of your clan in the Highlands where I grew up, and learned early never to trust one of them. Tell me, then, why I should trust you."

"Nobody asked you to trust me," she reminded him. "You're the one who carried me out of the university library and brought me here. You're the one who's insisting I stay. I don't even know you. Why should I trust *you?*"

His lip curled, defining that sneer of his even further. "As I'm the one who saved your pretty backside from a hungering demon, I'm thinking I've earned the right to demand the trust of a Campbell. Yet, I warn you. If there's a Campbell involved in demon treachery," he went on as if she hadn't spoken, "I'll discover the truth of it. You can no more hide the truth of it than you can hide the blood that runs in your veins."

Emma refused to have this conversation sitting at his feet and looking up at him. She stood, stabbed her index finger at him and said, "My mother is a Campbell and is one of the nicest human beings on the *planet.* Don't you talk about her like that. And while we're at it, I'm the one who should be worried about trusting *you.*"

"I'll remind you yet again that I saved your beautiful hide, didn't I?"

Beautiful? Not to mention *pretty backside?* She shook her head. *Concentrate, Emma.*

"I could have handled him myself," she argued. "Eventually."

He laughed and the sound nearly rattled the windowpanes. "Lie to yourself all you want, woman. But don't expect me to believe it. You were a tasty morsel to the demon and well you know it. If not for me—"

"Which begs the question," Emma interrupted, "what were you doing there, anyway? How come you were so handy to the scene? For all I know you were working with Derek the Troll."

"You accuse me of being in league with a demon?" He looked astonished at the idea.

"How do I know?" She waved one hand at him. "You're the one carrying a sword for God's sake. You're the one who kidnapped *me.* I didn't ask for any of this. And besides, we know I wasn't working with that thing. It almost killed me, remember?"

"He could have, but didn't," Sinclair told her, studying her carefully as if looking for some sign that she was what she claimed to be. She saw wary suspicion in his eyes and Emma stiffened. "He wanted something from you."

"Well, I don't know what. What could a demon want with me, anyway? I'm a student, for pity's sake," she muttered, then narrowed her eyes on him. "And I'm pretty darn disappointed in Scotland, let me tell you. I've dreamed about coming here all my life and never once did I dream about *demons.* I thought this was going to be a fun trip to a gorgeous place and all of a sudden it's a nightmare."

"Edinburgh is not all of Scotland," he said, dismissing the ancient city with another of his sneers. "'Tis a city like any other, with too many people and too many cars and too much noise for a man to think. There's good and bad here, like any other city of its kind. If you want beauty, you must go to my true home. The Highlands."

For one brief moment, her heart fluttered. It was the way he said the word *Highlands.* Like a man missing a lover. She heard his affection for the place in his tone and knew that this at least was one thing they shared. Emma had been reading about and dreaming of the Highlands of Scotland for as long as she could remember. But she only said, "You're no Highlander. You don't talk like one."

He frowned at her. "How am I supposed to speak, then, lass?"

"You know—" she waved one hand at him "—doona, dinna, canna, willna…"

He stared at her for a long minute and the flames crackling in the hearth were the only sound in the room beyond the pounding of her own heart. Then he laughed again. He threw his head back, planted both fists on his hips and laughed loud and long, the booming music of his laughter echoing off the walls, the ceiling and settling down over her like a warm blanket.

Despite her anger, Emma felt something inside her stir in response. Her blood heated, every nerve jangled in anticipation. There was something old within her. Something ancient. Something that recognized this man. She felt as though she'd been waiting for him. She didn't understand, but as she watched him every cell in her body leaped to life as they never had before. She *knew* Bain Sinclair with a bone-deep knowledge that had no explanation.

She'd never experienced anything like this before. Emma's earlier worries about being with him disappeared as she realized that through the fear and the worry and the confusion one thing rang clear in her mind. This man was where she belonged. This man was sanctuary.

This man was *everything.*

When his laughter finally died away, he looked down at her, still grinning, and Emma's heart stuttered painfully in her chest.

"That's foolishness, lass," he said, looking directly into her eyes. His gaze was steady and so pale a blue Emma felt as though she were looking at pieces of the sky.

"No Highlander talks like that. At least, not anymore." His smile faded as he led her to a nearby sofa, sat her down and then seated himself beside her. "Centuries ago, perhaps." He looked toward the window, but his gaze was fixed on something much farther away than the night outside. "Many things were different then. We walked our land as kings and fought and held it against countless enemies. But times change and a wise man changes with them."

"We? Centuries?" Her voice was a whisper. Her gaze locked on his profile as he seemed to stare into a past she could never fully understand. Was he really saying what she thought he was saying?

She swallowed hard. He spoke as if he'd seen those changes come and roll past. Had personally ridden the tide of history. It didn't make sense, but then what about tonight's happenings did? Why shouldn't she be sitting in a veritable palace in Edinburgh with a Highlander who was as mystical and mysterious as the feelings he engendered inside her?

He turned his face to hers, looked deeply into her eyes and said only, "Aye, lass. Centuries."

She met his gaze and saw the truth shining there at her. Of course he was centuries old. Of course he was part of the magic of Scotland. Breath caught in her lungs, she whispered, "How many?"

"Several."

Her stomach did a quick pitch and roll before cautiously settling again. It seemed impossible, of course. No one lived forever. But what about that night so far *had* been possible? Emma gave herself a mental pat on the back for accepting this latest piece of craziness so easily. Was her brain just giving up the fight for logic? No, she thought, with another good look at Bain Sinclair. It wasn't hard to believe in what he was saying because he was exactly the kind of man legends were built around.

He met her gaze squarely, silently, as if giving her time to adjust. But in a very weird way, knowing that he was centuries old made perfect sense. He was simply too *male* to be a modern-day man.

"You're telling me you've lived hundreds of years." Her gaze moved over his features, cataloging them carefully, etching the harsh planes and angles into her memory. Unnecessary, though, she thought, since a part of her recognized him. Knew him. He looked no more than thirty-five, yet his eyes were as ancient as time itself. "How is that possible?"

"I'm an immortal."

"Immortal." His features were calm, almost dispassionate, and she knew instinctively he wasn't lying. She took a deep breath, blew it out and dragged in another one. "Oh, God."

"I'll not hurt you, Emma," he said, then frowned slightly, "unless I find you're in league with that demon, after all."

"I'm not, but you…" She pushed both hands through her short, red hair and rubbed at her scalp as if she could somehow slow down her racing thoughts with a quick massage. "How—when—why?"

Still keeping his gaze locked on hers, he said softly, "I died in 1046 and was made an immortal Guardian. We few protect this world from the demons trying to destroy it."

"Immortals. Demons," she whispered, caught in the heat of those amazing eyes of his. "Guardians, for Pete's sake. One of us is really crazy, Bain. And I don't think it's you. So what does that say about me?"

"That you're a woman with a cool head on her shoulders," he told her, one corner of his mouth tipping up. "One not willing to take things at surface truth. A woman who trusts her instincts."

"Right." She blew out a breath, scrubbed her hands up and down her forearms and felt the bandages he'd applied as soon as he'd brought her here. He'd saved her from

Derek. Treated her cuts. Fed her. Was offering her protection. And now, he'd trusted her with a secret she knew instinctively he didn't share with many others. She was being pulled into a world she never would have thought existed and somehow…it felt *right.*

"I don't understand any of this," she whispered. Emma looked at him and knew that everything he was saying was the absolute truth. But her heart was at war with her brain, that still screamed for logic.

Flames snapped and hissed in the hearth; somewhere in the house a grandfather clock bonged out the hour, and outside in the city the world rolled on. While Emma listened, Bain talked. He told her everything. Told her about life in the eleventh century. How he'd died at the hands of a Campbell who'd sold out their cause against the British for a handful of gold coins and a new castle.

She saw it all; the past was alive and vivid, as if she, too, had lived in the world he described. As if a part of her had always been with him.

Then he told her that at the moment of his death he'd met a being called Michael and was given a choice. His soul could continue on to whatever awaited it, or he could live as an immortal and battle evil through the centuries. Bain had accepted the challenge and made a home in the Highlands where he'd lived off and on for hundreds of years. This house, where they stayed in Edinburgh, belonged to another Guardian, Karras, who was off now on business of his own.

That was the only reason Bain was in the city. He was

watching over the portals until Karras returned. Then Bain would go back to his home in the Highlands.

By the time he finished speaking, Emma's head was spinning. She heard every word, watched his face, the shifting emotions flashing across his features as he told her of the passage of time. How he'd lived, alone, in a castle near his ancestral clan.

The Highlanders there didn't ask questions of a man. Didn't wonder why he never aged. The people there still believed in magic and the world of the Fae. They understood that not all of life was simple black and white and that there were no answers to some questions—so they didn't ask them.

"And you live alone," she said, feeling a tear in her heart at the thought of him existing in solitude for eons. Everything in her wanted to reach out to him. To somehow ease the loneliness that must be clawing at him. Surprised by the strength of her reaction to him, Emma tried to rein in her own feelings as he answered her question.

"Yes, I live alone. I've never felt a hunger to change that." He turned his head again, to look at her now. "Until you."

"Me?" Her heart shivered, but still she shook her head. "You don't even like me. I'm a Campbell, remember?"

"Not something I'm going to forget, lass. But the heart of it is, you call to me and I know you feel the same."

"I do, yes," she said, scooting back on the couch as he shifted to lean toward her. "But it doesn't make sense, Bain. We just met." Love at first sight only happened in the movies, she thought. Or in books. It wasn't real life, and even if it was, it wouldn't happen to *her.* "I don't know what I feel," she hedged, her heartbeat quickening as he reached for her hand.

The instant his fingers touched hers, the moment his palm slid against hers, heat slammed through her. It was so much more than desire, though. This felt like her entire body was awakening all at once. As if she hadn't even really been *alive* until this moment. There was something inevitable about it. As if she'd been made for him. As if her body had only been waiting for him to show up so it could welcome him.

How could she fight something so elemental?

"Do you feel that?" he asked, his deep voice a raw hush of sound. "The fire between us? The flash of lightning?"

Instantly, heat spilled from him, slid into her and sped through her veins like flames dancing atop a river of gasoline. She burned. She ached. She felt a connection to him she'd never known before. And when she looked into his eyes again, she knew he felt it, too. What was the point in denying it? "I do. What is it? What does it mean?"

"If it means what I think it does, you'll not be leaving me. Ever."

"Hold on here, Bain," she said, needing to put the brakes on, for her own sanity's sake if not for anything else. "There's no way I can just stay here forever. I hardly know you. I have a life. Parents. A brother and—"

He kissed her.

Emma's brain shut down and her body took over. Its

needs supplanted everything else. Words died. Thoughts splintered. The touch of his mouth on hers dissolved everything but the very sensations it created. One corner of Emma's mind fought to hide what she was feeling, but Bain wouldn't allow that. He gave her more, demanded more. His mouth, his tongue, his breath, all worked together to drown her in more soul-shaking sensations than she'd ever known before.

Wrapping his hard, muscular arms around her, he leaned back on the sofa and drew her with him until she was wrapped across the top of him. She felt every square inch of his huge, amazing body and that only fed the flames already licking at her insides. His hands slid down her back to her behind and pressed her to him until she felt the rock-hard length of him and she knew exactly how much he wanted her.

She groaned as his tongue tangled with hers. Sighed as he lifted his hips into hers and she wiggled atop him as if trying desperately to get even closer to him. That tiny, logical voice in the back of her mind shrieked even louder, demanding that Emma stop. Think.

But she wasn't the one who called a halt to what was the most sensuous experience of her life.

Bain pulled back from her, breaking the kiss even as warning bells sounded in his mind. There was more here than simple lust. More even than the slender threads of connection he'd felt ever since first laying eyes on the woman. This was deeper, richer, unlike anything he'd ever experienced with any of the countless women he'd been with during the centuries of his life.

His heart thundering in his chest, Bain sat up, gently easing Emma off his chest and away from the aching erection that was demanding he get closer to her, not farther away. But he'd be damned if he allowed his cock to be making his decisions for him at his age.

It wasn't just lust pounding through him, Bain told himself as he fought to keep from reaching for her again. His gaze locked on her, he noted her swollen lips, her disarranged clothing and her quick, uneven breath.

He groaned inwardly as he silently admitted that he'd been right in his suspicions about the attraction he felt for Emma. From the very first moment he'd set eyes on her, he'd felt it. The *bond* that had leaped to life the moment she was near him. Now, Guardian legends raced through his brain—tales of Destined Mates. The one woman meant to be with a certain Guardian. How his body would know hers. His soul would recognize hers. How their connection would strengthen a Guardian's powers even while tying him more closely to the human world he protected.

Bain had to acknowledge that he hadn't put much faith in the legends. After all, a man living centuries alone could make himself insane, waiting and searching for a Mate that would never appear. Instead, Bain had put the legends from his mind and focused his energies and his great strength on the task given to him. Fighting demons.

Now his world had changed in the fast blink of an eye. She was here. In front of him. A woman from modern times that called to the ancient warrior within him. Was Emma the one? Was this woman his promised Mate?

There was only one real way to know for sure. According to legend, only his Destined Mate would be able to hear a Guardian's thoughts. He looked into her eyes and sent her a mental command.

Take off your clothes.

She laughed shortly and straightened her shirt before pushing one hand through her tousled hair. "In your dreams."

Bleeding, buggering hell.

The Fates were ever trifling with a man. But this was too much. To send him a Destined Mate after centuries of solitary life would seem a gift to some. But the fact that she was a Campbell proved that those very Fates had a most perverse sense of humor.

"Do you realize, lass," he said on a sigh, "that I didn't say that out loud?"

A moment passed, then two. And finally, her eyes widened, her mouth dropped open and she stared up at him. "But I heard—"

"Aye, you heard my thoughts. And that can only mean one thing. You're mine, lass."

Chapter 4

She was his.

Three days later, Bain's words were still circling in Emma's mind and she was no closer to being able to accept them. How could she? How was she supposed to believe that she was Bain's Destined Mate? The one woman in the world meant to be with him?

"Not that you'd know it from the way he's treating me," she muttered to no one. Three days she'd been locked away in the Edinburgh mansion with the one man in the world who was supposed to be destined for her and had he made one solitary move since that amazing kiss?

No, he hadn't.

She wasn't disappointed, though. It wasn't as if she *wanted* to jump into bed with a virtual stranger—well, okay, maybe she did. But if he was right, then he wasn't really a stranger, either, was he?

And if she *was* this legendary Destined Mate, how could it possibly work out for them? He was an immortal. She wasn't. So was she supposed to stay with him until she was old and wrinkly and then what? He moves on, looking for another "mate" while she checks into the Old Mates' Home?

She sighed a little and walked into the garden of Bain's elegant mansion. Beyond the gray brick wall surrounding the back garden lay Edinburgh, the city she'd dreamed of visiting. The city she'd always felt drawn to. Now she had to wonder if her longing for Scotland had been her own subconscious trying to get her close to Bain. Was it possible that she once had been a woman in love with Bain, and was now reborn to get another shot at a happily ever after?

"God. It sounds like a bad plot in a sappy movie." But what other explanation was there? How did she know so much about him? How had she seen glimpses of his life? How had she read his thoughts? Why did she feel a "bond" with him?

Had she somehow known that coming here, to Scotland, would give her the opportunity to find the one man in the world she belonged with? And if so, *why?* To torture herself? Even if she was his Destined Mate, nothing could come of it. He was immortal and she was mortal. And that was just the beginning of their problems.

She was also an American with a family back home waiting for her. She couldn't just settle down with a Scotsman they'd never even met! And what was she supposed to do about school? She hadn't finished her degree yet and no way was she going to stop before she had.

Already because of this bizarre situation, she'd missed a couple of classes she couldn't afford to skip. But every time she thought about going back to the university, she pictured Derek the Troll showing up and trying to drink her blood or something even more disgusting.

Emma sighed, tried to push those thoughts out of her mind and focused instead on everything that had been happening lately. She'd called her parents to check in, not that she could mention anything about the weirdness of her life at the moment. What was she supposed to say about that, anyway? *Mom, Dad, I've met an immortal and we're supposed to be together forever.* Oh, yeah, that'd go over well. They'd have her on the first plane home, and from there to a lovely rubber room.

It wasn't easy talking to people you loved and lying to them. She felt terrible about it, but she honestly couldn't think of a way around the situation, either. Then, after calling home, she'd contacted the university to let them know that she would be missing a few classes. God knew how many, of course, but that was something she didn't want to think about yet.

Just as she didn't want to think about the whole Destined Mate thing.

The way Bain had explained it to her, once Mates made love, they were each of them strengthened. His powers as a Guardian would be enhanced and whatever innate strengths she possessed would also be made stronger.

There would be a physical and mental connection between them. She could already hear his thoughts as he could hers—which was uncomfortable, but if they were to have sex, that psychic bond would become stronger, too.

That was probably why he was making such a concerted effort to avoid her. She already felt more connected to him than she ever had to anyone else in her life. She couldn't sleep at night without dreaming about him. She woke up every morning aching for his touch.

Scrubbing her hands up and down her arms to dispel the chill racing along her skin, she wondered how she would ever be able to live without Bain if they ever did make love. Wouldn't she miss him for the rest of her life? Wouldn't she ache for him and pine for him and in general lead a long, miserable life all alone? And when she died a, hopefully, old woman, he would still be as he was today. Young. Strong.

Gorgeous.

And alone, she added, letting her gaze sweep across the tidy gardens and neatly clipped hedges. She knew Bain wouldn't be able to find another Mate. She was it for him. So when she died, he would be left to just keep going and going, continuing on through eternity, so alone. So solitary. So separate from the very world he fought so hard to defend.

Her heart ached for him, as if she were already feeling the pain that he would be forced to live with. But nowhere in his description of the Mate thing had he said anything about *love*. So what did that really make her? Bain's own personal battery charger? Not only would he get sex, but he'd become stronger. Was that why he wanted her here? Was it really not about protecting her, but strengthening Bain? And how would she ever know for sure?

"How'm I supposed to deal with this?" she wondered aloud, tipping her head back to stare up at the heavy gray clouds.

"You think it's easy for me, then?"

Emma whirled around and watched as Bain stepped out of the house and walked with long strides across the patio. He wore his black jeans, a black shirt, and as his long black coat flapped around his knees, she caught glimpses of the sword still strapped to his side. She knew instinctively that he'd been out in the city, demon hunting.

And how weird was it that she was getting used to that phrase?

A cold, damp wind lifted his black hair off his shoulders. His pale blue eyes shone with fierce determination and his mouth was a firm, straight line. Just looking at him made everything inside her burn with a need that was nearly overwhelming. She wanted him. More than she'd ever wanted anything. Was she supposed to ignore that? Ignore the tug of something so fundamental?

God, she wished she knew what to do.

"I didn't ask for this, either," he said, his voice as soft and warm as the wind was cold. He stopped beside her and looked down into her eyes. "I'd long ago accepted that I would not have a Mate. Centuries since I've allowed a faint thought of finding the one woman meant for me to haunt me. To torment my dreams and fill too many solitary hours. But at last, I decided it was no way for a Guardian to live. How could I keep my mind on my duties if indulging in thoughts of a selfish need?

"No, I put the very idea of you aside, Emma, long ago. Now, when the notion of a Mate no longer even crosses my mind, you appear. A Campbell, no less." He laughed shortly and the sound tore at her. "Fate, I've learned, is at times, a vicious bitch."

"Well, that was flattering," she muttered, whipping her wind-driven hair back from her face. "Thanks very much."

"You feel the same and you know it, Emma." He shook his head. "Will you not admit at least that the Fates have played you as strange a hand as they have me?"

Reluctantly, she had to smile. "Okay, yes, I can admit that. I came here to take a few classes. To see Scotland. Demons and Guardians weren't exactly in the brochure."

"It's odd for you, I know. But," he added, "you've accepted it far better than most mortals would. It's the Scots blood in your veins. Makes you more open to the possibilities."

"It's Campbell blood," she reminded him.

He winced. "Aye, I know. But still Scots."

She smiled inwardly at the discomfort on his face. He really didn't like the Campbells. That would make his meeting her mother really entertaining. But, she told herself, that wasn't likely to happen, was it?

Shaking her head, Emma asked, "Bain, what does all of this mean for us?"

"It means we're meant."

He said it so easily, yet Emma knew he, too, was torn about this. She felt it in him. There was doubt in his mind and heart. There was concern for her—with the threat of Derek the Demon hanging over her head. And there was hesitation in him about changing the way he'd always lived his life. His duty to defend humans from demons was a huge part of him and she knew that he was wondering if he could do it as well as he always had if he allowed himself to care for her.

He was wondering, too, if perhaps the Fates hadn't made a big whopping mistake.

"You say that," she said, "but I'm picking up enough stray thoughts from you to know that you're not exactly thrilled with all of this."

He scowled at her as if he didn't like being reminded that she could read what he was thinking.

"Besides. We're meant? For what, Bain? For a lifetime?" She threw her hands up and her voice hitched a little higher. "Whose? Mine? Yours? You're immortal. I'm going to get old and die."

He reached for her, laid his big hands on her shoulders and pulled her in close. In spite of everything, Emma felt the heat of him flow into her body, easing away the chill in her blood. The cold in her soul. She snuggled in close to him, resting her head on his broad chest, listening to the steady thump of his heart, and she felt…*right.* As if she was exactly where she was supposed to be.

"There must be a way for us," he murmured, resting his chin on top of her head. "I will find it."

Emma wrapped her arms around his waist, hung on and asked herself if she really wanted him to find a way for them. God knew it would be easier if she could simply walk away from Scotland and pick up her old life. But she'd never be able to do that. Not knowing that Bain existed. Nothing was ever going to be easy or simple again, she thought with a rueful smile.

Because, yes, she did want Bain to find a way through this mess. A way for them to be together. To claim whatever it was that linked them so intricately together. It made no sense, of course. But it was as if she'd known him forever. As if she'd been born with these feelings for him and had only been waiting for them to flower.

She knew his thoughts, how he felt. She saw what kind of man he was. Who he was. And she admired him. Wanted him. Cared for him.

But she couldn't say if she completely trusted him.

He kept part of his mind closed to her. Pieces of himself he denied her. Once they made love—and she knew they would; it was inevitable—would she be able to see all of those hidden pockets inside him? Would she be able to unravel the mystery of an ancient Highlander? Or would he still find a way to keep himself separate from her?

And a part of her wondered if she would be this drawn to him if she were still living in the dorm room at the university. If she were still going about her everyday life, would she be as intrigued by Bain? How could she be totally sure of anything? He'd swept her away from everything familiar and settled her down in a palace. Protected, perhaps, but cut off, with only him to lean on. How could she really know her own mind until life returned to normal? Until she could take a step back and look at everything objectively?

But what if that never happened? What if he kept her here indefinitely? It's not like she could escape him. Mr. Ancient Warrior was probably a pretty good tracker, too. He'd find her wherever she went. And so, undoubtedly, would the demon. So she was trapped here. Forced to trust Bain whether she was ready for that or not.

God, could her life get more confusing?

"Your mind is a jumble of thoughts," he said softly, lifting one hand to push a handful of red curls off her forehead.

"You shouldn't be peeking, anyway," she snapped, and hoped he hadn't been able to read any one thing in particular. People shouldn't be able to read each other's minds, she told herself. Thoughts were private and, sometimes, embarrassing. For example, the fantasies she'd been having the past couple of days all starred Bain Sinclair. Images raced through her mind, leaving her staggered even as he groaned.

"If you keep having thoughts like those, lass, I'll not promise to not look at them."

"Oh, great." She closed her eyes, mortified. When

she looked up at him, he was smiling. "Just because my thoughts get a little X-rated now and then doesn't mean I'm ready to jump into the mating bed with you."

"Fine, then." He inclined his head with a regal nod. "The mating bed, as you call it, can wait. Tell me what troubles you."

"God," she said with a choked-off laugh. "Where to start? You said that finding your Destined Mate would make your strength, your powers, grow."

"Yes."

"Is that why you're keeping me here? To use me?"

"No."

She leaned back and looked up at him, but his face gave away nothing of what he was feeling. Emma tried to look into his mind, but he'd shuttered his thoughts from her. That told her one thing, at least. He didn't completely trust her, any more than she did him.

"That's it? Just *no?*"

He sighed and tossed his hair back from his face. "If my only reason for having you here was to use you, I'd have already bedded you, lass. Sex with you will give me increased strength. Whereas this constant torture of wanting and not having is only driving me around the bend."

"Torture?"

"You doubt it?" He pulled her closer and Emma felt the hard, thick length of him pressing into her abdomen. "My body aches for yours. As yours does for mine. You think to hide it from me, but your need pulls at me. Your fantasies are all too clear. Would you lie now and pretend otherwise?"

Her eyes closed on a wave of something hot and delicious. Just having his hard body pressed to hers made her damp and more than ready for him. Every cell in her body wanted him and it took every ounce of her strength to not give in.

"Of course I want you. I'd have to be dead not to," she told him. "But it doesn't change anything."

She pulled out of his arms, took a halting step back and tried to regain whatever pitiful sense of control over this situation she could. And while she waited for her heart to stop pounding, she waved one hand at the sword he still carried strapped to his hip. Deliberately, she changed the subject. "Did you find the demon?"

"No." His features slipped into a mask of frustration that, for once, had nothing to do with her. "The portal at the library is silent, and there were no trace energy patterns nearby. He's not come back yet."

"Yet?"

He nodded, his gaze fixed on her. "Yes. He will return. And I think I know why."

Judging by the look in his eyes, what he had to say wasn't going to make her happy. But Emma had to know. She'd already figured out that ignoring all of this wasn't going to make it go away. And until this situation with the demon was settled, then nothing else in her life would be, either.

She waited for him to speak, keeping her gaze locked with his.

"I spoke to Karras," Bain finally said, "the Guardian who lives here. He told me there was word of an archaeological find newly placed in Edinburgh University."

"What kind of find?" Apprehension roiled inside her at his tone. This wasn't going to be good and she knew it.

Scowling, he pushed both hands through his shoulder-length hair and stared into her eyes as if he could somehow bolster her courage by sheer force of will. "It's a cup. Bronze, they say, etched with what my friend claims are demonic runes along with the clan name Campbell. The cup dates to ancient days. To before my time."

Before his time meant pre-eleventh century, Emma thought, amazed that she could actually *have* that thought without freaking out anymore. Demonic runes? What were they? And why the Campbell name? Oh, this couldn't be good.

Emma felt as though the ground beneath her feet was tipping and she was left to scramble to keep her footing. She took a breath and asked, "What does that have to do with the demon wanting *me?*"

He looked into her eyes and a shiver swept over her. She'd seen lots of things in his eyes in the past few days, but until that moment, Emma had never once seen even the slightest flicker of fear. But it was there now.

Fear for her.

"It's to do with how the cup is to be used, Emma." He reached for her, but she skipped back, shaking her head.

"Oh, God." Emma swallowed hard. "I'm not going to like this, am I?"

He moved closer to her, and this time laid his big hands on her shoulders and let his body heat drain into hers. "The demon needs Campbell blood, Emma."

Bain paused, gritted his teeth until his jaw looked as tight as steel, then added, "He needs *your* blood."

Chapter 5

Her breath hitched in her chest.

Panic coiled in the pit of her stomach and immediately sprung loose, shooting bone-deep fear throughout her body. Even with Bain as close as he was, she felt cold right down to her soul. This was so much worse than she had thought.

Not just any Campbell? Me, specifically? God, why?

"Your mother," he said, answering the question she'd only whispered in her mind. "She's a descendant of those who first forged the cup."

"Oh, God." Her mind was racing, and even if Bain was reading her thoughts, she knew he wasn't getting much. There were too many images and emotions flashing through her brain for anything to make sense.

Emma struggled for air while fear clawed and chewed at her insides. The demon needed her blood. *Her* blood.

All because of something that had happened more than a thousand years ago? How was that fair?

"Michael, the being in charge of the Guardians, checked into your history for me." Bain ran his powerful hands up and down her arms in a rhythmic motion designed to soothe. But she was beyond comfort, well into a panic zone that was so deep and so all-consuming she couldn't see a way out.

"My history?" she repeated.

"Your family's, that is," Bain corrected. "He sifted through the threads of time and found those tying you to the cup. Your mother's people once made a pact with a powerful demon. They were given the cup to use in… ceremonies."

"What kind of ceremony?"

His eyes met hers and held. "Blood rites."

"Sacrifices, you mean," she said, her voice as hollow as she felt. The chill sweeping over her was so deep that not even the heat of Bain's hands could dispel it. *Blood rites* was such a clean phrase, she thought, for something so ugly. "The ancient Campbells made sacrifices to a demon. For power?"

"Aye," he said, "and for land. Money."

She staggered back, tearing herself from his grip, covering her mouth with one hand as if she could bottle up the scream fighting to get past her throat. This was all too terrifying. Too real. "So what? The demon's been waiting for me to come here? If I'd never come to Scotland…"

"It would have found you eventually," Bain said, walking toward her with careful, easy steps as if he expected her to bolt. "And I wouldn't have been there to protect you. So it's better that it happened now. Here."

Maybe, but if she'd had anywhere to run to, Emma might have. But she didn't. She was alone in Scotland, but for Bain. The man standing between her and a demon who wanted her for—

"Why me?"

"You are the youngest of your bloodline," he explained. "It's how the curse was worded. The youngest of the clan retained the power."

"But I don't have any power," she argued frantically. This had to be a mistake. How could decisions acted upon centuries ago, made by people she'd never heard of, have anything to do with her?

"Your blood does."

"Of course it does," Emma muttered. She shoved her hands through her hair and shook her head, as if by denying all of this she could make it go away. "What does he want my blood for?"

Again, Bain looked as though he'd rather do anything but answer her question. But he did, his voice low, reluctant. "He fills the cup with your blood, spills it onto the portal and it becomes an open gateway for eternity."

She swayed in place. "So he'd use me to destroy the world."

"Yes." He reached for her again, holding her tightly enough to help her stand beneath the burden of all this information. As if he knew her knees were wobbly and her head was spinning. But then, he probably did, Emma told herself. He could read her thoughts. Hear her terror. Feel her desperation.

"The demon would open a permanent gateway from his dimension into this one," he said, his voice a low rush of sound that seemed to reverberate deep inside her. "There would be no way to stop it. No way to halt their invasion. They would run riot over this world, its people, until they destroyed everything."

Vivid images of rampant destruction rose up in her mind in response to that statement and Emma wanted to run, but knew she couldn't. Because of the mindless stupidity of her ancestors, she was now the key to a demon's plot. How was she supposed to deal with this? "My blood does all that?"

"Aye." He pulled her closer, wrapping his strong arms around her and holding her with an iron grip that shut off her air and oddly comforted her at the same time. "But I will not let it happen. We will get the cup and destroy it before the demon has a chance to use it. Or you."

Emma nestled into his embrace, needing the comfort, the strength, he could give her. She felt adrift on some wildly rolling sea, with wave after wave crashing down over her as she struggled to breathe. Three days ago, her biggest problem had been picking out the right outfit to wear to her first pub. Now, she was the key to the destruction of the world.

"How?" She needed to know everything. "How do we destroy it?"

"Living flame," he murmured gently, his tone more soothing than his words. "A Guardian may stir the fires of eternity, but it's a dangerous task. One mistake and those flames will burn forever, endangering everyone. It's not a thing we do lightly."

Living flame. It even sounded dangerous.

"What happens then, Bain?" Her words were whispered against his chest, as if she were half-afraid to have him hear her. "If we stop the demon, what happens to us?"

"I have told you. We will find a way."

And what if there isn't a way?

Then we will take what we can while we can.

Speaking to him with her thoughts built an incredible intimacy she never would have believed possible. It was almost as if they were one person. Two halves coming together to become complete.

She looked up at him, into his now-so-familiar eyes and felt a rush of something hot and thick pouring through her. He was right.

For three days, she'd been here, living with him, avoiding him, ignoring the heat that lay between them. Why? Because she didn't completely trust him? Because she was afraid that they had no future? Because she was so far out of her element here that taking one more step might push her over the edge?

Yes to all three. Yet there was more, too. She was afraid that if she gave in to what she felt for him, she'd never be able to let him go and where would that leave her? But the bottom line was, whatever they shared was real. It was now. And wasn't denying it only punishing both of them?

Yes, his voice whispered in her mind, *a punishment neither of us deserves.*

She narrowed her gaze on him. Though it was sexy at times, knowing he could read her thoughts was still a bit unsettling. "Seriously? You've got to stop dipping into my mind whenever you feel like it. It's creepy."

"'Tis natural between mates. We can have no secrets from each other."

"Oh, there's the path to happiness," Emma said wryly.

"What do you fear?" he asked, stroking her cheek with one fingertip.

"The demon. Me. You. This. Everything." She stepped out of his embrace and instantly missed the feel of him pressed against her as she would have an arm or a leg. He was already so much a part of her, Emma didn't know how she would go on without him in her world. Yet, how could she stay in his?

"You fear me?"

Shaking her head, she looked up at him, stared into those ice blue eyes and said, "No," she corrected. "It's not really fear. It's… I don't even know."

"Three days I've given you to grow used to the fact that I am your Mate." His voice was a low growl. Naked desire was etched on his features. "You say you care for me, but you do not admit that we belong together. Three days I've wanted you. Ached for you. No more."

"Bain…"

No more.

That single thought roared through her mind as he grabbed her again, pulled her in close and kissed her as though his life depended on the touch of her mouth to his. And maybe, she thought wildly, it did.

Her body felt electrified. Visions swam in and out of her mind, images of him wielding a sword in a soft, gray mist. Leading a charge of screaming Highlanders into battle. She saw him die and her heart ached for him, her soul crying out to save him. Then she saw him through centuries of solitude, fighting demon after demon.

She saw him at his home, a rugged stone castle high on a hill. And she saw him the night they met in the library with fear and horror standing between them. The night his gaze collided with hers and sent Emma's world spinning off its axis. She actually *felt* what he had when he realized she was his Mate. She felt the elation, the pride, the roaring hunger racing through his system, and she felt her own match it.

Closing her mind to everything but the feel of him, she gave herself up to the wonder of his touch. He did things to her no man had ever done. Made her want as she never had. Made her need more than anyone ever had.

"Ah, Emma," he whispered, tearing his mouth from hers to bury his face in the curve of her neck. "I've been in such pain the past few days, tell me you'll welcome me now."

"I will," she said, barely able to form the words. Eyes wide open, she stared up at the leaden sky and only then realized they were on the patio, in complete view of anyone in the house who might glance out a window. "Not here, though."

"Aye. Here. Now." He straightened briefly, waved one hand and the air surrounding them rippled like the surface of a wind-blown lake. She reached out one hand, felt a barrier there and turned to look up at him. "This is what you did at the library that night."

"Aye," he said, reaching for her again, hunger flashing in his eyes. "Now we're invisible to the world outside this bubble."

She glanced at the house, then shifted her gaze back to his. It felt as if she'd known him always. He was the missing piece of her heart. Her soul. And for however long she would have him, Emma would savor it. Revel in what she found when they touched. What he made her feel when he looked at her as he was now.

He must have been reading her mind again, because in seconds, he'd stripped her out of her clothes and pulled his own off, as well. He was immense, her Highlander. Broad chest, heavy arms, with a Celtic cross tattooed on his right bicep. He tossed his black hair back over his shoulder and stood proudly naked, giving her time to look her fill. So she did. Flat stomach, bronzed skin, long, muscular legs and… Her eyes went wide and she felt the first flutter of nerves. "Um…"

I can see your thoughts, Emma. His laughter rippled through her mind along with his words. *Have no worries. We'll fit. We were meant.*

"Meant. Yes." She was meant for him. She knew it. Accepted it as a bone-deep knowledge that needed no proof. No explanation. Whatever else happened in her life, her world, this moment with Bain Sinclair was one she'd waited all through time for. Banishing that trickle of nerves, Emma threw her arms around his neck and held on tightly, sliding her palms up and down his back as he kissed her thoroughly. His lips and tongue drew gasps and moans from her.

He slid his hands over her body in a frantic dance of exploration as if he couldn't wait another moment to have her beneath him. Emma felt the same. Electric. Dazzled. Shaken. She needed him. Now.

Her body was hot, ready, and when he laid her on the cool, damp lawn, she shivered as the tender blades of grass caressed sensitized flesh. Then he was kneeling between her legs, his gaze locked on hers as he lifted her hips, positioning her body perfectly.

"You're a wonder, lass," he said, sliding his big hands up and down her thighs until she writhed with the need clamping down on her.

Emma held her breath and looked up into those amazing blue eyes of his. Fire flashed in their depths and she knew that his desire for her was quickening into an inferno. She felt his want rippling off of him in thick waves and felt her own body responding. She'd never known such immense hunger. It was as if she'd been starving all her life and then suddenly was offered a banquet.

"Come to me, Bain," she whispered, lifting her arms to welcome him, parting her thighs farther in invitation.

She kept her gaze fixed on him as he entered her with a swift rush of tenderness and strength. He had been right, of course. They fit. Beautifully. She felt her body stretching to accommodate him, even as she locked around him. Every last glorious inch of him claimed her in a way no man ever had before—and as no man ever would again.

Instantly, he set a rhythm she raced to follow. He bent his head to take first one of her nipples, then the other, into his mouth. His lips, teeth and tongue worked her sensitive flesh until she could hardly draw breath. There were too many sensations coursing through her at once, each of them demanding her attention.

And then there was nothing but him. The friction his body created with hers. No lingering foreplay and no need for it. The ache was all. The astonishing rush of sensation overpowering. He loomed over her, an ancient warrior, long black hair a curtain on either side of his face. His hard mouth was lush and glorious as he claimed a kiss while his body claimed everything else.

Again and again, he pushed her higher, faster, wilder than anything she could have expected. Emma's mind touched his. She felt his need as well as her own. Read his astonishment at what was happening between them. Saw herself through his eyes and felt his raging desire like a storm. She *felt* his pleasure as if it were her own and sensed that he was experiencing her own discordant thoughts and emotions.

When the first thundering crash of her climax dropped on her, Emma screamed his name and locked her legs around his hips, holding him to her. Her body rocked beneath his as she rode the hard, fast currents of an orgasm that threatened to splinter her heart and mind. Then moments later, his body clenched as hers had and Emma experienced his soul-shattering release as completely as he did.

Bain felt the very foundations of his life shake beneath him. He'd had no idea that the connection between he and his Mate would be so all-encompassing. Bracing himself over her, his body still locked deeply within hers, he felt the connection they shared become as indestructible as bands of iron. Once-fragile bonds tightened like invisible coils, drawing them together, making them one.

He felt her heartbeat as his own. He looked into her mind and read the same stunning sense of wonder that had left him shaken. He felt her touch, her fingers on his face, as a blessing, a kind of miracle that he'd never known in all his long centuries of life.

His soul trembled. His heart opened and his eyes were seeing his world as if for the first time. All the long years of emptiness he'd survived were now no more substantial than autumn leaves, lost in a cold wind. Here was all. Here, he thought, looking down into green eyes shining with the wonder of what they had just experienced, was *everything.*

Cupping her face in the palm of one big hand, Bain looked deeply into her beautiful eyes and solemnly swore, “I will never let you go.”

Chapter 6

Edinburgh by night was a magical place.

Lamplight glittered on rain-wet cobblestone streets. Laughter and music spilled out of pubs, drifted on the cool wind and floated along the streets, a pied piper's siren song to the young, or the lonely. Ancient buildings, some tipped weirdly as if leaning against each other for support, lined the roads and cars were parked half on and half off the sidewalks.

The narrow alleyways, or "closes" as they were called here, looked shadow filled, forbidding and every bit as haunted as the city tour guides insisted they were. Edinburgh Castle, once home to a doomed queen, sat atop a hill looking down on the city it had stood watch over for centuries. Moonlight shifted in and out of existence as the ever-present clouds chased one another across the sky.

Bain's footsteps were soundless and Emma tried to

match him. But even in her tennis shoes, she managed to make noise. Alongside a man who moved with such stealthy confidence, Emma felt clumsy in comparison.

Her hand firmly in his, she felt his strength pouring into her and read the steely determination in his mind. She knew he'd wrapped them in an invisibility bubble again so that they could move through the darkened city undetected by humans. But still she felt as though there were unseen eyes watching them.

"Tell me again why we're doing this at night," she whispered, whipping her head around to stare down the long, empty street behind them.

He briefly squeezed her hand. "Because there'll be no one in the archives to gainsay us as we search for the cup."

"Right. Right." She knew that. And it made sense, of course. Even invisible, they couldn't really snatch an artifact, build a living flame and destroy it while there were people in the building. Then she thought of something. "Can we do the flame thing while we're invisible?"

"No." One word. Harsh. Sharp. And Emma saw in Bain's thoughts he wasn't happy about that. "Maintaining both spells at once is difficult. I can't risk the flames spreading."

So they'd be out in the open where anyone could see them. Fabulous. But the archives would be empty and the demon wouldn't be there. Or maybe good old Derek would be hanging out in the library waiting for her return. That was never going to happen. Emma doubted she'd ever be able to go into any library ever again without ropes of garlic, a cross or two and maybe Bain's sword, just for good measure.

They are not vampires, Emma, Bain chided with a deep-throated chuckle. *Merely demons.*

Merely? There's nothing "merely" about demons, O great and powerful Highlander.

Thank you. He shot her a long look and a half smile. *It is good to know you see me as I am.*

Emma laughed, as he'd meant her to, and it felt good no matter how briefly it lasted. Honestly, she'd never been more aware. More alert.

Beside her, Emma's warrior moved with a deadly sort of grace that made her heart flutter and her hormones sit up and shout hallelujah despite how scared she was. Ever since they'd made love in the yard the day before, they'd scarcely been apart. Sex had never been like this before.

Every time they were together, their hearts, their souls, their minds became more intertwined. Now, it was as if she couldn't tell where she left off and Bain began. She was closer to him than she'd ever thought it possible to be to anyone and still…there was something he wasn't telling her. Something he kept locked behind a wall in his mind that she simply couldn't see past.

And that worried her.

He had full access to her thoughts. She felt him, a shadow in her mind, all the time. And now she wondered how she'd ever lived without that intimate touch. She knew he was aware of just how scared she was. How sad she was that she could see no future for them. How absolutely she loved him.

Yet despite her feelings, she'd yet to say the words. Even knowing that he could read them in her thoughts wasn't the same. If she said *I love you* and then had to walk away, Emma wasn't sure she'd be able to survive their separation. So she couldn't say it. Couldn't make that last commitment.

"You worry."

"You betcha," she said, shooting him a glance, then once more looking over her shoulder. The street was empty, lamplight shining like tiny globes of gold in the darkness, spreading pools of light across the damp cobblestones. Pins and needles scampered up and down her spine.

She could swear they were being watched.

"There is no need," he said, and stopped long enough to pull her close to him for a tight, one-armed hug. In his free hand, he held his sword, ready for battle. "I will protect you. We will find our way."

"I really do want to believe that," Emma said, staring up into those icy blue eyes that could hold her captivated with a glance.

"Then do."

She laughed shortly and huffed out a breath that ruffled the short, red curls on her forehead. "Okay. What was I thinking? I'll believe."

One corner of his mouth tipped up and Emma's body turned to liquid heat as erotic images flashed through her mind. Clearly, her body didn't care that they were in danger.

Instantly, Bain groaned low in his throat. "Guard your thoughts, Emma. You can't tempt me here. There are other things we must do."

"Me tempt you?" She smiled wryly. "Just looking at you makes me want to—" Another very explicit image rolled through her mind. *Her, straddling him, arching her back as he lifted his hands to cup her breasts. Her body encasing his, her hips grinding against him, taking him deeper, higher. Sweet friction as he moved within her. The sweeping sensations of a soul-shattering orgasm ripping through them both...*

"Enough!" He cupped the back of her head, pulled her close and kissed her, hard, long and deep. When he was through he pulled his head back and each of them fought for air. "Let us finish this and then I will show you *my* thoughts."

Emma trembled with the miniquakes she now recognized as foreplay shocks. Almost as good as the real thing, they rippled through her with tiny jolts of expectation that nearly made her forget they were on the trail of a cursed cup designed to hold her blood.

Nearly.

"Okay," she said, nodding as that thought went through her mind. "Back on track."

Without another word, he crossed the street, taking her with him, leading her toward the darkened university. A scant few windows shone with the soft glow of lamplight.

Mostly, the blackened windowpanes of the school stood out as darker shadows in the gloom. Sort of like empty eyes staring into space. And over all, the hint of danger lay like a thick fog.

"Don't you feel it, too?" she asked, turning her head toward Bain.

"I do." His eyes glittered in the light and his features were shadowed, harsh. "There are demons near. They sense the energy barrier." His hand tightened on hers. "As I can see the trace energy signatures they leave behind, they can sense mine."

"So the invisibility thing is pretty much useless?" She glanced around, even more nervous than before. "That makes me feel better."

He squeezed her hand briefly. "The energy field is not a defense against demons. It's only to protect us from prying human eyes while we do what needs doing."

But there are no humans watching us. Emma's frantic gaze swept the darkness, searching in the shadows, even as she hoped she wouldn't see a thing. Knowing demons were out there, staring at her, was completely different from actually *seeing* them.

Her stomach jumped, her nerves seemed to sizzle in warning. Suddenly, she felt those watching eyes even more fiercely than she had before. There was dark power out there and it was focused on them. Was it Derek watching them? Or a different demon? Or even worse, a *troop* of demons, all working together to kill Bain and her? And what if the demons didn't know where to go at all? Were they simply leading the demon threatening her to exactly what he needed?

"Bain—"

"I feel your fear," he said softly, gaze still moving over their surroundings, scanning, watchful for the slightest movement that might constitute a threat. "Don't allow it. If the demon follows, I'll dispatch it."

"So you're expecting Derek to show up." *Great. That makes me feel fabulous.*

"I always expect trouble," he countered. *That way I am rarely surprised.*

But Emma felt as if she'd been nothing but surprised for days now. She didn't know how much more adrenaline her body could take without just imploding.

Then the university loomed before them, the old buildings, constructed of gray stone, boasting mullioned windows, looked like an ancient fortress rather than a school. And, for some reason, that made Emma feel better. Maybe because the man she was with had come from before the time this place was built? Maybe because he belonged, not in a city but on the ramparts of a castle? If anyone could get them through the dangers of tonight, Emma knew it was her Highlander. Pride rushed through her in a wave almost strong enough to quash her terror.

"When this is finished, Emma," Bain promised, "I will take you from this crowded city and show you the Highlands. You will love it."

Emma looked at him and hoped he was right. Oh, she knew she'd love the Highlands. How could she not, with her very own Highlander to show her the country, to make her see it through his eyes? But what she didn't know was if she'd be alive to go with him. Even her pride and faith in Bain wasn't enough to convince her that she had a future past tonight. And should she live, how long would she have with Bain before she was forced to leave?

A scuffle of sound reached Emma and ended whatever she might have said to Bain. Before she could react, the world seemed to explode.

Stay down!

Bain's voice was harsh and loud and brooked no argument. Emma dropped to the cobblestones, their damp cold seeping into the knees of her jeans as she watched three demons rush Bain from the shadows. They were pale, their faces white as bone, their long arms ending in hands curled into claws. One of them howled and the sound seemed to echo up and down the street, sending shivers along Emma's spine. Her mouth went dry and everything inside her iced over. Fear was a living, breathing entity within her. She felt helpless and didn't like it.

She never heard Derek approaching from behind her until it was too late.

He snaked one hand around her mouth, and with the other grabbed her hair and viciously yanked her head back. Naked throat arched toward the sky, she sent one quick mental scream.

Bain!

She caught only a glimpse of her Highlander's furious eyes when he whirled to see Derek with his hands on her.

Then the other three demons pounced on Bain as Derek carried her off toward the university…and the waiting Campbell Cup.

Bain was filled with a fury that nearly choked him. Roaring his rage, he tore through the demons he now realized had been sent to distract him. It had worked. He'd been so focused on protecting Emma from this, he hadn't sensed the *real* attack coming from another direction. Derek had used Bain's own concern for Emma against him and Bain had fallen for it. That only infuriated him further. It was *his* fault Emma was now in danger. *His* mistake that had put her in danger. Now all he could do was end this battle and get to her as quickly as possible.

Derek would use Emma to open the portal and keep it open. Preventing that from happening should be the most important thing to him and yet, after a thousand years of protecting humanity, Bain realized he didn't care about the damned portal. If it was opened and he was forced to stand guard over it for eternity, he would. Battling one after the next, every demon hell spat out at him.

The portal was unimportant. The only thing he worried about now was Emma's safety.

Once that doorway was open, Derek would have no further use for her.

She would die.

Unless Bain prevented it.

With single-minded determination, Bain emptied everything he had into the fight with the three demons. His blade sang as he swung it with fierce abandon. His muscles bunched and cries of agony filled the still night air. A demon claw raked along Bain's arm and blood flowed freely. He didn't notice. Another of the demons kicked out at his legs and Bain leaped into the air, avoiding that pitiful attempt to bring him down.

Again and again, he squared off against the three, his body moving in long familiar moves even as his mind sought Emma's. But her thoughts were closed to him. Was she too afraid? Was she unconscious? There was another explanation, but Bain refused to accept that. She wasn't dead. Not yet, anyway. Derek had need of her and so would keep her alive. For now.

That thought gave him the impetus to finish the fight in a few blindingly fast moves. First one, then another, then finally the third demon succumbed to his blade until all three opponents were writhing on the street, wet cobblestones shining black with the stain of demon blood.

"You're too late, Guardian," one of them managed to say, its words coming garbled from a mouth sliced open by Bain's sword. "We have the woman and the gates will open."

He paid them no heed. They were merely the distraction and he wouldn't be drawn away from his objective.

"She dies tonight," another one promised, grunting as Bain gave it a kick that sent it sprawling into one of its brothers.

"You lose!" the first crowed, then moaned, clapping one hand to its ruined face.

"We shall see," Bain muttered, draping the three demons in the finely meshed, silver Guardian netting. The harder they struggled against the net's hold, the tighter they would be caught. The perfect trap to keep them detained and unable to hurt anyone else. Bain stood, grabbed his sword, then waved his free hand across the demons, wrapping them in an energy field that would hide their presence from all but him.

When he was finished, he spun, faced the hulking black shadow of the university and raced toward the woman who was now the center of his life.

Chapter 7

"You stupid bitch." Derek yanked at her hair until Emma's eyes watered. "You won't stop this."

He forced her through one of the oldest buildings on the Edinburgh campus, using her like a divining rod. He faced her first one way and then the next, down long, empty corridors of what seemed to be an ancient section of the university. When he didn't find what he was searching for, he dragged her farther along the darkened halls.

Now that her time was running out, all Emma wanted was the chance to tell Bain she loved him. To let him know that the past week—despite everything—had been the most amazing of her life. That she would love him forever. That maybe, one day, she'd be born again and they'd have another chance.

But even with that, she kept her thoughts closed to him, afraid of distracting him while he was fighting. He would come to her. She knew it. *Believed* it. All she had to do was stay alive long enough for him to come storming to her rescue.

Then her racing thoughts crashed to an end. She jolted in Derek's grip as something dark and ancient awakened in her blood and made it buzz as if it sizzled just beneath her skin. Evil wasn't just a word, she told herself as she felt the black stain of it slide through her system. It was alive and hungry and calling to her as if to a lover. Emma moaned and pulled back, instinctively trying to distance herself from the source of that power.

Derek laughed in her ear and his voice was a hiss of sound. "I knew you'd find it for me. Blood calls to the cup. Soon this will be over. Soon, my brothers will own this world and all of you will service us."

Oh, God.

Fist still in her hair, Derek dragged her down the hall, enjoying her struggles to get free. The dark heat emanating from the cup was more intense the closer they got and Emma's body erupted in a sheen of sweat. She couldn't breathe. Couldn't force enough air into her lungs to keep from feeling light-headed, dizzy and disoriented.

At last, her mind helplessly sought out Bain's. *It's here. Derek found it. Help me.*

Emma!

The roar of her Highlander's voice in her mind was a momentary comfort. Finally, though, Emma's body seized up at her nearness to the cup. A faint, tight moan slid from her throat and Derek laughed. Throwing the closest door open, he stepped inside and spotted the very thing he was searching for.

Emma dropped to the floor, trying to make herself a smaller target. She curled into herself, trying to ease the racking pains shuddering through her now that she was so close to that damned cup.

It was no use, though. Just being in the same room with the thing was killing her. She felt her bones shrieking. Felt her soul cringe and her blood boil. There was ancient power in that cup. Dark and evil.

She looked up as Derek took the cup from a low shelf and ran his long, pale fingers over it in slow, loving strokes. The ancient bronze cup was battered and stained, its once-pristine surface blackened through time and the evil that had brought it into existence. The inscription etched around its rim was barely legible. But when Derek lifted it, those faded symbols suddenly illuminated with a dark red light that seemed to burn into the bronze, rejuvenating the cup into what it had been in the beginning.

A dark promise of death and power and change.

"You see?" Derek sighed. "It reacts to me. It knows its time has come."

Emma watched him smile at the damn thing, and for a moment, she half expected him to kiss it as sports champions kissed a hard-won trophy.

He slanted a look at her. "The demon world has long sought this cup. Forged by your ancestors for use when worshiping the old ones."

He walked close and crouched beside her where she

huddled on the floor. His burning, maniacal gaze speared into her eyes. "It was lost centuries ago. Even my kind couldn't find it. Buried and forgotten, the cup lay hidden beneath the earth. Until a new housing project was begun. It was freed from the muck and brought here to wait for your arrival. Now it sings to me."

Pain welled and blossomed inside her. The closer the cup was to her, the deeper the agony twisting within. How could her ancestors have forged a bargain with whatever had created that cup? How could they have thought, even for a moment, that anything was worth the fetid stench of the thing being brought into this world?

She shuddered, lungs collapsing, brain burning, and still she managed to look into Derek's eyes and whisper, "Bain will stop you."

"That's where you're wrong, bitch." He smiled. "Your Guardian is as good as dead."

"Not quite yet."

Emma heard Bain's voice and reacted instantly. Fighting the crippling pain inside her, she took advantage of Derek's momentary surprise. She reached out, batted the cup out of his hand, then watched as it rolled across the room toward Bain. He kicked it out of reach, lifted his sword and smiled at the demon. "Your plan is finished."

Her hand burned where she'd touched the cup, but already, with distance, the pain she felt began to fade just enough to make drawing breath easier.

"I'll kill the bitch!" Derek dragged her to her feet, and stood behind her, using her body as a shield. He grinned at Bain and said, “So you see, your plan ends, as well, Guardian.”

Before Emma could figure out what Derek meant by that, he bit her.

She screamed while white-hot pain lanced through her throat as his teeth dug deeply into her flesh. This, she thought wildly, she hadn’t expected. Her eyes met Bain’s horrified gaze and she felt agony spiral through her system like a tightly wound string suddenly released. Heat, then cold, washed over her, *in* her, as if something hideous—something alive—was racing through her bloodstream. Her gaze locked on Bain, she saw fear dazzle his eyes before the edge of her vision began to go gray.

Over, she thought. *All over now with no hope of a happily ever after.*

A shout of pain, raw with rage, tore from Bain’s throat as he watched Emma slide slowly to the floor at the demon’s feet. He heard her last coherent thought and his soul wept for her even as his body and mind raged with the need for vengeance.

Her green eyes were glazed, her already fair skin going pale as milk. Blood stained her torn throat and ran in bright rivulets down the front of her blue T-shirt. His heart shattered, Bain felt her agony as his own, took the pain inside him and used it to finish the demon that had brought all of this down on them.

Cup forgotten, the demon laughed. “You can’t kill me on this plane, Guardian, but I’ve killed what’s yours.”

Bain had no time for conversation and no wish to talk

to the smiling beast standing over Emma. Instead, Bain rushed him, lifted his sword and swung it in a wide arc. The razor-sharp blade sliced through Derek's neck in one clean stroke. The demon dropped to the floor and Bain kicked the body away from Emma.

Weakly, Emma clapped one hand to her neck. "Thought you said they couldn't be killed."

Bain spared the body a quick look. "It's not dead. Like a lizard, it will regenerate whatever it needs."

"That's…gross." She let her hand fall to her lap, glanced at the bright red blood coating her fingers, took a breath and said, "Not vampires, huh?"

Stop talking. He tore his shirt off, ripped at the fabric, then folded a strip of the material into a thick square and used it as a pad, holding it to her injured neck. Too much blood loss, he thought, even knowing that the blood wasn't the real problem. There was no way to keep the truth from her. *You have been poisoned.*

"Poisoned? Great. How long do I have?" Her eyes held his, demanding truth when he would have preferred a more gentle lie.

His heart twisted in his chest. The love of his life was so near death it terrified him. He, a Guardian who hadn't known the bitter taste of fear in too many centuries to count, now felt it overwhelm him.

"Tell me, Bain," she insisted in a voice that was barely more than a hush.

"Not long." Fresh fear as well as despair jolted through Bain. He was going to lose Emma permanently unless he acted. Soon. But the "cure" was not a sure thing. How could he risk it? Yet how could he not?

I love you, you know.

Her voice sounded in his mind and he wondered frantically how he could go on throughout eternity never knowing the touch of her thoughts again.

"I know," he said, kissing her forehead, sweeping her curls back from her pale face.

She laughed shortly, painfully. *Not the response I wanted.*

"Then I will give you what you need to hear. What I need most desperately to say. I love you, Emma Campbell Madison," he told her softly. "And trust me when I say I never thought to put the words *love* and *Campbell* in the same sentence."

She smiled, as he'd hoped she would, then closed her eyes on a soft moan. Time was ticking past. Every moment lost brought them that much closer to an end that he could not even contemplate. How could he be expected to go on through the eons without Emma at his side? Without her smile, her laugh, her touch? How could he face a long eternity of darkness with no promise of love or laughter to warm him?

He could not. *Would not.* Bain knew he had to act quickly. But first, he must tell her what he was thinking and then convince her to take the risk. To chance life. With him.

There is a way to perhaps defeat the poison.

She slowly, painfully, opened her eyes and looked at him, waiting for whatever else came next.

"Living flame." He said the words aloud, as if testing the sound of them on his tongue.

Clearly confused, she frowned and asked, "How?"

"You must walk through it." She blinked at him and he heard her thoughts, scattershot through her mind. More than that, he felt her fear, her reluctance to leave him, and he felt her waning strength. He waited, though, for her to speak her doubts aloud.

"Through eternal fire?"

"Yes," he said, pulling her to her feet, supporting her weight easily when her knees buckled and she slumped against him. He cradled her tightly to his chest and knew that he would do whatever was necessary to keep her there. With him. Where she belonged. "It is dangerous. But it should work."

"Should?"

She was even paler now, her skin nearly translucent, as if she were already beginning to leave him and this world behind. Everything in Bain was a defiant fist, refusing to let her go.

He cupped her face in his palm, forcing her to look up into his eyes. "Hear me, Emma. There are no guarantees in life. Not even when one is immortal. Yes, there is a risk to you. The flames could kill you. But without them, you will most surely die and I find I can't bear the thought of it."

Her eyes shone with unshed tears and she tried to lift a

hand to touch his face. But she couldn't quite manage the task. "You do love me."

"Aye," he muttered thickly, "I do at that and seeing you in pain is tearing at me. I won't lose you, Emma. But, ultimately, you are the one who must choose. Choose life, Emma. Choose the risk. If the eternal flames don't kill you, the poison will be gone from your system and you will be immortal."

Just like that?

He caught the flicker of hope in her mind and clung to it.

"Standing in the fire is not an easy thing," he warned. "The flames will consume the poison. Consume that damned cup. Consume your mortality."

"What'll be left?" Her voice was barely a whisper now, as if she were nearly too far gone already for him to reach.

"You," he insisted. "You will be left. The essence of you. And you will be with me. Always. There will be *us*. It will work, Emma. I will stand in the fire with you. I will take as much of the pain as I can, but you will have to trust me, Emma. Do you?"

Instead of answering, a question simmered in her mind and slammed into his.

You've been hiding something from me, Bain. Something in your mind you don't want me to see. So before I answer your question, tell me what that is.

His arms, so strong, so capable, felt useless as he cradled the only important thing in his world. He sensed her body shutting down, the demon's poison slithering through her blood, infecting tissue and bone. Draining the life from her inch by inexorable inch. All Bain knew was that she must survive, so he gave her the one thing he'd kept from her.

"I didn't want you to know that an immortal may give up eternity. Become human."

"What?" Her eyes were clouded now, nearly opaque as her eyesight failed. Her breath was coming in short, irregular gasps. "You could become human?"

"Yes," he said, ashamed now that he'd ever thought to hide it from her. "Guardians can choose to give up the life of battle, become mortal like their mates. But I didn't wish to. A warrior is all I have ever been. I could not step away from my duty, Emma. Not even for you."

You big dummy.

His eyebrows arched high on his forehead.

She sighed heavily. "I wouldn't want you to be less than you are, Bain. I fell in love with my Highland warrior. Why would I want him to be anything else?"

"I am a fool."

Yeah, pretty much. Her laughter was fading now, too, the soft sigh of it in his mind more of an echo of what it had once been.

"We can't wait," he announced. "The demon's poison spread faster than I expected."

Her head lolled against his chest. *I trust you, Bain. Build me a fire.*

He did. Holding her propped against him with one arm, with his free hand, he sketched ancient symbols in the air.

His fingers drew light and magic from the cold, drafty room, and as he whispered words of an ancient tongue known only to the Guardians, the very air around them shimmered and twisted with power.

It seemed to Bain that it took forever to make the magic happen. The urge for speed crouched in his chest and howled at him to hurry up. The sane corner of his mind warned that one misspoken word could turn living flame on the world and create as much destruction as a demon's incursion. He could afford no mistakes—not only for what it might cost the human world, but for the reason that he would not have the time to cast this spell again. If he didn't get it right the first time, he would lose the woman who was everything to him.

The spell for eternal fire was a difficult one and his worry for Emma made it that much harder to concentrate. Still, he focused his energies, drawing on centuries of life and power to do what he must. This was the only chance she had. The only chance *they* had.

Emma felt a magical wind tousle her hair, then she opened her eyes to watch her Highlander. He looked too good to be true, she thought, a weary smile lifting one corner of her mouth. She wanted another hour with him. Another night. An eternity.

She couldn't bear to lose him just when she'd found him. But she was so tired. So empty. Her bones were mush. Her strength was nearly gone. She listened to the steady, hard beat of Bain's heart beneath her ear and told herself that it wasn't such a bad way to die. In the arms of the only man she would ever love.

Hold tight to me, Emma! His thoughts crashed into her mind, allowing her no chance to slip away. He simply refused to accept her surrender to death. *There will be no leaving me, do you understand? Turn from the abyss tempting you. Return to me, Emma, and stand beside me as you were meant.*

Then light erupted into the darkness.

Emma forced her eyes open as magic electrically charged the air in the room. Shadows danced on the walls and heat licked at them as an inferno roared into life. Dazed, she stared at the wall of living fire in front of her. The flames danced and twisted and writhed against one another. Colors burst from the heart of the blaze—orange, blue, red, green, yellow.

It really *was* alive, she thought, and the heat was its heartbeat.

All around them, the shadows slipped away, unable to stand against the vivid brightness of a light so otherworldly. The Campbell Cup, so long coveted by the demon races, skittered noisily across the floor, as if drawn by the very heat of its destroyer. It was swept into the flames and was obliterated in an instant.

Oh, my God.

He must have heard the fear in her voice. He looked into her eyes and whispered, "The fire vanquishes evil, Emma. There's nothing evil about you. You *will* be saved.

I will allow nothing less, do you understand? I love you. Through all time, I will love you."

Emma smiled despite the weakness dragging at her and said softly, "Just don't let go of me, okay?"

Never. His promise echoed in her mind as he walked her into the heart of the firestorm.

Heat ripped through her and Emma gasped, throwing her head back, expecting to feel the excruciating pain of being burned alive. She stared into Bain's eyes and felt him with her. His heart, his soul, were so entwined with hers, it was impossible to feel the fear that should have been racking her.

Their hands met, palm to palm, and fingers locked. They stood, two halves of one whole, in the center of a fire that blew hot with the breath of eternity.

Heat, incredible heat, flashed through her veins and Emma felt the poison bleed from her cells, her muscles, her bones. As the flames danced around them, snapping, hissing, twisting around their limbs, tangling in their hair, all traces of the demon's venomous bite were consumed, leaving Emma alive in a way she never had been before. Her body awakened. Her soul swelled, blossoming with the promise of eternity, and as she stared into Bain's eyes and watched him smile, she knew.

It had worked.

Their desperate gamble had given them forever.

He pulled her close, murmured words both ancient and beautiful, and in the space of a single heartbeat the flames disappeared, winked out of existence. As if they had never been.

"It's over," she whispered, tipping her head back to grin at him in the sudden stillness. "I feel…different."

"As you should," he told her. "You're an immortal now, Emma. Just like me."

Immortal. The word sang through Emma's system, and for just a moment, she enjoyed the thrill of having eternity stretching out in front of her. She imagined watching the world change around her and always being able to reach out and touch the hand of the man who had saved her life—and that made that life worth living.

As you did for me, Emma, his mind whispered into hers. *For centuries, I was a man alone, and now, there is you. A priceless gift to one such as me.*

She smiled up at him, cupping his face between her palms. "I'll remind you of that the next time you're furious with me."

"I know you will, lass," he said, turning his face to kiss her palm. "What a fine time we'll have."

They would, Emma thought, since she now had an eternity to be with the man she loved more than anything. Then, she realized there were one or two things that had to be said. She poked him in the chest with her index finger.

"No more secrets, okay?"

"Agreed." He kissed her, nearly shattering her train of thought.

"And I'm going to finish school. Get my degree."

"If you wish."

"That means staying in the city during the school year, Mr. I-Can't-Wait-to-Get-Back-to-the-Highlands."

He frowned, but nodded, stroking her hair back from her face with gentle fingers. "I will find a Guardian to keep watch at my home until we return from this blasted city."

Emma wrapped her arms around his neck and went up on her toes. "*And* you have to come home with me to meet my family."

His scowl deepened and she laughed.

"I see nothing funny about this," he told her as his arms came around her, holding her close.

"I know." Emma gave him a quick, hard kiss, then grinned again. "Oh, I think my mom's going to love you. But I warn you, my dad can be pretty protective."

"As a man should over his children."

"My brother will probably want to come back to Scotland for a visit with us."

"Aye," he muttered, rolling his eyes. "They're all welcome in our home, Emma. For as long as any of you like."

"I knew you'd say that," she said, still smiling. "You're a softy, Bain Sinclair."

He pulled her in tightly to him as if to dissuade her of that notion entirely.

Her eyebrows lifted as she pressed closer, rubbing her hips against his. "Okay, not a softy."

He bent his head to kiss her but she stopped him with one finger over his lips. "There's one more thing. You do realize, that for the rest of our eternal lives together, I'm never going to let you forget that I walked through fire for you."

"Leave it to a Campbell to find a way to torment me." He smiled at her and Emma's body went into overdrive.

She ran one hand across his bare, muscled chest until he shivered with the desire claiming them both. "Let's go home, Highlander, and I'll let *you* torment *me* for a while."

"I willna ever let you go, Emma. I doona think I could bear eternity wi' out ye."

A delighted laugh shot from Emma's throat as Bain gave her the Highland dialect she'd expected when she first met him—that seemed like a lifetime ago. And when he swept her into his arms and kissed her, she knew that an eternity spent with this man wouldn't be nearly long enough.

* * * * *

A Vampire's Vindication

Alexis Morgan

Chapter 1

"The daughter's already on her way home?"

"Yes, sir. Keelie started back as soon as she heard."

To buy himself some thinking time, Griff refilled his glass from the carafe of blood on his desk. Well aware of the half-blood chancellor watching his every move from the video screen, he sipped the O neg with a calm he wasn't feeling. The blood gave him an excuse for his fangs to show other than sheer temper.

From the day she'd left the clan to work for Lydia Bronson, his cousin Dorothy had been ordered to maintain silence about their family connection. So far, she'd held to their bargain.

"Are you sure Lydia will tell her?" He flashed his canines at the screen."And, cousin, I will know if you're lying."

Dorothy's shoulders slumped in defeat. "Lydia has been refusing all of her medications to keep her head clear, and she's quit confiding in me. Even so, I think her intent is to tell her daughter everything."

"Keep me posted."

Griff disconnected the call, deciding he'd showed amazing restraint by not bashing the computer against the wall. Son of a bitch, the timing couldn't have been worse, but then Lydia had never been concerned about the devastation her rash actions had caused others.

He pinched the bridge of his nose and prayed for patience. He was already under attack on another front. All he could do was hope that Lydia managed to quietly pass into the next world without adding to his problems.

But knowing her, that was probably too much to wish for. Stubborn didn't come close to describing that chancellor when it came to her own agenda. Hell, her arrogance would have done a pureblooded vamp proud. Lydia Bronson would hold off the specter of death with nothing but sheer willpower until she was damn well ready to go.

He considered his options. If he were to show up at her house uninvited, maybe he could stave off the impending disaster that would ensue if she broke silence after all these years. Damage control was everything.

With Lydia about to die, that left him the only other person who knew the truth behind the events of twenty-five years ago. Maybe the past could be laid to rest for good. Then again, perhaps not.

Griff studied the file he'd spread out on the desk, his eyes once again drawn to the pictures of Lydia's daughter, Keelie. Her looks favored her late father Kenneth more than her harpy of a mother except for that distinctive eye color: not quite amber and not quite brown, but somewhere in between, like the color of fresh caramel, rich and sweet.

Not that Bronson women of either generation were either of those two things. Lydia worked, but her part-time teaching job at a small college didn't pay enough to maintain her lifestyle. To make up the difference, she'd been feeding off his finances for years.

Then there was the daughter, an environmental scientist and a born crusader. She'd scrutinized every enterprise his clan was involved in since she'd finished college. Keelie had kept Griff on his toes, knowing that she was waiting to pounce at the first hint that any of his clan's actions threatened the native flora and fauna.

Although it certainly pissed him off, he admired her persistence. It was her way of striking back at the vampire she held responsible for her father's death. Oh, yes, if Lydia opened her mouth, his world wouldn't be the only one to be turned upside down. Keelie Bronson was in for a major shock.

Rather than watch his life unravel from a distance, he'd confront Lydia and try to talk some sense into her. Soon the sun would set, and he'd be on his way.

Keelie slammed her transport into Park and ran for the house. She hadn't slept more than a handful of hours in three days as she'd hiked, flown and then driven like a madwoman to get back home. Exhaustion burned like acid in her brain, leaving room for only two questions.

Had she made it in time? And how would ever she forgive herself if she hadn't?

The front door swung open before she was halfway to the porch. Dorothy, the family housekeeper, stood framed in the doorway. There was no need to ask if the past few days had been hard on her. It was written there in the slump of her shoulders and the sorrow in her eyes. Even so, she answered the question that Keelie couldn't find the words or the courage to ask.

"She's waiting for you."

Relief tasted sweet. Keelie slowed to a stop after reaching the porch, reluctant to enter the house. Once she crossed that threshold, brutal reality would have to be faced, acknowledging her mother was dying.

Leaning back against the railing, she struggled to compose herself. It wouldn't do to go charging into her mother's bedside in a full-out panic.

"Tell me what happened."

Dorothy glanced back over her shoulder before joining Keelie outside, pulling the door closed behind her.

"Saturday she worked in the garden. She always says digging in the dirt soothes her spirit after a week full of dealing with fools."

Dorothy and Keelie exchanged smiles. They both knew Lydia had zero tolerance for idiots or incompetence. It was one of the things that Keelie shared with her maternal parent.

"When I looked out, she'd collapsed. The doctor had warned her to take it easy because the lymphoma had progressed to the point that this could happen at any time."

Shock sent a painful jolt straight through Keelie. "When did he tell her that? Why hadn't she told me?"

In fact, why hadn't Dorothy?

"Your mother doesn't tolerate weakness in anyone, least of all herself. I would've told you myself, but she threatened to fire me if I did."

Dorothy's eyes filled with tears. "Seriously, Keelie, the way she was acting, I've been afraid she'd actually throw me out in the streets."

"She wouldn't have." Maybe. One of the symptoms of the disease was erratic behavior bordering on paranoia. Dorothy stared out toward where the sun was slipping down beyond the horizon. "There's nothing to do now except keep her comfortable. She's been refusing any pain medication, claiming she needed to keep her wits about her until she talks to you."

The housekeeper gave Keelie a considering look. "Whatever she wants to talk to you about must be powerfully important."

Each word stabbed like a dagger into Keelie's heart. It was bad enough that she'd been off playing when her mother's illness took a turn for the worse.

"I don't have any idea what it's about. Do you?"

"No, she quit confiding in me months ago." The hurt in Dorothy's voice was obvious. "We used to be friends."

Keelie threw her arms around Dorothy and gave her

a fierce hug. "You're still her friend, Dorothy. It's the disease talking, not Mom."

Dorothy stood back, her hands on Keelie's shoulders. "How did you grow up to be so smart?"

"I had the good fortune to have two terrific role models, Dorothy. You and Mom."

It was time. Facing what was waiting for her inside wasn't going to get any easier.

"Is she in bed?"

Dorothy nodded. "She's too weak to sit up more than a half an hour at a time, but maybe seeing you might perk her up some."

Keelie braced herself. "Look, I'll sit with her for a while. Why don't you take a break?"

Dorothy led the way back inside. "I do have errands to run. I won't stay gone long, though, and I'll bring dinner back with me."

"Dorothy, you're a godsend. Go run your errands and then relax awhile."

The older woman still hesitated. "Are you sure?"

Keelie forced herself to nod. "We'll be fine."

That was a lie, and they both knew it. Nothing would ever be fine again.

Chapter 2

Keelie stood over her mother's bed in the gathering darkness, her heart breaking. The strong, vibrant person she'd always known was gone, replaced by a frail ghost of the woman Lydia Bronson used to be. Her life could now be measured out in hours and minutes, and the clock was ticking. Soon Keelie would be alone. Yes, she loved Dorothy, but it wasn't the same. She and her mom had been close and for good reason.

After her father's brutal murder, they'd turned to each other for comfort. His killer had never even been brought up on charges for her father's death. Because Griffon Tyler was a member of a wealthy vampire clan, no one had questioned his claim that the death had been accidental. For Keelie's father there had been no justice, no vengeance, no retribution. She closed her eyes and fought against the familiar burn of hatred.

Because of that vampire, Keelie had grown up without a father, and her mother had grown colder as the years had gone by. Maybe it had been the disease that destroyed her mother's smile, but more likely it had been grief and bitterness.

"Mom."

No response. Keelie would've been scared, but she could sense the faint flutter of her mother's pulse. The only question was if her mother was asleep or if she'd slipped into a coma. Did she really want to know which it was? No, but walking away wasn't an option.

Touching her mother's shoulder, Keelie gave it a light shake. "Mom, I'm back. Dorothy said you wanted to talk to me."

This time her mother stirred, her eyes fluttered, then opened wide to stare up at Keelie. At first there was nothing but confusion reflected in their amber depths. Keelie gave her mother a few seconds to gather herself.

Finally, there was a glimmer of recognition and her mother's mouth offered a hint of a smile. "You're back."

She gathered her mother's frail hand in her own. "Sorry it took me so long to get here."

"Dorothy?"

"She's out running errands. She won't be gone long, but she just left."

"Good." Lydia struggled to sit up. "Must talk."

Keelie lifted her mother up enough to tuck another pillow behind her. Even that much effort left the older woman struggling to breathe.

"Take it easy and rest, Mom. We can talk later after dinner."

Her mother grew more frantic, more insistent. She squeezed Keelie's hand with a chancellor's strength. "No! Now. Before she's back. Dorothy will tell him. I know she will. She doesn't know I heard her talking to him."

Him? She must mean her doctor. He'd warned them that the natural progression of the lymphoma could bring on paranoia and unexplained agitation. Keelie fought to present a calm façade to her mother, hoping to soothe her fears.

"Mom, please, Dorothy is your friend. She'd never do anything to hurt either one of us."

Lydia's head jerked back and forth, adamant in her denial. "She works for him. I know she's been lying to us. You need to know the truth about everything. Before it's too late. I'm so sorry. My fault. Should have said something before now."

"Said something about what?"

Tears trickled down her mother's papery cheek. "That night. Back then…seemed right. But the lie spun out of control."

Feeling shaky herself, Keelie sank down to the floor next to her mother's bed. She brushed her mother's hair back from her face, buying herself a few seconds. Dread settled in her stomach, sending cold shivers of fear scattering along her nerves.

"What night, Mom?"

Although she knew. There was only one night that could carry such dread weight in her mother's voice.

"You know. That night. When I…when Kenneth… death and blood. So much blood."

As the words faded away, her mother licked her lips and her eyes lost their focus, perhaps seeing the past so much more clearly than the present. Just as quickly she was back, looking at Keelie with burning intensity.

"I left a letter. It explains everything. Tell him…sorry, so sorry."

Her mother paused to catch her breath. When she didn't continue, Keelie prompted her, knowing her mother wouldn't rest easily until she got it all out.

She couldn't mean Keelie's father. Surely she wasn't that confused. "Tell who you're sorry, Mom?"

Lydia started to speak and then her eyes widened in horror as a deep voice answered the question for her.

"I suspect she means me."

Keelie lurched to her feet, planting herself firmly between her mother and the vampire standing in the doorway. Her fangs dropped down as she stood ready to defend them both if he took one more step into the room.

Griff didn't know whether to laugh or applaud Keelie Bronson's determination to protect her mother from him. Not that he'd make the mistake of underestimating her. The North American Coalition employed chancellors to police both humans and vampires for good reason. She might just be able to take him in a fair fight, but then he never fought fair.

Right now Keelie hovered on the brink of attack, those caramel-colored eyes boring straight into his in full challenge. His own predatory instincts bubbled to the surface. Under other circumstances, he might've tried to coax her into channeling all that high-octane emotion into a different, more pleasurable direction.

Right now, if he even so much as hinted how aroused he was by her display of temper, she'd be on him, no holds barred. He eased back half a step, forcing his shoulders to drop and his hands to dangle at his side, hoping she'd accept that he posed them no immediate threat. Slowly the tension sizzling in the air between them settled down to a more manageable level. Barely.

"Who the hell are you?" she snarled.

He arched an eyebrow and offered her a small shrug. "Don't play games, Keelie. Even if we've never spoken in person, Lydia's reaction should tell you who I am."

He let a hint of his own fangs show when he spoke. "Besides, considering all the injunctions you've filed against me over the past few years, I can't believe you don't recognize me."

"Griffon Tyler."

Lydia whispered his name, the words so faint that only those with vampire DNA would've been able to hear them. Her daughter certainly had. Keelie flinched and stepped back closer to her mother.

"Don't worry, Mom. Mr. Tyler is leaving."

Griff leaned against the doorframe and crossed his arms. "No, actually I'm not."

He hated to ramp up the tension again, but he wasn't going anywhere before they settled a few things. Damn Lydia for putting Keelie through all of this. If the woman had dealt with their mutual problem sooner, Keelie wouldn't be the one stuck in the middle.

Keelie glanced at her mother before turning her angry gaze back in his direction. "You will leave and leave now. Can't you see that she's sick?"

Damn, he hated the pain in Keelie's voice, the one innocent in all of this. "We'll compromise. I'll go as far as the living room."

Before he did, though, he had one more thing to say. "Lydia, she's going to find out. Wouldn't you rather she hear the truth from you?"

As he spoke, his hand reached out toward the daughter in a futile attempt to offer her some kind of comfort. She clearly wasn't interested. He couldn't blame her.

On his way out, he gave her his parting shot. "Come talk to me when you're ready."

Then he walked away before Keelie could argue the point any further.

Chapter 3

Griff Tyler was no longer in sight, but Keelie could still feel the power of his presence echoing throughout the house. She'd actually taken a couple of steps as if to follow him before catching herself. Staring at the empty doorway, she wondered at her strong reaction to the vampire. He certainly wasn't what she'd expected. In the past, they'd dueled via legal documents, never over the phone or in person.

Certainly, his arrogance had come across quite clearly in their correspondence, but that hadn't prepared her for the impact he'd have on her senses. Her own temper had heightened her awareness of him as he'd filled the doorway with his tall frame and broad shoulders. He wasn't the pretty-boy spoiled heir she'd pictured. Instead, he had those predator's eyes that saw too much and a nose that had been broken once too often, making his face rugged rather than handsome.

She doubted he smiled often. But when he did, she bet it was devastating, especially with that impressive set of canines he was sporting. She shivered.

Her mother drew Keelie's attention back to her. "Keelie."

Lydia's hands worked the edge of the blanket, clearly agitated.

"Mom, what is it?"

Although she didn't want to know. Once again she knelt at her mother's side, wishing all of this would just go away.

A strange calm settled over her mother's expression, erasing years off Lydia's face. Her eyes dropped to half-mast, her hands still at last. When she spoke, there was a resurgence of strength in her voice.

"I'm sorry, Keelie. I was a coward then, and I'm a coward now. I loved your father, and I love you. I see so much of him in you."

Her hands went back to tugging at her covers. "I left a letter in my desk. You know, the secret compartment. Remember the game we used to play so you'd know how to open it?"

Keelie nodded. The hidden door could only be released if the desk drawers were opened and closed in the right sequence.

"Good. Find the letter. Read it. Take any questions to Griff. He'll know the answers. He's strong."

"Mom, you're scaring me."

On so many levels. She knew a goodbye when she

heard one, but was her mother really asking her to trust the vampire she'd spent the last twenty-five years reviling? Was this the disease speaking? Somehow Keelie didn't think so.

She captured her mother's hands, hoping to calm her. They were cold, too cold. Lydia stared up toward the ceiling, a smile slowly spreading across her face.

"Kenneth, I knew you'd come."

The words floated on a whispered breath—and then her mother breathed no more.

The cry of anguish had Griff running for the bedroom. He'd sensed the nearness of Lydia's death, but doubted Keelie had. She'd been too intent on understanding her mother's confused words to realize that Lydia had been slipping away.

When he reached the bedroom door, he found Keelie huddled on the floor, her chest heaving with huge, wracking sobs. Dorothy would've been better suited to comfort the young chancellor, but his cousin had yet to return. Griff did the only thing he could think of. Grabbing a quilt, he wrapped it around Keelie and then muscled her up off the floor.

He hated—HATED—dealing with a woman's tears, but it would take a lot bigger bastard than he was to drop Keelie in the other room and bolt out the front door. Cursing himself for a fool, he settled them both on the sofa and wrapped his arms around her as she soaked the front of his shirt with her grief.

After a few seconds, he began rubbing her back with one hand, mumbling a bunch of nonsense, hoping the tone of his voice would soothe her even if his words didn't. When the torrent slowed to a stop, he loosened his hold on Keelie, but she made no effort to move away.

"Keelie?"

She'd fallen asleep.

"I'll be damned." He studied the lump of female passed out in his lap. "Now what do I do?"

If he were careful, he might be able to lift Keelie off his lap. At least then he'd be able to track down Dorothy and contact the authorities to report the death. But Lydia wasn't going anywhere, and Keelie obviously needed a few minutes of oblivion to deal with the situation. Why else would she let down her guard around her sworn enemy long enough to fall asleep? He cradled her closer and let her doze.

A short time later Keelie finally lifted her head, her face still blotchy from crying. Her eyes blinked in surprise, as if confused about how she came to be on his lap. He relaxed his arms, allowing her to decide what to do next, hoping she'd make up her mind quickly before he did something stupid. Like kiss her.

Too late.

Griff took it slow, brushing his lips across hers, offering comfort, tasting her tears, and wishing the circumstances were different. He was hardly an innocent when it came to the female of the species, but this was different. Through the growing fog of passion, he fought to put a label on what he was feeling. No luck. The best he could come up with was that somehow she just fit: in his arms, on his lap, maybe in his life.

No, don't go there. Under the circumstances, it was understandable that emotions would run hot. That was no excuse for letting his imagination rampage out of control. He was just feeling overprotective. After all, Keelie's late father had been Griff's best friend. Despite his differences with Lydia over the past twenty-plus years, he'd kept an eye on his boyhood friend's daughter, but always from a distance. Not like this, crushing her against his chest, his tongue down her throat.

But damned if he could find the strength to stop, to call a halt to this headlong rush of heat. He brushed his thumb across the soft skin of Keelie's cheek. Reluctantly, he lifted her off his lap, trying to ignore the brief flash of hurt in her caramel-colored eyes.

He was never at a loss for words but found himself struggling to string together even a simple explanation as to why they needed to stop. "Keelie, we can't…we shouldn't."

Then a noise outside gave him that final push of common sense. "Dorothy's back."

With more regret than he could believe was possible, he walked away.

What had she been thinking? Her mother dies and what does she do? Jump the vampire who killed her father? Keelie's face burned in shame. She watched as Griff Tyler stopped Dorothy to break the news. Two grocery bags hit the ground as the housekeeper reeled in shock. Her grief-stricken eyes looked toward the house as she listened to whatever Griff was telling her.

Finally, Dorothy slowly walked away from the vampire, heading for the porch. Griff remained in the yard, making a call. Keelie opened the door and enfolded Dorothy in her arms as they both dissolved into tears. When the storm had spent most of its fury, Dorothy drew a shaky breath.

"Griff said he'd make the necessary calls. I need to go see to your mom."

Now wasn't the time to ask Dorothy about Lydia's assertions that she'd overheard her old friend talking to Griff Tyler. That would come later. For now, they had a funeral to plan.

"I'll go with you."

Chapter 4

"Your mother will be missed."

"Thank you."

Keelie managed a small smile as she accepted yet another in a long line of condolences. Would the line ever end? She appreciated everyone honoring her mother's memory, but it wasn't as if Keelie knew many of them well.

Her emotions were stretched to the breaking point. It wouldn't take much to shatter her composure completely. Knowing that Griffon Tyler was lurking along the back edge of the crowd didn't help. He'd kept his distance, but she could swear she sensed every move he made.

She'd tried several times to catch him watching her. But each time her eyes had strayed in his direction, he'd been engaged in conversation with one of the other high-ranking pureblood vampires on the guest list. Griff was definitely working the crowd.

The question was why? What was he after?

None of that would matter if he would conveniently disappear from her life as quickly as he had appeared. Once she settled her mother's estate, Keelie would return to her job where the only contact she had with Griff was through his attorneys. But those same instincts that made her so good at tracking down threats to the environment were screaming that Griff was up to something. He might walk back out of her life, but it would be on his terms, not hers.

Her fingers strayed to her lips, as she relived that moment of weakness when she'd let him kiss her. That had been bad enough, worse was the knowledge she'd kissed him back and was still thinking about it three days later.

And of course, this time when she glanced in his direction, he was looking straight at her. Judging by his slight smile, he knew exactly what she'd been thinking. The egotistical jerk. She wondered again what was contained in the thick envelope she'd found in her mother's desk and what it had to do with Griffon Tyler and the events that had led to her father's death.

Since she couldn't be sure how much Griff had heard of her last conversation with her mother, she'd been reluctant to leave the letter in the desk. As soon as she'd had time, she'd removed it and now carried it with her for safety's sake. Eventually she'd find the courage to open it, but not today and maybe not tomorrow.

The last of her mother's associates paid their respects

and then moved on. She thanked them for coming, but all she really felt was relief that she was done playing hostess. Or was she? A late arrival stood in the doorway, looking around the room as if he owned the place. She didn't recognize him, but there was no mistaking the vampire's arrogance and wealth.

He surveyed the room, his lip curled just enough to express his disapproval when he spotted Griff. Who was he? She rose to her feet. The tension between the two vampires spread across the room, making the other guests stir restlessly. Several made a discreet exit.

What was going on? Keelie started across the room, noting the instant that Griff realized she was on the move. He cut through the crowd, heading in her direction. Figuring better the devil she knew, she allowed him to intercept her. He offered Keelie his arm, leaving her no option to refuse without insulting him. She managed to maintain a calm demeanor, but just barely.

"So who is he and why is he here?"

Griff set a roundabout course through the crowd that would eventually take them by the newcomer. He stopped at the buffet table to pick up two drinks; blood for him, wine for her.

"My cousin, Becan Tyler," he finally answered when they were again on the move. "As to why, you'd have to ask him that. He avoids me."

She smiled at Griff over the rim of her wineglass. "One of those nasty little vampire family feuds we hear so much about?"

Griff's eyes turned icy. "A family disgrace is more like it. Becan is hoping you now have proof that would destroy my position in the family. If that happens, he inherits control of the clan's business holdings."

"And I'm supposed to think that's a bad thing?"

Griff's fangs flashed. "Damn straight it is. Trust me on that."

"I have no reason to trust you on anything, Mr. Tyler."

Griff's eyes hardened to the color of jade. "Fine, Keelie. I get that. True, I might be a coldhearted bastard, but Becan makes me look all warm and fuzzy. If you don't believe me, talk to the few humans who've managed to escape from his estate and lived to tell about it."

Despite her mother's strange behavior, Keelie hadn't forgotten Griff's ties to her father's death. She might have kissed the vampire in a moment of weakness, but the last thing she wanted was to be entangled in his clan's politics. She removed her arm from his and put some distance between them.

"Thank you for the information. Now if you'll excuse me, I need to greet my guest."

Chapter 5

Griff should just let her go. She didn't need him. After all, Keelie Bronson was all grown up, a chancellor in her prime. If Becan were the type to attack directly, she might even stand a fighting chance against him. Unfortunately his cousin had perfected the skill of the sneak attack. If Keelie somehow thwarted Becan's efforts to oust Griffon as clan leader, the bastard would kill her without hesitation, and her death wouldn't come easily.

Griff watched her approach his cousin, telling himself he was merely concerned for her safety, the same as anyone who might be seen as a threat to Becan's plans. That much was true, but Griff tried never to lie to himself. He'd spent the entire evening fighting the need to watch over her, to hover nearby, to find someway to drive away the shadows in those caramel-colored eyes. Maybe even kiss her again if the opportunity arose.

It would be better for all concerned if he kept his distance from both Keelie and Becan. His extended family hardly needed a fresh batch of gossip about the Tylers and the Bronsons circulating among the other vampire clans.

He'd already paid his respects by being there, which meant he could leave in good conscience. He'd wanted to talk with Dorothy about the letter Lydia had left behind but couldn't do that now. The last thing he wanted to do was draw Becan's attention to her presence. But come to think of it, he hadn't seen Dorothy since Becan had appeared. Good thinking on her part.

Elitist bastard that he was, Becan had made Dorothy's life a living hell when they were younger because of her mixed blood. As soon as she was old enough, she'd deserted the clan's stronghold to make a life for herself among the humans and other chancellors.

It was after the death of Keelie's father that Griff had encouraged Dorothy to apply for the housekeeper's position working for Kenneth's widow. The arrangement had worked out for both of them. She'd needed the job, and he'd needed her to keep an eye on things for him.

Unfortunately distance wasn't working for him now. He couldn't hear what Becan was saying, but Keelie's body language was all too clear as she emphatically shook her head and took a step back. Damn it, didn't the woman know never to show a sign of weakness to a predator?

Griff set his glass aside to free up his hands. The crowd scattered in front of him, showing a well-developed sense of self-preservation. No one in their right mind got in the way of a vampire on the hunt.

He openly displayed his fangs as he approached his cousin. Becan stopped talking as Griff headed straight for them. He smiled, but it wasn't friendly, especially with his own impressive set of canines fully extended.

Keelie looked back over her shoulder to see what had brought on the vampire's aggressive reaction.

"Griff, did you want something?" she asked.

Something in her voice caught his attention. It wasn't fear, at least not exactly. Relief, maybe. Either way, her eyes were pleading with him not to make a scene. For her sake he'd try.

"Keelie, I see you've had the questionable pleasure of meeting my younger cousin, Becan."

He met the challenge in the other vampire's eyes with a small smile. Becan hated being reminded of the three-day difference in their ages that had given Griff the decided advantage in the power structure within their clan.

Becan shrugged a shoulder. "I thought someone from our clan should offer their condolences to Miss Bronson, preferably someone who wasn't involved in the death of her father. Tell me, Griff. Any truth to the rumors that you were also present when poor Keelie's mother died?"

As he spoke, Becan's hand snaked out to brush against Keelie's cheek. She flinched, clearly hating the feel of his touch. She backed away, stopping only when she bumped into Griff.

Her eyes blazing, she glared at Becan, the tips of her own fangs showing. "You need to leave. Now."

The other vampire read her message loud and clear. Griff was welcome. Becan was not. This time his hand snapped out as if to slap her. She deflected the blow before Griff could do it for her. That didn't matter. Becan would pay for trying to harm Keelie.

Griff's rage burned hot. Between one heartbeat and the next, he slammed Becan against the wall, choking the bastard. How dare Becan touch her? Keelie didn't belong to him and never would. She was Griff's alone to claim. To protect. Griff's fangs ached to rip into Becan's throat and drain him dry.

Before he could act on the thought, Keelie grabbed his wrists, using her considerable strength to loosen his hold and allow Becan to suck in enough air to live. What a damn shame. A lot of Griff's problems would be solved if Becan breathed his last.

"Griff, I don't know what's going on between the two of you, but stop this now."

She glared at him until he released his cousin. Becan rubbed his throat and snarled. "You will both pay for this."

Keelie pegged Becan with a hard look. "Either walk out now or I'll toss you out. Right now, I don't really care which it is."

Becan jerked his head toward Griff. "If I go, he goes."

"That's not your decision to make." Keelie took a step closer to the irate vampire. "You weren't invited, he was."

Not really, but Griff wasn't about to argue the point, not when it meant he could stay. His cousin moved as if to go on the attack, but then clearly thought better of facing off against both a pissed-off chancellor and an enraged vampire. That showed more sense than Griff would have credited his cousin with having.

Finally, Becan's resolve broke. He quickly backed out of the door and disappeared into the night.

Becan's departure left Griff with a shitload of aggression and no handy target for it. He stepped outside, drawing a slow breath to test the night air to make sure Becan was really gone. Keelie joined him. Not good. His control was already shaky. With vampires, aggression was aggression, whether it was directed toward an enemy or a potential lover.

He looked around. No enemies in sight.

That left only one possible target: Keelie. The last thing he should be thinking about was taking her up against the brick exterior of the reception hall. At her mother's memorial service. What the hell was wrong with him?

Stupid question. His instincts were thinking how the soft curves of her body would cushion the powerful sex drive of a vampire lover whose temper was running hot. That her mouth, right now set in a grim line, was perfect for long, wet kisses and so many other things.

"You need to go back inside. Now." Before it was too late.

She got right up in his face. "One thing you haven't

seemed to figure out, Griffon Tyler, is that I don't respond well to orders. Care to tell me what that was all about?"

Clan business was supposed to be kept secret, but she should know what she was mixed up in. "Becan wants to take over the clan and is looking for any ammunition he can find."

"And you just had to go toe-to-toe in front of my guests?"

"He started it."

Okay, that was real mature. At least his childish remark had softened Keelie's mouth, as if she were fighting the urge to grin. It also made her look ever so kissable.

"I apologize for dragging you into our family problems, Keelie. I won't apologize for going on the attack when he tried to hit you. Next time, I'll kill him."

She looked up at the moon overhead, as if praying for patience. Finally, she looked up at him. "Griff, I handle my own battles. I don't need you to fight them for me. Now everyone inside thinks you were fighting over me like two dogs with one bone."

He liked that she wasn't afraid to challenge him when she wanted to make a point. Unfortunately, it also had the effect of ramping up his predatory nature even more, taking it in a whole different direction.

Damn, his fangs burned to taste her life's blood, knowing it would pack a fiery kick. But not here, not in a parking lot. If he ever bedded Keelie—no, make that *when* he bedded her, it would be someplace private where he could savor each moment, making sure she took as much pleasure from their joining as he did. He let some of what he was feeling show, tracing the graceful curve of her neck with his fingers.

For the first time, Keelie looked a bit nervous. "Griff, what are you thinking?"

He tongued the sharp tip of his fangs. "You're a smart woman, Keelie. Figure it out."

She backed away in a hurry. Once again, she should've known better than to retreat in front of a vampire. He followed her step for step, not wanting to scare her, but unable to stop himself, not with the urge to mate clouding his head.

"Damn it, woman, stand still before I do something we'll both regret."

He closed his eyes and fought for control. Finally, he crammed the lid back on his temper. He stepped back and bowed slightly.

"I apologize again. Now go inside and make nice with your guests. When you leave, make sure you're not alone. I wouldn't put it past Becan to come sneaking back. He doesn't handle being thwarted very well."

"And you do?"

At least she was smiling. "I'm not sneaky. If I want something—or someone—I'm far more direct in my approach."

Those caramel eyes reflected both the moonlight and a bit of curiosity. "Is that a warning?"

"More like a promise. Now go before I rethink my decision to behave."

Then she surprised them both and grabbed his lapels to drag him down for a kiss. They were both breathing hard when she finally broke it off.

"That still doesn't mean I trust you."

Yes, it did or she'd never have let him stay, much less kiss him.

Rather than point that out, he said, "We still need to talk about whatever it was that your mother left you."

The light in Keelie's pretty eyes immediately dimmed. Perhaps a cloud had passed over the moon, but he was pretty sure that he was the one responsible for that flash of pain.

"I'll be at your house tomorrow sometime after sunset."

She jerked her head in agreement and walked back inside.

Once she was out of sight, he picked out a place where he could watch over the parking lot without being seen. Yeah, she could take care of herself, but it wouldn't hurt for her to have some backup in place. Just in case.

Chapter 6

Keelie stared up at the ceiling. After her alarm had gone off, it took her a few seconds to figure out exactly where she was. Finally, she remembered checking into the hotel just before dawn.

It had only made sense to stay in town rather than drive all the way back out to the house. Her aunt's attorney had approached her last night after the memorial service asking her to meet with him. With everything else going on, she'd tried to put it off until next week. But he'd insisted the matter couldn't wait, so she'd reluctantly agreed.

Something was definitely going on, but she had no idea what it could be. If it were just her mother's will, surely that could have waited a few days. Nothing was making any sense.

She'd been so tired that she'd barely taken note of her surroundings before tumbling into the bed and falling asleep.

Unfortunately, her dreams had been anything but restful. The image of Becan Tyler's fangs haunted her as he lunged at her throat. When Griffon thwarted his cousin's attack, the flash of his fangs had a totally different effect on her. After vanquishing their mutual foe, Griff had led her in a dance of celebration--as in some of the most amazing imaginary sex she'd ever had. Even now, she ached with the need to finish what her dream self had started. Or maybe she'd kick-started the dream herself by giving into the impulse to kiss Griff last night. What had possessed her to do something so foolish?

She closed her eyes against the confused torrent of emotions flooding through her. How could she be thinking of that vampire in those terms while knowing he'd been involved in her father's death? It made no sense. Had her mother been thinking clearly when she'd told Keelie to trust him? Was Griff a good man and not the monster she'd always thought him to be?

Thinking in circles accomplished nothing. It was time to make some plans. First, she'd get dressed and eat. Then off to see the attorney before going back home. She'd have the place to herself because Dorothy had requested some time off before returning to her duties.

The house would be doubly empty with both the housekeeper and Keelie's mother gone. At least she'd have some privacy while she sorted through things, deciding what to get rid of and what to keep. And maybe she'd finally find the courage to read the letter her mother had left for her.

Time to get moving.

Keelie dug her nails into the palms of her hands, needing that small bit of pain to convince herself that she wasn't caught up in a nightmare. No, she was really sitting across from her aunt's lawyer, who'd just succeeded in destroying her life.

"I'm sorry, Mr. Fogarty," she said, although why she felt the need to apologize for anything escaped her. "Would you repeat that?"

The elderly lawyer sighed and turned his eyes back to the document in his hands. "The aforementioned house belongs to the Tyler vampire clan. You have one week to evacuate the premises, at which time you will turn the keys over to their legal representatives. Failure to do so will result in immediate legal action."

Finally, he set down the thick sheaf of papers and took off his glasses. "I'm sorry, Miss Bronson. I've only been your aunt's attorney for the past five years. She never mentioned any of these arrangements to me. On the plus side, at least she did leave you a tidy amount in a trust fund, enough for a down payment on a place of your choosing."

He sighed heavily again. "As much as I'd love to tell you there's been a mistake, I can't. I've studied this file and even consulted with my partners. There are no loopholes and no explanations why the courts gave Lydia free use of the house for her lifetime."

That's because no explanations were necessary. It had been Griffon Tyler's way of assuaging his guilty conscience.

She was absolutely furious, but the attorney wasn't a suitable target for her anger. If her mother was still alive, they'd definitely be having words over this, but she wasn't. That left one person—Griff Tyler.

And she'd kissed the bastard. Twice. She fought the urge to scrub her lips with the sleeve of her jacket to wipe away all memory of his mouth pressed against hers. She settled for a breath mint.

Rising to her feet, she picked up the copies of the legal documents that Mr. Fogarty had provided her with. "Thank you for..."

Her words drifted to a stop because she couldn't think of one thing she was grateful for.

"I'll be going now."

He followed her to the door. "If there's anything I can do for you, please don't hesitate to contact me. I wish things could have been different."

"Me, too, Mr. Fogarty. Me, too."

Keelie parked her transport in front of the house that was no longer her home while she tried to decide exactly what it was she was feeling. It felt like—nothing. She was numb. She'd lost too much, too fast, for her mind to be able to process any more pain.

For the moment, all she could do was stare at the two stories of wood and glass where she'd lived with her mother since the death of her father. It had never occurred to her to wonder how her mother could afford such a place. As a child, she'd accepted everything at face value, but she'd outgrown that excuse years ago.

She couldn't sit outside all night. There was a ton to pack and not much time to do it. She'd called ahead to have a local moving company drop off a shipping container and a load of boxes.

Time to get started.

After grabbing her suitcase, she headed for the front door. About halfway to the house, the back of her neck started itching, as if someone was watching her every move. When she reached the porch, she set her bag down and slowly looked around, hoping whoever was watching her would think she was simply taking time to enjoy the spectacular sunset.

As soon as she turned, the feeling disappeared. If someone had been out there, he was gone now. Maybe she was being paranoid, but then considering how screwed up her life had become, she had good reason to feel that way.

Time to get the pile of flattened boxes inside and set the deadbolt. She'd feel a whole lot better with the stout thickness of the door between her and the outside world. After half a dozen trips carrying in the packing supplies, she locked the door and headed for the kitchen. She'd eat a quick meal before boxing up her life.

An hour later, she set her dish in the sink. She'd lingered too long over a simple sandwich. No more excuses. It was time to take that first hard step. After picking up a stack of boxes, she eased through the door into her mom's room. Bracing her load against the doorframe, she flipped on the light.

One look at the room and her lungs froze in her chest. The boxes slipped from her hands, clattering to the floor as she stared in shock at the chaos that lay in front of her.

What had happened? The drawers had all been upended on the floor, and the closet had been stripped bare. Even the mattress and box springs had been slashed apart, the stuffing thrown around the room like clumps of dirty snow.

One part of her was in fierce denial at the sight of so much damage, but her heart knew the truth. Far too much hatred and anger had gone into the total destruction for it to be a simple break-in. The intruder had been searching for something. She had to think he hadn't found it. That was the only way to explain the broken and battered remains of her mother's collection of porcelain wolves.

She knelt down to pick up the only one that had somehow escaped unscathed, drawing comfort from its familiar shape. When she could bear to look up, she studied the mess. Where to begin? Calling the police certainly, but they'd want explanations, ones she didn't have.

She'd check out the rest of the house and then decide what to do. Her chancellor hearing would've warned her if someone else was still inside. She peeked into Dorothy's room off the kitchen. Neat and tidy, just like always. Either the intruder didn't think Dorothy had anything worth stealing or else he'd run out of time to search her quarters.

Upstairs, Lydia's home office was a mirror reflection of her bedroom. There wasn't a single surface left unscathed, not an item left unbroken. Keelie ached with grief over so much wanton destruction as she moved down the hall to face her own room.

The door stood ajar. Even from a distance she could see the floor was strewn with a trail of debris. Gathering the tattered remnants of her courage, she took a leaden step forward. Things. They were just things. Not all could be replaced, but she'd still have her memories.

She pushed the door open with her fingertips, still hanging back as far as she could. Eventually she'd cross the threshold, but not yet. Maybe when she could draw a full breath. Maybe when the knot in her stomach loosened.

Maybe never.

Somewhere downstairs glass shattered. A second later, it happened again—closer this time. One more time and she was bolting for the stairs, her fangs running out and demanding a blood price from whomever was out to destroy her life.

She hit the bottom step as a cloud of black smoke came roiling out of her mother's bedroom. Thick and oily, it ghosted through the hallway, consuming all the breathable air. Its mate came slithering out of Dorothy's room, blocking the way to the back door.

Survival instincts took over, thinking for her when she couldn't put a coherent thought together. Choking when she hit the solid wall of smoke, Keelie dropped to the floor and crawled, hoping to buy the few seconds she needed to reach the front door.

Desperate with sure death dogging her footsteps, Keelie crawled over broken glass, grateful for the thick denim of her jeans. In the living room, she grabbed her purse and the overnight bag from the bench by the front door.

Only then did she open the door and go stumbling outside, leaving the nightmare behind her as she ran out into the darkness.

Chapter 7

Griff yanked the steering wheel hard to the left, sending his transport barreling toward the ditch. Even with his vampire reflexes, he only narrowly missed Keelie as she stumbled out in front of him.

Was she out of her effing mind running out into the road like that?

Then she wheeled around and dropped to her knees. His vampire eyes, better suited to the night than the day, saw all too well the tears streaming down her face as she hugged herself and keened in heartbreaking grief.

What was wrong? Sure, she'd just lost her mother, but that didn't account for why she'd choose to cry in the middle of the road. Even allowing for the fact there wasn't much traffic out this far, she wasn't that stupid. He slammed the vehicle into Park and took off running.

That's when he noticed her face was reflecting a red

flickering light. He slowed to a stop in stunned silence. The crackle and pop of a fire raging out of control overrode the normal night sounds. The flames were licking at the roof of her house, the interior already an inferno. Hell, even her vehicle was burning.

He reached for his phone to call it in. It was obviously too late to save the house, but hopefully the fire department could contain the damage to the immediate area. If the flames reached the grasslands behind the house, there would be no stopping it.

While he provided the necessary information, he cautiously approached Keelie. She was clearly caught up in the throes of a powerful emotional meltdown. That was understandable, but it also meant she might not recognize friend from foe.

"Keelie."

No response other than her tears slowed. In stark silence, she stared at the raging dance of the fire lighting up the night. He stripped off his jacket and gently settled it over her shoulders, wishing there was more he could do to ease her pain.

He knelt down on one knee, putting himself at eye level. "Keelie, honey, are you hurt? Were you inside when the fire started?"

She drew a shuddering breath. He still wasn't sure if she really knew he was there, but then she spoke.

"Why would you burn the place, Griff? You ordered me evicted from the house, but the lawyer told me I had a week. Do you really hate me that much?"

Her words, an equal mix of anger and hurt, battered at him over the roar of the approaching fire trucks. He leaned in close to make sure she heard his response.

Gently cupping her chin with his hand, he tipped her face up just enough to make sure she heard him clearly.

"You haven't known me all that long, but that doesn't mean you don't know me well. I have three things to say, and you'd better damn well believe me."

He held up one finger. "First of all, I don't know a damn thing about any eviction notice."

Two fingers. "Even if I had wanted you to move, I wouldn't set fire to the place and risk destroying my only chance of reading that letter your mother left."

When he raised the third finger, he narrowed the distance between them until only a breath of smoky night air separated them. "And I sure as hell don't hate you."

Then he settled his lips over hers, letting his kiss speak of things he wasn't yet ready to put words to. She moaned under his gentle assault, her hands frantically seeking something to hold onto. He guided them up around his neck as he settled her against his chest. When she didn't fight his embrace, he slowly rose to his feet, taking her with him.

The fire department had turned out en masse. Obviously Griff's name carried enough weight to pull out all the stops. Within minutes the road and driveway teemed with men and women carrying axes and dragging hoses. At least no one offered false platitudes about their chances of saving anything as they hosed down the burned-out shell of her transport.

All she had left in her life was her purse and an overnight bag. Well, and a borrowed jacket and a vampire's arm around her shoulders. When she shivered, he pulled her in closer to his body. It felt good. Too good.

She had to be out of her mind. How did she go from mourning the loss of all that she had to once again kissing Griff Tyler like there was no tomorrow? As much as she'd like to blame it on a near-death experience, she couldn't. Terror may have sent her running into the night, but that didn't mean she should seek sanctuary in Griff's arms.

But that's exactly what she'd done and, what's more, she couldn't muster up either the energy or the desire to step away from him. Right now one of the yellow-coated firemen was looking in their direction, a chancellor, judging by the flash of fangs when he spoke to the fire chief. A second later he started toward them, his face grim, his dark eyes suspicious.

"Mr. Tyler, I'm Inspector Collins. I understand that you're the legal owner of this property even though Miss Bronson and her mother were the residents."

Griff nodded. "Actually, it belongs to my clan. As friends of the clan, the Bronsons were given use of the place years ago."

Friends of the clan? That was news to Keelie. Before she could say anything Griff gave her shoulder a slight squeeze. A warning? She casually stepped away, unwilling to let Griff control the conversation. Maybe the chancellor hadn't picked up on the silent communication, but Griff had read her message loud and clear.

Or maybe she was wrong about that. The investigator's eyes narrowed as he studied the two of them.

"Do either of you know of any reason that someone would burn down the house?"

Images of Griff's cousin Becan popped into her head, but once again he warded off anything she might have said. "No, we don't, Inspector."

The man clearly wasn't buying it. "How about you, Miss Bronson? Any problems with anyone? When you came home, did you notice anything out of the ordinary?"

"I've been gone since early yesterday. When I came home I had the strangest feeling I was being watched." She shivered again. "When I didn't see anyone, I went inside."

He nodded and then pointed toward the shipping container. "I take it you're moving?"

"Yes." She stared past him at the smoldering skeleton of the house. "I stayed in town after my mother's memorial service ended to meet with her attorney today. I found out that she left me a small trust fund. I plan to buy a place of my own, so I ordered the container and boxes to be delivered. I've only taken a short leave from work and needed to get started."

"Why don't you walk me through everything that happened from when you got home?"

"I decided to fix a sandwich and unwind a bit, so I went straight to the kitchen. An hour later, I couldn't put off facing my mother's room any longer. That's when I discovered her room had been vandalized."

She stopped talking as the memory swept her back to the pain of that moment.

"Everything was smashed or ripped to pieces. Everything."

Inspector Collins looked up from the notes he was taking. "Did you call the police?"

Keelie shook her head. "I decided to check out the rest of the house first, so I ran upstairs. I would've sensed if the intruder was still in the house, so I figured I wasn't in any immediate danger."

"And was the upstairs vandalized as well?"

"Yes, everything was trashed, but I didn't get much of a chance to look around before I heard glass breaking downstairs. By the time I got back to the first floor, the house was already filling up with smoke. It came from several directions. I dropped to the floor and crawled out the front door."

Griff had been leaning against the side of his transport. He straightened up and rejoined the discussion. "Wasn't the back door closer?"

"Yes, but the smoke was coming from the back and both sides of the house. The front was bad, too, but clearer than the rest of the lower floor." She had a sudden urge to cough, maybe to clear even the memory of smoke from her lungs.

The investigator nodded and then continued writing for several seconds. "What happened next?"

"I got outside and ran as far as the road before I stopped to look back. I never saw anyone around the house, but then it was after dark at that point."

"When did you arrive, Mr. Tyler?"

Despite the calm way he asked the question, Keelie frowned. She didn't like the barely veiled suspicion in the inspector's voice. She might have her own problems with Griff, but still she defended him.

"He pulled up right after it happened. As I said, last night was the memorial for my mother. He'd promised to stop by right after sunset to see if I needed anything."

"She was kneeling in the road when I drove up. I damn near hit her."

As he spoke, Griff reached out his arm to her again. He might only be trying to present a united front to the authorities, but she allowed herself to sink into his side. If nothing else, the warmth of his body helped keep the chill of the night air at bay. Not to mention she'd reached the breaking point after a day full of shocks.

"If you don't have any more questions, Inspector, I'm going to call a cab to take me to a hotel."

He held out a card to each of them. "Here's my contact information. I've got both of your numbers when I have more questions."

Interesting that he said "when" and not "if." Right now Keelie was too tired to do more than wonder about what he might be thinking. When the inspector was out of hearing, Keelie pulled out her phone. Griff placed his hand over hers before she could dial.

"I'll take you to a hotel if you insist, but I'd feel better if you came home with me."

"Why?"

"The security is better for one thing. The other is I never sleep well in hotels, and I'll be damned if I'll let you out of my sight before we get to the bottom of this."

Maybe she was crazy. She had no reason to trust Griff, but she liked that he left the decision up to her. Well, except that he planned to be right beside her no matter what. But the truth was she was afraid, deeply afraid, to be alone right now.

"Fine, but let's be clear about one thing—I'm sleeping alone when we get there."

"It's a deal. I'll put your bag in my vehicle."

He pressed a quick kiss on her cheek and walked away, leaving her second-guessing her decision and wondering about the gleam of satisfaction she'd seen in his eyes.

Chapter 8

Griff would kill the bastard that put the fear in Keelie's eyes. While dealing with the aftermath of the fire and all the questions, he'd kept a lid on his temper, but just barely. The last thing she needed to deal with right now was an enraged vampire intent on murder. But once he had her tucked safely away in his home, he'd start hunting for the culprit.

Becan better hope he had an ironclad alibi or he was a dead man. Griff glanced up at the sky and realized how late it was. The search would have to wait until tomorrow night. Right now he had more important things to do.

Like getting Keelie tucked up safely in his bed. Yeah, he'd promised she could decide where she slept. If she insisted on separate rooms, he'd live with it.

Griff carefully steered around the clutter of fire trucks and headed for his house on the Tyler clan estate. It wouldn't take long. As he drove, Keelie stared out at the darkness.

"I'm sorry this all happened."

"Did you torch the place?" she asked without looking at him.

A flash of hurt anger had his fangs running out. "Hell no."

Keelie finally turned in his direction, her own fangs gleaming whitely in the night. "Then you have nothing to be sorry for, do you? But, when I get my hands on the bastard who did, there'll be no quarter given. No matter who it was or what his last name is, blood will run."

He grinned. She was a bloodthirsty wench. He liked that about her. "Can I watch? Or help?"

"This isn't funny, Griff. Someone destroyed everything and for no reason."

He took her hand in his and kissed it. "No, it's not funny. I was smiling because you remind me of me. I was just thinking how much I was going to enjoying ripping the bastard into little bloody shreds."

"This is my battle, my duty."

He understood that as well. "And I'm on your side. Never doubt that."

As they drove through the security gates, he could feel her still watching him. She waited until he pulled into the garage before she finally responded.

"Just so you know, I do believe you."

Inside the house, Griff set the alarms and made a couple of quick calls. He had friends living on the outskirts of his estate whose special abilities made them well suited to the task of guarding his house in the daylight hours. They promised to come as soon as possible.

"Thank the pack for me."

When he hung up, Keelie was watching him, a curious look on her face. "The pack?"

He opened the fridge and pulled out sandwich makings for Keelie and a blood pack for himself. "It's, um, a nickname for a special security squad I use for daytime surveillance."

"What's special about them?"

"They're a canine team." True enough, except they worked with timber wolves, not dogs.

She accepted the sandwich he'd put together for her. "Thanks. I didn't realize how hungry I was."

He let her eat in peace, fixing her a second sandwich and then one for himself. After cleaning up the mess, he picked up her bag.

"Ready to go downstairs?"

An unexpected knock at the door had him dropping the bag and palming the gun he had tucked in his waistband. He motioned for Keelie to get back before he peeked outside. He jerked the door open and motioned for his friends to come inside.

"Keelie Bronson, meet Garrett and his partner Kipp. They'll be patrolling the estate while we sleep."

She started to smile but then she blinked and took a closer look at Kipp. "That's a timber wolf, and a big one at that."

Garrett grinned. "You've got a good eye. Most people just think he's a big dog, and an ugly one at that."

The wolf nipped at Garrett before shoving past him to lick Keelie's outstretched hand. Griff wasn't much for sharing, but that was the first real smile he'd seen on her face all day.

"He's not ugly. In fact—"

She pulled something out of her pocket. When she opened her hand, there was a small figurine of a wolf, one that was an exact match for Kipp.

"My mom and I collected these. We both love wolves." Her smile dimmed. "This is the only one that survived the destruction in my mother's room."

"Well, if you like wolves, you've come to the right place, Miss Bronson." Garrett shot a glance in Griff's direction. "Any time you want to spend time with a wolf, you just let me know."

Griff was going to wring his friend's neck for him. "Don't you have something better to do than stand around in my kitchen keeping me up? Or did you actually have a reason for being here?"

"We caught Becan's scent. He's definitely on the estate."

Keelie looked up from petting the wolf. "I get first crack at him."

The wolf woofed and Garrett laughed. "I think I'm in love."

Okay, enough was enough. "All right, you two, that's

enough. Get going and find him. I'll catch up with you at dusk."

He shoved them out the door and threw the lock. At least the close-up encounter with the wolf had brightened Keelie's mood. Unfortunately watching her take such sensuous pleasure in running her fingers through Kipp's fur had him wanting to howl himself.

Time to go downstairs. Now, before he did something stupid like trying to coax Keelie into trying out the kitchen table. Despite his earlier plans, he knew she needed some rest. They both did. He'd offer her the guest room next to his bedroom, but that was as much distance as he could stand between them. He'd come too close to losing her, and he'd only just found her.

So tonight he'd sleep alone. But once the dust settled, all bets were off.

Keelie followed Griff down to the basement level that had no windows, no outside access to endanger him during the daylight hours. Maybe she should be thinking about something other than the way those jeans showed off that fine-looking backside of his, but she couldn't help herself. With her family history, she'd never expected to be attracted to a vampire, much less the very one rumored to have killed her father. Somehow, she knew there was more to the story than the few hints she'd managed to garner over the years.

Griff stopped halfway down the hall and opened a door.

"This is your room. Mine is right next door. You should be able to find anything you need stocked in the bathroom."

When she started past him, he quickly backed away. His abrupt departure startled her and made her wonder at the reasons behind it. He'd certainly not been reluctant to touch her before this. She'd certainly expected at least another kiss. Maybe even hoped for another kiss or a reassuring hug.

Inside the bedroom, she set her purse on the dresser and got her first clear glimpse of how bad she looked. No wonder Griff hadn't wanted to kiss her. Her hair was a tangled mess, her skin and clothing covered in sooty streaks. She probably smelled as if she'd bathed in wood smoke and burned oil.

A knock at the bedroom door interrupted her pity party. She peeked out. "Yes?"

Griff shoved a stack of clothes at her. "I thought you might need something to sleep in."

She accepted the gift. "Thanks. I appreciate it."

Then he was gone again. The vampire was a constant surprise. More than ever, she needed to know his truth. But first things first. A hot bath was calling her name.

When Griff finished his shower, he could still hear Keelie moving around in the room next door. Images of her soaking in the oversized tub, her skin slick with soap, had him hard and hurting. He groaned and leaned his forehead against the cool tile. He hadn't been in this constant state of sexual arousal since his teens when he first became fascinated with the female half of the population.

The phone rang, providing him with a welcome distraction. A few seconds later he slammed the receiver down. Somehow Becan had managed to elude Garrett and his pack. The vampire's scent trail had ended abruptly when it crossed a road. Their best guess was someone had picked him up. None of the gates had opened, so he was still on the premises.

For now, they were pulling back to Griff's house to reinforce the security there. He trusted his friends to keep him and Keelie safe for the next few hours, but come nightfall he'd hunt. He needed to end this, to lay the past to rest, because for the first time the future held something he wanted.

Would she never settle down? Every move Keelie made jarred Griff awake. He flopped over onto his stomach and covered his head with a pillow. No good. His nerves were scraped raw with the need to charge next door and demand answers or, better yet, demand satisfaction. Whatever kind she was willing to give him.

An unexpected sound had him jerking upright in the darkness. He reached out with his vampire senses. Someone was sneaking around upstairs in the kitchen.

He rolled up to his feet, prepared to defend his home and his woman. After easing his door open, he moved through the darkness toward the soft glow of light at the top of the stairs. At the bottom of the steps, he sniffed the air. One kind of tension drained away only to be replaced by another as he realized who he was tracking—Keelie. Vampires were predators at heart, and she was rapidly becoming his favorite prey.

He deliberately made noise going up the steps to avoid startling her. Even so, with her chancellor hearing she'd probably been aware of his approach since he'd left his room. She was already pouring a second cup of hot chocolate when he walked into the room.

Her eyes were so damn sad. "Sorry if I woke you."

He wrapped his hands around the mug she offered him. The warmth felt good, but it also gave him something to do with his hands besides hauling Keelie straight into his arms.

Her wearing his oversized T-shirt and flannel boxers shouldn't have been sexy, but try telling his hormones that. He kept the counter between them to hide his body's response.

He said, "The real question is what is keeping you awake?"

She stared down into the depths of her mug for several seconds. Even from across the room he could see the ripples dancing in her drink.

"I almost died today, Griff." Her smile trembled almost as much as her hands. "And I don't even know why or what I did to make someone hate me that much."

"Keelie..." He started toward her, but she held up a hand to stop him.

"Griff, we both know that whatever is going on started

the night my father died." Her fangs were showing now. "I want to know what really happened. I deserve that much."

Maybe she did, but he knew she'd hate the truth once she knew it. Before he could say another word, she picked up an envelope and tossed it down on the counter between them.

He blinked several times. "Is that your mother's letter? I assumed it burned up in the house."

"No, I've been carrying it with me since the night she died, trying to find the courage to read it."

He didn't blame her for feeling that way. She'd lost so much in the past few days, but running from the truth never worked for anyone. He had his own selfish reasons for wanting the facts to come out, but he'd lived with the lies so long now he didn't much care what the rest of the world thought. Only Keelie mattered right now, and he wanted no more lies between them.

He walked around the counter, needing to touch her, to ease the pain she was already feeling and the rest that would come the second they opened the envelope. To his surprise, she met him halfway, her hands sliding over his chest.

"Kiss me, Griff. Please."

Damn, he had no business taking advantage of her when her defenses were down, but he needed her touch as much as she needed his. He kissed her soft and slow, fighting against his instincts to take her right then and there, fast and hard, claiming her as his own. It didn't help his resolve when she moaned and practically climbed him, ending up with her legs wrapped around his hips, her core solidly against his erection.

This had to stop. Afterward, they could pick up where they'd left off if she could still stand his touch. No more lies.

"Keelie, honey, we have to stop." He gave her a tight hug first, hoping she'd know that he didn't want to let go of her even though it was the right thing to do.

She froze in his arms, leaning back enough to look him straight in the eye. "You don't want this?"

His laughter held little humor. "More than you can possibly know. I'm skirting the far edge of crazy wanting you."

He supported her with one arm while he snagged the envelope off the counter. "We'll deal with this first. Ignoring it won't make it go away."

Then he carried her downstairs to his bedroom. They needed someplace quiet and safe to deal with the storm that was coming the second she read her mother's letter. Granted, the living room upstairs would've been more neutral territory, but the wolves were at the door. Literally. And although their sense of smell was their strongest sense, there was nothing wrong with their hearing.

He set her on the bed and wrapped a blanket around her shoulders. After turning on enough light for her to read by, he sat down in the easy chair across the room, giving them both the space they needed.

"You read. I'll listen and then answer any questions that I can."

Chapter 9

Keelie winced at the sudden brightness in the room and stared down at the envelope in her hands. As long as the light was soft and the shadows thick, she could hide her embarrassment and pretend she hadn't practically begged Griff Tyler for some hot sex. But evidently her best efforts had been all too easy to resist.

"I wanted it, too, Keelie. I still do. Never doubt that."

Her head jerked up. Was he some kind of mind reader? Feeling more than a bit defensive, she lied. "It was a mistake."

There was a lot of heat in those grass-green eyes when he smiled at her. "Only in the timing. Once we deal with that blasted letter, and you even hint that you still want what we started in the kitchen, I'm all yours."

She swallowed hard and tore open the envelope.

Keelie read the letter once and then a second time. Finally, she looked up from the paper that had just torn her world apart. "She killed my father? You helped my mother get away with murder?"

Griff was up and moving before she even finished talking. He knelt down in front of her, taking her hands in his. She didn't know why she let him.

"Your father was my best friend. He died way too young, and I miss him to this day. Your parents went through a rough patch, and Kenneth made a mistake. When he confessed to having a brief affair, your mother lashed out at him. As a human, he was no match for the strength of a chancellor. By the time I got there, he was dead, and she was hysterical. Lydia was terrified they'd take you away from her. If the court didn't buy that it was an accident, they could've even executed her, leaving you an orphan."

He threaded his fingers through hers. "We staged it to look as I was the one who killed your father. With my clan's influence, the court ruled it accidental death and ordered that I support your mother for the duration of her life. Looking back, maybe we could have handled things differently, better somehow. But once we set things in motion, there was no going back."

But that wasn't all of it. How much worse could it get?

"Over the years, your mother slowly twisted the truth in her own mind. Maybe it was the disease, but somehow she decided I really had killed your father. She tried to get the courts to review the case, using my own money to pay for an endless line of lawyers and petitions. For the past ten years, my own clan has suffered because of the constant financial drain. That's what Becan's using against me to try to take control of the family fortune. If he could prove I murdered your father, Becan would get it all, and then God help us all. No one will be safe, but especially anyone who isn't pureblooded vampire, starting with my friends you met earlier."

The wolves and their owners? Heartsick, she held out the letter. "Here's your proof for the courts so you can clear your name once and for all. And, Griff, I'll pay you back every penny, beginning with the trust fund Mom left me."

She looked around for a clock. "The lawyer's office should be open. I'll call them now and get things started."

For the first time, she saw Griff angry.

He rocked back on his heels, jerking his hands free from hers. "I don't need your damn money, Keelie. There are only two things I want, starting with keeping the people I care about safe."

His hands settled on her thighs, spreading them far enough apart enough for him to settle between them. The blatant move sent a jolt of heat bubbling through her body.

She suspected she knew what else he wanted, but she needed to hear the words. "And?"

He leaned in, crowding her. "And I want you. You okay with that?"

Where had the air in the room gone? She settled for nodding. As soon as she did, he tugged her down off the edge of the bed to straddle his thighs. His hand tangled in her hair, angling her mouth to mate with his.

And for the first time in days, maybe in forever, Keelie's life felt right.

* * *

Griff couldn't stand another second without getting skin-to-skin with Keelie. He'd always been in control. Not this time. He wasn't going to just pleasure her, he was going to claim her in every way he could think of. Take her every way he could, branding her with his touch, with his body.

As much as he loved kissing her, he needed more and soon, before he lost his mind completely. When he broke off contact, she pouted, her lips red and swollen. Oh, yeah, he wanted more of that, but not yet.

"The bed offers more possibilities," he told her as he tugged her flannel boxers down as far as he could before lifting her back up onto the mattress.

Then he peeled them the rest of the way off. Her scent taunted his control as her racing pulse had his fangs aching for a taste of her life's blood. Each thing in turn. He cupped her full breasts through the soft cotton of her shirt. She sighed and leaned back on her hands, a siren's smile on her face.

"I want you naked, Griff. Naked and up here with me."

Who was he to deny an invitation like that? He stood up and dropped his sweats. When his cock sprang free, she gasped in what he hoped was a combination of appreciation and anticipation.

"Ooh, let me get a good look," Keelie said.

Then she scooted to the far edge of the mattress just out of reach. That so wasn't happening. He crawled after her, a predator intent on claiming his mate. He caught her ankle and dragged her back to where he could take his time.

He captured her other ankle and lifted both high over his shoulders. He kissed the inside of her right thigh, grazing her soft skin with the sharp tips of his fangs. His woman clearly liked that. He repeated the maneuver with her left leg, leaving her moaning and him so hard he hurt.

Positioning himself to join his body with hers, he held back. "I've been waiting a long time to find my mate."

He rocked against her, testing and teasing them both. "This is a claiming, Keelie. Make no mistake about that."

He pressed even deeper. "Do you understand? Because I keep what's mine, Keelie, and you are mine."

Those caramel eyes were running hot as he thrust deep and hard. "I claim you, Griff Tyler. You're mine, too."

Then she held out her arms, pulling him close and arching her neck to the side, offering him everything she had to give. He pressed a kiss to her pulse point as the pounding rhythm of their hearts and bodies reached a crescendo. Then, as a blinding ecstasy burst over them, he sealed their connection by tasting the rich flow of her blood and then offering her his vein in return.

Griff shifted away from the woman sleeping curled up next to him, trying not to wake her. Neither of them had actually slept much, but he wasn't complaining. Their life together was definitely starting on a high note.

But there was still the problem of Becan and whoever had set fire to Keelie's house with her still in it. This time when his fangs ran out, it had nothing to do with sex and everything to do with vengeance and retribution.

He'd let Keelie sleep while he went on the hunt. He reached for his jeans and a clean shirt. Before he could get dressed, Keelie was up and heading for the bedroom door.

"Griff Tyler, don't think you can leave without me. It will only take me a minute to throw on some clothes."

He caught her arm. "I'd rather you stayed here where my friends can keep you safe. I hunt better alone."

"If we're mates, we're partners. Deal with it."

She punctuated her declaration with one of those long, hot kisses he'd already become addicted to.

"You don't fight fair." He kissed her again, almost giving into the temptation to head straight back to the bed.

But the distant pounding on the door upstairs put that idea on hold. Garrett wouldn't be disturbing them this long before sunset without good reason.

"Meet us in the kitchen."

Keelie nodded, and then she was off and running.

Chapter 10

When she reached the kitchen, Griff was making coffee and talking to Garrett. Tension was definitely running hot in the room. Even the wolf was on full alert, his ruff standing at attention.

"What's happened?"

"They're pretty sure Becan's gone to ground some distance from here. We have to hurry if we want to get there before the sun sets, and he can take off again."

Were they forgetting what even the dying embers of the sun would do to Griff?

"But how can you go out in the daylight?"

"I'll ride in the trunk until we get there. By then, the sun will be down."

"Okay."

That might take care of one problem, but she knew facing a cornered vampire wouldn't be easy, even with backup. It was doubtful he'd come at them with just his fangs. But it was time this ended. For the sake of greed alone Becan had trashed her home, robbing her of the memories it had held.

A few minutes later, they all piled into the transport, Griff curled up and uncomfortable in the trunk. Keelie sat in the backseat with a pair of wolves while their handlers rode in the front with a pile of weapons. Evidently she wasn't the only one concerned about cornering a desperate vampire.

The ride took almost thirty minutes. When they drove the transport off the road and into a clump of trees, the top edge of the sun was just barely visible on the distant horizon. The instant it dropped out of sight, Griff popped the trunk and climbed out.

He did several stretches. "Remind me not to make a habit of traveling that way."

Garrett held out an assortment of firearms and a couple of knives. "Here you go, boss."

"Got any extras?" Keelie asked, surprising both men.

"Sure." Garrett offered her a pair of automatics. "Take your pick."

She chose the bigger of the two, checking it over with the ease of familiarity. All three men, and apparently even the two wolves, watched in amazement.

Garrett grinned. "I'm guessing that's not the first one of those you've held."

She gave them a smug smile. "Nope, and I've got the marksmanship medals to prove it."

Griff wasn't happy. "Just remember, targets don't shoot back. Aiming at another person isn't the same."

"I haven't shot anybody, but I've spent much of my professional life out in the wilderness. I've had to defend myself a time or two against varmints."

When one of the wolves growled, she added, "Most had two legs. The few that didn't, I aimed high. None of them were wolves."

When the wolf padded over for a head scratch, she laughed. "I swear, these two seem to actually understand every word I say."

Garrett grinned at her. "You have no idea."

Griff wedged himself between her and the wolf, giving the animal a dark look. "Back off, furball. She's mine. Now let's get going before Becan bolts again."

They fanned out and started forward, the wolves ranging ahead, their noses to the ground. Just over the next rise, Kipp stopped and tested the night breeze. When he growled low and deep in his chest, the other wolf joined in. Griff's two friends joined the animals, their eyes gleaming oddly in the moonlight.

What had they found? She inhaled deeply and knew the answer. The night air carried the scent of death.

Becan was dead. Griff knew it as well as he knew they were walking into a trap. The pungent smell of old blood and dead vampire made it impossible to pick up any other clues as to who was waiting up ahead. Using hand motions, he signaled for the pack members to circle around behind the cluster of boulders.

Keelie eased up next to him as they waited for the men to get in position. "Griff?"

"I'm guessing Becan isn't the one who burned the house down."

He looked down at her. If his suspicions were right, Keelie was in for another shock. "The night of the fire, you never realized anyone had been in the house until you actually saw the damage. Is that right?"

At first she seemed puzzled by his question, but she slowly nodded. "That's right. The scents were normal—Mom, me, and Dorothy."

Her eyes widened. "Dorothy? You think Dorothy burned the house down? Why would she do that?"

The woman in question answered herself. "I wanted to destroy everything Lydia held dear."

Dorothy strolled into sight behind Griff, a rifle pointed straight at Keelie. Cousin or not, she'd just signed her own death warrant. No one threatened Griff's mate and lived. *No one.*

Keelie's voice rang with pain. "But why? You and my mother were friends. You were family."

"No, actually I was your father's mistress. He promised to leave that bitch for me. Instead, she murdered him in cold blood and your lover covered it up. She never suspected who I was or what I'd meant to Kenneth."

"Why would you work for her all these years?"

"It's easier to poison someone when you cook her meals. I wanted her to suffer long and hard for what she took from me."

Keelie gasped. "She wasn't sick? That was your doing?"

Dorothy looked proud of herself. "It took me a long time to find the perfect poison, one that acted slow and mimicked a disease. No one ever suspected. At least right up until the end. I knew she'd hidden a letter for you. I couldn't risk anyone finding out, so I burned everything."

"The letter had nothing to do with you. And why kill Becan?"

As she spoke, Keelie shifted slightly farther away from Griff, making it harder for the other chancellor to watch them both at the same time. He mirrored her movements, putting even more distance between them.

Dorothy's lip curled back off her fangs, only emphasizing the crazed look in her eyes. "I proved to him once and for all which of us was the superior being. Of course, by the time he believed me, he was only a breath away from dead."

Griff's turn to keep the conversation going. "Okay, I understand why you'd go after him, but why me? Why Keelie?"

Her eyes flicked back and forth between the two of them. "I can't afford any loose ends. Griff, you've always been decent to me, so I'll make it fast and easy for you. But either way, you're going to die along with Keelie. A lover's quarrel, you know. Kind of funny, history repeating itself that way."

She brought the gun to bear directly on him, clearly thinking he was the bigger threat.

Keelie stepped toward the housekeeper, her own gun

aimed at Dorothy and momentarily drawing her full attention. "Pull that trigger, Dorothy, and you're a dead woman. Walk away while you can."

"You don't have the guts to kill, Keelie. I do."

Just as she pulled the trigger, Griff charged forward, ignoring the burn of the bullet grazing his shoulder. Dorothy was so intent on taking another shot at him, that she missed the blacker-than-night body leaping through the air as Kipp latched onto her wrist and bit down.

Her scream echoed through the night. It only lasted long enough for Griff to finish the job his furry friend had started.

"Hold still."

"But that hurts."

"Most gunshots do."

Keelie pressed the last piece of tape in place. "I still think you should see a doctor."

"I'll heal."

She turned away, trying to hide the tears. She'd cried more in the last week than she had in her entire life. She was tired of it.

Griff caught her around her waist and pulled her down in his lap. Careful of his sore shoulder, she buried her face against his chest.

"I was terrified out there, Griff. For all of us."

He held her tight. "I know, but it's over now. We're safe now."

Yeah, she was. "I know."

But there was still something that needed saying. "Griffon Tyler, as the sole remaining representative of the Bronson family, it's my duty to make reparations for the trouble we've caused you."

Her lover jerked as if she'd hit him. "Damn it, Keelie, I've already told you I don't want your money."

She let her hands do a little wandering. "Yes, you made that perfectly clear. I was thinking of paying you back in some other way. I'll have to make installment payments. Lots of them."

His breathing picked up its pace, his pulse racing to keep up as her hand slid down between them.

"I'm sure we can work something out. Of course, you'll have to live here with me to keep up the payment schedule."

She adored the deep growl in his voice. "Only if you admit you love me as much as I love you."

"I'll even put it in writing. Tomorrow, though. Right now, I think we should work out the details."

The heat in his eyes had her wanting to purr. "I'm up for it if you are."

"Oh, rest assured, I am."

Then he set about proving it to her.

* * * * *

Vampire Lover

Linda Thomas-Sundstrom

Chapter 1

The heat hitting Kelsie Connor in a wave was like a second-degree sunburn on midwestern-pale skin, but she refrained from touching her bare shoulder with the cool rim of her martini glass. Movement of any kind could prove suicidal beneath a moon like the one in tonight's balmy June sky, if the legends were true.

The majority of Homo sapiens might not perceive anything abnormal about the blaringly bright full moon lending a reddish cast to the sidewalk, but humans weren't the only species calling Miami home. And not all humans were unobservant.

Certainly not herself.

Tonight's moon had a special name. *Blood Moon.* A moniker for the second full moon in a single month. Not a Blue Moon, as some people called it. This particular one, appearing every five years, looked more like the sun viewed through a layer of smog. Nothing remotely white or silver or blue about it. Not so benign.

Rumor had it that this moon brought out other two-legged, night-loving species besides Miami's usual sleek human glitterati. Legends foretold these Others could smell movement, as if *action* was another word for *bouquet.* Not only that, it was said that Others had internal directional beacons spliced into their genes, and just flat out knew where to find fresh meat or fresh blood or whatever their particular dietary needs dictated.

"Disgusting…"

While poor human saps like herself had be lucky enough to utilize all of their senses, and then scramble to find two or three more in order to keep on the good side of the separation between life and death on any night in a city this size.

Kelsie took a second glace up at the strange, unearthly phenomenon overhead and rode out a ripple of internal heat at the thought of what that moon could do for her career if she was right about what might happen beneath it.

The thought actually turned her on a little.

Moisture gathered between her thighs.

This definitely wasn't the night to be strolling around, looking for a stray ocean breeze. Nor was it opportune for taking shortcuts on dark, under-populated side streets. Five years ago, during the last Blood Moon phase, ten people had gone missing in this part of Miami alone. Maybe not so unusual in a decadent city on a steamy summer night, but she had crunched some unpublicized numbers, turning up the names of at least twenty more MIA's that had fallen beneath the radar.

What happened to those people?

As a fact-finder for the *Miami Tribune,* Kelsie knew that numbers, and the ways to get them, were her game. She was damn good at her job. Now, though, like all wannabe writers who longed to move up in the world of journalism, she needed a break.

"So here I am, in the market for a monster." An *Other.* A creature out of legend that would help her get that elusive byline.

What she wanted was a werewolf.

With a grin, Kelsie leaned back against the warm brick on the outside patio of the Havana Club, untasted martini in her hand, trying not to call attention to herself. Her gray silk camisole and black skirt amounted to camouflage in this chic crowd. She had understated her makeup; nothing too red or too vibrant. Her shoulder-length blonde hair was down, straight and combed off to one side.

As a matter of fact, she might have gone a tad too far by understating everything, she acknowledged, watching the dancing, flirting hordes of men and women making the scene. By keeping her distance and blatantly showing her indifference to the art of the pickup, she might actually stand out a little.

Still, if anyone could find a werewolf—given that there were such things—she was determined to do so. If anything could lure a werewolf out of hiding, a Blood Moon would be the ticket. Her senses were keen enough to sniff out a story, honed by her journalism background and the attention she paid to her surroundings. She tried to process details in a manner similar to the way she supposed werewolves sucked up moonlight. Taking it all in.

Thus far, at this club, however, she had only come across wolves of another sort. The usual kind. Problem was, there were too many people jammed into a tight space to see individuals clearly. The hum of voices had escalated over the thump of the music as bar drinks flowed.

Kelsie scanned the crowd, darting hopeful glances here and there. For what? A bit of fur showing on the back of someone's neck? Like finding a werewolf would be that easy?

Closing her eyes briefly, she enjoyed the arrival of a rare ocean breeze. The night was glorious, even if it proved to be monster-free. She loved the dark, the stars overhead, the night heat that seared her lungs. Miami was like no other place on earth, and about as far removed from her family's Irish heritage as was possible.

Ireland hadn't held anything interesting for her in some time. Living in the States made it easier to chase interests and follow her own path. She just needed this one little *monster* in order to get ahead. A hairy one, preferably.

"Is that too much to ask for?" she said aloud. "Kelsie Connor, on the prowl. Trolling the dark in search of adventure." *Needing to ferret out the rumors and put my strange compulsion to find Others to the test.*

"Maybe you, big guy?"

Her gaze latched on to a man in a floral shirt, well beneath the club's blue awning. *A decent candidate for a werewolf?* Tall, broad-shouldered, with abundant auburn hair and a perfect tan, he moved with an animalistic, lumbering step as he stalked a woman sucking down a lime-green, nuclear-hued appletini.

Hell, he actually looked like potential, the epitome of something unmorphed. After all, Weres could be anybody, anywhere, without a full moon to trip their DNA switches. Recipients of gene splicing/coding between humans and wolves could either be complete fantasy, or an actual syndrome affecting a small segment of the population. She hoped for the latter. Because if there were such things as werewolves, one informative bio in a newspaper column would make this freaky Blood Moon worth her weight in gold.

"Tonight's the night. I feel it."

Squeezing her thighs together to fend off the thrill Kelsie figured she shared with most reporters about to close in on a story, she scanned the crowd again. Her grin faded as she riffled through the rest of the legends.

There were, of course, other Others. Vampires. An altogether scarier breed. The walking dead. As bloodlusting bloodsuckers, out only at night, they'd have to show up as pale anomalies in this city, and stand apart. As did pasty-hued tourists among the Miami sun and sand natives.

The thought of vampires in the area was a sudden deal-breaker, chilling the blistering night. Kelsie felt that chill waft in now, like a cold breath on the back of her neck.

Unlike werewolves, vampires weren't humanlike most of the time. None of the time, in fact. They might walk like humans and talk like humans, because that's what they had been once upon a time, but when the life had been drained out of them, they became animated cadavers who tended to pass on that same trait to people who came into contact with them.

The stuff of nightmares.

To make matters worse, there was more than one kind. Besides double-dead vampires, there were living vampires who possessed human traits and heartbeats.

"I'll take a werewolf, please," she said aloud, trying to dislodge the chill that seemed to be sticking around and was now dribbling down her back, making a point to hit each vertebra, ending on the one closest to her butt.

Vowing never to even think the *V* word again, Kelsie leaned more weight on the brick, allowing the rough surface to scratch at her slinky gray silk, needing to cut off that chill. She took a good-size sip of her martini before remembering she didn't drink, and coughed. The alcohol had been purely for looks. A prop. Connors never had been able to manage their liquor.

And damn it, the pesky chills were unwarranted, since there was no way a vampire could be around others and virtually blend in. She didn't want one of *those.* Why would anyone go out of their way to find a vampire, when a pair of fangs could etch the word *lethal* across a jugular vein?

But wait! she thought with a healthy dose of sarcasm.

Vampires were supposed to be cool-skinned, right? Considering tonight's hundred degree swelter, rubbing up against one might be so bad, after all.

She grinned widely. Pressing the martini glass to her throat, she muttered, "One good story is all I need. Something unique, and not too life threatening."

A werewolf would do. In particular, a werewolf hit by the light of a Blood Moon. *Think of the headlines!* If any man-wolf accidentally stepped out from beneath the awning, lured onto the moon-brightened patio, she'd be waiting.

"Come on, wolf boys, show yourself. Do it for me," she whispered to the blur of moving bodies inside the doorway, even though the damned chills persisted, despite the summer heat wave.

It felt suddenly as if a fog bank had rolled in. As if she was being watched.

Uncomfortable, curious, with little hairs standing straight up on her arms, Kelsie turned her head, surprised to find she had company. A man. Several feet away. His gaze intent on her—probably because he'd heard every silly thing she'd said.

What have we here?

Hayden Flynn's interested gaze slipped over the female across from him in a sensual glide. From her shining hair to her sexy high-heeled sandals, the sassy young blonde should have captured the interest of any male with properly functioning body parts, yet this woman was alone, set aside.

A beautiful wallflower.

He observed her carefully, drawn for reasons he couldn't put a finger on. There were plenty of attractive women in the club tonight, and prettier females within twenty feet in several directions. This one wasn't outstandingly beautiful by today's standards, though she was striking.

She had a narrow, heart-shaped face, big eyes, plus a sensual mouth turned up at the corners and perhaps a bit too large for the rest of her delicate features.

A mouth most males would know how to abuse, he noted.

Her body was exquisite. An expensive haircut swung her hair softly over well-proportioned shoulders. Her choice of clothing showed off lots of smooth skin—neck, shoulders, chest, arms. The outline of firm, rounded breasts pressed against her filmy drape of gray silk.

She was incredibly sexy. Mouthwatering.

Hayden was sure he hadn't seen her before, yet felt as if he had. A stray thought, deliciously tantalizing, suggested that she might be waiting on this patio for him. *Wishful thinking?*

Hayden studied her further, intrigued.

On the surface, her body language was loose. She was enjoying herself, comfortable with her solitary status at a notorious pickup club. The glass she held was full, though she had been holding it for some time.

Cheap date. The cheeky notion brought on the rise of his own thirst, which he tamped down for the time being, fascinated by the strange things she was doing with her glass.

She pressed the glass again to her lips, but didn't drink. After resting the rim briefly against her cheek, she closed her eyes, then slowly slid it down to a bare tanned throat the color of honey.

The sliding glass routine was erotic, as was the nakedness of her throat. Naked, that is, except for the twinkle of a fine silver chain that picked up the patio's torchlight.

Hayden felt a pleasurable sensation run through him that was equal parts lust and intrigue, due to the challenge of silver so close to the woman's veins.

Pangs of that lust beat at him. He hadn't ever experienced this kind of immediate attraction. The woman had to be special, somehow. That uniqueness separated her from the other women here tonight, and called to him as surely as if she'd wrapped her glossy lips around him. His entire body was alive, and on standby.

Breaking visual contact with her, Hayden sent his senses outward. He inhaled deeply, frowned, then refocused.

Yes, something is here. Something strange.

The air around the attractive wallflower was as disturbed by her musky scent as he was, as if her presence agitated the night. This sort of air displacement was usually reserved for creatures like himself, but this female was human, live, mortal. Her soul's song was low-pitched and vibrant, emanating from her like radio waves. A strong, steady heartbeat surrounded the twang of her soul, in the manner of an accompanying bass drum.

Why did she affect the darkness surrounding her?

Hayden searched his memory banks for an answer to that question, hunting for a word to explain the phenomena. He caught one quickly because it was a concept he knew intimately.

Hunger.

The woman was burning up with hunger. Her inner fires were stoked. Her carefully cultivated, languid exterior hid a scrambled ball of energy tucked inside. It was as though her honeyed skin acted as a barrier between her outward persona and a roiling inner chaos that could escape with one good sneeze. This was evidence that she wanted one thing, while her soul wanted something else. The pretty blonde was not only at odds with the night, but at war with herself.

If he hadn't been completely attracted before, Hayden was fully captivated now. He inhaled again, smelling the complexity of her desire, now that he'd pinpointed her secret turmoil. The scent was dark, like the tumbling incarnation of a summer storm.

Adrenaline spiked as he took in every detail of this storm in her gray silk cocoon, as he followed the line of her short skirt to shapely legs, knees and ankles. Black polish, the color of midnight, tipped her toes, as did two tiny silver bands.

He continued to stare at her openly, growing more

aroused by the second. Soon she would notice him. Would the games then begin, or be over before thirst overruled his curiosity?

He wanted his hands and mouth all over this woman. He wanted his lips on her long golden neck. These longings made him feel like the animal he'd never really been or accepted as part of himself.

His fangs were descending, and he knew better. Vampires had to exist on the periphery of mortal life, unexposed. Now was not the time or the place to explore his attraction to the woman. He had to be careful not to call too much attention to himself.

Leave now, before hunger obliterates good judgment.

Hunger was, in fact, circling, like a pack of snapping wolves. But he continued to search her face, noting that her eyes were a light jade-green and hooded by dark lashes. Familiar eyes?

The silver chain at her throat flashed as her head began to turn. Hayden winced, jolted by another surprise. Surely the little charm hanging from that chain, lying in the soft cleft between her collarbones, wasn't what it appeared to be?

Couldn't be.

Damnation, now that he'd seen it, he'd have to know for sure. Because if it was what he thought it might be, all hell was about break loose on the patio of a nightclub, and his move to America had been for nothing.

Forcing stale, steamy air into his lungs to maintain his composure, Hayden walked toward the woman, driven her way, fascinated beyond description, careful to keep his lips closed over the dagger-sharp teeth that defined him.

He is making a move?

The man heading Kelsie's way was tall, fair-haired and handsome, even in the shadows. Big, lithe, with aristocratic features and a fluid grace, he was, upon first glance, a poster boy for the term *sex appeal.* The whole package.

He was also a serious distraction from her task at hand.

His blond hair was worn on the long side, with just the right amount of curl. He was scrumptiously masculine in casual black slacks and a blue linen shirt that she hoped matched his eyes.

Males like this one were trouble to every female hormone on the planet. Except maybe for hers, tonight. Tonight, she was on a mission. A career-building quest. Her entire future depended on ignoring distractions like this one, no matter how flattering they were, and in spite of the way her treacherous body might react to the guy's appearance.

Remember the job, Connor.

Despite the reminder, her heart skipped some beats as the stranger stopped in front of her, blocking her view of the doorway. A full two heads taller than herself, Kelsie had to look up to address his untimely intrusion.

"Sorry. I'm waiting for someone," she said, hating the fact that he was so classy, close up, and that she had to ignore it. He was, in fact, one of the most gorgeous men she had ever seen.

"I'm sure you are," he conceded in a voice that matched his exterior—deep, rumbling and private in a way that jump-started her chills all over again.

"Already have a drink." Kelsie held up her glass before noticing that her hand was shaking, and so was the glass. The back her of neck prickled, again with that cool rush of air.

Premonition, maybe?

Although most Irish people were superstitious about such things, Kelsie fought the impulse. She was young and moderately attractive, so guys routinely tried to pick her up. She was adept at giving a decent brush-off to pursuers she wasn't interested in. Yet damned if she didn't feel tongue-tied right then.

She bit her lip hard and tasted blood. She watched his eyes immediately go to her mouth, as if the blood had enticed his attention. With the arrival of more chills came suspicion.

Maybe this guy was too perfect to be human.

All of a sudden there didn't seem to be enough air on the patio. Her chills mounted, as did the inexplicable feeling that her wishes for the appearance of a creature of the night had been heard by the wrong person in charge.

Please let him be a werewolf!

She barely got that thought off before the man's face blurred, and his mouth touched hers.

Chapter 2

He had tasted the woman before introducing himself, teased by the drop of crimson on her lip.

The mistake shot past Hayden's awareness. He was a vampire. Finding blood was what he was designed to do. *But not here. Not like this.*

Her bead of blood spread, slick as silk, as he pressed his mouth to hers. The heady scent of that single drop roared through him, tickling his veins, tightening his muscles.

Other body parts sprang to life, heating up from the inside out, as if he had just clamped on to a flame. Deep in the back of his mind, though, the talons of mystery coiled around his spontaneous action. He had meant to get away from her, to avoid this very thing. How, then, had he ended up in an unwarranted embrace?

Now that he had, though, sensations zoomed in, one after the other. The blonde tasted unusual. Hotter than most. Wetter than most. Her blood held a hint of aluminum, normal fare in humans, as was the anticipated sugary sweetness. But another, hidden component, drenched in a musky casing, also played on her soft lips. More hints of that storm brewing, plus a heady aftertaste of secrets.

Hayden's fangs began to ache. His pulse quickened as he held himself back from a full-out assault on the woman's taut body. She remained motionless. Although she had a mouth like liquid desire, it didn't respond to his. She didn't pull away, but neither did she bend or cave to this sudden hedonistic act of seduction. Shock ran through her body in ripples. She didn't breathe.

Hayden touched her teeth with the tip of his tongue as her blood curled into him, spreading throughout his body with the poignancy of a fire alarm. The moment was exotic, dangerous. Her blood was an instant aphrodisiac, an addiction to one who hadn't tasted the blood of a human since his awakening.

One slight flex of his jaws now, and he could bite right through the flawless skin. If he did, though, he would become something he'd vowed he would never be.

Darkness enclosed him as his urges raged. He knew that a multitude of people were close by, mere steps away. Still, he wanted other things from the woman who tasted of fire and sweetness, more than just her blood. He wanted it all, in that moment. All of her. Silver-clad neck to her black polished toes, and every moist, luscious space in between. Right here. Stretched out against this wall.

If her mouth was this hot, he could only imagine what

the rest of her had to offer. Unimaginable bliss. An inferno to slide himself into. Heat like hers was a turn-on, an inescapable draw for a creature unable to bask in the sunlight.

Below his belt, he began to throb with need. His jaws tensed, desperate for more than a taste despite the warnings his brain was sending to stop such thoughts. He didn't do this. He didn't bite, hunt, maim or kill. Those actions belonged to others of his kind who were less civilized. To the undead.

But as this woman's presence pulled at his baser instincts, spears of confusion struck him. Need versus want. Want versus sanity and the protection of his kind. The only way vampires could exist was in complete anonymity. He could do nothing here, and was behaving badly.

A sound reached him, bubbling up from the woman he had pinned to the wall. Hayden opened his eyes, dazed to find his fangs grazing her throat. A throat encircled by the stinging burn of silver.

Seconds of silence followed, in which neither of them dared to react. Then the woman's hands were on his chest, pushing.

Hayden leaned back, separating himself from what should have been sheer bliss with a viable partner, if he were merely a man. The finding of a lover on a warm, lovely night, who had very nearly succeeded in compromising his vow of blood celibacy.

Who is she?

The question repeated as he inched away, seeing something with this slight distance that he had missed before. This woman's aura was outlined in red, as if traced by a crayon. Her agitation swirled in the air between them like a live entity. Her eyes flashed green fire.

These changes had been mercurial, and a warning that she might be much more than she seemed. The blonde looked normal, but wasn't. Not completely. His uninvited advance had unlocked a clue about her true nature, setting part of her inner chaos free. That chaos had a name as black as her toenail polish.

"Slayer," Hayden whispered with distaste, just before she slapped him hard with her open hand.

The monster had her by the neck, unaffected by her slap, moving with a frightening speed. His eyes bored into hers.

She was up against the brick wall, held there by the brute strength of his arm. The situation had gotten real messy, real fast; a worst case scenario coming true.

Her glass fell to the ground and shattered.

Moonlight melted over this stranger's features, highlighting his cheekbones, casting shadows. If he'd been a werewolf, he would have been toast by now. But then she had already realized what he wasn't, leaving just one other category to describe the speed, strength, looks and attraction to her blood.

Vampire.

Her heart gave one giant thump. Keeping both hands raised to ward him off, hoping that vampires possessed a thread of common sense, contrary to the legends, Kelsie said breathlessly, "Back off! There are a hundred people here, all of them witnesses."

She should have been scared out of her mind. She should have shouted for help, but his hand on her throat was a caution against it. Staring back at this creature, Kelsie felt the kindling of her anger, in spite of the threat. There wasn't any way to make this work, jobwise. She hadn't wanted *him,* damn it—this creature who was unearthly handsome because he *was* unearthly. He was interfering in a damn good stakeout.

And—

She might not live to have another thought of any kind if she just stood here.

Luckily, he wasn't pressing too hard on her neck, but using just enough pressure to keep her from squirming free.

"Surely you wouldn't be stupid enough to bite me so close to a crowd?" she protested.

"You were waiting for me." His tone was accusatory. Darkness slipped behind the blue of his irises like free-flowing India ink.

Kelsie's stomach dropped at the sight. Her heart was beating so loudly, she couldn't hear anything else. She knew she had to hang on to her anger. If she didn't, she'd be totally helpless, totally screwed. No way did she want to become part of those missing-people statistics.

"Vain, much?" she snapped, her fingers tugging on his.

The vampire's head angled. One raised eyebrow suggested he questioned her response.

"I don't want *you,*" she said. "I'm looking for a wolf."

His hold eased. Visibly perplexed, he said, "Wolf?"

"Why are you here, in public?" She didn't sound so very panicky, she thought. If his grip loosened more, she could tear herself away.

"I think you know the answer to that," he said.

His tone was as seductive as the shadows, seeming to caress her chill-riddled skin everywhere at once, in sharp contrast to the reality of the situation. He had just sampled some of that reason for being here from her punctured lip. *Blood.* An appalling thought, yet she'd be damned if she would show her reaction. Animals were attracted to weakness. Vampires were predators.

"I'm not part of the snack bar," Kelsie said. "And none of your business."

"On the contrary, your presence is of great concern to me."

"Said like a true homicidal maniac. But I didn't believe you existed. I'm not sure if I believe it now."

"You know who I am?"

"Don't you mean *what* you are?"

His eyes sought to deepen the connection. "You weren't waiting for me?"

"Get over yourself."

He considered that reply. "You'd find a maniac preferable?"

"Infinitely."

The handsome devil gave her a stunning, if uncertain, grin, without offering visual evidence of his species. Kelsie didn't have to see fangs to realize how serious her situation was. Each passing second made it more obvious that he wasn't going away.

He was toying with her.

Vampires, Kelsie remembered, were little more than tricks of darkness and light, occupying the gray space between life and death. Not here fully, and not there. It was anyone's guess how they survived at all, or why blood kept them activated.

This one's mouth had been on hers before she'd known it—a strange kind of introduction to the threat of impending death by blood loss. But she was still alive.

"Why do you want a wolf?" His eyes were keen and demanding, daring her to explore their baby-blue depths.

Kelsie refused to answer. She hated being trapped by anyone or anything, anywhere. Her grandmother had raised her to be independent long before turning her loose on Miami. Years of martial arts would help her in another minute, she was sure, if she didn't drop from fear or fangs first.

"Wolves haven't helped your kind in a century," the vampire added. As if that made any sense at all.

"Why don't you have to wear a big V on your forehead to warn people who's in the house?" Kelsie snapped, flicking her gaze upward briefly to see the darkness behind his eyes nearly overwhelm the blue.

That darkness was a warning, she intuited. She had to

power back her anger or risk further inciting his. A big sucker like this would be way too powerful to get away from if he marked her as a target. He could probably bite her and be gone before anyone noticed.

So, why hadn't he already done so?

She swallowed hard. "Go away or I'll scream."

The threat sounded anemic.

"Perhaps you're right," he said.

His voice was way too suggestive, deepened by unspoken sexual promise. Instead of backing off, though, he leaned more of his weight into her and whispered prophetically, "We can meet at a better time."

The vampire, she was astounded to find, was solid, and hard all over. His arousal was evident. The fact that vampires could be sexual creatures came as a shock to Kelsie, since most people would tend to think the only thing to worry about were the teeth.

And as he leaned closer, the night…

The night seemed suddenly to extinguish the light of the torches, blackness blending with the red tint of a disturbed moon. She and the vampire were drenched in moonlight that seemed to stick in her throat, choking off her next breath.

When her eyes met his, all peripheral movement ceased. The club scene fell away into the distance.

Adrenaline shot through her veins as the vampire's blue eyes searched hers, seeking something. The intensity of their locked gazes was almost painful. Kelsie wanted to run, and keep on running, but couldn't move a muscle.

She wanted to nail this bloodsucker to the wall with his own teeth, ripped from his preposterous mouth.

The moment was both deadly, and extremely erotic. A spark of wild attraction flared inside of Kelsie, burning as hot as the vampire's touch. Hot, and intimate. She couldn't look away to save her life.

Her chills were history.

The damned vampire didn't back off or let up. He met her heat, degree by degree, with his hips tight to hers. His body called to hers seductively. The distant part of Kelsie still connected to her brain realized that this could very well be the end of her life and the loss of her soul, and yet she stood there. As he did. He seemed to be waiting for something with obvious wariness. What? A poke in the chest with a sharp stick?

In spite of thoughts of retaliation, Kelsie hadn't gotten in so much as one solid punch. With each passing second in his wicked embrace, she lost more of the will to fight him off. Her anger had been twisted, maneuvered, and he had to be doing this, using that mesmerizing voodoo vampires were rumored to possess.

She was in serious trouble. Already, her hips pressed back against his, independent of the inner red flags. Her unmentionable places dampened further, as if they might lure his greedy attention there. An uneasy feeling grew, deep down inside of her. The very core of her body wanted to know what this vampire had to offer. Chances were, the little devil on her shoulder whispered, he would have had years to perfect his bedroom skills.

Not. Good.

Needing to save herself, Kelsie scrambled for a last hold on reality, and found one. Facts. She was good at facts. And the main one here was that there was something decidedly wrong about a sexually charged vampire. Totally unfair. Slightly creepy.

"Dream on." She said the words defiantly, resolutely. "Not with this girl. Not tonight or any other night."

The realization of this statement being insincere was more frightening to her than anything else, and another hint that the fantasy heat trick the vampire had going for him was melting her judgment and inhibiting her ability to think straight. Why else would her imagination be conjuring up dangerously indecent thoughts? About him?

Damn it, she was wavering, and not nearly scared enough!

In the midst of all the crashing thoughts and illicit cravings, while Kelsie's mind reached for a firmer grasp on how to get out of this, the vampire's lips brushed hers a second time, almost ghostlike.

She closed her eyes.

A brief pinch of pain woke her from her stupor. Ready to shove the damned vampire away, and back into the coffin he belonged in, Kelsie opened her eyes to find him near the doorway, looking at her over a broad, muscled shoulder.

"Connor," he said soberly, as if he'd just caught her name out of the ether and it didn't sit well. His eyes glinted. His blond hair settled to stillness against his chiseled cheek.

Kelsie just stared, teeth clenched, face flushed, fear and anxiety and embarrassment merging into a tight ball of aggravation. He'd been the one to break the spell.

And he knew her name.

He'd be able to find her in the future, if vampires used phone books or the Internet. Hell, having tasted her, he might be able to find her in some other revolting way.

He couldn't have missed the way her body reacted to his. He might assume it was a permanent invitation.

Seemingly in afterthought, the Other she hadn't been expecting spoke again, with a glance up at the moon.

"You want a wolf? Why not just call them?" he suggested.

Then he was gone.

Giving in to the weakness in her knees, Kelsie slumped against the wall, lucky to be breathing. She'd had a serious mental and physical lapse. The arrogant bastard had gotten too damned close, and she had allowed it.

She swiped at her lip with the back of her hand to erase the feel of his mouth, and felt wetness. Glancing at the spot of blood on her knuckle, she swayed. It was a monstrous find—blood made to appear darker by the ghastly moonlight.

Her heart slammed against her ribs in protest. Both hands went to her neck. No blood there, thank God, but she did find a scratch that made her head go light.

The bloodsucker had tried to bite her!

Her gaze flew to the empty doorway. It took another minute to be able to speak. Tossing her hair out of her face with a quivering, bloodstained finger, she said with a rise of her Irish temper, "Yes, run, you lousy, bloodsucking son of a bitch."

"Connor."

Hayden pushed through the throng of people without stopping to return the attentions of the women eyeing him appreciatively.

He needed time to think.

It was absurd that after all these years he would stumble across one his old enemies. In Miami. In a nightclub. *The* enemy. One of the hellish Connor clan. The bane of his family's existence for as long as he could remember. Connor—the Irish equivalent of the Terminator in slaying his kind.

No wonder the air had been disturbed and his attention captured. The question plaguing him now was why he hadn't perceived the extent of the threat, even when it came in a delicious package. He had been all over her. Hell, he'd been aroused.

What was a Connor was doing so far from Irish soil, anyway? She had to have followed him, lured him to her on purpose. It was the only explanation for the meeting.

"Connor." Hayden reached the sidewalk without looking back, but didn't get any farther. Her perfume wafted upward from his hands and his shirt. Her sweetness sat on his lips. His hand still smarted from closeness to that silver chain she wore.

He glanced down the street. She would pursue him, no doubt about it. It's what Slayers did.

"You are a good liar, Connor. An actress of the highest caliber." Hayden closed his fingers over the burn on his palm. "You said you weren't after me, and I nearly believed you."

She had, in fact, seemed as shocked as he had been. She had allowed him a taste, and he still felt the aftermath.

Slayer blood was said to be a delicacy. But surviving any sort of closeness to a Slayer was unprecedented, and highly unusual. No vampire he knew of had survived such a forbidden assignation.

Still, the flicker of his excitement was tempered somewhat by a wave of residual resentment. A reminder that he had come to Miami to get away from the old feuds. He thought he had escaped the problem of ancient vendettas by leaving them and the blood oaths behind. Now he had to deal with this young Connor incarnation. Nothing had changed.

This Connor was part of the family that had hunted his family for centuries. Connor killings had been swift, brutal, until his family was all but extinct.

He was the last of his bloodline.

Of course, it was no secret that his family had enjoyed their share of Connor blood, in return. A blood oath went both ways. He had known there were two Connors left in his part of the world. One of them was old, nearly blind and feeble, in County Clare. The other one, this youngest Connor, had left Clare and against all odds was here. Not only in the same city, but blonde, youthful and as sexy as anything on two legs.

And she was a Slayer.

She'd inherited the gene that Connor men had for centuries scoured the countryside for. Connor men sought out and married women with a special gene they called "Sense," perhaps hoping to shore up their own family's longevity. The DNA that produced a Slayer was a delicate one, preferring to be housed in women. But rarely was it passed on from mother to daughter.

Except here, it seems.

This Connor was the daughter of Katherine, the Slayer who had taken his father to an early grave.

Hayden had to ignore the jumping pulses of interest, because the feud had merely changed continents. Against nature, Connors had found a way to pass the gene along, by birth. He hadn't escaped his past at all.

Damn it, he should have recognized the shade and shine of her green eyes. He hadn't been prepared. How could he have been? Even with the name Connor, she should have been normal.

So, who was the real *sucker* in this bit of introductory foreplay?

What would transpire when she came after him?

"What will it be then, Slayer?" This time when his fangs extended, Hayden bared them with a sad, questioning smile.

* * *

It took Kelsie five more minutes to gather herself sufficiently to move, and then it was only to step over the broken glass.

Her trembling had lessened. She felt steadier, though oddly distanced from the world around her. Her anger had finally burned through some of the bullshit. She had peered into the eyes of the wrong beast. A willing sacrifice, for the sake of a newspaper.

"Thanks for nothing," she muttered to the moon.

Now she was all too aware of *him.* Although the vampire had gone, his presence lingered, wrapped around her like sticky, muscular, invisible arms.

Out of habit, she fingered the chain at her neck, pressing on the pendant her mother had given her on her tenth birthday, just hours before her mother had died. Touching the charm made Kelsie breathe easier. The necklace was all she had of her mother, and a reminder that although she may have been the first Connor to leave Ireland, roots ran deep. She was never to take the necklace off. Her grandmother had requested that she not do so, and Kelsie never had. And Connors, she had been taught, never ran away from a fight.

So, what happens next?

Would the monster come back for her? Would her grandmother know what to do, if Kelsie called?

Maybe she'd whittle some stakes in the meantime, just in case. Having hooked a vampire, was she dead meat?

The patio torches sputtered beside her. Kelsie looked

there, then again to the doorway, hearing an echo of the vampire's voice.

"You want a wolf? Why not just call them?"

A shiver of apprehension arrived as she thought about that. The pendant seemed suddenly weightier in her fingers, and icy to the touch.

Nothing was as it was supposed to be. Silver was supposed to ward off vampires, but this vamp had ignored it. Vamps were supposed to be pale, gaunt creatures, yet this one could have been a movie star. What else had the legends gotten wrong?

Why had this vampire left her alive and breathing? He hadn't really tried to harm her…much.

She glanced at her knuckle, at the smear of blood, and wondered if the scent would lure more nighttime creatures. She wasn't up for that, no matter how badly she needed a byline.

But the moonlight seemed to tug at her chest, as if attempting to pry free a rib bone. The vampire's eyes had pried something loose as well, by delving into hers. For a minute there she had felt different—defiant, belligerent, slightly dangerous and as though she carried someone she didn't recognize hidden inside of her. The vampire's unholy mouth on hers had started all of this strangeness, and his disappearance hadn't lessened the effect.

She felt…*off.*

"Wolves haven't helped your kind in a century," he had said. "Why not just call them?"

"What the hell." None of this made any sense, anyway.

Focusing her attention on the doorway, Kelsie said loudly, firmly, "Wolfmen. If you're there, come out now."

A hot breeze rose to circulate fallen leaves on the patio. Kelsie's heart rate notched up tenfold.

Light-headed again, she put a hand to the wall for support. How lame was calling werewolves with the expectation they would come? How ridiculous was it to take the advice of a bloodsucker? The encounter on this patio had turned her into an idiot.

She fought off another wave of distress, thought, *What sort of person can call werewolves?*

She frowned, trying to recall the term this vampire had used that had struck her anxiety cord, and shouted for the hell of it, "Weres! Come out!"

When she looked up, it was to find two men beneath the awning. Big guys. Their chests and arms rippled beneath their shirts like a freaky muscle mirage. Their curiously bright, animal-like eyes were trained on her.

"Shit!" she swore, as she raced for the gate.

Chapter 3

After taking a good long look at the moon, Hayden turned his attention back to the nightclub, half a block away. A heated breeze ruffled his hair as he waited.

He had given her every reason to come after him. He had scratched her skin, bringing up the blood necessary to identify her. Now that he had placed her, he could hear his dead ancestors crying out for retaliation against the atrocities her family had performed on them in the past.

Hayden fought that notion, as he always had. More questions consumed him. Were Slayers always this attractive? He wanted her to come after him for reasons having less to do with what was wired into him, and more to do with the excitement of meeting a female strong enough to face him. A female with a shared past. One who already knew about him.

Wouldn't that be a relief?

In spite of the time she had spent in Miami, this Slayer still tasted like County Clare. She wore the Connor crest at her throat—a heart with a stake through it.

Cheeky Connor bastards. This wasn't a game, after all, or a date with a viable partner. It was the unexpected meeting of a Connor with "Sense" and a Flynn, whose name in old Irish, Flann, meant blood-red. This meeting was a continuation of a terrible, centuries-old war.

A Connor Slayer would have to come after him. Her own blood would demand it, if not her soul. So why prolong the inevitable? He would wait for her right here, tonight, and get it over with.

He'd love to get his hands on her again.

And his mouth.

Hell, he did want to bite her. His soul cried out for that. No Slayer, or anyone else out of the fold, knew how seductive a fang slipped into dewy skin could be, or how incredibly erotic that physical metaphor was.

The longing for intimate blood sharing had a name. A Dark Surrender was a ritual that took place when a vampire found a mortal woman willing to take him in, body, blood and soul. Becoming like him. Leaving one life behind for another. The continuous line of Flynns was proof of the viability of the ritual. The offspring of that kind of liaison became what he was. A living vampire.

Not one of the undead, per se. Some special quirk in Flynn blood, long tended, allowed the vampires in his family to live and breathe and age as mortals did, with beating hearts in their chests. A unique side effect in the invisible manuals of vampirism.

He wasn't immortal. Unearthly strong and powerful, certainly, but susceptible to a stake or a silver bullet that might only slow the true undead down. After Flynns were killed, if they weren't immediately beheaded or cremated they became monsters, undead vampires, like the rest of the fang-bearing breed. For this reason, his family had always taken precautions against an unwanted afterlife.

It was likely a Slayer from County Clare would know all about that, too. A Connor was certain to comprehend the nuances of a Flynn's existence. As the last Connor Slayer standing, this one would have been raised on the propaganda, fed it on a daily basis, along with her porridge.

Probably she had been hoping to throw him off balance with her silky, sultry aura. If that had been her agenda, she had reached her goal.

Hayden licked his lip. Catching a slight trace of the Slayer's sweetness, he pulled a face. This Connor was a forbidden delight. No one had mentioned this might be the case, or that he would be so attracted to the very being set upon this earth to destroy him.

He wanted to touch her, all right. *Needed* to touch her. For all the wrong reasons. Never would he have considered that a Flynn might want to take a Slayer to bed, instead of putting her under the ground. His fangs ached with a dull persistence. Not for the thrill of a bite, but being near to *her* again. The enemy. Like it or not, Hayden

Flynn had been sidelined by a Slayer, and he was going to have to do something about that.

"Come and get it, then, Connor," he said, knowing she would hear him, wherever she was.

Hayden's body gave him a swift heads-up. His awareness filled in the rest. The Slayer had left the club. The night carried her presence: a whiff of blood in the air, sweet as nectar.

She had left the lights and the crowd to enter the realm of the beast. Who but a Slayer would dare confront the darkness?

He was feverish with anticipation. If she sought him, knew him, had a bead on him, the outcome seemed bleak. One of them might die.

He focused on the sidewalk, saw her. She kept close to others on the street, her footfalls tentative, the gems on her sandals throwing off random glints of colored light as she passed beneath a streetlight. She looked wary, agitated and...inspired. If she was anything like her ancestors, this woman was Death in a pretty capsule, her outward appearance designed for a reason.

He waited by the side of a building, near the sand, observing from the shadows.

Can you feel me, Connor?

She paused midstep and turned to look straight at him. Hayden's blood boiled in his veins. His thirst beckoned. The Slayer's green eyes, though unfocused, held an unsettling, haunted quality that was alarmingly innocent. Almost vulnerable.

The unusual thunder started up again in Hayden's chest. Anticipation? Withheld aggression? Misplaced lust for an old enemy? He was still hard. His fangs were sharp against his lower lip.

Theirs was to be a unique duet, it seemed: a mortal woman with special strengths and a vampire with a plan that didn't include draining all her blood. Both sets of parents would roll over in their graves at this last thought.

Yes, here. He sent the message to her, anxious for closeness and at the same time dreading it, if she meant to fight.

Clearly sensing him, she crossed the pavement, heading his way, hesitating twice as if to think things over. Determination crept over her features as she continued on. Her silk blouse clung to her breasts enticingly when she picked up her pace.

Stopping just a few yards away, and in full moonlight, his beautiful nemesis spoke around the people on the sidewalk. "What do you want?"

Hayden scented the blood on her hand and on the scratch he'd made at her throat. His thirst responded with a roar that nearly kicked him sideways.

The Slayer took an unconscious step backward.

Fighting for control, Hayden growled, "Shouldn't I ask the same thing of you?"

"Why would you?"

"You're nothing like I expected," he said.

"Neither are you," she admitted warily.

"You did expect me, then?"

"Does anyone expect a vampire? Should I be flattered by the attention, or speed dialing 911?"

Clearly tasting her fear, but liking the exchange, Hayden said, "Ah, that's the question, isn't it? Which of us will be left standing?"

She blanched visibly. A puzzled expression crossed her face.

"For the sake of my ignorance, why don't you explain why only one of us will be left standing. Is it your blood-lust?"

Her act really was good, Hayden decided. It had to be one. He recognized her. The air around her swirled, caressing her slender form as if it knew her, too. The silver talisman at her throat was icing on the cake.

"We're opposites, are we not?" he said.

"That's your explanation?"

"Old enemies," he elaborated.

"How can that be, when I don't even know you?"

The Slayer's weight shifted back and forth from foot to foot, evidence of her nervousness. Each move she made stirred the air, pushing the lushness of her scent to him. It really was a toss-up for him as to what to do. If she wanted to play games, Hayden decided, he'd play along, see where this went.

He pointed to her throat. "I recognized the Connor crest."

She fingered the charm. "You had to bite me to see it."

"I didn't bite you," he corrected.

"No? What would you call this?" She tilted her head to expose the scratch marks. Hayden's hunger exploded when he saw the nip he'd used to place her. *Sweet as nectar...*

He struggled to speak past the gnawing thirst, wondering if that thirst might be conceived more of emerging emotion than a desire for blood.

"I'm a vampire. You're a Slayer. I'm supposed to bite you," he confessed. "Or die trying."

Connor flinched, and tilted slightly on her pretty feet as if she'd been struck. She rallied quickly. "Go to hell with this Slayer business. But before you jump back into that hole you sprang from, tell me how you knew this was my family crest, and how you knew my name."

"Everyone in Clare knows about the Connors, and what that crest stands for."

"Clare?" She seemed confused. Her forehead wrinkled in thought. "County Clare? You're from there? Yes, I hear it now in your voice. Do you know my family?"

"You're the first Connor I've met in person, although our families have been at each other for years," Hayden replied.

"At each other?"

"Maybe arch enemies is a better description."

"Hardly any of my family is left."

"True. Yet you're here, and in the presence of the one being you were born to kill."

Hayden watched her rock back. Noticed how her breasts

pressed against the shimmery silk as if straining toward him. Either she was as attracted to him as he was to her, or the thought of taking down a Flynn turned her on.

"Kill?" Her reply emerged slowly, and after a pause. "You're saying that due to an old argument between our families, you want to hurt me?"

"Just as you want to fight me. The blood feud is branded into us, Connor, served to us on a plate whether we want it or not." Hayden didn't mention how much the idea sickened him. He still wasn't sure about Connor's intentions.

"I don't want to fight you," she said.

"Then why are your hands fisted? Why are you here, so far from the club? Why haven't you already called the police?" He took a step forward, spoke around his fangs. "It's who we are. What we are. What I find strange is that I want to resist the temptation bred into me."

He was, in fact, wrestling with urges arising from a source outside of himself that told him to tear into her neck with the fever of a fiend. Part of him had been preset to eliminate whatever Connor he might find. But he had always been different. He had grown up hating the destruction, carnage and stories of sadness and loss the rest of his family had known.

He wanted this Connor for other reasons. She was radiating her own kind of pheromone, fascinatingly feminine and musky. He was sure that her green eyes, though half clouded by doubt, beckoned for him to fall into their emerald Irish depths.

Not only did he not want to kill her, the urge to bite her

took on a whole new meaning, plumped up by desire of another sort. Bite for pleasure. Indulge in the splendor he was sure he would find here. Together, they might find new ways to vent the frustrations bred into them. *Love, not war.*

"Connor." Hayden pitched his voice lower. "It's what we are that finds us together."

"What we are?" she said, obviously perceiving the hunger in the intensity of his gaze, because she took a stance as wide as her tight skirt would allow, and raised her hands to fend off any movement he might make.

In her eyes, Hayden saw a flash of green fire that was contrary to the tremble in her voice as she said, "I suppose it's way too much to ask for somebody to tell me what the hell is really going on!"

Chapter 4

As soon as the vampire repeated the word *Slayer,* the air had gone right out of Kelsie, dragging her into a tunnel the color of pitch. She fell, folding into the darkness, with the night closing in after her.

In the darkness she heard whispers, though meaning skipped past her awareness, as if she'd dropped into a memory too painful to confront. Yet out of the murmur of voices she caught the word *vampire.* And seconds later, *Flynn.* The concepts swirled around and around, forming the image of a tall, light-haired man with a chiseled face and the teeth of a demon.

She blinked and came to, shaking, tense, cold to the bone. The vampire had set something into motion with his talk about Slayers and enemies. As she stood with her hands raised, looking at the handsome representation of the devil standing across from her, in his prime and in his element, Kelsie said "Flynn," with the inflection of an oath.

Yes, she knew that name. Had heard it before. Flynn was a cursed name tied to the very soul of the legends in Clare. And also, if she was right, tied to the creature across from her.

Not just a vampire. An ancient Irish one.

She lowered her hands slightly, her need for answers outweighing everything else. How had she known his name? What did this mean?

"You're one of *them,*" she said. "I suppose Ireland's too small for the likes of you these days? Big city, easy pickings?"

"Again, couldn't you answer that question as well?" he replied.

They were alone on a street corner. No help was to be had if she shouted. She had made a huge mistake by wishing for monsters this night. She was no more a Slayer than…

"I don't know what you're talking about," Kelsie said. But thinking about the term *Slayer* produced a tingle of rightness she couldn't completely ignore. Was that a title for the thing she felt growing within herself? *Vampire Slayer?*

Absurd!

She was keyed up and ready to get off a potentially damaging roundhouse kick out of sheer frustration. This vampire hailed from the same county in Ireland as herself, and talked nonsense. He'd told her they had been born to take each other down or die trying. Just moments ago, she had called werewolves out of a nightclub, wolves who were hogtied to an awning by a full moon.

Her dizziness wasn't going away. She had to dial things back, hoping the vampire would maintain his distance until sanity intervened. It was important to understand why this was happening, how she could wind up here with him and why she hadn't sprinted in the opposite direction.

"If your perceptions are so evolved," she said, testing her voice, "maybe you'd be kind enough to enlighten me further. Did you come all this way to find me, in particular, or was our meeting coincidence?"

The vampire smiled again, this time showing a flash of pure white fang. Stunned by the sight, Kelsie stood her ground. A fresh jolt of introspection occurred with the sight of those fangs.

Maybe the desire to find these creatures hadn't been just an idea for an article, after all. Maybe it had been an ongoing compulsion, and the Blood Moon over her head was the excuse she had used to act on that compulsion. She had never been afraid of the dark. Had never been truly afraid of anything.

Irish people were nothing if not superstitious. It wasn't a stretch to wonder if it might be possible for a Blood Moon to affect more than just things that went bump in the night. Including in the mix the things that chased those night creatures, for whatever reason. Breakout article or… the need to slay them?

A shudder racked Kelsie. Why? Because the vampire

was right. She had come out here alone, looking for monsters. What did this say about her? That she really might be a Slayer, and didn't know it? She might have an alter ego she hadn't been aware of until now?

"If it's confession time, Connor, you start," Flynn said. "It was the other way around, wasn't it, and you were looking for me?"

Kelsie shook her head. "I was looking for a wolf."

"By the way, how did that turn out?"

His question had the ring of irony in it. The question she had asked herself minutes ago rose up again, as bright as the demon moon overhead and twice as discomforting to face.

What sort of person called werewolves, and didn't fear vampires nearly enough?

"Slayer," she whispered, short of breath, her gaze rising to meet the blue eyes that were now considerably closer.

Call me foolish, Hayden thought, but Connor didn't appear to be faking the surprise that turned her face an ashen-white. She was riddled with quakes. She did look vulnerable.

Without a second thought, he closed the distance between them, pinning her arms to her sides as a precaution, holding her tightly against his body—a move that primed his thirst to savage levels and sent his libido spinning into overdrive.

The fragrance of her blood filled him—heady, fierce, scintillating—as her body molded to his. In his arms, she seemed small, slight, though he knew looks could be deceiving.

When her body convulsed, he held her tighter.

Connor. Are you really a Slayer who doesn't know anything about herself? Truly as fragile as you seem at the moment?

His thirst nipped at him as mercilessly as a thousand slashing teeth, painful, terrible, new, sending the heat of apprehension across his nerve fibers, calling the beast in him over the line. His head angled toward her neck. He rested his lips against her soft, moist skin, independent of his will to stand firm against the urges, and shut his eyes.

Her protest gave him pause. Though it shouldn't have mattered, Hayden lifted his head, saw that Connor's teeth were chattering. She'd split her lip again. A final straw. All that blood… A vampire could only take so much.

She was up off the ground and in his arms before her next breath, and struggling like a wildcat to get free. He carried her over the sidewalk and into the enveloping darkness of a beach protected from the moonlight by line after line of old palm trees.

He set her on her feet near one of those trees, and pushed her up against it, waiting for her struggle to ebb. The fragile skin beneath her left ear lifted with each heartbeat, moving the silver chain ringing her throat.

"You haven't been taught well enough," he warned, his accent and fangs in full evidence now that he'd given in to the emotions gripping him. "The reputation of the Connors has markedly slipped."

He touched the tip of her earlobe with a finger, and

watched the chain beneath it vibrate, as if it recognized an enemy when its wearer didn't. He could tear the chain from her in a second. Yet the delicate silver strand was a reminder of his adherence to a personal vow. *Harm no mortal.*

He had to let Connor go. He had to let her run, no matter what he was feeling or what he perceived in her.

A twist of pain stirred him from his thoughts. Hayden glanced up to find Connor digging her small white teeth into the flesh of his wrist.

He was hit by an overwhelming urge to laugh at the irony. Searching her gaze, he found it openly defiant. But her green eyes held a hint of another emotion not so insignificant to get around. The Slayer's hunger was upon her. She also felt this attraction, and was…*willing.*

Heaven help them.

Forcing his thirst down with all of his might, leaning into Connor's young body, Hayden opened his mouth… and let the laughter out. Then he ducked as her fist came at him, faster than a mortal's normal reaction time, though not quite fast enough. He caught her fist easily in his, reveling in the meeting of skin on skin.

Pressing her arm to her chest, slipping his hand over the silk cloth, he noted how hard her heart was beating, felt the uplifted swell of her breasts. This time, when he kissed her, the night came crashing down.

Kelsie melded to the vampire's heat, thinking to fight, but parting her lips to receive him, sure she would burn in the same hell he had come from, for doing so.

This kiss was blazing, ferocious, rich. His mouth did terrible things to hers, provocative and mind-numbing things. His hands were fluid, touching her here and there.

The pleasure was extreme.

Caught up in the fire, Kelsie snaked her hands up his back and over the carved muscle beneath his shirt, bringing from him dangerous growls of delight.

If they were old enemies, these actions were insane.

The kiss deepened when she wouldn't have thought it possible. He devoured her, monstrously. Frightening new longings filled her. Inner fires ran rampant, her neck, chest, belly and hips lighting up like tinder.

"Flynn." She formed the name against his lips, her hips sliding against his invitingly, seeking a further connection in this ravaging of the senses.

He understood what she wanted. She felt the slow slide of her skirt over her thighs, followed by the sound of lace tearing.

She cried out when he entered her with a passionate thrust, and thought she might be losing her mind. But she gave in to the fever by wrapping her legs around him. Trapping him to her. Growling with her own wicked delight.

She wanted this. God alone knew why.

Flynn reached the core of her body with his next series of thrusts, slickly hitting the crucial spot over and over again. Kelsie clung to him as the sky threatened to explode, as the night went from red-drenched black to gray to white, and back to velvety darkness. She sent her hips to meet his, the crescendo deep inside growing steadily stronger, and arriving as a blisteringly hot orgasm that left her reeling.

She gasped, cried out, but wasn't so far gone that she missed the sharp prick of fangs dragging across her throat.

She slammed back into herself with a lucid warning. *One bite, and it will all be over.*

Fear of that sort of ending cut right through the passion and the desire, bringing up another chilling thought. Perhaps Slayers and vampires were shaped from a single stone. Designed to hunt, taught to kill each other to avoid this very situation, this very thing: the merging of their flesh and blood and souls that might mean the creation of some new abomination.

The spark of that possibility shook her. Her hands flexed. Her spine snapped straight. Kelsie broke from the flames of greed awkwardly, panting to get her breath back. With a strength she didn't know she possessed, she knocked the vampire away, got both feet on the ground and stood facing him, shaking so badly she could hardly stand.

He seemed as dazed as she was. His expression turned questioning. She could see how his body shook. But this separation allowed Kelsie enough distance for her anger to return, and for the new thing he had called her to unfurl.

Slayer.

Chapter 5

It took Hayden several seconds to realize what was going on. They'd shared something intimate, ultimate. Now, Connor suddenly looked formidable.

Her eyes were bright rings of color, her stance none too stable. She gave off a new vibration. Their union had caused some sort of untimely transition. Either that, or the vampire lover routine had been an act all along, and she'd used him for some nefarious purpose.

Not trusting himself to speak, his head spinning with the hastiness of the separation, Hayden gathered himself together. His hunger hadn't lessened, nor had the desire to possess her. After tasting all that heat, he wouldn't be satisfied until he had more.

He wanted to yank her back. Wanted to take her all over again. He'd nearly touched her soul.

"Connor?" he finally managed to say.

She stood with her hands on her hips, not bothering to press her skirt into place to cover herself, looking no less splendid in her flushed, disheveled state.

"You were going to bite me. The sex, the moment, wasn't enough."

"A bite doesn't make you like me," he said. "You should—"

"Know this?" she finished for him.

"Yes." Hayden held up his hands to placate her, watched her own hands fly to her neck—to search for what? Fresh bite marks? Or maybe just to protect herself?

"I'm not one of the undead," he said. "I'm a living vampire, and as alive as you are. This union is—"

"Sacrilege," Connor said through bruised, quivering lips.

"Only if you're a—"

"Slayer?"

She sounded unsure of the word, Hayden thought, as if it had stuck in her throat. He took two cautious steps toward her, hesitated when she stepped back. The confusion on her face seemed real.

"It wasn't an act," he said, trying to believe that. "You wanted this as much as I did."

Her eyes flared a brilliant green. The atmosphere around her grew thicker, as if she'd gained more substance. Yet she had invited this sudden union. She had participated. Would a Slayer do that?

She stood there, beautiful, different, silent. When she moved again, it was to touch her mouth. After that, she ran her hand slowly over her torso, her fingers trespassing over every one of her curves, ending in the valley between her legs. She looked down at herself, pulled at the shreds of the black lace panties he had torn out of the way, her face now devoid of expression.

Hayden's attention was riveted. He couldn't take his eyes from the woman he'd been inside of.

"Yes, I wanted this closeness," she admitted. "Why?"

"You tell me. Isn't it a strange time to come to your senses?"

"Better late than never, is the saying," Connor responded soberly. "But then, it doesn't take into account the lapse that occurred in the first place."

Truly perplexed, Hayden grinned ruefully. "You are good, Connor. Very good. You had me going. I wonder for what purpose?"

She contemplated his question, looking as though she truly had no idea what he was asking. If this sudden onset of innocence was some sort of taunt-the-vampire routine, he should applaud her performance. She had, in fact, gotten him good. So good that his body continued to be racked with quakes.

"The woman kissed me back," he said. "What will the Slayer do?"

"Walk away."

That was the thing he wanted the least, and the answer that surprised him the most. He was riled up, overflowing with need. After an intimate affair with this woman, whatever else she might be, could he just let her go? Would he?

"I'm way too attracted to you," she said. "Your pull on me is too strong, unnerving. It's obvious I can't trust myself."

She hadn't blamed him. Connor, Hayden decided, was becoming more interesting by the minute. After that confession, even her hand on those filmy panties came in a lagging second place to the sheer wonderment of what she might do or say next. Although his hunger continued to rage, he was also curious.

"Another time," she said. "We can set a date, meet again."

Hayden knew he could be on her before her hand stopped fluttering, if he chose, Slayer or not. He'd been a vampire for a long time. Fifteen years ago he'd been handed his fangs and the thirst that came with them. He had passed through the fire of loss, losing his family in the flames of their final death. He was the last of his kind. The last of the Flynns. And he hated the curse that ensnared him.

He hated that this Slayer's mother had killed his father.

This Slayer he had just…

"Date?" he repeated. Now that they had been as close as any two beings could be, would it be back to fighting? Sex as foreplay?

"Dinner first, perhaps?" he suggested.

"In the manner of a last supper, you mean? I'll pass," she replied.

"More's the pity. It would have given us time to get to know each other even better." The words tasted bitter, and rang with unintended sarcasm. Hayden wanted a repeat engagement, her naked body hot against his and smelling of desire. His sense was that she wanted the same thing and would ignore it—for what? Taking care of business?

"Funny how things change," Connor said in a steadier voice. "An hour ago, all I needed was a story to further my career. Now I need the skills necessary to deal with a vampire, so that I can continue with a career of any kind." She paused, then added, "Do you want to kill me, Flynn, whether or not I am what you think I am?"

Hayden found her question absurd, having had his tongue in her mouth and her legs spread apart.

"You said you were supposed to," she pointed out.

"I have never harmed anyone," he confessed, knowing his answer might allow this Slayer an edge. "I'm not what I am by choice, Connor. I've never had an urge for violence. Taking out a Slayer might make me worthy of my name, but I have no desire for that. What about you? Do you want to remove me from the world?"

"No."

"What do you think of when you look at me?"

"Sex," she said.

Unable to help himself, Hayden laughed at her answer. It was the second time he'd laughed in an hour, and it made him feel lighter, somehow.

"Is that a compliment?" he asked.

"Yes. And very un-Slayerlike, I'm sure. Also, though,

part of me wants to break your teeth and string them on a necklace. That feeling is new."

Her eyes shone with interest. Her creamy skin gave off an almost supernatural glow, reflecting the dappled moonlight streaming through the palm fronds overhead. Hayden didn't know what to think. Indecision kept him silent.

"So," she said, rolling her skirt over her hips. "I need to find out what this means. What that name you called me entails. Can you give me time?"

He nodded. *Now what are you up to?*

"Meet me a week from tonight. At the castle on the cliffs of Clare," she proposed.

When she turned from him, Hayden felt a stab of regret so painful, he winced. He saw also that Connor moved slowly, and perhaps with some discomfort. Their intimacy hadn't been gentle. He regretted that.

She spoke over her shoulder, as if knowing he was thinking about her, and sensing that he would let her go, for the time being.

"One week from tonight," she repeated, then walked off into the red-tinted moonlight like the ghost of Hayden's own botched bloodlust.

Chapter 6

It took five hours of driving to get from the airport at Shannon to her grandmother's cottage. Tired, wet from the rain shower, Kelsie found herself heartily welcomed into her grandmother's fragile arms, and wanting to cry. Homesickness hit her hard. Familiarity was all around. But this was the same grandmother who might have kept things from her. Important things. She looked at Gran with new eyes, loving, and also silently accusing.

The weathered, feisty eighty-five-year-old, with her gray hair braided in two thick coils, had once possessed a strong, capable body, now softened with age. Cliff Cottage, with its view of castle ruins and the sea, had been her grandmother's home, and the home of scores of Connors before her, for as long as anyone could recall. Was it now also a house of secrets?

"Gran, I've come home to ask you a question," Kelsie said.

Seated in her chair by the window, her grandmother gazed at her quizzically, as if she might have perfected the trick of reading minds and body language. Connor green eyes, a slightly watered down version of Kelsie's own, examined Kelsie's face as she sat on a stool at her feet.

"Isn't it a fine welcome, then," Gran said. "You've not come to see an old woman, but to pump her for information."

Kelsie found the straight-to-the-point dialogue both uncomfortable an necessary. Nevertheless, if she was going to meet a vampire on his own soil, she'd need all the help she could get. The basics would be a good place to start.

"Gran, I'm wondering if you have withheld important information from me."

"Why would you think that, child?"

"I've been called a name I'm unfamiliar with."

"And that name might be?"

"Slayer."

Her grandmother's face seemed to age further in an instant. The intelligent, gray-green eyes narrowed, and Gran's lips twitched, as if there were things she wanted to say, but didn't know where to begin.

"Ah," Gran said, visibly disturbed. "I see. So it's true, then."

Feeling sick to her stomach and desperate, Kelsie said, "What's true?"

"You were sent away to someplace safe, in case this happened," Gran said, with maddening disregard for answering a question directly.

"Evidently not safe enough," Kelsie said. "Does the name Flynn ring a bell?"

Her grandmother looked up. "There are none left with that name."

"There's one," Kelsie corrected. "He will be here in a few days to meet a woman he called 'Slayer.'"

In the quiet following her statement, Kelsie heard the ticking of the mantel clock. Had time, she wondered, become as much of an enemy as the vampire? What did her grandmother know about all this? Were these few days all Kelsie had left?

She hadn't been able to stop thinking about Flynn, and what they had done. To her shame, not a minute went by that she didn't want to do it again. She had to get to the bottom of this, so that she could either call his bluff or… not.

"The beginning, Gran," Kelsie said. "What is a Slayer?"

"A Slayer is a vampire hunter," Gran said reluctantly. "With the sole purpose of hunting them down."

"Where do Slayers come from?"

"Only a few people are chosen for such a path. The ability comes through females most often, and is unavoidable once it settles in."

"Damn it, Gran." Kelsie had to work hard to keep from shouting. "Do these abilities run through me? Do I have them?"

"Did this Flynn recognize you?" her grandmother asked.

"Yes."

"He called you by that name?"

"Yes. He knew I'm a Connor."

The fact that her grandmother nodded was like a spear to Kelsie's heart. "Then it's true, child," Gran said. "And I'm so very sorry."

Sorry? Kelsie had to get this straight, wrap her mind around what seemed so ludicrous. "How, Gran? How can I be one?"

"I don't know," she replied simply. "It's an ability that's rarely passed down."

"Passed down? What do you mean?"

Gran's expression flattened further. "If you are a Slayer, one of the chosen few, it's because you are like your mother."

The sickness in the pit of Kelsie's stomach threatened to erupt. *Like your mother?*

Blackness opened up in the part of her mind containing memories. Her sweet-scented mother had died on Kelsie's tenth birthday. A car accident while on an errand, or so she had been told. Was that a lie?

Maybe not an accident? Kelsie thought with a frightening snap of perception. God. Had her mother been a Slayer, and died in some other way? Perhaps at the hand of a vampire?

Kelsie couldn't make herself ask the question. Her hands were visibly shaking. Her face felt numb. If her mother had been a Slayer…and if her mother had met her death at the hand of a vampire…had that vampire been a Flynn?

Like mother, like daughter. The phrase rang in her ears.

"She…she was one?"

Gran nodded, keeping her focus on Kelsie.

"You encouraged me to go away," Kelsie said, recovering enough to speak. "Was that to protect me?"

Her grandmother nodded again.

"So," Kelsie began, almost inaudibly, "Connors have a blood feud with the Flynns? That's real? If there are vampires and werewolves in the world…" her tone sounded slightly hysterical "…why not Slayers?"

She wished with all her heart that her grandmother would admit that none of it was true, and nothing more than a good bit of Blarney. No such luck was to be had, though. The seriousness of her grandmother's expression struck terror into Kelsie's soul.

"My mother hunted them? Is it what the title has to mean? Fighting and killing? The Flynn I met seemed so sure."

Her grandmother spoke at last. "I hoped, since the Flynns were gone, that you would never need to know about your family's history. How was I to know what you might become, or that the remaining Flynn had left for far-off shores that would turn out to be the same as yours? I perceived no danger for you if you left here, Kelsie. Please forgive me for not explaining sooner. I'd thought to save you from this. Keep you from this." Gran's voice rang with heartfelt emotion. "How did you find him?"

Her grandmother had said *him,* not *it.* She knew this Flynn wasn't one of the undead, that he was a living vampire. The distinction was clear. Kelsie held the sickness down, her energy draining with the effort.

"In a nightclub," she said.

Her grandmother's eyes went to Kelsie's neck. "Lord. He didn't—?"

"No." She knew what Gran was asking, and also that she could not mention how their physicality had gone way beyond a damned bite. Or that now she dreamed of him inside of her. How his closeness remained a nagging heat despite the distance and the terrible information she'd just gleaned.

"The ability isn't handed down?" she asked, at length.

"No. Connor men have sought women through the ages with this special ability."

"Why?"

"I've come to imagine it was to keep the damage local. To keep Ireland from being torn apart by creatures unlike ourselves by marrying women who could face the creatures down."

After that, her grandmother sat silently for a while, her gaze on the window, her only movement the tap of arthritic fingers on the arm of her chair. It was several minutes before she spoke again.

"Will this Flynn come home to destroy the last young

Connor, is the question in need of answering," she finally said.

"If I'm a Slayer, am I his enemy, Gran?"

"Yes."

"Do I have to be?" She was afraid to meet her grandmother's gaze, fearing her grandmother would see other things—such as how Kelsie had run her hands over the vampire's body, and opened herself to him.

Instead of addressing or answering her last question, though, the old woman got up from her chair. Taking a cane from against the wall, she said, "I don't want to be the only Clare Connor left on God's green earth. Come on then, child. We have work to do before he arrives."

But as Kelsie got to her feet, she couldn't dislodge the lump in her throat or the tears flooding her eyes when she imagined the fate that might have actually overtaken her mother.

Like mother, like daughter.

Katherine Connor had been a Slayer, and there was little comfort to be had from that fact.

Hayden disembarked from his private plane and paused to look around the tiny airfield. The one useful thing about inheriting family money carefully gathered over the centuries was the protection it afforded him. He could come and go as he pleased. A car waited to pick him up.

As the scents of home hit him square in the face, he took in a deep, overdue breath. He'd forgotten how much a part of him this land was, but still approached the car with reluctance. He was home because of Kelsie Connor, and returning to Ireland was dangerous for them both.

Hayden nodded to the driver before climbing through the open door. Noting how few lights shone in the distance, he settled on the leather seat. After the illumination of Miami, with its circus-style neon and continuous noise, the utter darkness of the rural countryside, coupled with the total absence of sound, caused a pleasant ruffling of his senses.

He could hear himself think. His thoughts turned to *her,* as they had every waking moment for the past week. As the car started off into a nighttime landscape lit only by stars and the car's headlights, Hayden envisioned Connor's face and tried to reason with himself.

The dilemma was driving him mad. She couldn't have been faking, he was almost sure. Connor's arms and legs had wrapped around him. She'd been like nothing he'd ever encountered, but did she have an ulterior motive for her behavior?

He lowered the window to cool off his face, and tried to think about something else. Home. Ireland. An ancient land ruled by ancient edicts and timeless grudges. No one had dared stand in the way of the Flynn-Connor feud in all the years it had been going on. No one had put a stop to it. The two remaining recipients of that deathly grudge were supposed to have been raised to hate each other, and trained to fight to the death. But from what had already transpired between them, neither he nor Connor appeared to have the heart for this war. Quite the opposite. She'd have him think she didn't know what she was.

He remembered the night her mother had died, because he had lost his father at the same time. Each of them—his father, Connor's mother—had died by the other's hand.

Hayden closed his eyes, let his head fall back against the seat. Fifteen years ago, Kelsie Connor would have been a kid. By now, though, a staff member for the *Miami Tribune* with a Connor grandparent of long standing in the Irish community, would have to know the score.

She would have to know that his father had gone after her mother, and that her mother had taken his father with her to the grave. Still…would Kelsie Connor have invited Hayden close if she knew those things?

Inhaling the familiar green smells, he thought he could smell Connor's sultriness in the cool, fresh air. Connor, damn her beautiful hide, haunted him in ways no female had. He couldn't wait until they met again. *Opposites, yet with so much in common.* Like himself, she had fled from a place that held too many memories. The land of her ancestors. It was ironic that he had stumbled upon her, thinking to go far out of his way to avoid that very thing.

Serendipity? Fate? Had those things played a part? Was the feud to end here, either way? Death, or a second embrace?

Kelsie Connor had some kind of mysterious hold on him. She was a warm ray of sunlight on his face, though she wore a curse around her neck. She had called this meeting, dictated its terms, he reminded himself. For revenge? In order to own her birthright? To get back at him for giving in as much as she had?

He should want those same things for himself, but didn't. Never had. He'd thought to relegate the battles to the past. He had made a vow to leave the next Connor Slayer alone. That it turned out to be Katherine Connor's daughter had been a shock. Now, anyway, their lives were impossibly intertwined.

What is that?

Memories scattered as Hayden jerked to attention. He inhaled again, frowned, felt his fangs drop, and moved his lips in silent acknowledgment of what he'd found in the breeze.

Bloody hell and back. Although he was the last of the Flynns, he wasn't the last vampire on earth, or in Ireland. The stink of the undead cruised tonight's wind with the fervor of an awakened banshee.

It was a sure bet those others would scent a Slayer in their midst. Quite possibly Connor's safety was the reason her grandmother had sent her away. If she truly hadn't been aware of him, and therefore ready to destroy him, then she'd been telling the truth.

His Slayer was in more danger than she knew if she had just begun to find herself and her strength. If she hadn't known what she was until he had gotten close, he was partly to blame for bringing her here.

He just couldn't cut a break. All he wanted was…her.

As well as whatever gross oversight Fate might offer up that would allow for past sins to be forgotten.

"Take care, Connor," Hayden said, with his head in his hands. "For me."

Chapter 7

The wind on the cliffs was unrelenting as it whipped through Kelsie's hair. The late evening sky was a deep charcoal-gray. Rain had retreated over the ocean.

What she needed was more time to think, and didn't have it. She had seen the family book, and in it the long list of Connor and Flynn destruction dating back to the Middle Ages, the names meticulously penned by enemies keeping track of each other.

All those Irishwomen, Murphys, Connelleys, Malloys and more, brought into the family to do their duty and protect their land from an invading species. Like Darwin's noted laws, Slayer abilities might have been developed over time to deal with vampirism.

In Gran's book Kelsey had found her vampire. Hayden, a lyrical, melodious name, so like him. A derivative of Aidan, after Aodh, the Celtic god of sun and fire. Funny,

Kelsie thought, that a creature who couldn't exist long in sunlight carried the name of a sun god.

Gran, when pressed, had explained things about the Flynns, though not everything, and not to Kelsie's satisfaction. Suspiciously missing were the main points, like in most old arguments. Not even Gran knew the origins of Slayer mysticism, nor the secrets and rituals of dealing with a vampire rival.

Gran's daughter had been born with this gene. A boon for the Connors, who didn't have to go looking for it, and also an anomaly, since Slayer "Sense" didn't usually run in families. And now, seemingly, another anomaly had appeared: Katherine Connor had passed this Sense along to her own daughter.

Surprise!

Yet Kelsie now understood it to be true. A kernel of internal memory had been awakened by her acknowledgment of the existence of vampires. This newness was as weighty a burden as it was mysterious. She waited anxiously for the full impact to make itself known, realizing that in order for old feuds to dissolve, the bad blood between families had to end here, on these cliffs. It was up to her to see that it did.

Was it reasonable to think you could discuss things sensibly with a vampire? Point out the negatives of this ridiculous relationship? See Hayden Flynn without wanting to end up in his arms?

It wasn't helpful to surmise why he had attracted her instead of killing her outright, or why their moments of intimacy had birthed a Slayer—even though those questions plagued her.

The biggest question of all: Why had she liked it? Liked him?

As for actually being a Slayer…could she refuse the title? Shun it? She didn't plan on hunting anyone, not even a gorgeous vampire from a family who hated Connor guts. Not even for a promotion. Hayden Flynn had said that he didn't want to harm her, but could a vampire be trusted to tell the truth or keep his word?

As an insurance policy, she carried in her skirt pocket a sharpened stake that she'd discovered in her mother's trunk. If Hayden Flynn came after her, she'd try to defend herself, yet she hoped it wouldn't come down to kill or be killed. If Hayden Flynn wasn't prone to violence, maybe it was possible for them to call a truce.

When Kelsie looked up again, it was to see that night had fallen with the quietness of fine snow, and that the walls and broken towers of the castle ruins opposite the cliffs had been lit by a single torch.

She hesitated. She wasn't ready to see him again, might never be ready. But she was, in spite of everything, her mother's daughter. She had set this date.

It took her only two more steps toward the castle to realize she was indeed in the presence of a vampire. Vamp scent was everywhere.

But it was the wrong scent.

The wrong vampire.

* * *

Hayden saw the glint of light on the cliffs as he moved along the path after Connor, keeping her in view, as he had for the past few days. He sniffed the air, whispered "No!" The reek of the undead filled his lungs. Without a Connor present to protect his land and hold the chaos at bay for all these years, Hayden's worst nightmare had come to ground on his own damn soil.

Trespassers.

Rage filled him. Power surged through his muscles, fueled by the thought of losing Kelsie before he'd had the chance to know her. Before he'd had a chance to explain about himself.

He ran for all he was worth toward the castle, utilizing a speed mortal eyes couldn't have perceived. The savageness of his anger crackled the air as he reached the keep. He heard her voice as he entered.

Not too late!

Relief flowed through him. But an extraneous thought nagged as his boots hit stone. The old dilemma resurfaced. Had Connor been faking her naivete? Covering what she was? He could find the truth now, if he was careful. She would face another creature here, and he would know about her for sure—if he could hold off that long, when she was in danger.

He climbed the western tower wall quickly, hand over hand, until he stood on a decimated landing above what once had been the great hall. Looking down, he saw her and nearly shouted her name.

A big sucker had Connor cornered—an old thing, tall, gaunt to the point of emaciation, hungry as any depraved, ravenous beast. Against the threat, Connor stood rigidly upright, fear etched onto her features, her green eyes open wide.

Hayden's heart pummeled him mercilessly. Every muscle in his body seized with the need to move, to help, but he waited, barely able to keep himself back.

"You don't belong here," he heard Connor declare bravely.

The creature beside her didn't respond. Hell, Hayden realized, maybe it couldn't. Maybe it was so far beyond hungry as to be complctcly mindless.

Careful, Connor, my love!

Love. The emotion swirled around him as fiercely as the wind.

Three feet of distance separated the Slayer from her viable target. Hayden had been that close to her, once. Closer. They'd been glued together, mouths and hips and everything in between. It had been sublime.

"I don't want to hurt you," she told the beast. "God knows you've been through enough already. Still, I will defend myself."

The vampire lurched forward. Equally as quickly, Connor's hand rose, with a speed her expression registered as a complete surprise. Then the monster blocked Hayden's view.

Wait, Hayden told himself, his boots edging the gap in

the floor above her, his muscles tense with strain. *Hold tight. Wait and see.*

"Connor," he wanted to shout, *"what are you doing to me?"*

Kelsie's senses reeled with input that was sudden and overwhelming. As if she'd jumped into a fire pit, feet first, her skin exploded with heat. Nerves blazed.

She knew this reaction, and also knew what it meant. Something that didn't belong in this world faced her. A thing apart, independent from the reality most people saw.

The torch, its flame flapping furiously and smelling of oil, gave the area beneath the castle's moss-covered arch an otherworldly aura. In the dim light, the monster edged closer.

She recognized the difference between this creature and Hayden Flynn immediately—not only in looks, but at a deeper, more intrinsic level. This one felt *wrong.* It stank of rotting flesh. Its white face shone like a clown's. Its eyes were empty black sockets.

The creature made no sound when it moved. It didn't appear to use its limbs, more or less floating on its own evil stench. Kelsie's heartbeat tapped out a fast staccato. With the monster right in front of her, she almost went down, the horror was so great. Her fingers held tightly to the weapon in her hand, the smooth wood foreign to her touch and not nearly as comforting as a revolver loaded with silver bullets would have been.

No time to be sick!

The monster's fangs were as black as its glaring eyes. It came on like a slippery darkness, fast as a blink. Like a spider. Two hands, cold as granite, tore at her sweater, tugging her toward its tattered chest. Its mouth gaped open.

Adrenaline kicked Kelsie into gear. She jumped sideways, landing on both feet with her hands still raised. The sharpened stake she clutched gleamed in the torchlight, catching the bloodsucker's attention. Angry at this show of resistance, it attacked.

Swinging to the right, ducking quickly, Kelsie hit the wall hard with one shoulder. Pain crashed down, hot, terrible, but she straightened in time to ward off another blow. Ducking again, she came up behind the vampire before remembering that the place where its heart was supposed to reside was on the opposite side. The fangs side.

The monster whirled before she finished the thought, and had her by the throat. The momentum of its attack sent them both stumbling into another wall. A rain of stones hurled down on them as Kelsie stabbed at the gaunt, sunken chest with all her might, without penetrating the flesh.

The vampire tumbled back, flailed its arms, hit dirt and bounded back up as if its backside were made of springs. Kelsie shuffled forward with another shallow breath, but her attention was derailed by the sense of another intruder.

Had this bloodsucker brought a friend?

No. This scent is familiar.

As fast as her fleeting thought, a secondary dark figure appeared between herself and the gaunt bloodsucker. Tall, dressed in black, with his blond hair shining against the backdrop of cold gray stone, Hayden Flynn glanced at her briefly, grabbed hold of her sweater and carried her out of the keep.

He tossed her the last little way, onto the grass, onto her knees. When she looked up, Flynn had already gone.

She stumbled to her feet and sprinted toward the hall, hearing scuffling sounds and a long, piercing wail. After that there was nothing. Dead silence.

Sides heaving, and with the stake clutched in her fist, Kelsie stopped beside the torch, breathless, seeing nothing of the gaunt monster. Only one vampire occupied the ancient space now. Hayden Flynn. His blue eyes were on her, as dangerous as she'd remembered them, and flashing evidence of his hunger. His lips were open, showing her a glimpse of fang.

He didn't shout, growl, or move toward her. He stood there, unmoving, as if trying to get a grip on himself. Then he said in a deep rumbling tone, "You weren't lying."

Chapter 8

The Slayer looked so small, standing there, her face highlighted by the fire from a torch, as it had been when he had first laid eyes on her. She was no less striking for all her disarray.

The stake she held was aimed, point out, at him. She was scared, and rightly so. His heart went out to her.

"Just another night in the life of a Slayer," he said, observing her expression carefully.

"You came," she said, breathlessly.

"It was an invitation I couldn't refuse."

He felt twitchy, wanted to ease her tremors, but was unsure of how to go about it. After seeing her grandmother, Kelsie Connor might have bought into the ancient-enemies scenario.

"Why did you help me?" she asked. "To save for yourself the pleasure of having a Slayer?"

"You haven't yet grown into that stake in your hand, so where would the sport be in that?" Hayden said.

"I know about you. Did you come after me, all the way to Florida?"

"I left Ireland to avoid the word *Slayer* altogether. To avoid this moment, in particular."

He watched her think that over. Her lush lips parted. "I didn't know about myself," she said.

"I get that now."

She eyed him suspiciously.

"You fought like a girl," he said, grinning. "Not like a Slayer in tune with her talents."

The wide-eyed Connor didn't let the comment anger her. Although her face was as white as a sheet, she offered a hushed "Thank you." Two simple words that Hayden saw she meant. A sentiment that had the similar effect to a stake through his heart. Because with those words she'd uttered, the war was over.

"You're welcome," he said.

Her eyes met his. "What now? We just go on our way, hoping that someday we won't want to take up where this left off?"

"Do you think you might change your mind?"

"No."

"Can you walk away this time, and forget about me, Connor?"

"No."

Hayden studied her more intently, his pulse still erratic at the thought of what that bloodsucker might have done to her. The depth of this emotion was new, and unusual. He felt protective. The big bad vampire wanted to watch over the same Slayer more or less assigned to seeing to his demise.

"Then I think you owe me," he said, trying not ruin the effect of his statement by offering her the smile that tugged at his lips… Because he was completely certain about how she could make this up to him. And it involved a bed.

Love thine enemy...

"Go to hell on the *owe you* thing," she said. "And what's so amusing?"

"I was wondering if you'll forget that I saved you?"

"No one ever forgets their first."

Ah, Connor was sassy, all right, Hayden thought, if somewhat out of her league now, with that stake visibly wavering in her hand.

He could smell the scrapes in her skin from her tussle with the undead. The accompanying scent of blood was adrift, and tempting, but not nearly as tempting as her shirt, torn open at the neckline to expose a triangle of creamy, unblemished skin.

Skin unadorned by the special silver necklace.

Hearing the sound of wood striking stone, Hayden knew that Connor had dropped her weapon. He tried to understand what this meant, mentally, but his body had no such problem in translation, and took him toward her before he thought to pull back.

Her eyes were on him, disconcertingly green. Within

her gaze was a strange, knowing light. Intelligent. Calculating. Nothing innocent about it.

He looked at her uncertainly. With twelve inches separating them, doubt again crossed his mind. *Have I been had?*

"Let me see," he said, testing his theory. "You don't really fight like a girl?"

"Not usually."

Was she hiding a grin?

"You aren't going to tell me that—"

"I knew you'd come, and wanted to see what you'd do? See if you would jump in to help me, true to your word about not wanting to see me harmed?" Connor said.

He raised his eyebrows questioningly.

She went on. "That I figured you would be doing the same thing? Waiting to see if I'd stake the monster or not?"

She let him sweat that out for a beat, then shook her head. "The answer is no to all of those things. It would have been something I'd do, though. Just so you know."

Hayden said, with relief, "You didn't know about being a Slayer."

Connor made a face as she moved a sore shoulder. "I had no idea."

"Now you do?"

"Oh, yes. I'm getting more and more used to it as the hours fly by."

"Do you want to end this here, as I do, Connor?"

"I do *not* want it to end here," she replied.

He took stock of that.

"We're the last hope for the old feud, so I'm told," she went on, stepping closer to him, looking up, her sultry scent punctuated by that saucy touch of musk.

Hayden knew that scent, and what it meant. His heart missed a beat or two as his fangs fully extended. Doubt melted away.

"Do you have an idea of how this is to go down?" he asked, wrapping his fingers in her hair, gently tugging her those last inches closer.

"Don't you?" she countered.

His mouth hovered above hers. She didn't pull away.

"This feud could have been stopped at any time. All it took was for one Slayer to cross the line," Connor pointed out, licking her lower lip to moisten it, then adding, "Or one Flynn."

Hayden's fangs began to ache. Temptation was a millimeter away. When Connor's warm hands caressed the sides of his face, he nearly came undone right there.

"What I have to say about the whole Dark Surrender thing, vampire, is *dream on.* Why should a Connor agree to give in?" she said.

"A vampire can't change his stripes. I am what I am, by blood."

"As am I," Connor whispered, her mouth rising to meet his.

In the next second, Hayden had her on the ground, with her arms raised over her head and her body stretched out beneath his. Her heat burned right through his clothes. She didn't resist, even when he looked longingly at her neck.

"Where is the necklace, Connor?"

"Safe."

When she smiled, Hayden smiled back. Looking into her eyes with renewed respect and more than a little awe, he moved his hips teasingly. "You're saying you planned *this,* Connor?"

"Did you assume I'd also think like a girl, Flynn? I'm a woman, as well as a Slayer."

"Truthfully, I didn't care what you *thought* like."

"I get that now," she said, mocking his earlier reply. "You're not one of the undead."

"Indeed not, since you didn't use that stake."

"You're capable of everything a normal man is."

Although she knew some of this already, firsthand, Hayden said, "And more. Much, much more. As long as my partner is a—"

"Slayer?"

"Maybe not quite a match made in heaven," Hayden admitted. "But it'll do in a pinch."

His mouth silenced her response, hungrily. Meeting his drowning kiss with ardor of her own, she flicked her tongue sensually across his fangs…

Then Hayden was on his back, with Connor on top and smiling down at him.

"Just to be clear," she said, "I might not have known about the Slayer gig, but I've never been a weakling."

"Point taken," Hayden conceded.

"When I love, it will be forever."

"Most commendable."

"There will be no surrendering here, dark or otherwise, on anybody's part. Just understanding. And plenty of sex."

"A Slayer after my own heart," he agreed.

Of course, he wouldn't tell her that he had allowed her get the better of him, this once. That he had seen her move coming, and that his strength would always be superior to hers. Getting him on his back had been a concession to the future. His own kind of surrender. And now she owed him twice over.

Trying not to laugh out loud over the hand Fate had unexpectedly dealt him, Hayden glanced at Kelsie Connor's smooth neck, currently flushed pink, so very inviting and silver free. He watched her skin pulse over her blue-tinted veins with each excited beat of her heart.

As her hips began to move against his, and she gave a low, sensual chuckle that he likened to the call of the wild, Hayden thanked those Fates again, seven times over, for this strange, lovely, unexpected, extraordinary gift.

With an answering growl, deep in his throat, and a firm hold on Connor's hips, he decided that this old ruin on the cliffs of Clare was as good a place as any to show a Slayer what miracles a vampire could perform, if given the opportunity.

She'd find out later that a vampire's libido, not unlike his thirst, was insatiable.

* * * * *

Vampire in Her Mysts

Meagan Hatfield

Chapter 1

"Where am I?"

Yuri Feodorovna forced his eyes open, his keen vampire senses instantly tasting damp earth and blood in the night air. He lifted his head off the ground. An unbearable ache pulsed through his veins and a fine layer of sweat coated his body. Both sensations were something he usually experienced after a battle.

Pressing a palm into the velvety earth, he pushed himself up to sit.

"Ahh," he gasped at the spear of agony jabbing through his rib cage. He covered his tender side with his hand, wholly unsurprised to see his palm covered in red when he lifted it toward his face.

"That's my blood," he groaned, letting his head collapse against the tree behind him. "That's…a lot of my blood."

What in Fatum's veil happened?

Clutching his waist with one hand, he used the other to push himself up. Standing sent a fresh wave of dizziness through him that threatened to pull him to the ground. Blood seeped between his fingers and streamed down his pant leg. Yuri bit down on his jaw at the current of pain streaming through him. The tip of his fang nicked his lip and the coppery taste of blood flooded his mouth.

"Dammit," he said on a growl, spitting the mouthful on the grass. As if being ginsu'd across the abdomen by some wannabe samurai blood hunter last night hadn't been bad enough.

Yuri stopped. An icy cold hand grabbed his heart, as memories of the past few hours came together…the fighting, the clanking of swords and slicing of flesh. In particular, the tattoos embedded across his adversary's forearms scared into Yuri's brain. They identified the sword-wielding vampire who attacked him as a *vanator*. A vampire blood hunter.

Yuri knew those tattoos well.

He should.

He'd worn the same ones for more than a century.

One mystery solved. A *vanator* had done this to him, he thought, inhaling an uneasy breath. Too bad owning that little bit of knowledge didn't make him feel any better. He could think of a dozen other beings he'd prefer trying to kill him rather than a *vanator*.

Before Yuri's brother Nikolai took over the *Mysts*, *vanators* were known as blood hunters—trained killers who assassinated their own from within. Blood hunters took out those vampires deemed not to be following the auld ways. Kings, queens, Dark Council members, corrupt politicians and aristocracy—no one had been safe from the *vanators* and everyone in their realm respected them and their missions.

Yet now, they'd become little more than bounty hunters. Duty-bound by an undying blood oath to Nikolai, a false ruler and the brother Yuri had been covertly fighting against for the past decade. Ruthless, brutal, the *vanators* relentlessly stalked their mark. They would not stop until they succeeded in delivering their target, dead or alive, and collecting their bounty.

Now they hunted him…and in the *Mysts,* of all places.

The holy vampire lands beyond the *Fatum*, Earth and every supernatural realm in between, the *Mysts* were a perpetual dark haven where day was never truly day and vampires could roam freely. For that reason alone, this place had always been dangerous territory for any vampire to enter.

Well, it had been pure and utter madness for him to come here.

Yuri dropped his chin to his chest and closed his eyes. Exhaustion warred with the need to act, to take out his opponents before they could regroup and strike again. He stumbled to the lake, pushing aside the marsh grass and shrubs. Collapsing at the edge, he sank to his knees. Cold water leached into his clothes, sending a chill up his already blood-drained body. He groaned, a tired and weak sound that made him cringe.

Dipping his arm in the pool, Yuri washed the blood

away. The caked-on redness seeped into the lake, revealing the tattoos forever embedded on the underside of both forearms from elbow to wrist, marking him *vanator* to anyone with the gift of sight.

He twisted his arms slightly, exposing the marks forcibly inked alongside his old ones, branding him a traitor to the *vanator* brethren. His stomach soured. Assassin scum was more accurate. Blood hunters, true *vanators* were brother to no one. Masters of disguise, they frequently changed personality, occupation and appearance to the point of being chameleons. They always worked alone. And they always hunted their prey until they were either captured or dead.

And for the first time, Yuri was the prey, not the hunter.

A twig snapped in the forest behind him.

Yuri froze. Instinct had him sinking lower into the grass seconds before his brain registered the order. Eyes alert, he scanned the darkness. A thick cloud passed before the moon, shutting out what little light there'd been. Yuri breathed out a curse as night's veil cloaked the forest around him, further concealing any would-be attacker. Careful to not make a sound, he floated his hand inches above the velvety lawn toward the dagger holstered at his thigh. Holding the weapon in his palm, Yuri fisted the hilt tight and waited.

If it was a *vanator* who hunted him, he wouldn't have to wait long.

He swallowed, his grip flexing on the weapon.

The darkness not forty yards behind him suddenly

parted, revealing the pale flesh of a woman's leg. An astonishingly long, slender leg. Yuri blinked. Certain he must be hallucinating from the loss of blood. Yet he remained fixed on the spot, waiting for the apparition to show herself once more. A heartbeat later, a bright flash of red fabric swished in the night, followed by the second bare leg until the woman stepped into full view.

Although the heavy cloak she wore obscured her form, the brief glimpse of red ceremonial robes beneath it identified who she was.

A *Kalu*.

One of the holy women from the *Samostan*, a women's temple devoted to the worship of the Goddess.

Yuri regarded the girl intently, remaining alert even though she posed no real threat to him other than alerting any lurking *vanators* to his presence.

With feline grace, the woman walked toward the water. The pads of her feet rolled from ball to heel with the elegance of a dancer. His sight in line with her ankles, he studied their delicate structure, the dip and curve of bone and flesh. Each step slid the cloak higher up her legs, first past her knee and then her thigh. Yuri eagerly explored each inch as it became visible. The curve of her calf, sway of her knee and slender thigh, each inch more enticing than the last. For a woman devoted to prayer and books, her body was more muscular than he would have thought.

An arm reached back and up. In a deft move, the woman removed the hood, settling the fabric back on her shoulders. His gaze slid to her profile. Skin, so white and pure in the moonlight it could be translucent, glowed with the perfect luster of a pearl. In stark contrast, wave after wave of ebony hair flowed down the enticing curve of her back, resting at the dip of her hip. She looked ethereal. A goddess reminiscent of the one she worshipped.

The female bent to the water's edge only a stone's throw away. With the grace of a soaring hawk, her pale arm arced over the water. Yuri caught sight of her wrists, slender and elegant, before she dipped her hands, plunging them into the lake and scooping up water. A moment later, the cloak fell off , pooling to the ground around her feet.

Yuri's heart skipped. Sweet Goddess, if he thought her magnificent before, she rendered him speechless now.

He'd heard of the alluring, borderline erotic *Kalu* garment, but had never seen one. Slaves to the Goddess, the *Kalu*'s attire reflected such. Red arm covers swathed her forearms from wrist to bicep. A narrow piece of fabric crisscrossed over her breasts and curved, wrapping once around her waist, leaving an enticing amount of flesh exposed from her rib cage to her navel. Panels, no more than ten inches wide, hung between her legs to her ankles on the front and back. Deliciously bare, her hips and thighs were concealed by only two ribbons tied in bows at her hipbones. Another slim red ribbon collared her delicate throat.

A sliver of moonlight peeked down from between the clouds, casting a hint of light upon her skin. Yuri's eyes widened with each new inch of flesh the moonlight exposed.

Tattoos.

This beautiful creature was covered in them. They peppered her flesh, her abdomen, arms, chest and no doubt her back too if he had the opportunity to look. Suddenly, the desire to bare this female to his gaze and study her marked body besieged him.

Unlike humans, who used tattoos the way a male peacock struts its plumage, in the *Mysts*, each tattoo told a story about the vampire who bore it, for good or ill. Some were put on the body by right, some by force and none were taken lightly. Every mark had meaningful and thoughtful placement. They spoke volumes about those wearing them. The tattoos identified where they were born, what class or horde they belonged to, what specialties they owned, or where their affiliations lay.

In the same vein, if someone placed false tattoos on their bodies, claiming to be someone or something they were not, they would bring shame upon their clan, and in most cases find themselves exiled. That is, if a disgraced family member did not find and kill them first.

Yuri looked down at his inked forearm, studying his own marks. The intricate design rippled as he flexed his grip on one of the weapons of his trade. Yeah, he knew all about those tattoos. But why did she have so many? *Kalu* were said to be marked as such, but he couldn't imagine so heavily. Whatever her tattoos spoke about her, Yuri had the clawing urge to read, to learn, to know.

Curious to see if his keen eyesight could make out any symbols or patterns in the darkness, Yuri glanced toward the woman again. His mouth slackened at the sight of her. The female had undone the ties around her neck and now bathed topless by the water. Even in the dim light, Yuri had no problem making out the perfect shape of her bosom. A small tattoo sat nestled in the valley of her chest. However, the flesh of her breasts remained unmarked. Crimped and tight, her nipples looked succulent, two raspberries ripe for the taking.

A hammer of lust began pounding in his veins. A dangerous undercurrent of hunger rippled through him in its wake. The need to feed, to heal, overwhelmed him. His canines throbbed, lengthening on their own volition. A haze of red blanketed his vision. Yuri pinched his eyes shut, trying to get himself under control. He swallowed, groaning at the raw slide of his throat.

A loud female gasp filled his ears.

Yuri cursed beneath his breath. He'd been discovered. If the girl ran, in the state he was in, he'd never catch her before she reached help. Goddess knew what would happen if she sounded the alarm and let the entire *Mysts* know he was here.

Out of options, Yuri grudgingly utilized the last resource he owned and readied to overtake the girl's mind.

Zeroing his gaze on the female, he focused on her eyes. Heat bored into his skull and within seconds, his *medji* self bombarded her mind and took control.

Being one of the last psychic vampires in existence had its perks. But wounded as he was, he knew he couldn't hold her still for long. He was already getting a sense of this woman and she did not like his mental invasion at all.

Bracing his hands , Yuri pushed up to his knees, feeling pain crawl through him anew. Weak and wounded, Yuri forced himself to appear anything but to the female as he approached her. If the vibrations he picked up from her thoughts were even remotely accurate, she was skittish as a feral cat and had claws just as sharp. Yuri held his back ramrod straight as he neared her, even though his shoulder burned in protest and the unbearable need to vomit rolled through his gut.

After two more steps, he stood in front of her. As his telepathic powers instructed, she remained motionless. Yuri wrapped his fingers around her upper arms, holding her physically as he prepared to release her mentally. But he stared into her face and hesitated.

Dewdrop-shaped eyes of a color he'd never seen before locked on his, a flicker of willful intelligence sparking in their depths. Her eyes seemed almost iridescent obsidian with flecks of color that shifted with each play of light, very unlike a vampire's flat black eye color. Her slender arching brows matched her high cheekbones. The sultry curve of her mouth instantly recalled the palace courtesans, lush, curvy and willing.

However, her mind intrigued him most. He'd entered her psyche easily enough. She had not been expecting his attack and he'd slipped her mental defenses without difficulty. Yet, the moment he'd gained access to her thoughts, he'd felt her mentally pushing him back. Hard. It had taken all of his concentration to keep her immobile until he could reach her.

Tightening the grip on her he'd let slacken, Yuri pulled out of her thoughts and released her mind.

Like a deer sensing a lion, she instantly moved away from him, trying to run in the opposite direction. However, Yuri held her tightly. Undeterred, she swung, her elbow nearly smashing his nose. Yuri used his years of combat training to efficiently immobilize her upper arms and pin her back flush against his body. When she fought to get away once more, he flashed the dagger he still held in his hand, covering her mouth with the other. She finally quit struggling.

"Don't make a sound," he said, fighting to keep his voice controlled and even. "Cooperate, do as I say and I will not hurt you. Do you understand me?"

The female glanced back at him and nodded. Those eyes of hers were big and yet calm, almost assessing in their stare as if she dissected everything about him. Yuri suddenly felt thankful for the darkness. Had this one seen the extent of his wounds, she might have tried to get away again and succeeded this time. And for the next few hours, he needed her.

It was all making sense. Why he'd journeyed to the *Samostan* in the first place. Why he'd been lurking just outside its outer walls.

Yuri hauled the *Kalu* to him. The sweet scent of her curled around him, enticing him, making his mouth water. He closed his eyes and dipped his chin to the space between her neck and shoulders, breathing her in. The beast within him responded, his nature sensing a way to heal. Yuri didn't fight it this time. Instead, he willed his fangs to lengthen, invited the blanket of red to drape over his vision. Yuri closed his eyes, a plan forming in some dark recess of his mind.

I need her. I need her. Those three words repeated in a prayer-like litany in his mind. Perhaps the Goddess had not abandoned him after all. Perhaps she'd dropped one of her servants in his lap to help him. After all, he could use this girl to escape this place. He could use her to get back home.

But first he needed her blood.

Yuri threw open his eyes. His vision zeroed in on the pulse fluttering wildly in her neck. His fangs ached, itching for that first taste of what he already knew would be sweet, hot and tangy blood.

The fingers around his arm tightened.

"Please," she breathed. The husky sound of her voice, soft and yet strong like steel and velvet woven together, shot straight to his groin. He felt alive with a lustful urge and need he'd not sated in…Goddess, probably as long as the female in his arms had been alive.

Dueling hungers began pulling at him from both sides. However, right now he could only focus on one.

"I apologize for this," he whispered in her ear.

"For what?"

Ileana Tarasova gasped, her body stiffening as razor-sharp fangs pierced the sensitive flesh of her neck. She lurched forward in an instinctive attempt to escape. However, the man grabbed her to him with a surprising amount of force for someone wounded as badly as he. His arms flexed, coiling tighter around her with each panting breath she exhaled, like a constrictor keeping its prey in place.

Trapped, Ileana's attention shifted to the bite, to the blood flowing in a hot rush from her body. A swell of panic rose in her gut. Again she wriggled, trying to break free, and again his hold only strengthened. She panted out a breath, her body slouching.

Helpless.

Goddess be damned, she was helpless to do anything other than wait for this monster to stop drinking from her. If he stopped at all. The thought would have made her angry if she didn't suddenly feel so woozy.

Light-headed, she felt her eyes flutter shut. With her sight cut off, her other senses took over. The intense warmth of his mouth on her throat intensified. The soft brush of the dark goatee framing his lips scraped against her skin. The heat of her blood as it rushed to feed him, and the wake of coolness it left in her veins. A massive shudder racked her body before she went limp in his arms.

Powerful and strong, his muscles held her upright, kept her clutched to his wide and muscular frame. Her chin slid to her chest. Ileana focused on the broad hand fanned across her abdomen just under her breasts. His fingers, elegant and manicured, palmed her flesh in a desperate grip with each pull of his sensual mouth. The curve of her backside heated, her softness molding against his hard build.

Beneath his hands, a deep burning ignited in her core. The seed of heat, no more than a tingling flicker at first. It began to flower and blossom until heat radiated outward in all directions, warming the limbs that had gone cold from blood loss. Her sex clenched and for a moment, Ileana could have sworn the flood of heat sluiced lower. Could have sworn she felt the stirrings of desire awakening inside her.

The man dislodged his teeth from her flesh with a heaving gasp. Ileana released a sigh of her own, one of both relief and strangely enough, of loss. Her neck ached and his warm mouth covered the throbbing skin, suckling and teasing before blazing a trail across her cheek toward her lips. She smelled blood on his mouth. Her sex pulsed, greedy, hungry.

In a daze, she became marginally aware of his long-fingered hands twisting her in his arms with ragdoll ease. Faced with his broad chest, she tilted her chin up. Ileana caught a brief glimpse of a much too gorgeous face and heated half-lidded eyes before he swooped again.

Only this time, he wasn't after her blood.

Chapter 2

Lips, warm and smooth and utterly male, crushed against hers. Hot and slick, his tongue twined with hers again and again, his mouth sliding over hers in a dizzying glide. At the faint taste of her blood on his lips, the vampire within her sparked to life. Renewed energy perked in her veins and Ileana kissed him back with an urgency and hunger she'd never felt before.

Some part of her brain screamed at her to battle him. The fighter inside told her she should give him one swift kick to the balls and run. Do anything except respond the way her body responded, with warmth and eagerness and lust.

Unbidden, her body sank willingly into his embrace, into his kiss. Then she was falling down toward the ground, her stomach in her throat. Hundreds of stars winked down at her against the pitch-black sky above.

Her lower back touched the earth first, followed by her shoulder blades and then her head, as the man laid her down and stretched out beside her.

It wasn't until he loomed over her that she saw the panic in his eyes, the self-loathing and remorse evident in his haunted gaze. She identified with the look immediately. It was the same one she'd become accustomed to seeing in the mirror.

Ileana shut her eyes.

Don't look. Don't feel.

Shaking her head, she tried to heed the mottos repeating in her mind. Yet she couldn't find the will to obey them. Cold, damp earth kissed her skin, sending trembles along her body. Something warm wrapped around her, lulling her to sleep. Ileana blinked rapidly, trying to stay awake. Trying to complete what she had set out here to do, to not let her guard down. But whatever effect his bite had on her, it still gripped her hard. Finally, she gave in and closed her eyes. Only for a moment, she told herself.

Ileana rocked her head to the side and then the other. A dull ache pulsed in her neck. Absentmindedly, she lifted her fingers to the hurt. Hot and sticky, her blood coated the tips of her fingers. She jolted upright, her hands instantly circling her armbands, ensuring they remained in place. Certain they did, she let out a sigh and tried to think through the sleepiness hovering over her.

She'd only closed her eyes for a moment. Hadn't she? How long had she been…

"You're awake."

Ileana gasped, spinning toward the male voice. It was the man who bit her. He sat on his haunches across from a low-embered fire. The soft light illuminated both his striking looks and his inherent lethalness.

"I am sorry for before, about feeding from you," he said, dropping his gaze to the stick he poked into the blaze. It hissed in reply, dozens of red sparks feathering into the sky like magical fireflies. "My wounds were too severe. I had no other choice."

Ileana glanced down at his side and back up, noting he did indeed looked completely healed. Again she clutched her neck, fingering the tender wound. Her other hand palmed her throbbing forehead. Closing her eyes, she massaged them both. Tried to wake up her senses, stoke her anger as this man did the fire. Ever since he bit her, it seemed the clawing drive for revenge that had driven her since childhood had seeped from body. The fact she'd lost her anger now of all possible times, made a slight boil surge in her blood.

Thank the Goddess.

"I swear on my beloved sister's grave," he continued. "I will return you to the *Samostan* as soon as possible."

Ileana's brow furrowed. "Why not return me now?"

The man paused, a question in his eyes. "My name is Yuri. What is yours?"

"You didn't answer my question, Yuri."

A shadow passed over his already dark features. "I need you."

"You *need* me?" she repeated, balking.

Yuri closed his eyes, obviously warring with what he had to do and what he had to say. "I need you to open the doorway to the outerworlds, so I may return home to mine."

At his admission, Ileana recoiled both internally and physically. The utter gall of what he asked her, or more to the point, *informed her* she had to do for him, astounded her. Unfortunately it did not surprise her. Everyone in the *Mysts* knew the blood of a *Kalu* served as a key to the outerworlds door should all other routes be closed. It figured a Feodorovna like him would put such a theory to test.

"You really are a monster," she said beneath her breath.

"What did you say?"

"And should I refuse to open a vein to set you free from the *Mysts*," she said in a voice loud enough for him to hear. "What will you do then? Will you kill me?"

He opened his mouth to speak, but closed it. Had she not been so full of self-righteousness, she might have feared the glint of anger burning behind his heated gaze.

"No, that's right," she said instead. "You won't have to bother dirtying your hands with such a task. You controlled my mind before. It stands to reason you could simply do it again. So, I guess that makes me your prisoner, *Yuri*," she said, placing her hands on her barely clad hips. "Now, what shall be your first task for me?"

An intense, dangerous glint sparkled in his eyes.

In one fluid motion, he stood and walked over to her. The sculpted quad muscles of his thighs rolled and bunched beneath his tailored pants. His arm muscles bulged in such a way she knew he clenched his fists alongside him as he walked. When he stood not two feet before her, she realized his fangs hung over his soft lips, sharp and aggressive. The wound in her neck twinged, remembering them embedded in her flesh.

Ileana shivered and wondered what he wanted, what he might do to her. She realized he could do anything he wanted and she would be powerless to stop him.

"Stand up," he ordered, his tone incensed. "And turn around, *Ileana*."

Unaccustomed to a female, any female, driving him to such a maddening brink of lust, frustration and vexation, Yuri fought to keep it together as the female did as he'd bade and stood before him. He didn't not know this woman, did not know the answers to the thousand little niggling questions whispering in his mind about her.

Though she looked the part of a young *Kalu*, every honed instinct in his body told him this was no simpering, Goddess-worshipping nun before him. So at her challenge, he decided to do what he'd been dying to do since spying her beside the lake. Yes, he could read her mind. In fact, he just had in order to discover her name, since she was being so stubborn. But right now, he wasn't interested in reading her thoughts. He only wanted to read her body.

The female stood still, her eyes looking up at him, her forehead barely level with his chin. Realizing she'd yet to follow his second order, Yuri circled his finger, motioning for her to turn. Although those intoxicating eyes of hers flashed defiantly, she kept them leveled on him and slowly spun.

Yuri's gaze instantly drew to a large back piece commanding her skin from the neck down to both shoulders. An elaborate weaving design encircled a skull, so faint it appeared to be superimposed on her skin. A chill, like death breathing down his neck, wafted over him. Ignoring it, Yuri closed the distance between them.

The body heat emitting from her small frame reached out to him, curled around him. Her scent, that lovely, delicate subtle scent of sweet flowers and honey, teased his senses. Yuri's mouth watered, recalling the rich flavor of her blood sliding down his tongue and throat. He swallowed hard.

"Tell me about your marks," he breathed, lifting his hand to the tattoo between her shoulder blades. She made a sound, a swift intake of breath, and tiny goose bumps peppered her skin. Finally, the fiery little nun with the sharp tongue had nothing to say. Yuri felt a smile tug his lips.

"This one looks old," he coaxed, his finger sliding gently over her skin.

Old and delicate.

Her skin was like a finely milled paper he feared tearing with his calloused fingers. Ileana shifted at his touch, her elegant chin dipping to her shoulder as she glanced back at him. Although he suspected she knew which marking he spoke of without looking.

"That was my first," she said, softly, definitively. "I was

nine. My family had just been slain mere hours before I arrived at the *Samostan*, afraid, alone."

Yuri's mouth slackened. *Slain?*

"The holy women stripped me naked and scrubbed my skin until it was aching and raw. I begged them to stop, cried for my mum. No one spoke a word to me the entire time. They would only chant the holy words and pray to the Goddess for forgiveness."

Yuri's heart tightened with each word, her suffering, her pain more sharp and real to him than the damp night air coating his lungs.

"I remember being relieved when they finally stopped," she said on a disbelieving laugh. "The respite however was brief. I had no idea who they were. What they were doing. No idea such women or such a place existed. Four of them pinned me down while a fifth marked my skin. Forever letting anyone know my family had been branded traitors and murdered. This one," she said, gesturing to the tattoo across the back of her neck, fanning out like wings on her shoulders. "It declares my life debt to pay back their sin."

Yuri cursed under his breath, the barbaric image of those vile women torturing a scared innocent scorching in his brain. He had heard of such a practice, but had never witnessed it firsthand. Then again, he gathered not many men ever had.

In that moment, Yuri felt the significance of her sharing her story. Her trust. Although it didn't make any sense, he wanted to thank her for telling him, apologize for the hurt she suffered at so tender an age, and murder the ones who'd marked her. Yuri had marks of his own. He'd received his first as a teenager, and he knew the pain. But to be so young and endure such a process made him despise the practice.

"I vowed that night to never become like them. To never forget the horror, the pain," she said, her voice softening. "To never believe the lies about my family."

Ileana shifted her hips and then her shoulders in an enticing wave. The thin ribbon of fabric draped over her shoulder slid to the grass beside her feet, baring her back. Yuri's throat dried. His palms burned to touch her. Not sexually, but for comfort. So much pain, so many trials. A life, written out like a play all over her body, and Yuri took his time reading every act. It was the most beautiful thing he'd ever seen. She was the most beautiful woman he'd ever seen. Pale skin painted with pictures, images and stories of her life. Hair the color of midnight, so thick and lush his hands would get lost in it.

Yuri leaned closer, breathing her in. Gods, she even smelled soft. Overcome, entranced, she drew him in. He closed his eyes and leaned nearer still. Until his lips almost brushed the downy skin of her tattoo.

Too close.

His hands flattened on her back, clutching her to him in a desperate grip. A breathy sigh passed her lips and Yuri could have sworn she melted back into his touch. Unable to restrain himself, he pressed his mouth full on her warm flesh. This time he was rewarded with a rich, husky moan.

The vibration moved through his entire being, like ripples breaking a lake's glassy surface. It rumbled his foundation until it cracked, releasing a need, a desire he had not felt since…

Yuri took a step back. "I'm sorry," he murmured, the apology a lie on his tongue. He wasn't sorry. In truth, he wanted more, wanted her. Here. Now. Instead, he moved away.

Ileana spun in his arms, her black eyes open and unapologetic. A soft hand covered his cheek, a long finger running down his neck, over his hammering pulse. When she leaned into him, so close her scent, her softness invaded every pore and inch of him, a sledgehammer of lust and desire pounded through him. Her fingertip continued its lazy glide back and forth along his collarbone, outlining the very tip of the tattoo that continued down both pecs and his ribs. He sizzled in a breath at the contact and swallowed hard before looking down at the female driving him into sensory overload.

"Now," she said. "Can I see yours?"

Chapter 3

The way he looked at her, Ileana wasn't sure if he would comply with her request or not. Truth be told, she didn't know why she had this insatiable urge to see.

Dark and guarded, his eyes stared down at her. Excitement, disbelief and if she read him right, a hint of regret lurked behind them. After a moment, he took a step back and then two. Ileana kept her gaze fixed on his, trying to read his thoughts. Then his arms lifted, his hands grasping the neckline of his shirt, tugging the fabric over his shoulders. Before removing the top from his head, he turned, putting his back toward her.

No longer able to keep eye contact, Ileana lowered her gaze to his waist, the first part of flesh he exposed. Her mouth slackened and a thick hum of desire pooled in her belly.

Goddess, he was gorgeous.

Broad, muscled shoulders tapered down to a slender waist. She had caught a glimpse of tight, dark nipples and his defined abs before he discarded his shirt. In fact, everywhere she looked, beautifully inked flesh concealed the chiseled muscle beneath it. Every inch of his abdomen and back appeared sculpted by an artist. And Ileana decided she'd never seen a more stunning piece of art in all her days.

Yuri stood motionless, fidgeting only slightly under her perusal. However, Ileana felt his nervous energy, saw his heavy swallowing. Although she tried, she could not deny the strong attraction pulling her to him, the almost uncontrollable need to see his markings. His body siren called to her and she obeyed. Tucking her hair behind her ears, she stepped toward him in almost a trance. Until she stood as he had behind her only moments before, her chin barely coming up to his shoulder blades.

Chewing her lower lip between her teeth, Ileana lifted her hand. Reverently, her fingertips touched his shoulder. The muscle beneath her hands jumped. Yuri turned his head to the side, his eyes meeting hers for a moment before looking forward once again.

"My father gave me that one," he said, his voice cool and icy. "It declared me a full-fledged adult male of my horde."

Ileana licked her lips, her hand moving lower to the horned demon on his rib cage. "Given to me after my first battle," he said without looking. "The horns represent the two men I killed that day."

"And this one?" she asked, her hand palming the intricate woven symbol that took up most of his back from ribs to waist.

Yuri cleared his throat. "That is the emblem of the *medji.* It was bestowed upon me after I was taken from my home to train with the seers."

"Your family did not try and stop them from taking you?" she heard herself ask before she could stop it.

He shook his head. "It was considered an honor for them to have a *medji* born son. I became a token, a trophy in their case to flaunt like some medal they'd won."

Ileana's heart tightened at his words. Both of them were scarred, physically and emotionally from their way of life, their families.

Dangerous.

By the Goddess, what she was doing was dangerous. She shouldn't be listening to his stories, shouldn't be touching his skin. But she couldn't stop. Slowly, her fingers followed every delicious curve, dip and hollow of his shoulders and back, then down his arms and back up, listening to the story that accompanied each tattoo.

Then she took the backs of his palms in hers, examining them. The hands she'd felt upon her skin looked as elegant and strong as she imagined. Her fingers threaded through his briefly before fluttering back up. When she grasped his wrist and turned his forearm to view the tattoos on the other side of his arm, her heart froze.

"What is it?"

Although she couldn't hear anything over the hammering of her pulse in her ears, she must have gasped aloud.

"Nothing," she breathed, dropping his arm and stepping back. "It's nothing."

"Ileana, are you all right?"

Yuri had turned to face her. She shook her head, unprepared for what she just saw and doing a damn fine job of showing it.

He moved to follow her but then stopped. One eyebrow lifted quizzically. As if solving the puzzle, he lifted one arm and then the other, looking down at his forearms before looking back at her with narrowed eyes. "You know these marks," he stated more than asked.

"No, I…" she said, shaking her head, knowing full well the implications if she did.

It didn't work. "You're lying." His eyes glowed red. Fangs dropped over his lips. Ileana held her breath as his handsome face contorted into what she imagined was the last thing his enemies saw before he took their life.

And then he charged her.

Yuri took the female to the ground, tossing her onto her back with enough force to take the air out of her lungs, but not enough to harm her. Ignoring her gasping breaths, Yuri pinned her arms over her head, pushing them into the grass. He covered her body with his, stifling a groan as his hard frame molded against her soft curves.

Using his body weight to keep her down, he captured her hands and pinned them above her head. Disbelief, adrenaline and the lingering pulse of arousal flowed through him with such force he couldn't think, until the truth of what almost happened crashed over him anew.

"You weren't coming on to me. You were trying to kill me!"

She wriggled beneath him enticingly, her pelvis pushing up against him in a way that made his balls throb. But he was too furious to care. "Who sent you? Who are you?" He had questions screaming through his mind and the little vixen wasn't coughing up any answers. Although his brain couldn't piece together the puzzle of her yet, no nun from the *Samostan* would recognize his *vanator* tattoos.

Ileana squirmed again and Yuri's grip on her wrist slipped. Compensating for the move, he clutched her armbands. Tugging the fabric to her wrists, Yuri thought to use them as an impromptu binding. Thinking he could at least keep her immobile until he could decide what to do with her.

"No," Ileana shrieked, redoubling her efforts to get free. Yuri pressed more of his body weight atop her, scanning her body, her face for the source of her alarm. Then his gaze settled on the pale flesh of the forearms he'd just uncovered.

His heart stopped, and then withered in his chest. The air sucked out of his deflated lungs. She glanced from him to her upraised arms and quit fighting.

"You're…"

"A *vanator*," she finished for him.

Chapter 4

Yuri paced around the clearing, twirling the short hairs of his goatee in one hand, cupping his elbow with the other. "So, you're one of the hunters my brother sent to kill me?"

Ileana pinched her lips together and looked away. Even tied to a tree she looked regal and beautiful. Her damned enticing curves that accursed robe hugged were displayed perfectly. Yuri turned from the sight of her, a low growl rumbling in his chest.

"I bet you're not really a *Kalu* at all, are you," he stated more than asked. "You lied so I would trust you, and then what? You were going to take me to him alive, or kill me and throw my head to the dogs?"

Again she offered no answer.

Fatum's veil! Her calm and stoic defiance infuriated him. He spun back around. "I hope you know the penalty for placing false markings on your body."

"It's not like that," she said between clenched teeth.

"Then what *is* it like, Ileana."

She whipped her head to face him. Long wisps of raven hair cascaded over her shoulder and concealed breast, the ends nearly coiled in her lap. "Stop calling me that."

"Why? Isn't it your real name?"

"Of course it's my name," she bit back. "I never offered that information, you stole it. But no one calls me by my given name. Not anymore."

Although her words pricked a nerve of intrigue in him, he ignored it. "Well, in case you haven't noticed, *Ileana,* you're the one tied up and captured. Not me. I make the rules," he said, pointing to his chest.

Goddess, he was acting like some primitive ape, beating on his chest to prove his dominance. Yuri ran a hand through his hair and then over his goatee. This woman infuriated him beyond all reason and measure.

Tracking back to her cloak, he started rummaging through her pockets, looking for something, anything that might prove she wasn't a cold-blooded killer. Prove his instincts hadn't been so wrong about her. When that yielded nothing, he tossed the cloak down and sat on a nearby tree stump. Reaching into his back pocket, he retrieved a strand of beef leather he'd put there earlier and snapped off a bite. He wasn't hungry, but he had to *do* something. Inaction wasn't doing his brain any favors.

"Everything I told you before was true." Her voice cut through the still night, small but strong. "I was a *Kalu.* But I ran away from the *Samostan* when I was twenty. I couldn't abide that place and swore the moment I could, I would leave."

Yuri flitted his gaze toward her, looking at her out of the corner of his eye. When she spoke again, he softened his chewing so he could hear her better.

"I had nothing. No family, nowhere to go. My hate for the world and the clawing need for revenge were the only things keeping me going," she said, her focus still, her gaze locked on some distant memory. "Becoming a *vanator* was the easy part. I already had more ink than most of the veterans. And I had a lifetime of bloodlust waiting to be sated lurking inside me. However, being able to pay back the man who killed my family has proven nearly impossible."

Yuri swallowed and stared at her. "What does any of that have to do with accepting a contract out on me?"

She looked at him as if he'd just asked her why the sky was blue. "You are a Feodorovna. You're part of the royal family line." She paused, her jaw clenching. "You're *his* brother."

Yuri sat up, taking notice at the mention of Nikolai.

"Disdain me all you want," she continued. "But your family doesn't do good deeds. They don't save lives. They destroy them," she spat. "I discovered that about your bloodline at a very young age."

Her words struck Yuri like a barbed hook through his lungs, ripping away his breath in one swift pull. "Goddess," he said. "Nikolai killed your parents."

"Yes."

At her answer, Yuri dropped his head in his hands. He didn't need psychic powers to tell him his brother had been responsible for her pain. He read it pouring off her clearly enough.

More blood. More blood on his family's already stained hands. His trembled with rage. If his twin hadn't been blocking their psychic link, Yuri knew for a fact he could have sent his brother into a coma with the pure force of hatred and anger he felt for him now.

However, hatred and anger never helped anyone. Yuri ran his fingers through his hair and glanced back at the lovely, strong and passionate young woman across from him. She proved as much. Look what hate and revenge did to her life. The seed his brother had planted inside her grew into evil, twisting vines, coiling around her spirit and threatening her very soul. The realization saddened him. To think of what this beautiful creature could have been if someone had shown her love, kindness, forgiveness.

Yuri sucked in a breath and knew in that moment what he had to do. Undoing the past was impossible. But perhaps her future was not lost.

"Ileana, I am so sorry for your pain, your suffering. If I could but undo it, I would."

Her eyes narrowed. "I don't understand. He is your family, your brother."

Yuri nodded. "My twin to be exact. Yet we could not be more different. As youths, he would kill a bird and I would try and bring it back to life. He would set a trap and I would make sure I was the first to walk through it so his machinations would not harm anyone else. I came to the *Mysts* to try and foil his latest plot. But this time he was one step ahead of me. I not only failed in my task," he said, his voice cracking. "He sent the *vanators* after me. They nearly succeeded in wiping me out. Would have, had it not been for you healing me."

She blinked up at him, her big eyes so wary and unsure. Yuri could almost hear the surprise in them. And why wouldn't she be shocked by his admission? Here she had thought killing him would hurt Nikolai. When, in fact, his brother was the one who hired her in the first place.

"I don't know about you, but I used to believe the Goddess had forsaken me. Taken everything from me she could and turned her back on me." He paused, weighing his words in his mind carefully before speaking. "I would be dead if not for you, Ileana. And Nikolai, his evil, would have won yet again. Perhaps she hasn't given up on either of us just yet."

Ileana's brow tightened. So many questions filled her mind. In his one admission, countless beliefs that comprised the web of her life's ideology and values unraveled. She couldn't think, couldn't grasp it all and connect the dots.

"When word traveled about a contract out on a Feodorovna, I thought my long wait was over. Thought I finally had a chance to avenge my family. I knew nothing about you except for your name. Had no idea Nikolai wanted to see you in your grave, as much as I want to put him in his."

How could she have been so wrong? How could Yuri not be like his brother? How could a Feodorovna be good? How could *she* be good for that matter?

Yuri glanced down at her, something warm and almost tender in his dark gaze.

Before she could open her mouth to try and explain herself further, a familiar flood of warmth rushed through her veins. It filled her head, sending a wave of sleepiness rippling through her. Ileana tried to blink, tried to hold it back. But the current overtook her. Yuri entered her mind with his ability, and held her captive. Without lifting a finger, he untied her bonds and laid her in the grass.

The strong hold he had on her mind kept her utterly immobile. Yet, unlike last time, she felt no fear, no worry for her own safety. No, this time she could only fixate on the sorrow in his eyes. She felt powerless to do anything to soothe it.

Yuri leaned over her, a slight smile on his lips. Gently, he placed her heavy cloak atop her prone body like a blanket.

"It seems we both have the same goal, my little nun. You wish to kill my brother and so do I. However I cannot endanger your life any further. As a *vanator*, even being seen with me is compromising to you. My family has brought your heart enough pain. I cannot bear to bring you any more. Please go in peace. May the Goddess keep you safe."

Ileana gasped and jolted upright.

Yuri's words rang crisp and clear in her head. His last sentence replayed over and over in her mind. However, the rest of her memories seemed foggy, as if their entire meeting had been a dream. She touched her neck, the bite mark, flinching at the twinge of pain.

No, not a dream.

Where was he? Blinking, she whirled her head from right to left, trying to get a sense of her surroundings. A faint part of her heart hoped she would see him beside the fire. Nothing, only the smoldering remains of burnt-out ash and wood. Like the faint wisps of smoke curling into the sky, he too had vanished.

"Well, what do we have here?"

Ileana spun. Her blood ran cold at the sight of the *vanator* behind her. Even in the darkness, she recognized him. Seven feet of towering hard muscle, and a face so scarred only one eye opened.

"Misha," she breathed. Her hand instantly gravitated to her thigh, where she normally stowed her weapon. A low curse passed her lips when she only met bare flesh. Damn *Kalu* robes. They hid nothing and she'd had to go weaponless in order to trick Yuri. Her heart seized at the thought of him. If Misha had found her, then it stood to reason he would find Yuri too....

"Looks like someone decided to go rogue."

Rogue? Ileana licked her lips, scanning the ground by her feet and then his for an escape route. "What makes you think I would go...?"

"Don't be coy with us, Ana," he bit out, stalking closer, almost clumsy in his confidence.

"I'm not—" She paused. "Us?"

A moment later, two more *vanators* emerged from the darkness. Ileana recognized them at once, Misha's little cronies. Goddess, she mentally chided herself. She had not even sensed them. Ileana rose to her feet, backing in the opposite direction. Her feet slipped on the wet mud beneath her bare feet.

"We saw you let him go. Saw him tuck you in for your little siesta and walk away."

They had been watching? Ileana took a deep breath. She had to play this cool. "If you saw the target leave, then why aren't you following him?"

Misha offered her a lopsided smile, his eyes undressing her in such a way it made her stomach turn. "Oh, don't worry. Sergei is tailing the mark. The one *you* let walk away without so much as a fight."

He made no mention of Yuri's *medji* powers being the reason she hadn't fought back. That meant they didn't know about his powers, and perhaps Yuri would get away after all. Ileana only briefly pondered the fact she cared more about his safety than her own before Misha lunged at her.

Hard and firm, his arms snatched her around the waist. He hauled her back against his front. "You know what letting the target go means to the brethren, don'tcha, Ana?" He snatched one of her armbands, ripping away the fabric, revealing the tattoos hidden beneath. His fingers bit into her flesh as he forced her arm up for inspection.

"These are going to have to get changed." Rough and clumsy, his hands slid down her arms, before veering toward her breasts and around her waist. "Mmm, but first I think this is going to have to come off," he said, pulling at the ties at her hip. "This is all going to have to come off."

Rage exploded inside her at the threat. Ileana kicked back her head, smiling when her skull crunched against his nose. He screamed and loosened his grip. The moment the arms around her fell away, Ileana ran forward. The defensive move gave her only seconds. She'd trained with Misha at the academy and knew he possessed an unnatural tolerance to pain. The blow bruised his pride more than his nose and he would no doubt relish the opportunity to make her pay for it.

Ileana made it three strides when a second *vanator* leapt in front of her, blocking her escape route. He swung his arm in a wide hook jab. Ileana bobbed and weaved, coming up with a hard uppercut to his jaw. Bone hit bone, her knuckles cracking against his skull. Gasping, Ileana again made for the tree line. If she could make it into the brush, she might have a chance to…

Something struck her hard between the shoulder blades. The blow forced the wind from her lungs and knocked her to the ground.

Dazed, Ileana tried to catch her breath. Behind her, the *vanators* whooped and hollered, as if they'd just taken down a trophy animal in a hunt. Propping her hands under her shoulders, she pressed them into the earth and tried to move, to get away.

Rough hands clawed her shoulders, dragging her upright and launching her forward at the same time. Her torso slammed against an unforgiving boulder. Her palms curved around the cold stone before fingers clutched each wrist, pinning them down. Misha's fingers dug into her scalp and tugged back hard. Ileana tried to scream, but he wrenched her neck back at such a harsh angle, it immediately stole her breath.

"Come on, Ana," he drawled, his free hand palming her naked thigh and squeezing her ass. "If you quit fighting now, I'll make sure you enjoy it at least a little."

Frantic, Ileana darted her gaze left and right. Her mind raced, searching for a weapon, a way to escape. Her thoughts were so focused on survival, she didn't register the men flying off her until she toppled to the earth.

The hysterical shouts and cries of the men filled her ears. Trembling, Ileana wondered what new devilry the *Mysts* might have conjured for her to face. She pivoted on her hip to look toward the clearing.

"Yuri?"

His back was to her. Fists clenched tight at his sides. His broad shoulders shielded her from the sight of Misha, who lay on the ground, rubbing his obviously sore jaw.

Scooting up to sit, Ileana glanced around for the others. Their broken bodies lay sprawled on the grass, limbs cocked in unnatural angles.

"Calm down, brother," Misha said, nodding toward Yuri's forearms. "There's enough of her to go around."

Yuri took two steps closer and threw up his arms, showing off the ink branding him a traitor. "I'm not your brother," he bit out. "And she is not interested."

"I beg to differ." Misha's gaze slid to her. His hand reached down to cup his privates. Fingers curling over the still-hard rod, he rotated his hips, his eyes shuttered as he stared at her. "In a few minutes, she would have been begging for more."

"Bastard," Ileana breathed.

Yuri's muscles were jumping behind his shirt.

Before Ileana could get to her feet, Misha began screaming, a high-pitched, earsplitting wail. Frenzied, his fingers clawed at his head with such force his fingernails ripped strips of flesh from his face. Heart racing, Ileana glanced from him to Yuri, unsure what was going on.

Yuri remained unmoving, his back straight, his muscles tensed. Focused. Ileana swallowed, her gaze traveling back to Misha writhing in pain on the grass. Realization dawned.

Medji powers.

Yuri had used his psychic abilities to attack Misha. Or rather, have Misha attack himself. A shudder passed over her skin at the sheer power Yuri possessed. The assault continued for only a few moments before Misha's body began seizing in convulsions and then quit moving altogether.

Yuri's shoulders dropped, his muscles relaxed. He

stared at Misha for a few seconds, his fingers flexing and closing before he spun around. The sight of him stole her breath. Unruly strands of dark hair whipped across his handsome face. His fangs hung down in lethal points, and a fierce bloodlust filled his eyes.

"Are you all right?"

Momentarily breathless, she nodded. "You came back," she finally said, her voice still laced with a low-grade panic she did not even try to mask.

He stepped toward her, his hands gently wrapping around her biceps. "Of course I came back."

Goddess, help her, but her heart fluttered at his words. His hands gripped her tighter, almost desperately. Then, unexplainably, the energy between them shifted. A change passed over Yuri's handsome face. The worried façade dissipated, leaving the mask of indifference he'd worn most of the evening. The one she had a feeling he always stoically wore even though the burden of it nearly killed him.

How she wanted to rip it off, beat and pound on it until it cracked. Until he cracked and leveled those fierce and passionate eyes on her again.

Ileana reached toward him, her hand cupping the side of his face. A low groan ached from him and he leaned into her palm. The façade splintered ever so slightly at just her touch. What would happen if she kissed him? If she peeled the robes off her body and stood bare before him? Thought after thought and countless what-if's crossed her mind.

Instead, she stepped into his arms. Tilting her head to the side, she tucked hers under his. He inhaled sharply, releasing the air in a shuddered breath. Ileana held hers as she rested her cheek against his chest. When his arms finally closed around her, his chin dropping on the top of her head, she smiled and closed her eyes.

Warmth, safety enveloped her such as she never felt. So much so, she wondered if he'd entered her mind again. She felt…

Home.

Something roared in the distance, a shrieking bellow that rent the sky and made the earth rumble. Yuri clutched her tightly as the sharp wailing continued. The sound cut through her, low and visceral. Ileana's bones quivered and the flesh covering them shrank in fear.

Keeping his hands on her upper arms, Yuri leaned back, scanning the woods and sky. "Oh, no."

"What's happening?" she shouted over the growing noise.

"Red wind." Wide and alarmed, his black eyes fixed on hers. "We must take cover. Now!"

"Red wind?"

"It's a sandstorm off the Zavodnica Sea," he said in a rush. "A giant wall of red will blow miles high in the sky, and move faster and further than an avalanche. The cloud will swallow everything in its path."

Ileana swallowed, her brain fighting to process the coming scenario. "How soon will it be here?"

Yuri whirled quickly, looking in both directions before settling back on her.

"Minutes."

Chapter 5

The word had barely registered in her brain before his hand clasped around hers tightly and he started running away from the noise. Legs pumping wildly, Ileana sprinted behind Yuri.

Although she knew she shouldn't, Ileana glanced over her shoulder. Ominous and blood red, the swirling cloud of particles raced toward them like a living thing bent on peeling the flesh from their bones.

"In here!" Yuri's voice screamed through the deafening pain racking every nerve in her body. Ileana glanced up in time to see a decrepit shack almost perfectly hidden from view in the overgrown brush. Only a few more steps, she told herself, kicking her legs faster, using the last reserve of strength she possessed. She was thankful that every stride, Yuri kept hold of her arm, kept pulling her along when she thought she might falter.

Finally at the crumbling building, Yuri tucked her arm against his ribs, easing her behind him as he kicked a booted foot on the door. The rotten hinges gave way and the door opened. Yuri ushered them inside and Ileana followed, releasing a grateful breath when Yuri slammed the door closed behind them.

Ileana bent at the waist. Bracing her hands on her knees for support, she pulled air into her lungs.

"We made it," she panted, the statement voiced more for her own ears than his.

Closing her eyes, she felt Yuri pace the small room. Knew he checked the two small windows she'd spied upon entry, assessing their ability to hold back the coming storm. Had she the strength, she would have done the same thing. Being meticulously thorough was something they had both been trained to do. Yet right now, Ileana couldn't move. Every muscle in her body felt like rubber. Her legs quivered and she wondered briefly if she might collapse.

"Are you all right?" Yuri's arms slid around her. Solid and warm, his hand pressed against her lower back, his other cupped the apple of her shoulder, guiding her into his arms. Offering her strength she didn't have on her own.

She nodded, opting instead to sink to the floor. A heartbeat later, Yuri crouched beside her, his body and arm arching around her like a shield. For the first time, Ileana became potently aware of his size, his solid strength and intoxicating maleness. She'd never needed anyone to protect her, never wanted to depend on anyone else for her own safety. Yet she recognized some inherently female part of her had awoken and thrived under Yuri's wing. And for the life of her, she wasn't sure it was a part she could dispose of, or if she even wanted to.

Still fighting to catch her breath, Ileana turned off the thoughts warring inside her and simply allowed herself to lean into Yuri's embrace. If he was shocked by the move, he didn't show it. Instead, the hand resting on her upper arm flexed as if in approval and pulled her tighter. Ileana followed his lead and rested her head on his shoulder. She focused on the calm tempo of his breathing and trying to match it.

The earth beneath them began to shake violently. The walls trembled, sprinkling years' worth of dust from every crack and corner. Pans vibrated and bounced off the counters, banging on the floor. Ileana's heart raced in time with the furious storm.

A horrible screech split through the sky, as the red wind screamed at the top of its lungs and swallowed the tiny shack. Ileana covered her ears with her hands and closed her eyes, unsure why this wind, of all things, frightened her. She could face *vanators,* dragon warriors, harpies—anything. But this screeching wind seemed to eat through her very soul like acid through flesh.

Large and warm, Yuri's palm made slow circles on her lower back.

"Shh, Ileana, it's all right," his voice soothed in a calming litany. A soft glow sparked in her stomach. Like a seed of light, it grew, expanding into her arms and legs until it filled her completely. And always there, always urging the warmth and lightness was Yuri's voice, telling her she was safe.

The storm, still rampant and wild in its rage, buffeted, sounding more like a freight train passing just outside the window. A sense of peace and calm washed over her, like a gentle wave cleansing the beach.

Realization dawned and she gazed up at Yuri. "You entered my mind, didn't you?"

A slight curve twisted his lips. "I had to. I couldn't let you be afraid."

"Couldn't let me?" she bristled.

Yuri sighed and reached out, smoothing a strand of hair away from her face. "I couldn't bear to see you afraid. Is that better?"

Ileana opened her mouth to snap back some witty reply, but closed it instead. Using his shoulder as a prop, she leaned her head against him and took in their surroundings for the first time.

"What was this building?" she asked, feeling an eerie chill travel up her spine. This shelter had obviously been someone's home at one time. Articles of clothing still hung on hooks by the door. Pans sat neatly arranged beside the stone hearth carved into the wall, and for the first time, Ileana noticed they sat on what may have once been regarded as a pristine rug, now covered in soot and dust.

"I don't know," Yuri replied. "But whoever left this place, left in a hurry."

Yuri tilted his head toward the ceiling and scanned the walls. Ileana couldn't help but admire the sight of him. The flickering red light from the window reflected off his eyes. They shone in the darkness, warm and almost colorful. Reminiscent of a raven's multihued wing tinged with striking layers of blues and reds that are imperceptible unless examined up close.

He swallowed and her gaze lowered to his strong jawline, now blurred by the shadow of dark hair that had grown in the past hours. Still trimmed, the smooth goatee perfectly framed his lips. She'd never noticed their shape before, the lower much fuller than the top, the smooth texture. Hers suddenly tingled, growing full, almost heavy. Ileana licked them, tucking the bottom one between her teeth, thinking the languid sensitivity delicious.

She sucked in a shaky breath, willing him to look at her. The arm around her shoulders tightened. The warm body next to her stiffened, before he looked down at her. The expression on his face seemed both concerned and hungry and was enough to send Ileana reeling to catch her breath all over again.

By the Goddess, she wanted to look away, wanted to apologize, wanted to sink into a hole and disappear. But the overriding desire to feel his lips on hers kept her eyes from turning away. Instead, she reached up to him, framed his stubble-roughened cheeks beneath her palms, and pulled him closer.

"Ileana," he said, his breath warming her lips.

Since her parents' death, she'd hated hearing her name.

Yet when Yuri said it, something cold and hard inside her dissolved. She loved to hear her given name on his lips. Loved how his *L* rolled off his tongue in a sensual purr. It made her feel feline. Made her want to rub her body against his like a cat against a scratching post.

"Ileana."

Goddess, he said it again. She mewled. Her needing whimper had Yuri claiming her face in his hand. His thumb brushed across her lips in a caress both rough and tender and her gaze dropped to his, willing his mouth to hers.

He smiled and tenderly bent his head to her. When his lips touched hers, pinwheels of fire licked her belly and every weary muscle in her body sprang to life. Instinctively, she knew what she wanted. What she craved.

"Use your powers on me, Yuri," she said when he pulled away.

He froze, the muscles beneath her hands tensing. "Why?"

"I want you to tell me what I'm thinking," she said with a coy smile. "What I want."

Yuri paused, his eyes boring into hers so reverently, so deeply she could feel his stare like fingers on her skin. "I…" He shook his head. "I'm going to build a fire," he muttered.

And in the time it took her to blink, he'd pushed to his feet and walked away.

Yuri tossed the wood into the hearth with more force than necessary. He had to do something to get his mind off Ileana. Goddess, didn't she know he didn't need to read her mind to see she wanted him. He only had to look into those heated eyes, taste her sweet lips.

Although fleeting, the quick look over his shoulder was enough to send another aching tug of desire through his body. A becoming flush highlighted the normally pale skin of Ileana's beautiful face. Her lips, still full and moist from his kiss, were soft and parted, revealing two tiny perfect fangs. Fangs he could already feel stabbing into his neck with sweet perfection.

He shifted his legs, trying to adjust the growing evidence of his desire for her. Angry with himself for reacting to her like no more than a green lad, he stabbed at the fire, relishing the pops and hissing he garnered in reply.

"Yuri."

Her voice was soft, breathy and his cock twitched in response.

"Yes."

"Turn around."

Unable to deny her with words, he shook his head instead. Busying himself with stoking the fire, he ignored the one building with the force of scorching hot bricks in his gut. A rustle of fabric sounded from behind him. The soft padding of her delicate footsteps echoed in the small room. He held his breath, waiting for her touch, sensing it coming.

Small and elegant, her fingers curled around his shoulders.

"Yuri, please," she said, tugging gently on his arms. "Look at me."

He bit down on his jaw, on the truth. "I can't," he ground out.

"Why? Is it your powers?" she asked sweetly. "Does it hurt to use them?"

Yuri thought of the night he held his sister in his arms. The night he told her promises he wasn't sure he could keep. Watched her murderer take her life and get away.

"Sometimes," he grated.

It did hurt, though not the way she assumed. It hurt to know things, to be able to control people and bend them to his will. To always wonder if people did things because you made them or because they wanted to.

"Yuri, please look at me."

Yuri gripped the shoddy mantel, feeling the wood splinter beneath his grip. "Don't ask me. Not now."

"Why not?"

"I cannot be what you need." *What you deserve.*

"How do you know what I need?"

Yuri whirled around, seizing her upper arms. Ready to tell her he knew everything about her from his brief glimpses into her mind. That he wanted more for her than he could ever give her. That she deserved to be treated like the noble princess she once was, not someone to be taken quick and greedy on a filthy cabin floor.

Then his eyes locked on hers. In them he saw every emotion he felt, but could not describe. Every unspoken want, desire, tangible need and unbearable loneliness permeating through his being for this woman, echoed in her beautiful eyes. It rattled him to the core and rendered him speechless.

The storm outside faded from existence. The walls stopped shaking and the entire world went quiet save for the sound of his heart thudding wildly in his ears. Yuri realized he hadn't taken a breath since he turned around, knew he needed to inhale and soon. However, it took a moment for his brain to register any need other than her. Once he taken the first breath and then the next, he realized the skin beneath his palms was bare. *She* was bare.

He paused only long enough to take in her perfection before he swooped down, covering her mouth with his own. Blinding heat sparked his mouth at the touch of her lips. She moaned, her body softening beneath his like wax melting beneath flame.

"Ileana," he said in almost a growl, as he dove down and took her mouth again.

Her velvety lips were moist and responsive, and he explored every inch of them. When his hand cupped her breast, a breathy purr rolled off her tongue. Yuri smoothed his cheek down her rib cage, kissing her soft belly as he went. His hands nearly spanned her waist and it hit him then. She was fragile, delicate, soft. No matter how hard and tough she pretended to be.

He wanted to ravish and worship her at the same time. Seduce her until she gave herself to him, mind, body and soul. Lay the world at her feet if he could. After hastily tugging off his clothes, Yuri placed them on the ground, laying her atop them.

Bending, Yuri placed a kiss on her welcoming mouth. Tasting and sucking her slick, full lips until his head spun and desire pooled in his groin. Everything in him screamed to plunge inside her welcoming body and make them both forget.

Ileana pivoted her hips, rolling her pelvis against his. A shock wave of pleasure jolted through him. The undeniable invitation to have her, to claim her, to own her if only for tonight sent his mind reeling. He reacted without processing, his hand skating down her side. So smooth, so soft. His gaze followed the trail of his fingers on her skin.

Reverent, he outlined the tattoo along her rib cage, smiling at her swift intake of breath. Again her body undulated in an erotic wave beneath him and his smile tightened. Yuri's cock pulsed. Long and impossibly smooth, her legs wedged wider. One knee dropped open, the other slithered up his thigh in a languid, silken glide. Yuri's breath hitched. Open. She lay bare and open. For him.

Mine.

This time he didn't hesitate. His hand slid between her legs, fingers parting her softest flesh. An approving groan slipped through his lips to find her wet, hot for him. His fingertip flicked her swollen clit. She cried out, leaning into his hand. Yuri repeated the move, again and again, his hand stroking her sex in a demanding spear that sent her eyes fluttering shut. Her mouth opened in a mute O as his fingers glided over the slick warmth of her, easily slipping inside and penetrating her.

The heat of her ignited and consumed him. So perfect, so tight, her sex hugged his finger, greedily taking it deeper. Jealous, his cock throbbed painfully as he continued to strum her like an instrument. Relishing every note, every tone of pleasure he could ring from her.

The delicious torment of both having and wanting this woman made his arms start to tremble, his vision go blurry. Again his groin tightened to the point of pain. Yuri wanted to take her, claim her, feel her and taste her. The sheer level of intensity with which he wanted to be inside her, frightened him.

"Please, Yuri," she breathed.

He looked down at the beauty beneath him. She reached for him, her fingers biting into his shoulders, pulling him atop her. When he gave in, allowing his body weight to sink against hers, she swallowed forcefully, a low whimper escaping her. The sound of her need proved more than he could stand.

Yuri entered her in one smooth thrust. Warm and incredibly tight, her body took him in. The feel of her turned every bone in his body to liquid heat. Closing his eyes, he allowed the bliss to consume him, allowed every pore, every nerve to sing out its pleasure from the top of his head to the soles of his feet. He eased out of her and slowly pressed back in, deeper this time. Again, he rocked inside her, each slide more luscious than the first. Friction, warmth, moisture, each sensation spurred him on.

Small hands palmed the expanse of his shoulders, her fingers gripping his flesh, searching the canyon column of his spine. Her legs wrapped around his hips, as her hot tongue traced a fire trail up his neck. Both acts urged him harder and faster. Two things Yuri had no intention of doing. He never wanted this night to end.

When he tried to slow the tempo, Ileana pushed on his shoulders, hard. Yuri rolled with the movement, pleasantly surprised when they stopped moving and she sat on top of him. Inch by unbelievable inch, Ileana sank atop him before resuming the pace he'd fought to decelerate. Desperate, his hands gripped her hips, working her up and down as his own body rose up to meet every one of her thrusts.

Soft and firm, her thighs clenched his sides. Her fingers spanned out on his chest. Waves of untamed hair cascaded down her waist, almost concealing the amazing sight of his cock disappearing inside of her over and over. The urge to release built faster and stronger with each delicious sway of her body. Fighting it, Yuri reached out, cupping her breast in his palm. Ileana closed her eyes, releasing a gasp as he began to knead and caress. Yuri couldn't remember anything more exquisite, more beautiful than Ileana perched above him. Yet right now, she felt entirely too far away.

Tightening his abs, he curled up to sit. First, his mouth closed over the tight nipple his hand had been neglecting. She cried out, her back arching into him as his tongue laved, his mouth sucked and his teeth lightly grazed the throbbing bud. He lifted away from her only long enough to grasp her face and crush his mouth against hers in a panting, teeth-clashing, hungry embrace. Half-mad with desire, Ileana rocked above him in a rapid tempo, and he loved every second.

Yuri knew they were both close. So close. Lying back down, he pulled her with him. His hands in her hair, smoothing it back from her face so he could see her. He wanted to watch her come. Watch the pleasure take hold of her.

Mouths open, frantically brushing with each panting thrust, Yuri felt a smile on his lips, felt another in his heart. Ileana smiled back, moving faster, harder against him. The tips of her breasts slid against his chest in a silken glide with each grind and snap of her hips. Warm and tight, her flesh hugged his cock. First in one strong fist and then butterfly pulses tightened around him, milking him.

Yuri moaned in her mouth. Her eyes slid closed, her back tensed beneath his hands. She tried to pull away, his name tearing from her lips in a desperate, heady sob. But he kept holding her, kept rising up hard to meet her next drive down and her next. Kissing her jaw, her cheek, Yuri made his way to her ear. He laved the sweet area behind it, sucking the shell into his mouth before telling her he had her, he was here and asking her to let go.

Now.

Chapter 6

A moment after his command, Yuri felt a powerful shudder quake through her slight body. A passionate gasp screamed from her lips and she came hard and forcefully. The sight, the feel and the sound of her climax cued Yuri to unleash his tightly reined desire. He let go, quenching the fire she'd spread like wildfire inside him. Hot and thick, his seed jetted inside her womb.

Groaning his release, he fisted the hair at her nape, hauling her neck down to him. Lost in a haze of desire and need, his fangs lengthened, stretching toward her.

Claim. Mine.

Yuri opened his mouth, piercing her sweet skin. Her flesh hugged his fangs with the same perfection as she sheathed his body. Their bodies joined, their connection, their oneness was stark and unshakable. He drew in her essence in long, sensual pulls. Each swallow of her sweet blood pulsed through his body, riding his pleasure out even further than he thought possible.

It took all the will he owned to pull away from her. With a soft kiss, he pulled back and turned his neck, offering himself to her. A shudder of anticipation skated up his spine, a cord of excitement knotted and tightened in his core. Featherlight, the tips of her hair danced on his chest before covering him in its silken blanket. Her breath warmed his neck, her tongue flicked out, sampling his skin. Even the simple touch had Yuri arching off the floor, his grip on her tensing. He felt her smile a heartbeat before he savored the sweetest pain and deepest pleasure he'd ever experienced in his long life. Ileana's sharp bite, and the heady rush of giving everything of himself and having it not only accepted, but unconditionally reciprocated.

After Yuri left to check the perimeter, Ileana found some clothes in one of the trunks. Although obviously meant for a young boy, she felt more at home and more herself in the leather jacket, tailored pants and holster than she had in those *Samostan* robes. Like armor, they shielded her from Yuri's heated gaze and her own sensuality that came out when he stared at her.

A minute later, Yuri stepped through the door. He held his jacket like a child in his arms, obviously carrying something although from this vantage point she couldn't see what. After securing the door lock, he kicked his boots on a small rug, knocking off the red dust that had accumulated on the soles. The domestic sight warmed her heart and put a smile on her lips.

For one brief moment she could envision a life with him, picture him coming home to her. Her smile fled almost as quickly as it came. Anger and resentment followed close at its heels. Would that image bring joy to her lonely heart in years to come or would it haunt her?

"What are you wearing?"

Ileana blinked, his query pulling her out of her thoughts. She glanced up at him, feeling a smile and the warmth of a blush on her face.

"I found them in that trunk, there." Standing, she brushed the dust off her pant legs and walked over to Yuri. He held an apple in his proffered hand and she hungrily accepted it. Although she tried, it was impossible to ignore his admiring gaze as it skimmed over her body.

"I think I miss the robes," he said, biting into the apple. His fangs pierced the fleshy skin in a way that made her sex clench and her blood thrum wildly in her veins. Last night she'd been that apple, captured between his teeth, a prisoner to his passion. An image of him taking her, her skin as white as the apple's flesh, their blood mixing into a fiery melding of reds like the fruits skin, flashed in her mind.

Her body thrummed, a wave of heat crashing atop her, the erotic current threatening to once again drag her into his undertow. How could she ever let him go today? Never look upon his face again? Never taste the intoxicating, hot sweet assault of his lips on hers?

A sandbag of emotions collapsed atop her heart, weighing her down. As if reading her thoughts, Yuri stepped forward. Strands of dark hair cascaded over his eyes. Eyes that held hers, watched her as if they could see straight through the flesh and bone to her soul. She shivered. Then they dropped to her neck, her collarbone, his finger following the path his gaze made.

"You're so beautiful," he said, his fingertip running along what she knew to be an outline of one of her tattoos.

Ileana shifted from his reach. "Stop."

"Why?"

"It's ugly."

Fingers hooked beneath her chin, forcing her gaze to his. "You're not ugly, Ileana. You're the most beautiful, perfect creature I've ever seen."

She tried to look away and he forced her chin back to him.

"Every marked inch of you."

At the solemn vow in his eyes, Ileana's heart stuck in her throat. She bit the inside of her cheek to keep from crying. Not from his words. But from the fact that, for the first time in her life, she believed something good about herself.

"Yuri, I…"

A riot of gunshots ripped through the cabin, piercing the windows and shattering glass all around them. Yuri pushed her to the floor, the weight of his body above her, shielding her from harm.

A low curse flew from his lips. "I must have been followed back here," he panted.

Ileana paused for only a moment before scooting from underneath him, and crawled toward the door.

"Where are you going?"

"We have to evade the *vanators* and get you through the veil," she said over the roaring blasts.

"You're leaving out the part about me needing your blood."

"Small detail."

He pulled on her arm, stopping her hasty move for the door. "Ileana, I won't do this."

Exhaling, Ileana wrapped her arms around his neck, sealing her lips against his. Yuri released a low moan and kissed her back. One hand dug into her hair, cupping her skull and keeping her a prisoner in his powerful arms. The other snaked around her waist, pinning her against his solid build. Hot and urgent, she kissed him with all the passion she felt for him. A kiss could speak if you listened. Part of her feared him paying heed to what her lips told him now. The other part needed him to know how she felt, for she was certain those three little words would never fall from them. Not in time anyway.

"Now," she said when they broke away. "Let's get you out of here."

Before he could protest any further, Ileana opened the door. Bending at the waist, she shielded her head with her arm and ran for the tree line, holding onto Yuri's hand with her other. As they had fled last night from the red wind, today they hurled away from a different threat, but one just as deadly.

Last night, Yuri served as the motor who kept them running, got them to safety. Ileana led them today. She ran until her thighs burned, sprinted even when there was no longer any sign of their pursuers behind them. Kept her grip tight on Yuri's and did not slow until they came to the stone garden. The one place she knew of with a sacred tablet, the porthole for creating a tear in the veil.

Now all he needed was her blood and he'd be safe.

"Ileana, stop!"

Yuri had been shouting for minutes, but she didn't listen until now. Releasing her grip on his hand, she pointed to the stone.

"There," she panted, her hands collapsing atop her knees as she fought for breath.

Yuri stared at the tablet and then back at her. "What about you?"

"I'll be fine."

"I'm not leaving you," he shouted. "Not after last night."

"You must. They'll kill you." Ileana winced. Without looking into his eyes, she could feel him opening her up, sense his *medji* powers pushing on her mind, attempting to manipulate her thoughts.

"Stop it, Yuri," she pleaded, squeezing her eyes shut as if the move could force him out too.

When the pressure in her head didn't cease, the probing ache in her mind wouldn't stop, helpless resignation swelled inside her. Ileana stopped fighting and sank to her knees on the grass.

"Please," she said on a sob. "I can't lose you too."

Yuri flinched. Her words snapped the connection he had on her mind at once, as if a light switch had been flung off. His heart hurt for her, for her pain and loss. To think he might contribute more suffering in her life made him physically ill. Forgetting everything, he rushed to her side.

"Forgive me..." he began. His words cut off when Ileana snatched the dagger from his thigh holster, slicing her palm open and smearing the holy stone with her blood before he even knew what happened.

"No," he breathed.

A deafening crack of thunder split the night. Winds kicked from the north, swirling her hair around her into a whirlwind of pulsing energy.

"What have you done," Yuri shouted over the roaring winds.

She blinked up at him. "What you needed me to do."

Lightning pulsed in blinding flashes, so bright Ileana had to shield her eyes with her hand. The sky split behind the stone, creating a whirlpool of blue, gray, purple and white mist that swirled in the heavens.

"A tear in the veil," she whispered. "You must jump, Yuri. Now!"

Instead, he stepped away from the ebbing whirl of light

behind him and toward her. "I'm not going without you. That." He pointed to the vortex. "*This*. Leaving. It's a reaction, not a solution."

"But the *vanators*," she said, her voice pleading. "They'll kill you if you stay."

"And you if I go," he replied solemnly.

Ileana shook her head. "What other choice is there?"

Yuri didn't hesitate. "Come with me."

"What?" she breathed. Her heart leapt out of her chest before plummeting back down on the jagged stones of reality. "I—" She swallowed. "I've never left the *Mysts* before."

Yuri smiled, his lips curving in that devastating grin that melted her heart and ignited a spark of arousal deep in her core. "I'll take care of you," he said, taking her hands and pulling her to her feet.

Goddess help her, but she believed him. "They won't stop hunting us."

"We will fight them," he vowed, tucking her arm to his chest.

Violent wind lapped at their bodies, but a sense of peace settled her usually turbulent emotions. The air currents licked his hair, kicking it in a boyish tousle that had her heart beaming. Voiccs shouted in the distance, more gunshots echoing in the wild sky. Whoever tracked them was close. Too close. Yuri pulled back and squeezed her hand.

"Are you ready?"

Ileana paused. Was she ready to trust? Ready to love?

Ready to let someone in? "More than I have ever been for anything."

Yuri exhaled, as if in relief. They turned to face the vortex, both the swirling unknown and their sanctuary.

"We jump on three."

Ileana nodded, her stomach floating wildly like a kite in a storm at the prospect of what lay before them. But she wasn't nervous or afraid. She knew Yuri held the other line and he wasn't letting go.

"One," he said.

"Two," she replied.

"Three."

* * * * *